JEWISH LATIN AMERICA

ILAN STAVANS, SERIES EDITOR

Like a BRIDE *and* Like a MOTHER

Like a Bride

ROSA NISSÁN

TRANSLATED BY DICK GERDES

INTRODUCTION BY ILAN STAVANS

UNIVERSITY OF NEW MEXICO PRESS

ALBUQUERQUE

Like a Mother

Novia que te vea © 1992 by Rosa Nissán,
Hisho que te nazca © 1996 by Rosa
Nissán
Translation © 2002 by the University of
New Mexico Press
Introduction © 2002 by Ilan Stavans
All rights reserved.

First paperbound printing, 2013
Paperbound ISBN: 978-0-8263-2364-4

17 16 15 14 13   1 2 3 4 5

Cover Illustrations: front, Nude with
Raised Arm © Brigitte Carnochan 1996.
Courtesy Peter Fetterman Gallery, Santa
Monica, California; back, Milling Around,
Handpainted photograph © Christina
Florkowski
Cover Design: Robyn Mundy

Library of Congress Cataloging-in-Publication
Data:

Nissan, Rosa.
[Novia que te vea. English]
Like a bride ; and Like a mother / Rosa Nissan ;
translated by Dick Gerdes ; introduction by Ilan
Stavans.
    p. cm.
ISBN 0-8263-2364-2 (pbk. : alk. paper)
1. Nissan, Rosa.—Translations into English.
I. Title: Like a bride ; and Like a mother.
II. Gerdes, Dick. III. Nissan, Rosa. Hisho que te
nazca. English. IV. Title: Like a mother. V. Title.
PQ7298.24.I77 A6 2002
863'.64—dc21

                              2001003717

To my mother, who taught
me to be courageous.
To Elena Poniatowska, to her
laughter—the one who opened
doors, colors, and taste for me.

Rosa Nissán

For Nadia,
Forever an Inspiration

Dick Gerdes

A popular song from Judezmo, a language based on Old Spanish, written in Hebrew, and spoken by descendants of Sephardic Jews expelled from Spain in the fifteenth century:

ah, the groom doesn't want any money!

He wants a bride who brings good luck.

ah, the groom doesn't want any gold coins!

He wants a bride with a good upbringing.

ah, the groom doesn't want any jewels!

He wants a bride with a jovial face.

ay, now the groom wants money!

and he wants a bride who brings good luck.

ay, now the groom wants gold coins!

and he wants a bride with a good upbringing.

ay, now the groom wants jewels!

and he wants a bride with a jovial face.

INTRODUCTION

Ilan Stavans

"Ma, ¿qué escrivites?" wondered the poet Myriam Moscona when *Novia que te vea,* Rosa Nissán's autobiographical novel, a title translated poetically by Dick Gerdes as *Like a Bride,* was released in Mexico in 1992. And Moscona, singing further praise to a storyteller of her same ethnic background, added: *"¿Ande tupates tanta historia, tanta memoria, tanta palavrica de las muestras? ¿Dí que queres arrevivir ista lingua casi muerta que conocites por la banda de tus padres y abuelos? ¿Quén te ambezó a dezir las cosas como las dices? ¿Escrivana salites?"* In translation, these queries appear mundane: "But, what have you written? Where have you, Rosa, found so much history, so much memory, so many of these words that are close to our heart? Do you want to revive this almost defunct tongue that you got acquainted with through your parents and grandparents? What urged you to say things the way you do? Have you turned out to be a writer?" Yet in the original, the utterance, of course, has magic; or better, it has zest. It is in a modified form of Ladino, the so-called Judeo-Spanish jargon with roots in the Iberian peninsula that probably date back to the thirteenth century, if not earlier. Moscona and Nissán, as Sephardic Jews from Mexico, came of age listening to it. The jargon appears somewhat prominently in Nissán's oeuvre, especially in *Like a Bride.* Curiously, it is not heard from the mouth of Nissán's protagonist, Oshinica, but by those in her entourage, most of them immigrants from Turkey and, prior even, from Persia.

¿Escrivana salites? is an accurate question to ask Nissán. Although she is unquestionably a novelist—aside from *Like a Bride,* she is the author of its sequel, *Hisho que te nazca* (1996), herein published in a single volume for the first time ever in any language; a travelogue about Israel entitled *Las tierras prometidas* (1997) that is also an exploration of her inner conflicts as a Mexican and a Jew; and a collection of stories, *No sólo para dormir es la noche* (1999)—her quest for a space and a voice came rather circuitously. That journey, in fact, is narrated in her books about Oshinica. With a plethora of tales inside but no way to articulate them, Nissán, as it were, enrolled in a creative writing course—*un taller literario*—with Elena Poniatowska, one of Mexico's most prominent women authors. This delayed encounter with her artistic self, it ought to be added, is not atypical in her ethnic group, where, as she herself explains lucidly in her fiction, the education of women until recently was if not forbidden, at least delegated to the status of non-essential. Indeed, it was Poniatowska herself, a non-Jew, who first recognized Nissán's energy and encouraged her to pursue her literary exercises. Soon those exercises turned into full-fledged narratives about the Sephardic idiosyncrasy, filled with humorous and linguistic puns. As in the case of most artists, her imaginative formulations might have represented an attempt by Nissán to distance herself from her community. But it is clear that, not only in the plot of her novels but in life too, as her people put it, *"la engrandecimos,"* her pilgrimage enriched her. The result, in the reader's hand, is, in my mind, unique in the shelf of Mexican letters and, equally, in the tradition of Jewish fiction in Spanish.

The uniqueness is twofold: first, I know of no other *bildungsroman* where the main character is a Sephardic female, whose odyssey is contemplated from adolescence to maturity; and second, the insertion of Ladino, not inconsequential, makes this a rarity. To understand these reasons I've just stated I ought to offer some context. To begin, it is illustrative to consider the question of why in the Jewish literary tradition Eastern Europe, in its rise to modernity, became the cradle for the novel. With the French Revolution came the emergence of the bourgeoisie as a major class, and the novel, as an artistic artifact, served as a thermometer of its angst. Ironically, *Don Quixote,* published in two parts in 1605 and 1615, is perhaps the first one to implement a reflection on actual change—internal and external—in human nature; its protagonist, Alonso Quijano, transforms himself from a loquacious *hidalgo* to a fool and back to a man of sense. But Cervantes's masterpiece stands alone as a door opener in Spain. The majority of groundbreaking novels, such as those written from Defoe to Diderot, were produced elsewhere in Europe. By the dawn of the seventeenth century, the Jews and also the Muslim populations of the peninsula had already been expelled. For this and other reasons, for years Sephardic literature focused on the liturgical and philosophical: the poetry of Shmuel Hanagid, Shlomo ibn Gabirol, and Yehuda Halevi, are highlights, as are the treatises by Halevi himself, Maimonides, and Hasdi Crescas. Fiction as such was not, in any significant way, an ingredient. Paloma Díaz-Mas, in the authoritative *Los Sefaradíes: Historia, lengua y cultura* (1986), embarks on an inventory of literature by Judeo-Hispanic authors that ranges from *coplas* to proverbs and ballads (e.g., *canticas* and *romansas*). About a fourth of her catalog is devoted to "adopted genres": journalism, narrative, theater, and "autograph" poetry. It is intriguing, though, that among the *romansos* (novels) she lists, almost all are described as *aranjados:* imitations. The earliest of these, released in places like Cairo, Smyrna, Constantinople, and Salonika, are traceable to the period of 1900 to 1933 but never before. In other words, while a distinct Judeo-Hispanic ethos is apparent in the Middle Ages—Abraham Joshua Heschel discusses it thought-provokingly in essays and, in passing, in his biography of Maimonides—its role in modernity is that of an addition, and not that of a source.

Nissán's *Like a Bride* and *Like a Mother* are not included in Díaz-Mas's register, probably because Hispanic America never became a centrifugal center of Sephardic culture. In fact, to my knowledge, the number of published Sephardic narratives in the region is minuscule; Angelina Muníz-Huberman, in her anthology with a Ladino title, *Lah linguah floridah* (1989), corroborates this statement: in the back matter of the book, a list of suggested further readings might best be described as *sparse*. (Muníz-Huberman, by the way, is the author of a number of memorable fictions on this topic, among them *Huerto cerrado, huerto sellado [Enclosed Garden]* and *El mercader de Tudela [The Merchant of Tudela]*. None, however, is realistic in tone, nor does any include the Sephardic dialect.) Hence, Nissán, at sixty-one years of age, is a *rara avis:* to employ an oxymoron, she is an *aranjado* novelist with an original voice, one that is modern, Jewish, and *muy mexicana*.

Plus, another asset of hers ought to be contemplated: in 1993, *Like a Bride* was successfully adapted into film by Guita Schyfter, her husband Hugo Hiriart, and Nissán herself, in a production of the Instituto Mexicano de Cinematográfia. This allowed Oshinica and the immigration she has come to be an emblem of to be better known in Mexico and beyond. (A succinct evaluation of the film is included in my book *The Riddle of Cantinflas* [1998]).

I might have an unruly, instinctual reaction to Nissán's protagonist and her Ashkenazic counterparts, but I shall refrain from indulging in an examination of them. It should suffice to say that, although at times over-sentimentalized, their inner world is not at all in conflict with the Jews I remember while growing up in Mexico in the sixties and seventies. The cadence of speech is captured astonishingly well and equally astonishing and vivid, too, are the various Spanish dialects recorded in the novel, each used by a different type of people. Indeed, just browsing through Nissán's pages makes me shiver with uncomfortable nostalgia for a milieu that formed me and which, with a dramatically different approach, I tried to evoke in *On Borrowed Words*. (A capacious study of Nissán's portrait of them is available in Yael Halevi-Wise's article "Puente entre naciones"

[Bridge Across Nations] in the journal *Hispania* [1998].) This, as far as I know, is the most comprehensive analysis by an academic of her work.) And of Nissán as a person I have even less to say, since our paths have not yet crossed. Instead, I offer a quote from Poniatowska that illuminates the fashion in which her education and worldview are in symmetry.

I've never met a person as natural and spontaneous. Rosa Nissán adapts herself to life the way a plant adapts itself to the soil or the sun. Her reaction is immediate. Her suffering and joy overwhelm her entirely. But there is reason for it, for *Rosita*
. . . is a total woman, rotund, her embrace wide, as wide as the patterns her legs create when she dances around . . . [Her] parents carry their Jewishness in their bone marrow, and they always enlighten Nissán's path with their seven-handed candelabra. She never sees any star other than the Star of David. Suddenly, though, she and her milieu were turned into star dust. [But Nissán] has returned to herself, but is no longer her parent's child, a child of Jews, the byproduct of schools for Jews only, and of the Centro Deportivo Israelita [Jewish Sports Center], of an isolated community. She remains the same star of Jericho, but her petals are fleshier, wiser, more vigorous. They have been expanded to embrace us all.

Escrivana she came out indeed, and full of pathos. Poniatowska addresses her as Rosita; I prefer *Rosica*. The former is Mexican; the latter is Sephardic. Either way, to the question "*Ma, ¿qué escrivites?*" she vigorously answers to her Spanish-language readers: a few God-granted words—*unas palavericas, como quisho el Dió.*

Like a

Bride

Rosa Nissán

Translated by Dick Gerdes

✻ GRADE SCHOOL.

Every night I kneel down by the window and look at a bright star that just might be my guardian angel. Then I recite "Our Father" to God and say a "Hail Mary" for the Virgin. I hope that one of them will protect me like they do my classmates, even though my parents are Jewish. Today I prayed that I wouldn't have to change schools. They want to put me in one only for Jews. Where do Jews come from, anyway? Dear God, please help me stay at the Guadalupe Tepeyac School, and please make sure that I'll never leave this place, and especially now that I'm going to start the last and most difficult year of elementary school. Only here, and with your help, can I make it. I promise to do whatever you want— follow the Ten Commandments, go to catechism on Saturdays, and whenever I die, I'll be a guardian angel for anyone you want. In the name of the Father, the Son, and the Holy Ghost. Amen.

At eight o'clock in the morning, just before beginning our studies, we pray. We put the palms of our hands next to our mouths, close our eyes, and recite the prayers together. I like the way it sounds. We make the sign of the cross with our right hand, and then we sit down to study. The school desks are neat—the part we write on lifts up, and we put all our stuff inside. I have a little

Santa Teresa picture glued on the top, in the middle, and other little flowered virgins are in each corner. I spend a lot of time giving them little kisses with my finger so they'll protect me.

After we do our lessons and finish our assignments, the nuns reward us with one more picture. Since I'm one of the best behaved, I have the most pictures. I have to hide them, because my mother doesn't approve of them. But she does see me make the sign of the cross every morning.

"I would rather you leave the room when they pray," she said the other day. But I don't want to. Then someone would ask me why I'm leaving the room, and besides, I like praying.

Yesterday at recess we were making sand castles, and when I moved to make mine bigger, I stepped on another girl's castle. She got so mad that she threw sand in my eyes and then yelled Jew! Jew! at me. Her yelling frightened me, because most of the girls don't know. Then some other kids formed a group, and in a flash a bunch of them were screaming, "You killed Jesus," and then they made the sign of the cross right in my face as if I were the devil. And I yelled back at them, "That's a lie. I'm not a Jew. I pray and go to confession just like you do."

It's almost one o'clock in the morning and I can't sleep—I just keep remembering how they threw sand in my eyes.

Dreams of hell. I dreamed the same thing last week, over and over, my bed's on fire. Even though it's dark, everything's lit up with yellow, orange, and red flames. Tombs pop open like Jack-in-the-boxes, and people rise up and start walking toward God. He's the one who's going to reward or punish us. I only see the lids pop off the coffin, and then the dead people start to walk.

"The Last Judgment . . . we'll all be there some day," said Sister María. "Then we'll know if we've won a spot in Heaven, or if we'll grow tails and sprout horns."

I know that those who have gone to hell play tricks on children so they'll be bad.

Last night the neighbors on the second floor came over and we played "Chance." I got the Devil and lost, because no one got the wicked card. That little red Devil with the wicked eyes danced around in my dreams way into the night—grasping an iron fork, he stirs the ashes around, then he comes and goes, does whatever he wants, casts a glance at me, shows me his horns and the red-hot edges of his pincers. I freak out when I imagine that this day could actually arrive. I hope it never does. Why would all of us who come back from the dead have to walk around nude? I don't like to be seen nude, and I wouldn't like to have to get up that day and have everyone see me like that. What a horrible punishment! I'll meet all those people from a thousand years ago—Benito Juárez, Napoleon, Miguel Hidalgo, and Costilla (my other grandmother), Cinderella, Cuauhtémoc. And how is he going to walk? They burned his feet. I'll bet he's going to rise up as good as new, everyone knows that with God nothing is impossible and . . . you know, it just might be fun, if I get to know so many people, but . . . nude? Oh, no! How embarrassing! And nothing to cover myself up with?

1. Thou shalt love God over everything else (I love him and I pray to him).
2. Thou shalt not take the name of God in vain (I'm not going to swear anymore, but when I do and I tell a lie, I'm going to cross myself, but not properly, so it won't be any good).
3. Thou shalt honor your father and mother.
4. Thou shalt honor the Sabbath and holy days.
5. Thou shalt not kill.

6. Thou shalt not fornicate (I'll skip this one, I don't even know what it means).
7. Thou shalt not steal.
8. Thou shalt not commit false testimony (I only tell a few lies, besides they're the worst thing that I can say to Mommy).
9. Thou shalt not covet thy neighbor's wife (I don't understand. Whose wife?).
10. Thou shalt not covet that which is not yours (that's easy, I never want anything that isn't mine).

If I can just manage to follow those rules, I'll go to Heaven for sure, and I'm really happy that the Ten Commandments are the same for Jews as they are for Catholics. Whew! They share something in common! At least I can repeat them in school just the same as at home. It's easy to obey them, because the thought of going to hell is terrifying. I want to go to Heaven. I'll be an angel like the ones in the pictures, and I'd like to be the one in the middle, invisible. Wouldn't it be great to be invisible! To be everywhere at the same time, flying from one place to another, without anyone seeing me? Then I could get close to those children and whisper in their ears, "Don't be afraid of the Devil! Spend your time on Sundays helping an old person, loan your crayons even if some kids are mean to you and break off the tips."

They say the Devil speaks to children through their left ears, telling them to play nasty tricks. And their guardian angel speaks to them through their right ears, advising them to be good. Those little blond angels, who are dressed in light blue and have transparent wings, live in Heaven. They can see God, the Virgin, and all the saints. They talk to them.

"Cross, cross, make the Devil go away and Jesus stay." Don't get near me, you ugly Devil. Get away! Leave me alone! I know that these little devils are very insistent and they're always at your ear, saying, "Steal that pen, hit your brother, pull her braids, make fun of her." Sometimes they are so convincing, because the Devil shows you how to be cunning. And they can be really mean.

My clothing will be pure white, I'll fly around from place to place, I'll teach children to be good no matter which country they're from . . . although I'm not sure I'd like to be an angel for a Jewish kid; maybe I'll adopt a Roman Catholic. Then one day I'll go to Heaven. Wings made of a delicate material like a bird's skin will sprout from me, and I'll dump buckets of water from the clouds on everyone below so they can feel the rain.

The girls in my classroom receive gifts and have parties twice a year—on their birthdays and their saint's days, but the Jews don't celebrate saint's day. The teacher asked me when mine was. The only thing I could think of was to tell her that I would ask my mother. I don't think there's a Saint Oshinica, but I'm going to look at a calendar and, if there's a Saint Eugenia, I'll be in luck.

Since we live right on Guadalupe Avenue, we can see the people streaming by on their pilgrimage to the Basilica. They're always singing, dancing, laughing, drinking, hugging each other, carrying their children and sick ones, food, and blankets. Each congregation has its leader who protects them so that the following group doesn't overtake them in the unending procession.

As soon as we hear them coming, we run to the balcony. We never get tired of watching them, and sometimes the groups are as long as three city blocks. As they amble down the street, it makes us feel sad. Now that we're approaching the saint's day of the Virgin of Guadalupe, there are so many different groups passing by with their banners, all of which have the image of the Virgin—

the mother of the Mexican people and their country—embroidered with golden thread.

They must enjoy it. They come from Toluca, Querétaro, Pachuca, everywhere. When they're right in front of our house they begin singing the traditional *Mañanitas*. They're happy because they're about to arrive at the place where the Virgin first appeared. Tears fill their eyes out of emotion, and they feel so close to each other. Some crawl on their knees . . . and they still have fifteen blocks to go!

The smell of hot tortillas invades the entire neighborhood surrounding the Basilica. On just about any step you can find women heating up corn tortillas, the small ones that they sell five or ten at a time, wrapped in cheap colored paper. I wonder why all those candles are for sale everywhere around the Basilica? They're slender and beautiful, and they're decorated with pink flowers.

Sometimes we would go into the church and listen to mass. We'd walk through the street with all the vendors' stalls and then climb the little hill, which we can see from our window. There's a small white house on top with a cross on the roof. That's where the miracle happened to Juan Diego, an Indian. Wasn't he lucky! I hope that happens to me someday. If it really was a miracle, then it can happen to me too. Afterward, we'd go back down the hill, and in order to get home, we'd take the trolley that runs up and down Guadalupe Avenue. That way we wouldn't be late and my mother wouldn't find out that we had gone to the Villa again.

I believed them, I truly believed my parents when they told me that the Jews didn't kill Christ.

"If they bother you again, just tell them that Christ was a Jew and had had his bar mitzvah."

"Oh, Daddy, do you think I would say that? They'd just get mad at me."

When my mommy went to Monterrey to see my other grand-father, Micaela quickly finished her chores and took us to the Villa again; we ran into some of her friends, and we walked together. Then I heard one of them say, "Listen, Mica, don't work there; the amount the Jews pay isn't much; they never pay much." I acted like I didn't hear anything, because I don't know what to think or do when I hear those things. And what if later on they start on this thing about the Jews killing Christ? Everyone already knows about it. Then we went inside the church on the hill for while, and I just stood there staring at Christ crucified on the cross. Look what they did to him! A woman who was kneeling next to us just sobbed as she stared at the blood flowing everywhere. Poor thing. Well, who wouldn't hate the people who did this? They're bad! And it was so long ago, and she still feels horrible about it. If that woman who is weeping finds out that I'm Jewish, she might even kill me. The good thing is that Micaela likes me a lot, and she doesn't really buy all that stuff, and you really don't notice that I'm Jewish at first. Honestly, I'd rather be Jewish than a black person. But even I get upset and sad! Look how they nailed him to a cross! Can you believe it? What monsters they were!

There's a fabric store at the corner where I live; Bertita and Bicha live in the back part of the store, and they're Mommy's friends. They make pastries and decorate them beautifully. I spend hours just watching them put layer on top of layer, and then there's always just one more. They make little doll-like figures, and using wire and icing they create the sweet little blue, yellow, and red flowers. Sometimes, when they finish a wedding cake, I say it's the most beautiful one they've ever made, but when they put the finishing touches on a birthday cake with the little figure in the middle standing on a pedestal, it always seems to be the nicest. I spend a lot of time with them, surrounded by vats of yellow, red, and blue icing.

The little figures don't look all that great until we make their clothes with little pieces of cloth and then stick them around the waist with some icing. We cover some of the folds with more icing, making it look like a waistband—then they look really elegant. Using some coloring, we decide if they are going to be dark-looking or fair-skinned, and they're just like we want them to be—poor things!—but they always turn out fabulous.

Bichita and Bertita are friends of a priest who teaches catechism at a church near our house on Saturdays. He teaches us to pray. A lot of kids go there. Ever since I've learned to cross myself, I can use my right hand faster, because it's the one you use to make the sign of the cross. Afterwards, they give us anise-flavored candies. I just love them. I never miss classes; the pastry ladies just tell my mother that I'm with them, helping to decorate cakes. So, I go to catechism secretly, because I want to have first communion, and they're the only ones who can help save me at the Last Judgment; maybe, just maybe, by saving me, God will forgive my whole family, too.

Several families from the old country live in this neighborhood called Industrial. They are my parents' best friends. They were already good friends before they got married. My mommy introduced Max to Fortunita, his wife. Now they have children too, and we're all very close. I'm the oldest. Today Mommy and some of her friends decided to go to a Hebrew school in the Valle district and see if the school could send a bus to pick us up where we live. When we got home from school, we found out they had enrolled us in that school.

Did all of these kids also kill Christ? They all seemed so gentle. I thought: it doesn't seem like they would do it. How could they even remember? They play marbles, ring around the roses, and everything we did at the other school. Are they the same, though? It's hard to tell if they're really Jewish. I don't know why, but I'm not interested in making friends with any of them.

Wow! Third year is really different. I'm learning the multiplication tables. And we're beginning to write in ink, which has been hard for me. It was easier with a pencil. Now we get everything stained—our notebooks, our backpacks, our fingers, and our checkered school uniforms. We bring ink bottles and blotters to make our lessons look better. With pencil, everything gets erased. Ink is better. This has been a big change for us. They treat us like we're older—we use ink bottles.

Our teacher, Mr. Gómez, is the most demanding teacher in the school, and he's the meanest, too. I'm in his room. For an hour, starting at eight o'clock in the morning, he makes us draw our circles perfectly. He imitates the action and then draws them all linked together on the board, telling us all the while that these are calligraphy exercises, and that he doesn't understand our scribbling. This is exactly the part I like best, and when we're working hard in class, that's when I'm not so afraid of the teacher.

My mother is really happy that he's my teacher. She says he's very demanding, and that's why he's a good teacher. Even if he is, he has an ugly face. That's why I sit near the back, half hidden, so he won't see me when he asks questions. The other day he asked me three times, but I didn't respond, because I didn't even hear him. I remember that the nuns were great. Then he calls out our names with a gruff voice, as if we were soldiers. I'll bet he doesn't even laugh at home.

The bus going to the Condesa and Roma neighborhoods continues on to Industrial. I've got a friend whose name is Dori. She's in my class and rides the same bus. We return to school in the afternoon to learn Hebrew, which is a strange language. You write it from right to left, exactly the opposite from Spanish. Now, whenever my grandfather scolds my father or my grandmother, I'll be able to understand him. Ah, I just remembered that at my grandfather's house they only speak Farsi. They use Hebrew for parties. Oh well, whatever!

Max and Fortuna moved to the Hipódromo neighborhood because they wanted to be closer to the Sephardic school and live nearer to their friends from the old country. The other families are looking for places to live around there too.

"What are you waiting for, Shamuel, don't pass this up! What are you going to do here by yourselves, wasting away alone? You and your wife who are still so young! Don't pass this up; let's move together, we'll take you there. There's an apartment on the corner near our house, it's not rented, it's on the fifth floor, and it's cheap! Come and see it on Sunday! It's great!"

I told Dori to check out the corner of Cholula and Campeche streets because we were probably going to move there. She got excited, because it's only a block from her house and the apartment building was beautiful. I can't believe it: I'll be living close to my best friend. Now I can't wait for the day when I'll finally be her neighbor.

Now that they're building a movie theater near our house, we're going to move. It took them so long to do it that we didn't even get to go to the opening. The only time I've ever gone to a movie was when Max invited us one Sunday morning. He took us to the Alameda. What a place! When it went dark inside, it seemed like we were in a dark street, and there were pretty little houses lit up on either side. I don't know if anyone lived inside them, I'm not sure, but maybe they were really stars on the walls. And what a movie! Max's children are so lucky to get to go all the time. My dad has never taken us to the movies. He's always working on Sundays, and then my mother shuts the blinds at six o'clock in the evening and puts us to bed, saying it's already nighttime and that no one goes out at night. I don't think I'll ever get to go again. If I could just see that movie over again . . .

This is the first night in our new house, and I'm excited. I want it to be morning already, because Dori is coming to take me to see her house. She wants to show me how close it is to mine. We're so lucky!

The building is nice. It's pink, which is my favorite color—after all, I'm a girl. That's the only thing I like about being a girl, we get everything in pink; it's prettier than blue. We have the whole floor to ourselves, because there are only five apartments in the building, one on each floor. We live right on the corner, so we have balconies that look down onto both streets. On the Cholula Street side, we get the sun when it comes up. That's where the living room and kitchen are, and you can see the Popo store from that side. The bedrooms are on the other side: one for my parents, one for my three brothers, and one for my two sisters and me. Now we won't have boys and girls sleeping in the same room. Too bad! It was more fun that way. If only Moshón could stay with me.

He's going to be bored with the two little ones. There are two bathrooms. One is small, and the other has a tub. The kitchen is so big there's room for a breakfast nook and the washing machine. And my mother put the banana tree on one of the balconies. The sitting room has a long balcony with flowers. When I look out the window of my brothers' bedroom, I can see the neon sign for a movie theater. It is divine (no one says divine, that's only for God, Our Father); I mean it's *neat* to have a movie theater so close. It's called the "Lido," and it's already open. This is a fancy neighborhood!

I've got a bunch of school friends who live around here; well, they're everywhere. Maybe there aren't any Catholics here, I'm not sure. Now all of us who used to live in Industrial live here, next to each other. Even my granddaddy moved from his house on Calzada de los Misterios and bought one in the Roma neighborhood, on Chihuahua Street, near a park that has a huge water fountain in the middle. What a house! It's really something else. It has an indoor patio, and the floor and walls are decorated with smooth tiles, and there must be over one hundred flowerpots on the floor and hanging on the walls. The flowerpots that I like the most are the ones decorated all over with pieces of broken dishes. They're like the ones we have at our house—they even have the same designs. And, by the way, the dishes that my mommy bought in La Merced market are a thousand times better than the old ones, because while you're eating your soup, all of sudden little animals—a bear, a dog, a duck—start to appear inside the bowl. It's fun discovering them while I eat! I hope these don't get broken very soon.

I don't know why my mommy's friends feel sorry for her because we live on the fifth floor. It's not too tiring to climb the stairs, and besides, we do little things to make life easier—if the mailman or the milkman or anyone comes with something, we just drop a little basket with a string tied to it over the balcony. That way we don't have to go up and down the stairs. When we get home from school, and before we climb the stairs, we yell up to the apartment to see if we need to buy bread or tortillas. On the days Mommy goes to market, she pays a little boy to help her because no one in the family can carry all those bags up five floors.

After having gone to the Sephardic school many times and eaten in a hurry while the bus waited downstairs where we used to live, it's been a relief to live in this neighborhood because when the bus drops us off, there are still a lot of kids on it. While they're taking them and then returning to pick us up again, we have time to play on the sidewalk with Dori and her two brothers who come to wait also.

Mommy didn't set aside her usual routine even when Dori came to eat. She sits the six of us around the table together and she lets us know that the belt is just over there; we don't talk; we eat quickly; we don't even argue; then she sends us down to the street to play; and she doesn't want us to throw anything. Fortunately, we can play ball or skate outside; there are always a bunch of kids playing in the street. I don't understand how all these things can make that silly Dori laugh. She said my mother is very nice and it's nice to have a bunch of brothers and sisters. Nice? It's horrible! And it's even worse when you're the oldest one and you have to stop them from fighting and they hit you really hard because you're the oldest. Look . . . she doesn't even have a mother. But my mother is nice? Well, she's even less than nice when she gets mad and digs her four nails into my arm, making it bleed. Now there are little scabs like fingernail scratches that were really visible last week, and when I said something to my dad that I shouldn't have, she did it again. How was I supposed to know that I shouldn't have said anything to him?

◇ ◇ ◇

Acapulco is really beautiful! And I never believed that the ocean could be so big! It never ends! I was lucky to be invited. I'm the only one of my brothers and sisters to go to the ocean. My Aunt Chela and I slept in one room and my grandparents in another. And my aunt took so long to get ready! She puts on one lipstick, then another, looks at herself in the mirror, makes a face, touches up her eye makeup, looks at herself again—this time from another angle—smiles, looks again, makes another face, then looks at herself out of the corner of her eye. After this ritual, she remembers that someone else is in the room with her—that's me—and says, "Oshinica, I'm ready, let's eat breakfast. If we don't, your grandfather will disown us, he'll think something has happened to us, or that I spend too long getting ready. Actually, I've spent less time here than back at home, mainly because I didn't spend so much time styling my hair."

I had already put on my long, flowered beach robe, the one my daddy bought from Chucho in the store across from ours in Lagunilla Market. It covers my bathing suit. Finally, we're all decked out for our entrance into the dining room where my grandparents are waiting.

"Good morning, Daddy," she says as she kisses his hand, and then greets my grandmother in the same way.

"Oshinica, aren't you going to kiss your grandfather's hand?"

The hotel is on top of a mountain and you can see the huge, beautiful ocean from the dining room. And right now I'm thinking about my aunt who looks so pretty this morning, knowing that she has an elegant bathing suit on underneath her robe, and another one that she hasn't worn yet in the closet. It has a picture on it, with a woman diving into the ocean and a bright sun in the background. I've never seen a more beautiful bathing suit! They buy her whatever she wants. My mother doesn't find it very amusing. She says they spoil her so much that she's useless. But, with me, she's great! She likes me as if I were her little sister. My daddy, her only brother, is fifteen years older than her.

Shabat always begins at six o'clock on Friday evening, just as the first star appears in the heavens, and it ends the next day with the first star. I sing in the choir at school because the teacher said I had a good voice; Moshón doesn't. That's why I go on Fridays, and if we don't, we won't be able to sing at weddings. They pay us to sing, too. That's the only way I can earn some money, but I also like to go to the synagogue because we always have fun there. Since the bus picks us up before prayer time, we've got half an hour to fool around. At the corner of Monterrey and Bajío, where the synagogue is located, between the bakery and the store, a woman is usually selling hot tortillas, but she's not always there. Our big thrill is to eat. First we buy some bread rolls and strips of cooked chile wrapped in paper. Then we put them together and have a feast. We continue walking with fire coming out of our mouths, and then a little later we buy tortillas (if we have any money left).

At 7:15 we take our places in the choir. The prayer begins with our singing, well, our *shouting*. I don't know why the people like our toneless voices—it's so silly to say that we sing nicely, and that our temple is the best one around because of the choir.

I don't like taking baths with my brothers and sisters anymore, because Dori laughed at me. My mother gets the four of us older ones into the tub, sits on the edge near the hot and cold faucets, soaps my head, scratches me with her nails, goes to the next one, Moshón, and at the end Zelda and Clarita, then back to me. Every eight days each one of us gets scrubbed down three times. I asked if we could bathe separately, but she says it's too much work. The next step is even worse: brushing our hair and making long braids for all of us girls. We begin crying from the very moment she begins brushing out the tangles. It's frightening to have to take a bath, but the good thing is that once our hair is braided, it doesn't get tangled again. During the rest of the week she just undoes the braids and sprinkles lemon juice on them so they won't get tangled.

Every day my daddy gets up early and goes to Chapultepec Park to do his rowing. But he doesn't leave until he sees us safely on the bus, and the only thing I don't like is that he makes me eat two soft-boiled eggs, which is the only thing in life that makes me sick to my stomach. Just looking at them makes me want to vomit, but I swallow them quickly, after which I always start running toward the bathroom as if I were going to throw up.

Daddy has a lot of friends at the park, like Don Gume, who has a clothing store in the Escandón Market, or another, the milkman, who lends my dad his bike. They're almost always together in the park because they take the same bus line: Chorrito, in Juanacatlán. First they walk together for a while, and then each one rents a rowboat. We go there on Saturdays, Sundays, and every day during summer vacation. We always have fun with him; Mommy doesn't like to have fun. Mothers only like to clean house. I like going there because we get to row the boat, first me and then Moshón, and afterward he buys us fruit drinks and pieces of papaya at a stand on the edge of the lake. While we're eating, he rows us around the lake really fast. I can row fast too, and when we pass through the tunnel underneath the street—the long one that goes to the other side of the lake—I don't even hit the oars against the sides. Since Moshón can't beat me, he gets all bent out of shape. I can even do more pull-ups.

"Hey, Dad, why don't we rent two rowboats tomorrow and we can race to see who wins?"

I want to marry my dad because he's really handsome. Or even Moshón will do.

"Like I was telling you, Ernesto, that's the way life is, my twenty-somethingth child, first it was a girl, impossible; you know Oshinica, my granddaughter, I adore her, she has my mother's name, may she rest in peace. I didn't say a solitary word, you know I've got good manners, I don't stick my nose into things; in fact, I had called the hospital several times to see if the girl had opened her eyes yet. Two years later, thank God, a boy. I was his godparent, and it was my right. He was named after my grandfather because in our religion, as you know, it's required that the grandson carry the name of the grandfather. My daughter-in-law didn't go to the circumcision ceremony; if the baby needed her, she was there, but she couldn't even give much milk; she has boys, takes care of them, raises them, and that's it. Anyway, to make a long story short, her third child was a girl. Only God knows what he's doing. And, eleven months later, lo and behold: another girl. She gave us a total of three of them. For the last two, the mother chose names from her people. Can you imagine? Three dowries! My son is going to have to work like a dog in order to get them married. Would you like some coffee? 'Hey! A cup of coffee for this man.' As I was saying, right now I would like for my daughter Chelita to get married, and I can vouch for the fact that she's a doll with a creamy-white face, a real sweetie-pie, and obedient. We've had some real pests come around, because those Arabs are asking for hundreds of pesos—and if the boy is from a good family, even as high as several thousand pesos. Between you and me, that's the way it is. I tell you these things because you are my friend; I've known you ever since I arrived in Mexico ... Ernesto, why are you getting up? It's still early; it's barely ten o'clock ... wait a little longer!"

My granddaddy got sick, and I think Dr. Ernesto did too, because as much as my granddaddy wanted him to stay, he left there quickly. What horrible things he said!

What a neat green rocker! It's cool the way it rocks back and forth. But I don't think they'll let me try it because last Friday after Moshón had gotten all comfortable in it they said, "Get out of that rocker! Your grandfather is about to come home, and he'll get upset."

I know they'll never let me sit in it. So my five brothers and sisters and I sat all squished together on a couch and, once we got absorbed in a TV program, we forgot about fighting for the rocker. Grandfather makes his appearance. We all jump up at once, just like when the school director comes into the classroom. Tall, standing erect, one hand in his pocket and the other ready to tweak our little chins, we take turns giving him kisses. Chelita, my aunt, is also standing, hunched over a bit, and speaking like a mouse to show him how insignificant she is compared to the superiority of her father. She kisses his hand and puts it on her forehead as if to receive his blessing. He puts his hand forward, and while we kiss it, he looks the other way. That's his way of doing things. Next, he takes his hand out of his pocket and changes channels on the TV. Once he has decided which program we'll watch, he sits down in his rocking chair.

Sometimes I just stare at the photographs on the living room walls. They all look so old. There's one I especially like of my granddaddy sitting at a table. I don't know how they took them, but there are other grandparents from different angles, some laughing and others very serious. What a funny picture! Next to the window there's a picture of us sitting together arranged by age: first me, I was laughing with my braids and a huge topknot, my mother really knew how to make those curls in my hair, too. I was smiling and giving Moshón, who was always handsome, a big hug; then Zelda and Clarita. We all look great together! Next to our picture, there's a map of Israel, and a blue and white flag with a Zion symbol in the middle, and it reads below, "Israel, nation of Hebrews." In the next picture, Aunt Chela is wearing a green dress and a protruding hairdo; then comes my father when he was still single, and above the chimney, which has never been used, there's a Mason diploma with silver and gold edging that my grandfather is really proud of. He says it's a secret group and some of his best friends are Masons. No doubt about it, my grandfather is really pompous.

Today I went upstairs to his room and on top of the chest of drawers there were a million oddly shaped and different colored bottles of cologne; one of them has a little black ball on top, and when you squeeze it, a wet, strong smell comes out. I adore going up to his room because it's as elegant as a king's chamber, and so is my aunt's bedroom: it's all hers, and it has a dressing table and stool. I've never seen myself from the front and the back at the same time before. Is that the way they see me when they see me from the side? I didn't really recognize this new Oshinica, and I think my nose is too big if you look at me from the side, but . . . what a luxurious bedroom . . . and it has a terrace with cane furniture. She has her own bathroom. It's violet with turquoise and white. Then I begin poking around in her chest of drawers. Wow! Is that neat or what? It's like getting inside my aunt's world. She has hose, invitations, spools of thread, little boxes; everything's a secret, but I just go about opening and closing doors and drawers.

Here there's plenty of room to store things; at our house all I have is the bottom drawer of the chiffonier. That's where my mom puts my folded underwear, so I can't really hide anything there. Oh, how I'd like to be able to lock it and have my own private space! Even if I just had a place to hide this diary, so I wouldn't have to live in fear that someone is going to read it. It's no one's business but mine.

A lot of times I hear the adults say they'd give anything just to be kids again. Being a kid is marvelous, we're supposed to be happy, not be in need of anything, and laugh at anything . . . and also, they begin gazing nostalgically. I don't understand it. What do they see that's so great about it? This is being happy? My mother yells at me, she spanks me, and at school they punish me. I still haven't finished writing "I must obey my parents and my teachers" five hundred times. For more than a month now, I've had to fill up page after page of the same thing. And they won't let me talk in class, either. The only homework I have time for is to repeat this writing, and I like it, especially when all the lines are connected. I can do it fast and they look great. I think that those adults who believe those things about childhood probably couldn't draw those lines, or their parents didn't scold them. And if that's true, will it be worse when I grow up?

Do I want to look like my mom, my grandmother, or my aunt? No, I'd rather look like my grandfather, my dad, or even my brother. Those women are so boring, and they're dumb as well! Well, I guess my mom isn't so dumb, but she's not all fun and games either. My grandmother can't even go to Sears by herself, and it's only two blocks away. But she goes secretly with Uba. Women are supposed to stay at home; it doesn't even occur to them to go rowing. My dad is really nice; the men go out to work and the women take care of the children or the brothers and sisters, like me. At least I don't get bored, because I can go outside and always beat the guys at soccer or baseball.

"That man dressed in blue, is he the groom?"

"I don't know, honey, but I think so. The other one looks too old, but let's go to the park, because your grandfather doesn't want anyone to disturb him."

"Is it really possible? That ugly guy wants to marry my aunt?"

"I don't know. I'll ask your grandma later. All I know is that your aunt has been jumpy lately, and who knows what they're going to talk about?

"When I brought the coffee, I heard them talking about the property in Polanco as a part of her dowry. But I shouldn't say anything; your grandfather would kill me. Let's take your little boat to the park, and we'll put it in the water; all the kids will be taking theirs. Didn't you bring yours with you?"

"Yes I did, Uba, and I like to come over here because then you always take us to the park."

When we got back, they were saying good-bye.

"That guy dressed in blue, the one with the straight hair," said my dad, "he's not going to marry your aunt."

I felt faint. Oh my God! What a shame! Everyone was mad. And my poor aunt, she's so pretty and he's really ugly. She was so embarrassed that she locked herself in her room. My father doesn't have any land or even a car, so how is he going to get *me* married? When we were leaving, I heard my grandfather say, "They're crazy! Is that all they think of her? They can go straight to hell! They don't know what they want. Well, I dare them ever to find any girl as beautiful as my daughter."

I don't want anyone to know that I cried all night long, or that

I bit my blankets out of rage. But what difference would it make if just one of us got mad? What did my aunt feel? What a shame, him rejecting her like that! How embarrassing! She had already gone out a few times with this guy, who had a beard and wore a black hat, and now, when they finally come to formalize the engagement, the deal is off. This isn't going to happen to Moshón. Maybe I'll just stay like a little girl. I don't want this to ever happen to me. It's horrible being a woman. If I'm stronger than Moshón and I can do anything he can, what's the difference? I don't want to even get close to an Arab. Yesterday, when those men arrived, my granddaddy, smiling with his gold teeth, said that I was his little granddaughter, and they said what everybody says: "Like a bride! A true bride!" That means good luck!

Why would I ever want to get married?

"Auntie, you're so pretty. Why would they want to do that to you?"

"Well," my mommy answers, "they're backward and stupid. They never let your aunt go out alone; they always hired a teacher to come to the house. They always made her seem like she was hard to get, and that's why she talks like that. Ugh! They didn't even let her have any friends. And those from Persia? They're all the same. What's the difference? Your grandfather has made a slave out of your father. See what I'm saying? Yesterday he told him to get the car out of the garage just as we were getting ready to go to the movies. That ended that idea. Heaven help him who doesn't do what he's supposed to. Everything will get ruined. And don't you see? If you're not high class, you don't have good clothes, and we're even without a car. In Istanbul, I used to go to the best schools, and our classes were taught in French. My mother's family, of course, was upper class."

◇ ◇ ◇

Two kids who ride the school bus to the Roma neighborhood began fighting; they had said a lot of bad words in Arabic to each other on the bus.

"I hope you swallow an umbrella and it opens up inside your stomach," said one of them.

"I hope you live 120 years in a hospital," said the other.

"A curse on the ship that brought your father here!" replied the first one.

I get scared when my daddy speaks Arabic to someone. He learned it in the Lagunilla Market and he speaks it from time to time, but not at home, of course—well, whom would he speak it with? Fortunately, no one at school has ever heard him speak it.

"Because of Queen Esther, we Jews were saved," said my mommy. It just so happens that the king of the Philistines, who wasn't Jewish, fell in love with Esther. As the king, he had all the young girls of the kingdom brought to him, and he chose her. Even though his prime minister did everything he could to prevent him from marrying her, it was her beauty that saved the people of Israel. And now we honor that marriage with the Purím celebration in March; at school we have a kermess charity bazaar with costumes; the mothers distribute bread and marmalade called "hamentachen," and they give us wooden rattles to liven things up.

They pick two candidates from each room to play the role of Queen Esther. On the day of the kermess, when they crown the queen, everyone really gets excited. Even the parents get drawn into it—they buy lots of votes so that their daughter will be elected the queen. How fortunate the chosen one must feel! They've never even considered me; besides, my dad wouldn't ever buy any votes. But still, when they come around to choose the candidates from each room, I always get a little nervous because they just might say my name. But it's never happened. I guess I'm not that pretty. And it's always the same girls. Last year, Dori lost by one hundred votes to the daughter of the school president. After the coronation, I like to go to the charity raffle, because the parents who own stores or factories always donate neat gifts. Then they reenact the moment when the king chooses Esther. Out on the patio, we dance horas in a circle around a bonfire. Then we eat. My mommy usually makes a huge bag of popcorn because she was assigned to a food table.

I wet the bed again, and my mommy had taken me half asleep one last time to the bathroom. I still do it, and I don't even feel it. I guess she has gotten used to it, because she doesn't scold Clara or me; she just leaves the sheets on the bed all week and the stain begins to look really horrible. Whenever we get a new maid, I'm always embarrassed, but then I shake it off—there's no way I can hide in my own house, so I just act like nothing's happened.

My sister and I sleep in either of the two beds and when we realize that we're wet, we just change our pajamas and get into the one that's dry. Zelda just frowns at us and complains that our beds stink; she thinks she's unlucky because she has to sleep with us. We don't do it because we want to, and I'd never be able to invite anyone to spend the night, and I'd never dream of going to someone else's house. Just think what would happen if everyone at school found out! My mommy's right in loving Moshón more than us. He's really clean. These kids that don't wet their beds—how do they do it?

Freddy wets his bed too. We could try putting those of us who wet our beds together in one room, and those who are normal in the other. We can do it, if my mommy wants to; if not, Zelda will have to make sure she doesn't get her bedding mixed up with ours; then she'll have to stop bothering us.

I was going to say that out of the three closest aunts I have, the one I like the best is Chela, although my mommy's sister who lives in Monterrey is nice too. I was sent to stay with them during vacation. I even went to my cousins' school, which I really liked, because everyone wanted to know who I was, and my cousins would act like they were important, saying I was from Mexico City. Just outside the school gate they sell jícama, oranges, cucumber slices with chile, crisp pork rinds, yo-yos, baleros, paletas, chocolates, pinole, well, you know, all the things my dad says are no good for you—ah, and some caramel-covered apples that you suck on until you reach the apple part. Sundays are the same for me as for anyone else: I love to buy, buy, buy. But it's not the same in Mexico City. There's nothing to buy because when we get out of class, the buses are waiting inside the school yard, and even if they *are* selling things outside the gates, we don't ever see them.

Alegre is five years older than me. She has a bedroom all to herself, and I like being her cousin. And she has so many friends! She does things the way she wants to, she wears checked shirts that have the necks and sleeves like a man's shirt, and she has a wallet for her money just like my dad's—ah, and she wears pants, too. On Saturdays, she invites three or four friends over to spend the night; we haul mattresses, pillows, and blankets down to the living room, turn up the record player, and stay up as late as we want. What a great life! At home, if we make any noise after my mom turns out the light, she yells at us, "Enough! Be quiet. Or I'll give you all a good whipping."

Aarón asked me if I wanted to swim; I thought he meant in a swimming pool, but no, he meant on the terraced roof behind the kitchen. We put a board in front of the kitchen door to keep the water from leaking inside. We started filling up the patio at eight o'clock in the morning, and by eleven it was up to our knees. Even though it was freezing cold, we swam in our underwear. I can't believe I even opened my eyes underneath the water and I could see the bottom. It was a fantastic day! When my aunt came home, I got scared, but she didn't get mad. She just laughed, put a towel around me, and said, "Girl, you're so crazy. Just look at you! Really, you do some of the silliest things."

Before I went to sleep, she said to me, "Tell me, have you heard the stories about crazy Ishodotro of Yojá? They used to tell them to us when we were little kids in Istanbul." I adore the way my aunt laughs. And she has that mischievous look in her eyes. It seems a little strange to me because grown-ups don't do pranks. I wanted her to tell me the stories, even though they're the same ones my mom tells us.

What a strange aunt! If she lived in Mexico City she might get along with my mom, and then maybe my mom would be easier on us.

This year, I'll finish sixth grade. It's the year when they start taking most of the girls out of school—this is the year they begin to live at home with their mothers. They take sewing lessons, they learn how to cook, make desserts, and who knows what else; but all of a sudden they become pretty and get married. The boys are allowed to continue their studies. Oh, heaven forbid! What if they do that to me? What am I going to do at home all day long?

There are two bakeries near our house, but we always go to the one on Nuevo León, even though it's farther away. My mom likes their bread better. The only bad thing about it is that to get there we have to walk past Rosi's house, and every time her mom's standing at the window, and when she sees us walking by, she yells out, "Are you going for bread, honey? For the love of your mommy, get me a couple of loaves, too."

And there's no way you can say no to her, right? So she's always taking advantage of my brothers, or me, and as a result, she always gets fresh bread brought to her door. And yesterday, when I brought her the bread she had even more nerve:

"Honey, dear, could you please help me move this table, and that plant, and this pot?"

And she asked Moshón to bring her some soft drinks from the store across the street. We're definitely not going to walk by that old bat's house anymore. No wonder they call Rashelica the brazen old . . . I mean, well, she has some nerve! Even though it takes longer, let's walk all the way around the block, and besides, why doesn't she send Rosi dear, as she calls her, to do those things?

Sitting at the window that looks down to Piedad Street, Aunt Cler helps while away the hours. She is accompanied by the sounds coming from a large oval-shaped radio. This afternoon we listened to the comedy programs on Radio XEW and XEQ. Between programs they play songs by singers such as Avelina Landín and Amparo Montes—"I'm walking down that tropical path/my eyes are full of passion and my soul feels like crying"— or something like that. And at six o'clock, *Doctor Heart*. It's a neat program that helps people solve their problems. I love hearing about things that I never knew existed. I'd like to write her an anonymous letter with a fake signature so that my mom wouldn't find out, but I bet they'd never pay any attention to an eleven-year-old.

"So long as you've got your health, the rest is unimportant; you should be thankful to God that you're not an invalid, blind, or an orphan," says my father. "The people who write to her have nothing else to do; they're just vain."

And do they have problems! I'd like to ask her what I need to do to quit wetting my bed or to stop my mom from yelling at me.

"Dear Friend, . . ." she'd probably answer. But what a lovely lady! How I wish someone would say that to me sometime! My father says people who talk like that are hypocrites and he doesn't trust them.

Is that really true? Maybe so.

While we listen to the programs, I watch Aunt Cler sew and sew, and I see that she's concerned about what's going on in the soap opera—if they had caught Esmeralda or if the daughter had deceived her father. Silently she changes the color of the thread, finishes the last stitch, and happily admires the juicy purple grapes that grew from her hands on the throw pillows that will adorn her couch in the living room.

My mom goes into the kitchen to fix that tasty dessert that old Aunt Cler makes from rolled orange rinds. Her maid is off on Mondays, that's why we go to see her on those days.

"She can't be left alone; what would she do if someone comes to the door or she needs to go to the bathroom? If no one is around, what would she do? Heaven help me if something were to happen to her. And, to top it off, she's in a wheelchair. Poor thing! She can wheel around a bit. Uncle David, thank God, will come this evening."

And that's the way it's been for two years, and ever since her daughter died, she's been paralyzed.

This Monday my mother couldn't visit Aunt Cler, so she sent me with the keys instead.

"That's very nice of you, child. Stay for a while! Let's talk, take your mind off things, you poor dear."

As soon as the train starts along Piedad Street, I try to spot her window from my seat. In that building, there's a window curtain with that starched pride and the elegant hand-stitched lace, behind which I spot aunt's little face with straight hair. I climb the stairs, taking a short rest on each floor; the stairwells and hallways are so wide that you could dance a hora in each one. I think: once she walked up those stairs for the first time, and she'll go down them on the last day of her life. I get the keys out and I'm in the living room. I look around everywhere, there are embroidered doilies all over the place, and you can see the work of her hand in every throw pillow, in every corner. I cross through the sitting room and reach the door of the little room where the sound of the dark wood radio fills the house and my aunt's life. I know that she'll be surprised to see me because she never knows which niece has been designated to visit her that day.

"Ah! Is that you?" she says without cracking a smile.

Those big, deep eyes that I thought would light up just stare at me, giving me the shivers. I don't appreciate her not saying something nice about me coming—not willingly, but here I am. I sit down in this small armless chair, directly in front of her, and I look toward the street. The sun is strong, but it's partly hidden, so we put the blinds down. I like to leaf through her embroidery magazines while we listen to the radio programs. In one of the old magazines, *Family Magazine,* I run across a beautiful cross-stitch and she says she'll show me how to do it. When she sends me to get the orange-rind dessert, I stop and linger in the living room without bothering her. My mom told me that Auntie cleans all of her decorations on the glass shelves herself. She doesn't trust the maids, everything has to be carefully dusted, right down to the last little corner and crack; that's why she gets them out. I take a peek into the bedrooms: I see a picture of her daughter, then a girl younger than me, and I get sad for my aunt who lost her daughter and for the girl who, had she lived, would have inherited the responsibility to take care of her sick mother. That daughter is with her when she's embroidering, watching other lives from the window, listening to the radio, and watching the trains coming and going up and down Piedad Street.

🏃 at grandma and grandpa's house.

"Hey, grandma, can you put a record on for me?"

"I don't know how to turn on the record player, dear."

"Should I ask grandpa to do it?"

"We only have Arabian music."

"Well, that's okay, whatever . . ."

"Just as soon as your grandpa comes downstairs."

"No, don't say anything to him," my father says, "it'll probably break, and then he'll just get mad at me."

"Oh, Daddy, don't worry! I want to hear how it sounds. Ever since I've been born, they've never played it. It's always been closed up, just sitting there by itself. Does it even work?"

"Be quiet. He's coming down now, and don't you dare say anything to him!"

Like always, my dad and I jump up from our chairs at the same time and proceed to kiss my grandpa's hand, which he then promptly sticks back in his pocket.

"Shamuel," he says, "this television set isn't working."

"I'll talk to the repair man tomorrow, Papa."

"And tell them to quit making a fool out of me, they say they fixed it but now it's worse. And it's happened four times this week."

"Here, let me take a look at it."

"What! You don't believe me? If I tell you it's broken, then it's broken."

"Mom has been watching a soap opera and she doesn't notice anything wrong with it."

"You don't see anything because you're ignorant. Look, the picture is horrible. Isn't that right, Luna?"

"Well . . ."

"Look, don't you see those lines across the screen?"

"Uh, where?"

"What do you mean where? Are you blind? Yep, it's true, the older you get, the stupider you become. Anyone can see them," he says, smiling toothily.

"Okay. Oshinica, you're smarter than your father. Don't you see the lines? I'm not crazy! Everyone around here contradicts me. Do me the favor of telling those jerks to come and fix this once and for all."

"Grandfather, what does the record player sound like?"

"Which one? That one? It sounds beautiful. It's one of the best record players around. The sound is the greatest. You know, of course, that your grandfather doesn't buy cheap stuff. But not now, dear, I'm tired, and besides, on top of what your father has put me through, my stomach hurts. Maybe on Sunday, if I'm feeling better . . ."

The wedding was very elegant, and the person Aunt Chela married turned out to be much more handsome than that other guy who couldn't come to terms with my grandfather that day. Too bad it had to be in the synagogue on Querétaro Street, but since he's from the Arab neighborhood, they do things their way. It makes me furious the way they put women on a pedestal, like birds in a cage. I don't know why my grandfather wears a hat, you couldn't see his face, all you saw was the hat and that's it. I got hyper and went downstairs for a while and hung onto my daddy's legs. The guy who seats everyone saw that I was overexcited, but since I'm still a little girl he couldn't send me back upstairs.

My grandfather looked very proud, holding the arm of his only daughter as they walked toward the groom who is now our uncle. The reception was in the Dream Hall, which is on Cordoba Street. My dad wasn't happy taking care of the drinks and looking after everyone, but it was probably because my grandfather spent a lot of money. My dad said, "Why so much fuss, everyone's going to end up complaining anyway." But I could tell that my aunt was very happy, and so was my grandfather.

I often come back from my grandfather's store stretched out in the back seat of his car. If it's still daytime, I know when we are going by San Juan de Letrán because of all the billboards and advertisements that I can see through the window, but I prefer to go at night, so I can see all the lights that go on and off. And I know when we get to Alvaro Obregón Street because of the trees with huge branches, the old houses, and the electric wires that I know by heart. When he's about to drive the car into the garage, I get up and hear him say, "Damn it, they take so long to open the door," while he's honking the horn and getting more and more furious. Finally, Uba comes running outside with her pigtails and that smile that she thinks hides her fear, wiping her hands on her apron, which is always wet around the waist. I know all about the terror that my grandfather's arrival causes, and where did he buy a horn for his car that sounds just like his voice? Inside, everyone is scurrying around. It's him! Raquel, take Teresita to the bedroom! Children, turn off those lights! Before going inside, Uba and I look at each other like accomplices, while my grandfather puts the stunning car into the garage. Just watch, he says, soon he's going to have to leave his pride and joy out on the street. My brothers and sisters run outside to greet him with hugs and kisses. He takes off his hat and walks through the garage and into the kitchen, stopping to take a look at the garden in the back because he always reminds everyone that the roses and orange trees belong to him. Wearing his standard suit, he checks the contents of the simmering pots on the stove and checks to see if the table has been set in the dining room. My dad won't be long in coming, and my grandmother is busy with her hands in a silver bowl, separating out the bad rice from the good. He's not in a hurry to get back anyway, because my grandfather always gets into an argument with him. For a long time now he has just said yes to everything.

Before greeting everyone, my grandfather goes to the small bathroom next to the kitchen. Later, when he comes downstairs, we eat. We all get seated around the table and begin to pray.

Ever since my aunt got married, my grandfather acts differently. He is very friendly toward his son-in-law. Within a few weeks my uncle began arriving late to eat, and now we don't start until he arrives. Now then, if my dad tried doing that, my grandfather would kill him right on the spot. Today he was about to blow up when my Aunt Chela almost began sobbing, saying in a tiny voice, "It's just that his mother gets upset if all of her children don't have breakfast with her, and they're really bad about praying. Don't get upset, Daddy."

After what seemed like hours of waiting, my young uncle, all smiles, shows up with the Shabat book in his hand. Can you imagine? While he's shaking the men's hands and telling everyone that the prayers at the temple where he goes always end late because they're longer and more complete, he's telling us that his Judaism is superior to ours because, according to him, we don't practice religion the way we are supposed to; and, besides, we drive cars on the Sabbath. Everything calms down once the chicken soup is served, and when it's time for squash, my grandfather is already offering avocado to my uncle, another piece of chicken, and he assures him it's kosher, like the wine, too. What's more, he's impressed with his son-in-law's style and intonation when he prays, which is the way they do it in Damascus. I don't understand the differences among the regions of Syria, and he responds with a laugh: "There aren't any. Just consider the people from Guadalajara who think they are better than people from Monterrey. It's that simple. In Syria there's a city called Damascus and another one called Halab. But you know how Jews can be."

I just can't stand the way he prays, and how he acts like he's better than us, and how he sits down at the table as if he were a king, telling me every five minutes, Darling, bring this, bring that. But I don't dare say no to him. And my aunt, ever since she became pregnant, shrugs her shoulders even more and speaks as if she's suffering from a lot of pain. At the dinner table we get to talk about different things; in the living room we only discuss religion. My new uncle loves to put on airs, and he asks how could we ever allow a microphone in our temple, which means using electricity, and that's a sin. And then he says Turkish rabbis are religious only when it's convenient for them.

My father doesn't dare say a word, fearing they'll take it out on my aunt, so I'm the one who responds the most, defending our people and our customs, always with my father's approving eye. Sometimes I feel like I'm speaking for him. Since I'm supposed to be like my granddaddy's mother, he likes me a lot and never scolds me. Even my mother doesn't make me shut up or pinch me to stop talking. They just laugh and then send me off to the kitchen to get something, anything, but hurry back as fast as possible. The women are always coming and going; they seem to talk a mile a minute. My uncle doesn't say much because he can't get a word in edgewise, and my aunt, embarrassed, laughs and says, "Oh, Oshinica, how do you come up with this stuff!"

Afterward, I go into the living room and look at all the pictures in the newspaper of people who got married that week. How fine the women look with those long trains flowing behind them! I wonder if I'll ever be in the newspaper some day, dressed like them, like a bride.

Every time I'm bounding down the stairs of the temple, I run into the old lady Mrs. Magriso, who's always grasping the handrail and stopping to catch her breath between steps. She'll stop whomever she can, so she always stops me, mainly because my dad has always taught me to be respectful, and even more so with older people. She tells me the same thing over and over every time I see her, and she doesn't remember that she always asks me the same thing every Saturday: "Ishica, who's your family? Which Sara is your grandmother? Of course I know her. I haven't forgotten that I was her neighbor in Istanbul, we grew up together, your uncle made clothes, she was just a youngster, and before long, one gets old. I'm sick, too. Say hello for me, honey," she said, as I watched her false teeth—and were they false!—smack against her pink gums. Then she kisses me on both cheeks and says, "You take after your mother, and you've got all her best features!"

Whenever it occurs to me to use just my dad's surname, some people never recognize who I am, and they repeat, "No, I don't know him, dear," and they just walk away. The reason is that just about everyone who belongs to this synagogue is from some place in Turkey, Bulgaria, Salónica, Esmirna, or somewhere near there. Here in Mexico, I don't think there are many Persians.

Once, during Yom Kippur, my dad took us to the Arab temple because sometimes Granddaddy liked to go there. They ask about me there, too, but for sure I wouldn't say I'm Sarica's daughter from Monterrey because they wouldn't know who she was. While the prayers are beginning, all of us from the choir walk all through the temple and meet up with the people who are just coming inside; then they look at us, trying to make out our parents' and grandparents' faces in ours and, finally, they ask, "Ishica, whose daughter are you?"

I was outside the temple when the first bride for today arrived. I liked her because she smiled at me, and I ran up the stairs to the choir in order to see her; they might not pay me afterwards, but I just stayed there: I was excited to see her enter the building. She got out of the car with her bridesmaids. The groom had already arrived to greet the guests.

Someday I'll also walk down the aisle holding my father's arm. The synagogue looks very imposing, now that they renovated it by putting three arches in front with two marble lions that hold up the sacred tablets. My fiancé will be waiting at the altar. What nerves it must take to walk all the way down the aisle while all those men and women have their eyes glued on you. They decorated the temple beautifully today. They must be rich; sometimes it's not fixed up so nicely. They've lined the entrance with roses, like at school when somebody important comes to see us.

I don't want to marry someone from another community because I won't be familiar with their way of getting married; then they'll probably bring their own rabbi and singer. I want to hear my own choir sing the songs I know by heart; and I'll save the first candies for the choir. I don't want to hear anything about how there weren't enough to go around. Ah, yes . . . and my bridegroom is going to be very handsome, not like this guy, who is really old.

The second bride was so natural about it all: the synagogue had been decorated since five o'clock, and now it was eight and still not much was going on. We were half asleep in our seats. All of a sudden the people who were sitting in the pews turned their heads. Finally! The bride has arrived! I squinted through the window: I can see her, even though she hasn't gotten out of the car yet. The choir director went downstairs in a huff to get our candy, and once we started eating the chocolates and almonds, we stopped dozing off. When the candy is wrapped as pretty as it is, like today, it makes me sad to have to open it up. They gave us little transparent heart-shaped boxes with white and dark chocolates inside; but as usual, we gobbled them up as fast as we could. How can these brides have the gumption to arrive so late in the evening! They charge them extra if they arrive after a certain hour.

When I get home so late, Mommy already knows that it was probably an Arab wedding, and she asks me who got married, to whom, if there were many people, and if we knew anyone there. Señora Magriso is always there because she lives just around the corner . . . and I ran into her again, so I tried to help her, and she said to me, "Don't worry about me, honey, I'm sorry to stop you. I'm just coming to watch for a little while. Thank you, dear child. May God bless you! Like a bride!"

My dad's and my grandfather's stores are next to each other right in front of Lagunilla Market on Comonfort Street. The gate is really pretty, and we go through a patio to use the bathroom in the back. The owners of the booths actually live there, and so I get to know a lot of the people, and they're always saying hello to me.

While my dad's store might sell ten coats for small girls, my grandfather will sell only one item, but even then he still earns more. He has really high prices; my dad sells low so he won't get bored. He says you can sell five, then another five, sell twenty, then another twenty. As for my grandfather's store, there are days when the customers don't even bother to look and yet he thinks he's important because he sells fur coats. He insists that he has the finest product in the entire market. And my mother says, "I can't stand those outdated styles."

When my cousin Aarón comes from Monterrey, he always makes fun of what's hanging in the window, and he pretends to hawk the clothes to passers-by: "Come in and buy something, fools! Come in and see the museum!" Then Moshón gets irritated, but he always ends up laughing too. Since my grandfather is hardly ever around, I always try on the different shawls and fur coats made of fox, chinchilla, astrakhan, and otter, which is black and smooth. I look at myself in the mirror and try to look elegant and arrogant, a real snotty person.

My grandfather's store is really luxurious; there are big lighted display cases on both sides. The mannequins are beautiful. Their eyelashes and hair are artificial, they are thin, their breasts are nicely shaped, and their waists make you jealous. They seem a little vain, but when a client wants to try on what they're wearing, they look so naked you feel sorry for them. It makes me sad to see them like that because when the men in the street see them they elbow each other and giggle. They're so stupid! I go over to the window and try to cover them with something, anything, just so they won't be so bare. I take one of their plaster arms off, but I'm always afraid they'll lose their balance, fall over, and break into pieces, so I usually decide to leave them alone, and if I can, at least throw something over their breasts. It's just too much when my grandfather, who is always in a rush, not only leaves the mannequins naked, but also bald; neither their little turned-up noses nor their false eyelashes can save them at that point. They look horrible, as if they were frightened or enchanted, with stiff hands, posing as if they were talking to someone, looking very aristocratic. I could just stare at those fair-skinned queens for hours on end, and the ones with dark hair, too, but they never say anything. In my dad's store we don't have this problem: the hangers are never bare and I don't feel ashamed.

I'm happy today because it's my birthday, and my Aunt Chelita and her husband gave me a radio, a small dark brown one. I put it next to my bed and it fits perfectly on the nightstand. It's already really late tonight, but I just love listening to my radio. I change the station whenever I want; in fact, I hope I don't get sleepy; I'd rather keep listening. The only person's birthday that my aunt can remember is mine, and I hope she never forgets it! The best programs are on Sundays on XEW and XEQ: *Laugh-a-Thon,* and the one with Cuca, the telephone operator. I just love her slow, sleepy voice: "Helloooow? Helloooow? This is your smooth operator. Helloooow?" And the other program with Rafael Baledón and Lilia Michel, always fighting like on the *Honeymooners,* saying

"Honey" to each other all the time. It's cute. Do you think they talk like that in real life? Can married couples have so much fun, say "Honey" to each other, and kiss each other so much? My mommy and daddy? Never. The others are different because they're artists.

But the program I love the best is *Women in Jail*. It begins with scary music, then you hear an old door creaking open very slowly, and you're about ready to jump out of your skin because you don't know what's going to happen next. Then it begins:

"Carlos Lacroa! Look out, Carlos, look out!"

"Shoot, Margot, shoot!"

I would love to be Margot and always be next to Carlos.

My dad forbade Moshón from reminding our aunt that it'll be his birthday in two months. He also wants a radio. What a bummer! He cried and cried. He's not allowed to say it to her face, and she probably won't remember.

Ever since we got a television set we watch wrestling together, and I practice all the moves with my brothers. Of course, I don't do them hard. When I do the flying leap I hardly touch them, and I pretend to poke their eyes using my knuckles instead. But knowing how to wrestle has come in handy. Take Juan, for example, the one who lives across the street: his dad is a wrestler, and he's one of those guys who wrestles before the big matches, so Juan thinks he's the top banana. Well, I pinned him down the other day after he had hit Moshón. He couldn't get loose, so I counted to three, and he gave in. Now, whenever he gets into a fight with my brother, Moshón tells him, "I'll sic my sister on you again." Then he backs off. I wish there were women wrestlers.

The Three Wise Men brought bicycles for two of us; in fact, we had even insisted on it. We always used to get roller skates, and it's not that we don't like them, but this time we wanted bikes.

Like every year, we spent the entire day playing with our new presents. My bike is a Hercules, and it's black, really pretty. Moshón's is a little smaller; it's red. My sisters got roller skates. The only problem with our bicycles is where to store them. There's no way we're going to carry them up five flights of stairs each time we use them. My dad says we should keep them at my grandmother's place, which is not far away, and since Mexico Park is nearby, we can ride there. That's our only option.

We've been riding our bikes for two days now. The only bad part is that there are two other kids in the park who have only one bike, so one pedals and the other rides on the handlebars, and when they pass by they yell, "Jews!" As for me, if the big kid keeps on bothering us, I'm not going anymore. But riding around on our bikes, we made some friends, and it turns out that their parents know ours. Their names are Reina and Elisa; they're from the same community, and they live right in front of the park, on the other side of my grandparents. They have a pretty house, but it's not as nice as my grandparents'. We've got the whole month of January to play with them. Classes begin again on February 7.

"Children, hurry up! It's almost three thirty, and we have to be there before four o'clock. Don't make us late. If you don't arrive before it starts, they'll make you pay a fine of five pesos."

Near the door, my mother buys us some candy. Smelling of garlic and sausage from the fifteen sandwiches we brought with us in a plastic bag, we go inside the movie theater. My mother asks the usher at the door if she can take us to our seats so she'll know where to look for us afterward. But it's not difficult to find us: all she'd have to do is follow the smell of garlic.

It seems like everybody from school is there; they may as well have dropped us off at school. Ah, but the principal and the teachers aren't around. It's so much fun! We run around everywhere, and that's why we get seats in the balcony toward the back—that way we won't bother anybody. No one—my mother, the kids at the movie, or me—cares what's showing. They always have two good movies. Many of them are in black and white, and they're about planes dropping bombs and crashing. When it gets to be too much for me, I get down underneath my seat and wait until the noise stops. Then I sit up again and barely take a peek out of one eye: if it's a nice scene, I sit back and take out a sandwich. When the movie is in Technicolor, I'm really happy, even more so if it's about Lassie or Esther Williams. I'll never get tired of watching her swim effortlessly with her flowered bathing cap, smiling and barely moving her shoulders. She is very pretty in that bathing suit with a little skirt. Many of the girls sit with the guys they like, and they date each other.

I've never seen a movie that I didn't like. Why do some people say sometimes that it was a bad movie? Whatever, we think they're just great and, anyway, my mom drops us off at the movie theater every Saturday because that's when she plays gin rummy with her friends and she only feels comfortable leaving us at the theater. Oh, my God, don't let me ever forget that my grandfather should never find out that she plays gin rummy. It's enough that he already says bad things about her, and it would be even worse if he knew she was abandoning her kids in order to play cards. At eight o'clock, we finally hear our mother calling for us as she peers into the dark. She's always in a hurry so she can get home before daddy does because he always expects us to be in bed by then; if we're not, he creates an uproar and demands to know why she has to go out and play cards with her rich friends (if they were poor, maybe he wouldn't get so upset). Afterward, Mommy takes it out on us.

◇ ◇ ◇

My mother is sewing; Moshón, stretched out on the floor, is sleeping (he can sleep sitting up too, but always with his mouth open); I'm embroidering; Clarita and Zelda are doing homework; Freddy is pushing his tricycle down the hall, making all kinds of noise, like some stock-car driver, braking on the curves without flipping over. We're watching soap operas on TV.

"Freddy, please stop making so much noise, I'm going deaf. Back and forth, don't you get tired? Leave the trike alone for a while. Why so much fascination with the thing? And you make so much noise! Come and watch TV, the cartoons are going to start. Moshón! Moshón! Wake up! It's about to come on. It's useless; he's in a deep sleep. Look how I'm shaking him. Moshón, my son . . . wake up! Don't you want to watch TV? You said to wake you up. Ugh, he's gone back to sleep on us. This kid would sleepwalk if he could."

I can't stand it when Señora Rashel shows up, and it's always just at the moment when the program is the most interesting. And she never shuts up, either.

"An ashtray, dear? Ah, I'm so tired today," she complains, falling into one of our easy chairs. "What are you watching? Ah, *As The World Turns!* I can't stand the emotion; I can almost feel it in my soul. Poor guy, the wickedness of that woman, damn her, she's worse than perverse."

"Señora, shh, shh, please . . ."

"Ah, praise be to God! And Freddy here? Why so much noise?"

"That's the way he is, Rashel. Be quiet. He cries during the soaps—gets it from his mother!"

"I can't stand it!" she says, pinching herself and putting her hands to her face. "I get so fidgety!"

"Shh, shh, Señora, let us watch the program."

Freddy gets up from the floor and hugs his mother while he cries. I think Moshón was watching the program, too. He had probably woken up, but we weren't paying any attention to him, and he looked like he had been sobbing as well.

"Only old ladies cry, dummy."

"The program's over, Rashel, now you can talk. You know, we all like to watch that guy's mishaps."

"For the love of my dead father's ashes that I've never seen, the program at five o'clock, a little before this one, is much, much better. At least there aren't all those strange husbands. Really, it's much more emotional than the other."

"María, are the sandwiches ready yet? Yes, put avocado and beans on them. Twenty should be enough; they're small. Just wait until you try them, Rashel, the good part about their mother is her sandwiches; and Shamuel won't be long in coming, so we can get in a game of cards."

"Ugh! Something smells."

We all look at each other to see who is the culprit.

"Moshón, put your shoes on! For the life of me, son, don't make us nauseated; put some of that foot powder on that I bought for you yesterday. I just don't know what to do with that child and his feet. What else can I do?"

Almost stumbling, Moshón gets up, still wearing that jacket that his father bought for him. It's dark red imitation alligator skin with black tassels, and it makes him look chubby. Is that the way he's going to turn out? He's always going around with his arms crossed over his stomach. He could sleepwalk, but his hair—smothered in gel—is always intact; in fact, when we play ball outside not one hair falls out of place.

"Hey, everyone, Shamuel is home!"

We all get up, give him a hug, and hang on his neck, making

him stoop over. When we finish kissing him, we take the packages from his arms. Before coming home, he always buys something for us to eat.

"But we've just served sandwiches," says Rashel. "Why do you have to eat again every time your daddy comes home?"

We quickly get organized and put a small table in front of the television set. We put out slices of Kraft cheese, ham, and pickles, each on a separate dish, with salted crackers to one side. We fix four crackers with a piece of cheese on top and pickles that my dad is slicing rapid-fire. We repeat the process, always putting a piece of cheese on top.

"Sarica, I'm still not full. What else is there to eat? Anything left over from lunch? Whatever you have is fine. What do you think, Rashel, shall we play some cards? I'm still hungry. I haven't had anything since three o'clock, and on top of it all, I'm tired: a client tried on everything in the store, drove me crazy, and then didn't buy anything. Well, I guess they're right; who's going to buy a fur coat in this heat? We didn't even get one sale at my dad's store, and he was fit to be tied."

Goyita's stand in the market is square-shaped. It's about six feet wide and six feet deep. She sits about three feet away, directly in front of our store. She says that one of these days they're going to come in and remove their stands. How awful it'll be to sit in front of our store and have nothing to look at across the way! When she lifts the curtain in front of her stand and hangs out some dresses, her place looks bigger than it really is. She has pretty dresses, some embroidered with beads, mock pearls, and sequins. They're charming, cheap, and chintzy. From ten to seven o'clock every day she sits on a trunk full of goods. To one corner toward the back she has a makeshift dressing room, and of course, there's hardly any room to move between the curtain and the mirror. When I sit on a stool in front of our store, her place is the only one I can really see. I must spend hours there watching her haggle with her customers, and by now I know the lowest price for everything she has. When Goyita goes to "Number 3" (which means she's going to the bathroom), I take over for her. I think her dresses are for older ladies. My mother never buys from her—even though she could get a dress at cost for something special, like a wedding or a New Year's party, she'll always have her dresses tailor-made.

"You wouldn't want me to buy a dress in Lagunilla Market, would you?" she said to my dad.

Our store is also about six feet wide, but it's a lot deeper; that's why my dad always says at the end of the day, "Let's close up the box now." We don't have display cases because my dad never wanted his store to look too ritzy. He believes that if it looks too posh, shoppers'll think everything inside is expensive and they won't even come in. Racks of overcoats are lined up at the entrance to the store; little girls' coats are to the right; on the other side, three-quarter-length coats with large checked patterns that are in style right now. Halfway into the store, there are two mirrors and a couple of small stools, then more coat racks–overcoats, raincoats, and those ugly *mursanadas* that are out of style. Just like in my grandfather's store, the dressing rooms have bamboo ceilings, and when the coats don't fit on the racks, we pile them on the floor. Before, there were curtains for the dressing rooms, and the clients would draw the curtains and try on the clothes—my father used to sell women's dresses. Then one day it was going to be only overcoats because he could make more money, and besides, he didn't want to compete with Goyita.

Without the curtains now, we can control thefts more easily. My father has already caught several fat ladies with big dresses who would try to hide the merchandise underneath their clothes.

Whenever fat ladies with coats on come into the store, my father always says, "Thieves!" And he won't leave them alone for a second, or he tells me to follow them around because when we least expect it, they'll try to hide something underneath their dresses.

Here in Lagunilla Market my father cashes checks for everyone. He loans people merchandise so they can sell it on their own, giving it to them at cost. When Goyita goes for lunch, my dad tells Moshón to watch her store until she gets back. He really takes advantage of her because, while she's gone, he'll always sell a couple of dresses without telling her. When night comes, we always wait until the stands in front of our store close first, so the owners can see with the light from our store.

Cata, who is the daughter of the cleaning lady in our building, is my friend. She likes to talk to me, and when I go to the bathroom, she escapes from her mother to go with me. We walk around the patio, and if a man comes by she keeps a lookout for me—but not for long, because if I'm gone too long my dad gets upset. She asked if it was true that I'm Jewish.

"That can't be," she said, "Jews are bad and they killed Christ."

"Yes, I am Jewish, but I don't believe what you say. The Romans killed him, and that was a long, long time ago." Why doesn't anybody believe it? Here, they talk about it a lot, Goyita agrees with me. But they still like my dad, they say he's nice and doesn't even seem like . . . I'm happy that you can hardly notice I'm Jewish—you can spot Semitic people a mile away, especially because of their hooked noses and rough features. Why doesn't anybody like Jews? I don't want anyone to know who I am; if they find out, something might change, or they won't treat me the same as before.

My dad was born in Palestine; now it's called Israel. They named me after my grandfather's mother, and thank God, in Spanish it doesn't sound bad at all: Eugenia. It sounds ugly in Farsi. "Oshinica" is a mixture of Turkish and French, and that's what they call me, even though my birth certificate says Eugenia. They named Moshón after my grandfather's father. Zelda got her name from my mother's mother, may she rest in peace, and Clarita was named after one of my mother's sisters who died in Turkey. Freddy got his name from my mother's grandfather, and my last brother got his name from my grandmother Luna's father: Raphael. Can you imagine that my great-grandfather knew that his great-grand-son had his name? He was a hundred and eleven years old. They say he cried with joy when he heard about it. Then he died a short time later. The way I see it, I'd rather give my children names that I like, but I'll only be able to do that starting with the fifth one. That's okay; it's better than nothing.

Yesterday I was in Reina Mataraso's house when her brother who calls us Jews came in; we're all afraid of this cocky guy. When he saw me he laughed, although he didn't say to me what he said in the park. That night I dreamed that he was chasing me, and in trying to escape from him, I madly rushed across Sonora Street to get to my grandfather's house. I almost got run over.

I told Reina about her brother and how he was always trying to push us off our bikes at the park, and when we did fall to the ground, he and his friend would run away making fun of us. Reina told me that her mother was Mexican, and when she had married her father, Reina acquired a brother too; he had been adopted, and his father was Jewish. She said Andrés hated Jews and that he was a real butthead. What a strange family! Not a nice situation.

I'm sure my grandmother has regretted a thousand times over that she agreed to let us keep our bikes at her house, mainly because we hardly ever go outside when we're over there—we just head for the kitchen to see who gets the baseball cards in the Corn Flakes box or maybe a glass of water, some fruit, or cookies like the ones my dad takes to work every day. Uba always gets upset.

Lately, Andrés hasn't been bothering us much. The day Reina invited me over for lunch, he was actually nice to me and I liked him. He was friendly, and when he sat down at the table he cut a large piece of cake for me.

"Damn it! It's despicable! They don't even go to the hospital to see my daughter; well, God is going to punish them. When they found out it was a girl, only her mother and father went to see her. It's not her fault. Is she responsible? She's been crying for two days now. My granddaughter looks like a little doll! I told you, Luna, why did we marry her off to that scoundrel? And he's the son of another scoundrel. Those men used to hit her. Just think of all the others she gave up for this jerk. Yesterday the nurse brought out the baby girl. I started to cry, seeing my daughter suffer that way. What a pity! She's just a little girl responsible for another little girl; if she had given birth to a son, the mother-in-law and her son would be right here kissing his little feet. Is this why we raise children?" my grandmother said, crying.

Only twenty-eight days until the sixth of January. That's when we get our toys. We also go to the matinee movie at the Lido. It's really nice there because they give out candy on the Day of the Kings.

Last year I saw "The Adventures of Robin Hood" with Errol Flynn. I hope they show it again this year! He's my favorite movie star: he dresses in green with tightly fitting pants, has a pencil-thin moustache and a divine smile (oops, I said divine again; only God is divine). But he does look like a prince—well, he defends justice, and he robs from the rich to give to the poor (he makes them so happy that they want to make him a king). With his band of followers who are all riding horses, they take the towns by storm, whoop it up, and give stuff away; then they return a second time to steal everything so that later on they can give it away to others.

I can still remember what happened last year. I was coming out of the bathroom and I saw my parents enter the house with our new bikes; after that, I couldn't sleep a wink. I acted like I was sleepwalking and went back to bed.

The next day I told them that I had seen them come in and they explained to me that because the door was locked, the Three Wise Men couldn't get in. Realizing they would probably leave the gifts in the hallway outside the apartment, my parents said they decided to open the door and bring the gifts inside so the children next door wouldn't think they were theirs. Maybe . . . well, I'm confused . . . do the Three Wise Men really exist or is this something my parents do? Finally, I said to Goyita at Lagunilla Market, "None of it's true, it was really my parents." But then she said, "They really do exist, and they only give to children who believe in them." I guess I'd better keep believing, then.

High school is a riot: a different teacher comes in for each class and there's a bunch of recesses all day long. Between yesterday and today, we've had about ten teachers and every one of them says the same thing: "Boys and girls, today begins a new chapter in your life; you are not children anymore, you are students responsible for your actions."

Someone has said this year they're not taking us on an excursion to celebrate Children's Day; they're not even going to give us any candy and soda pop. I can't believe it! So, what fun is it being a student, anyway? There isn't even a Students' Day. They say there is, but no one observes it anymore. And to think I'm only twelve years old. I'm still a little girl.

"How is Teresita, Uba?"

"Shh, shh, be quiet, child. Your grandfather is about to come down, and if he finds out he'll kill me."

"Where is she?"

"In my room, where do you think?"

"May I bring her down?"

"Hush, hush, child!"

"But why, Uba?"

"Your grandfather doesn't even know I had another child . . ."

"But, Uba, Tere is already six years old, isn't she?"

"Yes, but he doesn't know anything."

"But you always bring her down to the garden."

"Ah, but that's only after he leaves; when he's here, I keep her in my room."

"You mean he's never even heard her cry, even once?"

"Never, child."

"Uba, I don't believe you."

"It's true, child, and if he finds out, he'll fire me. That's why your grandmother and I have kept it a secret. I can't even tell you what happened fifteen years ago when Raquelita was born! If your grandmother hadn't begged him and cried, I wouldn't be here today. He sent her to the ranch. But she has lived here ever since she was small and at times, I thought your grandfather cared about her, but of course . . . you know how he is. Uh-oh, here he comes, hush, hush! No, better yet, run to meet him, give him a hug."

"Good morning, Grandpa, how are you today?"

"Better, child, a little better. I saw Ernesto yesterday and I exchanged some old pills for these new ones. My stomach hurts. Child, I haven't felt well at all. When someone doesn't feel well, all hell can break loose; that's why I didn't want to have dinner for Rosh Hashana or even have dessert at your father's house on Sunday. Oshinica, come sit at the table and have a bite to eat with us. Luna, didn't you see me come downstairs? What the hell are you doing in there? I'm going to the store. Give me a bowl of cereal and come sit down with me while I eat. You know that I don't like to be left alone. Who put this watermelon out? Don't you realize I've been dying from stomach pains? Do you want to kill me?"

I'm really happy I was named after my grandfather's mother! That way every time we eat at his house, I can sit next to him.

"Oshinica, come sit here, you know that I like to have my parents next to me: Moshón on one side and Oshi on the other. Isn't that why both of you are named after my parents, you after my mother and, you son, after my father? That's why you should be next to me."

My other brothers and sisters sit wherever they can, but it's always better to sit next to my grandpa.

"Shh, shh, quiet down and come to the table. Let's pray now. And Luna, where's the wine? Okay, Oshinica, everyone to the table. Didn't everyone hear me?"

"Grandpa, we're all here. Let's get started, we're hungry."

I'm so lucky! Last year, my Aunt Chela gave me a radio that I love to listen to at night, and now I have a record player that's all my own. Actually, there's an advantage to being the oldest, but I'm really tired of having to watch over my brothers and sisters—if something goes wrong, they always blame me. "But you were right here when they broke it! Why weren't you paying attention? These kids!"

Kids . . . well, that's not my fault! Whenever we begin to fight, my mother comes in brandishing a belt and puts things in order, and of course, the one who she lays into first is always me. By the time she gets to the last one she's tired and begins to feel guilty, but for whatever it's worth, it always hurts less than when my father spanks me; now *that* hurts because his palm always leaves an imprint on me. You can see the outline of each finger on our legs or arms.

"You can't go to Dori's house today because you have to take care of your brothers and sisters. Well, if you want to go over there, you'll have to take them with you."

"But, Mommy, how can I take them with me if they are such brats? None of my friends have to take their brothers or sisters along. Whenever you let me invite them over, they always come alone. . . . Oh, hi, Dori, I'm sorry but I can't go; I have to take care of my brothers and sisters. Are you sure? Them too? And what if they start fighting at your place? I can't believe it! Okay, we're on our way. Hey, Mom, can't at least Freddy and Rafael stay with you? Okay, you buttheads, let's go to Dori's house, but if you do anything wrong, I'll let you have it."

Every Sunday, since we don't have a car, my grandfather takes us out for a drive and we always end up at the same place: Chapultepec Park. It's really boring, driving up and down the same street. Why doesn't it ever occur to my grandfather—just once—to take us somewhere else for a change? There's a main road that cuts through the park, and everyone drives really slow, so we can all see each other. Some cars are filled with girls and others with guys, and they check each other out, laugh, hang about, waver a bit, then stop and get into each other's cars. Out of insecurity and fear, they joke and yell boisterously. A lot of our people show up, but we never get out of our car. We're always putting on airs, acting very serious, or else my grandfather gets upset. When we steal glances at each other, my mother always has to make some comment about it.

"You're silly," she said, shaking her head. "Decent girls don't come here; a lot of fooling around goes on here."

And my grandmother asks why else would the guys want them anyway: "One of ours wouldn't come here, right?"

The cars crawl along at a snail's pace; that's what we're doomed to do on Sundays. Everyone goes slowly in order to see everyone else and be seen. And there's a lot to see. Sometimes we'll turn and look at whoever is walking along the boulevard and then look to see who's coming from the other direction. We look at them; they look at us. Here, everything is too peaceful and it drives me crazy. Sometimes my father is so critical, other times it's my mother, but they always have to say something. And then we turn around and drive back, back and forth. During the second time, we look a little bit closer. Everyone begins to recognize each other.

Moshón can't stand the smell. When my father gave him the leather backpack, my brother said, "Oh, Dad, this thing smells horrible!"

"In time, the smell will wear off," he said.

But nothing he does helps. At night he has to hang it outside on the balcony, and whenever he forgets to put it out, we let him know, so he can't get away with leaving it inside. Wherever he goes, someone complains about it.

Clarita was crying all day long because she said she was fed up with those green velvet dresses with the half-circle neckline and skirts made out of that Irish cloth.

When my aunt got married, my mother had dresses made for all three of us. The neckline on mine was slightly different.

"Since she's a little older, she'll look prettier in this dress," the seamstress told my mother.

It wasn't long before it didn't fit me anymore, so it was handed down to Zelda, and from Zelda to Clara. This makes the third green velvet dress made of Irish cloth that Clarita has inherited, and since we don't wear those party dresses every day, she ends up wearing it for years before she gets a new one. But no one's going to realize that the latest dress, that is, *my* dress, has a different neckline.

"My dear Sarica, why don't you wear it more often? Why do you want to preserve it like a jar of cucumbers? Poor things, when are the three dresses going to get worn out?" Señora Rashel asked my mother. That's when I discovered that to be the youngest can have its disadvantages.

Now everyone is collecting silver chocolate candy wrappers again. I can spend hours taking the creases out with my thumbnail. They're so pretty! Everywhere I go, I'm always looking for chocolates wrapped in silver tinfoil with little pictures on them. They have to be unwrapped very carefully so the foil won't get ripped. I stick them between the pages of a nice book and flip the pages to see which wrapper pops up. Today, I got a blue wrapper with little stars on it. It's really pretty, and it's a hard one to find. I told

Dori I would trade half of it for the one with grapes on it. She didn't want to, but she gave me a little piece of one. I wonder where she got it, I can't find it anywhere. Maybe it's made in the States. I really like those wrappers so much that even though I probably shouldn't, I'm going to make a deal with her.

The English teacher—the fat one who smokes cigars—caught us exchanging wrappers; we were even sitting toward the back and being secretive about it, as if we were reading or had our faces pointed toward the blackboard. We've learned how to communicate by just glancing at each other. I've got the same wrappers she has, but she doesn't have any of the ones I have; I had some left over from last year and no one has them.

"Please, teacher! No! I'll put them away, I promise . . ."

I don't know what I would have done if he had taken them away from me. The wrapper with gold dice on a red background is at the beginning of the book, then small blue eyes on a yellow one, and the third is purple with little canes in five different colors. Even before I turn the page, I know which wrapper is next. I can't explain it, but I *love* collecting them. I hope this stays popular for a long time, like the spinning top did, which isn't popular anymore. Well, I guess it didn't last *that* long, but we sure had fun. I'm good at spinning tops but I'm lousy at making the yo-yo work; when I let it go, it just drops down and goes to sleep. I took my yo-yo with me everywhere, even to study; I couldn't let go of it for a second. At least I can do it better than Moshón. I wonder if my string is better than his?

Every day during vacation, and even on Sundays, I go to our store; I take lunch and stay most of the day. Sometimes my father gets irritated, especially if he hasn't been able to sit down and eat. He doesn't like his food to get cold, and all it takes is for him to spot the dinner pail coming. He gets really nervous if my grandfather's store hasn't sold anything. And then I get really scared. It doesn't matter what anyone says, he snarls at everybody. The employee will go out and sweep in front of the store again, splash some water to get rid of the salt, and sweep one more time. But it's useless. The closer it gets to when my grandfather returns from lunch, the more flustered my father becomes. When that happens he has no choice: he takes an overcoat from my grandfather's store and puts it in our store, which means that my father makes it look like someone has bought something; then he puts money in the till, and leaves the empty coat hanger in plain sight. That's the way my dad has avoided scoldings and insults from my grandfather for many years.

And then he sells it cheaper in our store.

"What? Only one item? Of course, you're worried about your own business more than mine. I'll bet you even steal clients from me. How can it be? I have the best merchandise in the entire Lagunilla Market and only one coat gets sold? Here's the problem: you're dumb. The older they get, the dumber they become. Look at you: six kids and you haven't changed one bit."

"Hey, Grandpa, why don't you get new stuff to sell? This is old fashioned."

"Shut your mouth! You don't know anything! Listen, do me a favor and go to the other store. Your father's made me so angry, my stomach hurts."

I checked the till and saw lots of change: nickels, dimes, and quarters. That means it's Saturday; during vacation there's always the same amount, but when there's more it means that the beggars will be coming around for some spare change. The same ones every Saturday: Señora Chuchita, Doña Carmelita, and Don Idilio.

They've been coming for years; Don Juan, at least, has been coming for four years; and the others, who knows how long, but they always stop by.

"Is Don Samuel in today?"

If they're tired, they'll sit on the little bench outside the store and then continue their march, giving us their blessings as they leave. When they stop coming, my father says they've probably died. He says they die because they're very old. When my dad's not there, they tell me what my father usually gives them; they're honest about it. We give less to the new ones. Lots of them stop by, all day long.

It's not very much fun owning a store in the Lagunilla Market. My father gets upset if I lose a customer. Moshón, of course, doesn't let anybody escape. But it makes me sad to have to fake a smile just to get a sale. My father isn't hypocritical, but a little hypocrisy doesn't bother him if it means he can sell something. And then there are those who come in with an exact amount of money, wrapped in a knotted handkerchief, saying they have only twelve pesos to spend. So you say it's worth thirty. And anyone can make an offer, but there's no need to go overboard. Take yesterday, for example; when I arrived, my father was in full form: "So, how much can you pay, ma'am?"

"Well . . ."

"Wait, take a close look at that cloth and compare it, why, it's pure wool, nothing synthetic. I'll demonstrate it to you. Do you have a match?"

And my father pulls a piece of thread from the cloth, lights it, and then says to the client, "Smell it? Pure wool."

And it's true—it smelled like burnt sheep to me.

"For you, thirty bucks. A steal."

"No, I'd better not, I don't have enough."

"All right, just to show you how much I want to sell you this coat, tell me how much you have."

"I can't tell you that, you'd get irritated."

"No, I won't. Go ahead, tell me."

"Well, I've only got . . . let me see . . . seven, eight, nine, ten, eleven . . . oh, dear, and I still need bus fare . . . I'm sorry, I just don't have enough."

"And you there, are you her friend? Can't you lend her the difference until she gets home? Then she'll pay you back."

"No, I don't have it either."

"Okay, since you people have been so nice, I'll let you have it for what you've got. Do you want it in a bag or are you going to wear it?"

"Oh, Daddy, how could you let it go for so little? And you didn't even let her talk you down?"

"They didn't have it, and besides, I'm hungry. Why are you late?"

"Mommy had to go to the market and I had to take two buses. I came as soon as I could . . ."

"All right, then, go stand at the door and watch things while I eat."

"Young lady (uh-oh, here comes a real doozy), what's this little coat worth?" (I was sooo happy that it was the same coat that my father had just sold!)

"Let me see . . . but go ahead and try it on." (I wondered how much I should ask for. She looked so poor.)

"Yes, it fits nicely. Well, how much is it?"

"That one is twenty pesos, but you can offer me twelve. Just don't tell my dad that I gave it to you for the bottom price. Do you want it in a bag? Hey, Dad! I sold one all by myself and really fast, too. I didn't take too long, did I?"

"Did you get a good price for it?"

"She bartered a lot, so I had to let it go for twelve."

"You did it again, silly."

"That's what you sold one for just now."

"Yes, but you need to try to get more for them, they cost me ten, and if I'm going to sell them for what they cost, we'll never make any money. Only the sun shines for free, my dear. There are more customers at the door. See what they need."

"They're just starting to look, Dad. Give them some time; they might get frightened and leave."

"No! You have to go after them, because they'll just go somewhere else. Don't you see that Jocobo is just waiting for them? He's very patient: he waits outside our store, and then he invites them over to his place. Watch how I get them to come into my store: "Ma'am, please come inside; it costs nothing to look. There's no pressure here."

And he lures them in. In hypnotic fashion, they follow his finger inside without even realizing it—right to the cash register.

Party time! Mommy bought the dough for fried bread; it's been forever since the last time she made it. Usually it's other Turkish food that no one wants to eat. She says she doesn't make this bread much because it's not good for you, but that's all her mother taught her to make back in Turkey. I ate four pieces and wanted more. She said that's enough and looked at me with those mean eyes of hers. Since Moshón didn't want his, I bought it from him. It was worth a nickel because it tasted so good. Tomorrow I'm going to ask the bus driver to stop at a store on Medellín Street so I can buy some gum; then I'll sell it at recess for a profit and pay off my brother.

Last time I made $1.30. I'm going to ask him to stop again today, and I'll buy twice as much. I'll sell each piece for 20 cents to the older kids and 10 cents to the younger kids. We're not allowed to sell things at school, but I don't let anyone see me doing it. It doesn't matter, because everyone knows that I'm selling something. Just so long as no one catches me.

I discovered that Mommy keeps a pile of magazines called *Confidencial* on a top shelf in her closet. There were twenty issues per month, and they came out ten years ago. Each issue has three love stories taken from real life. Although I've almost read all of them, I hope I never run out. They're the only things to read in the house. I adore those kinds of stories, but they're for adults. Plus there's a section in the magazine in which someone writes in about some problem to get advice. You can learn a lot. And there's another section on how to find a husband. I don't think any Jews ever write to the magazine. But it's fun to read. If only we had *El Tesoro de la Juventud* in our house, like Dori! When I go to her house and she's still in the bathroom, I try to finish what I'm reading but I never can. I've already read the fairy tales she loaned me, and I don't know who might have some Japanese and Chinese stories I could read. I've read *La Reina de las Nieves* and *Compañero de Viaje* like ten times already; no, it's more like twenty times, but I don't get tired of reading them.

In the morning I took my brothers to the barbershop on Michoacán Street and started flipping through the magazines they had on a table. I grabbed whatever was there, and I didn't even look at the cover. After a few minutes I opened up to a page with big pictures—the size of the whole page—of undressed women. I barely saw them before I quickly put the magazine down. My heart started . . . wow! I don't know what happened but I thought it was going to pop. Then I looked up at the barbers; they were busy with their customers. Since no one was looking at me, I discreetly picked up another magazine and started reading it as if nothing had happened. The magazine was called *Vea* and they had lots of them there. I'm ashamed to write this down, but there were all kinds of naked women—standing, sitting, and some even had their legs spread open. How disgusting! My God! How could they! Who knows what kind of women they are! Aren't they afraid that one day their moms or dads might see them in those magazines?

For the Jewish New Year, you have to dress up with the hope you'll look that way for the rest of the year. Mommy knitted some beautiful sweaters for us; she had never made them as beautiful. Mine is brown with yellow on the shoulders and brown diamonds. I'm going to wear it with a plain skirt. I'll bet we're going to be the best-dressed family of the whole synagogue. But here's the best part: The color and style of each of our sweaters are different. Finally, poor Clarita won't be bored with the same hand-me-downs.

Nowadays, I get around pretty much on my own. I know the Roma-Mérida bus line by heart, and the San Luis one as well. Both buses go downtown, but they take different routes. I get off at the corner of Tacuba and Isabél La Católica and walk down República de Chile, or I take any bus that's going directly to the

Lagunilla district. Along the way, I always buy some mangos, cherries, or apricots.

When I'm closer to home, I take the Santa María route. Those buses are brown with an orange stripe on the side. My mom says they take longer, but I like them better because they go by all the movie theaters—Gloria, Morelia, and Balmori—and even Becky's house, which is on Frontera Street. Sometimes we work it out so that I get on the bus at the corner where I live, she waits on Alvaro Obregón Street, and when she sees me waving from the window, she gets on. That way I don't have to buy another fare.

The Mariscal Sucre buses are blue-green and newer. I took one today, just to see where it went. I sat up front and discovered a million places I didn't even know existed. It goes down Amsterdam as far as the Insurgentes movie theater and even the Parisiana, the one that Dori likes so much. I also discovered that I can transfer to the Roma-Mérida line and make up time when I'm running late with my dad's lunch.

I don't like the train because it's too slow. I'll bet I know the whole city by now. I wonder why they call that green route the Mariscal Sucre?

While I was drying off after taking a bath this morning, I realized that I had grown two breasts like older women, only they're smaller. They're horrible, and I don't even want them. Did this happen because of the way I woke up or what? Yesterday, there was nothing there. This scares me! I don't want anyone to notice them. I couldn't really take a good look at myself because there's only one bathroom, and if I take too long everyone starts knocking on the door, and one of my brothers might miss the bus; so I just went flying out of the house. Since Moshón may make fun of me, I've got to act strong when we fight, play baseball, or do tricks on our bikes. I'll never give up and join the girls. They don't know how to do anything. And if I get hurt? It's probably going to hurt like it hurts wrestlers when they get pounced on.

If I don't change out of my school uniform, no one will notice anything. The good thing is that it's like an apron in front, and with my baggy blue sweater, it'll be even harder to notice. I have no problem with our formal dress uniforms because they're dark blue, and besides, we hardly ever wear them. And how am I going to hide them during gym class? Simple: I'll play volleyball with a sweater on. I hope my dad doesn't find out.

When there are no customers around, we talk with Goyita, even though my dad says she's jealous, especially when she sees that we sell a lot and she doesn't. Maybe that's why even when he doesn't sell much, she complains anyway, saying there aren't any customers.

"Goyita, will you let me see your magazine *Pepín*?"

"I've only got *El Chamaco* today. Do you want to read it instead?"

"No, not really. *Pepín* costs twenty cents, right? If I give you a few pesos every day, will you let me read it? I've started to follow the main story in it, and I can't put it down. Tell me what's happened to Esmeralda. Wasn't that old man about to trick her with something about her aunt being on her deathbed? I think he took her out for coffee and then took her somewhere because he had put a sleeping pill in her coffee. When she woke up, she was alone and undressed in a hotel room. Then she said, 'My God, what's happened, where am I?'"

"Ah, yes, now I remember," said Goyita, "he's just a dirty old man, that's all he wanted, just like all men, they only want to dishonor women and then dump them. That's why I refused to get married. They're all the same; it's better to go it alone. I live happily with my mother and niece. Anyway, that episode ended the story. What else did Esmeralda want from him? What more could he do to her? He abused her, he shamed her . . . he abandoned her. End of story!"

"Oh, my God, that's so horrible. Poor Esmeralda. Her mom probably threw her out of the house."

"Now there's a new one out; in fact, in yesterday's episode Claudia had left with her boyfriend on a bus to go to his hometown. And on the way they were kissing each other. That's the way it ended. . . . I haven't read today's episode yet; my niece should have brought it by now with *Pepín*. There she is! Didn't I tell you? She's reading it while she walks."

"Auntie, look! Look! Claudia just had a baby."

"What? So soon? But just yesterday they were on a bus headed to . . ."

I don't like taking the San Luis bus because it lets me off on Argentina Street—that's two blocks away from the store, but those buses come more often. Then I walk along Honduras Street where just about all the stores sell only wedding dresses. They must be very boring places; they're always empty, and the clerks stand at the door trying to snag customers. Do they really sell all those wedding dresses? I doubt it.

In *Pepín* they always disgrace the women by force or without them even realizing it. When are the mothers going to wear wedding dresses if they're still single? And who are the store owners going to sell them to? I guess there can't be many people who get married in Mexico, not many at all. Well, I'm going to be really careful: I'll never have a drink, so they can't disgrace me. I'll bet only Jewish people get married.

Today I went to a restaurant. The first time in my life. What an incredible place! It's called Sanborn's, and it's on Madero Street. I wonder if they're all like that? It's a palace. They took everyone in the choir, because there were two marriages, and since the second bride didn't show up on time, the chorus leader became upset and demanded they feed us, saying we were too young to go for a long time without eating something. The other kids felt right at home and knew what to order; I was the only one who was astonished by it all. The food was fantastic! Tamales, enchiladas, ice cream, milkshakes! The waitresses were so cute with their brightly colored dresses and little sombreros. I'm so happy I joined the choir! And I even earn money: fifty cents for each marriage. Sometimes we're really lucky: there was one last night, one this morning, and two more in the evening. Not bad! My dad almost never gives me money, and he'd never think about taking us to a restaurant. He says there's nothing like home cooking. He's got a screw loose! Mom doesn't even know how to cook—even he says so.

We have a dentist at our school now, and today he checked everyone's teeth in my class. He said I had twenty-eight cavities. He must be crazy! Do we even have twenty-eight teeth?

"It's highway robbery," said my dad, "He's shameless! Twenty-eight cavities! Well, he should just replace all of your teeth."

Now that I think about it, my teeth have never been checked. I didn't even know we were supposed to brush our teeth.

My mom decided that I was going to wear the yellow dress with the embroidered front. Yeah, it's pretty, but it doesn't have a blue collar. The only thing I'm concerned about is wearing a dress that has a large round collar, so it'll cover my breasts. Since the collar is embroidered, it's pretty too. I'm never going to wear this one, even if it was expensive. What a shame! If only they didn't show so much . . . and I don't want to go around without my sweater, that's ridiculous. I can still hide them pretty well, but they're still there.

On Sundays, we have only one clerk for both of our stores. My grandfather doesn't work, and since my dad can't run things by himself, I go with him in the mornings.

"It's strange! Everything's closed and it's already eleven o'clock. They must be sleeping off their hangovers," he says.

Chucho, who sells robes, is the only one who's open; he's more serious than the others.

What I heard was that there were two orchestras, and Doña Cata insulted Doña Soco, even spat in her face. And if it hadn't been for her husband, who knows what might have happened, and then this and then that. But, despite everything, I think they still enjoy themselves, and I'm always happy to go to the Christmas party, and I'd still like to have a Christmas tree; there's nothing wrong with that, but no Nativity scene, even though they are awfully pretty. I look at the ones they set up in the market, and I'm always tempted to change the donkeys for the ducks. I'm afraid to touch them; they might get mad if a Jew touched their things.

I got on the bus just three blocks from the store, and I don't know what happened next, but I dropped Dad's lunch container. Everything spilled all over the floor of the bus—macaroni, peas, everything. It looked horrible; it was all lumped together, like the way they give it to the beggars who go from door to door holding out their pots. I quickly grabbed the enamel container, which wasn't white anymore, got off the bus, and started crying. I didn't know which way to go—to the store or back home for more food.

❖ ❖ ❖

David likes that idiot Rina; all day long he says Rina this and Rina that, and I listen to him because I really want to be his friend. Well, I already am his friend: today he asked me to keep an eye out while they hid in the bathroom near the library; they were going to kiss and hug each other. I said okay, what else was I to do? If I don't, they won't trust me as a friend. I kept guard outside the door.

Sometimes David walks home with me after school; we go the same way, but I live ten blocks farther than he does. We walk down Insurgentes Street and once we cross the Nuevo León Bridge, we say good-bye. We have such a good time talking that the walk doesn't seem very long. I give him his backpack, and I continue walking down Juanacatlán.

I could hardly breathe today—my bra was too tight. And I felt strange all morning long, because I think my classmates have already figured out what's happening. My girlfriends had already said that it was time to use a bra so that my chest would look more attractive. They might be right, but I can't breathe; I wonder how the other girls can look so natural and breathe normally.

I ate at Becky's house today, and I met her mother's older sister. She lives with them; the poor woman never married. I told my mother about it, and she said the woman was destined to become a spinster, she was probably too vain; even with all the luck she had with suitors, still none of them seemed to meet her standards. Then she grew up . . . but who wants an old maid?

"The old men, if they've got the wherewithal, marry young women who haven't been spoiled, and they mold them to their liking," said my mom. "They're not stupid."

All the girls in my class have or have had a boyfriend—everyone except me. I'd like to know what it feels like, but if one of them tells me he wants to be my boyfriend, it'll be difficult to say yes. What am I going to do if one day David says that to me? But, after waiting for more than a year, there's no way I'll ever say no. It's been a while since we began buying the materials to decorate our school bus—little lanterns, flags, and streamers. We've always had the best float. I spent days and days making chains with crepe paper using different colors, but mainly light blue and white. I saw the parade on television. I can't believe how many people there were! And they even take their children with them. "That's dangerous! Aren't they afraid?" said my father. "They're all drunk, there'll be shootings, and people will die. This is the time to stay inside. I can't even imagine how they get down to the main plaza to hear the shouts for independence."

I was never allowed to go there for Easter or for All Saints Day. My grandfather arrives with the newspaper under his arm and declares, "Did you see how many died? This is not the time to be on the streets in this country."

Pepe came by today to tell me that David is going to make his move at the dance on Saturday. Oh my God, is it really true? I have to practice saying yes, yes, yes, yeeeeeeees!

We've already pooled our money: fifty cents each. The party's going to be at Becky's house because her mom is a good sport; she said she's going out with her neighbor so we can have fun. What a great mom! I went with Dori to buy ham and cheese for the sandwiches, drinks, potato chips, and other snacks. I like going with them to the supermarket and spending all that money on whatever we want. We brought a stack of records, but the ones we play over and over are "Frenesí," "Perfidia," "Adiós, my pretty little brunet, I'm going far, far away," and "Blue Tango, tadum, tadum, tara." Awesome! They're killer songs. I wonder if David is going to say anything to me? Or was Pepe just pulling my leg?

❖ ❖ ❖

"My dear little Rashelica, do you know where we can get a maid for grandmother? The damned woman just up and left yesterday afternoon, didn't even tell a soul. Don't mention it to your uncle. If they have no maid in the house, he won't be able to go to work. That maid, you know, was very good; really, you couldn't find a better one, nowhere. I feel for him, he's mortified."

"Well, I just know she's run off with her lover. Soon he'll dump her and she'll be back—and pregnant. That's the way they are, it's deplorable, they're born like that, and they've learned bad ways."

"That's okay, Rashel, I'll give her one of the girls. Just look at the situation your grandmother is in, oh dear, she won't be able to go very long without a maid. It seems like we always have the same problem. Well, I'm going to take a bath and go to bed. I'll send over some sweets tomorrow; I think they turned out really good. And what's up with your son? When is he coming home?"

"He's doing just fine, healthy as a horse. Don't even ask, Sarica, he has lots of clients in Mérida. He's taking a bus back tomorrow. The only problem is his crazy friend Enrique, who is there, and when they're together both of them are even crazier than he is. I'm really afraid when they're together. I tell my son, 'I'm not happy with that kind of friend,' and to my horror, he gets madder than a hornet. I'm so nervous about it that I'm going to Cuernavaca with my daughter. My brother lives there and he takes care of me. After getting married, he went to live there with his wife. Now I'm all alone! I eat alone; I drink alone. Enough! I'm going to rest for a while."

I can still feel David's cheek next to mine. No wonder everyone likes to dance like that. I can still feel how hot his cheek was next to mine. And "Perfidia," what a song! And David loves it too. As soon as it would end, he'd run over to the record player and put it on again. I'm amazed that a song can be so pretty. And then he'd put his cheek next to mine again. I'd close my eyes and the music seemed to overwhelm me, and his warmth too. Pepe's green eyes followed us all afternoon. I can only imagine that everyone in my class knows about David and me.

I'm learning how to dance the tango. Becky's older brother, who doesn't go to our school, knows how to dance it really well: three steps forward, then one backward, repeat, and at the end he bends us over backward and pretends to give me a kiss. I love dancing with him! Today, I ate at his house and then we danced. It was a wonderful afternoon! The other kids in my class are so dumb; they look like little stiff soldiers, they don't let loose, and they can't wait for the dance to end. It all seems like a gym class.

Professor Luvesky of the Hebrew School had a nervous break-down today. We've become the terror of the entire high school. We act as if we run the place—we laugh all the time, we always go into her class late, and we hide snacks that the cleaning lady sells us. Sometimes we don't have time to eat them between classes, so we end up being late to her class. But we also wait outside a little, because before the class begins she always asks for money for the Keren Kayemet, a reforestation plan for Israel, which is in a desert. I prefer to buy sweets. So, when class starts, we're still eating and laughing.

"Do you know what kind of marks are on my back?" asks the professor. "Well, it's full of whiplashes that I received from the Nazis when I stole a cucumber once. A cu-cum-ber! Do you hear me? And here you are laughing at me."

And then she went on and on, now almost berserk, while she showed us the number tattooed on her arm. She drew close to me, and shaking her finger at me, practically in my face, she blurted, "I'm here teaching you your language because you belong to a country that we never had, but you prefer to eat this junk and laugh at the teacher instead of going to Hebrew class. Do you know that I saw my family die in a concentration camp and that I was saved by a miracle? Do you hear me, Oshini? A miracle! I managed to escape during a heavy rainstorm and walked from place to place with my feet bleeding. Now that all that is behind me, I'm dedicating my life to teaching this language to Jewish children. And you people sit here and laugh at me! Look at my back! I have no one; I saw my family die! Can you possibly imagine what it was like?"

Then she went to her desk and cried. My candy and I shrunk out of shame.

"We have been fragmented into a thousand pieces, but we have made laws allowing us to survive in the Diaspora, without disappearing. This is why the Israeli people and their lands are still alive," she said in a more peaceful way, now that we were silent.

"We have had to place restrictions on ourselves, which is why we cannot assimilate; we are not superior, but we have to make sure that the Jewish people do not perish. Do any of you understand what it means to have a land where we can go and be welcomed?"

Then the teacher sat down at her desk. Her face was horrible, disfigured. For a cucumber, for a stupid cucumber, her back is full of whip marks. And there I was taking advantage of her. I can still see her face, and her eyes are focused on mine, her finger wanting to hurt me out of bitterness. It seemed like she would never stop talking, but I continued listening to her.

"Damnation, Oshini," she said, "dam-na-tion."

◇ ◇ ◇

I don't know how it happened, but all of a sudden I have this nice figure. For the first time, David said to me, "You're looking good." For one thing, I like myself better with a straight skirt on. I look different. I hate to say it, but I look pretty darn good. I'm going to make more skirts like that one. While he sat at his desk, he kept making crazy gestures with his mouth, as if he were biting something, and moving his head and closing his eyes, which looked like he was saying, "Oh-la-la." They say the same thing to me when I walk down the street.

I can't get anything right in algebra class, and I'm not going to understand anything if all I do is look at the teacher. While he teaches the class, I devour him with my eyes. I don't understand him, and I don't even hear him. Really, I don't have the foggiest idea what he's talking about. What's algebra good for in life, anyway?

I really like the teacher, but he's mean; he's always kicking me out of the classroom. Yesterday, as I was going into his class, he said, "Why are you coming in if I'm going to throw you out?" He hates me! I don't know what I see in this guy whose face looks like a pizza! Now I remember those movies with Rosita Quintana, the one who always fell in love with the guy who mistreated her. She'd pinch him and he'd swat her fanny. She'd act like she was mad, but she'd always go back to him. Pedro Armendáriz would laugh when he would do it to her, and he thought it was funny when things would backfire on her.

During summer vacation we go on field trips for five or six days. It's easy for the boys, but it's more difficult for us. Becky and another girl always get to go because their brothers, who are group leaders, watch over them. But for the rest of us, no way. I'm so jealous. This year they're going to Oaxtepec. The camp directors and the spiritual leader went to all the girls' homes to ask permission for them to go. They came to my house, too. I begged over and over and cried.

"Please, Daddy, it's not expensive, I promise I'll be good, come on, lighten up."

They said yes, but on the condition that my brother Moshón goes along. I don't know what he's going to do there: either he's going to be totally bored, or he's going to be stuck to me like glue the whole time. That won't work, but at least I can go.

We left early in the morning: four girls, twenty-five boys, two leaders, and the teacher. The advantage of fewer girls is that all of the guys are going to want to be with us. We'll be like queens. What does *reactionary* mean? As we were leaving my house, the leader said my father was a reactionary. What can that be?

We came upon a convent. There were mangoes everywhere—on the ground, in the trees, on the roadside, in the jelly, the desserts, and the cakes.

Today is the second day of the trip, and tonight I've been chosen to stand watch with Becky, Pepe, and David, from midnight until two o'clock in the morning. We guard against any attack or raid from some group like ours that's camped nearby. More than likely they'll try to surprise us and steal our flag. We can't ever allow that to happen. We stretched out on the ground and rested our heads on little piles of pebbles so we could look at the stars and talk in silence. We not only felt but could see the calmness, and hear not only our voices but, perhaps for the first time, the surrounding silence. I don't want anyone to interrupt this moment. The four of us are wearing pajamas. How beautiful to be alone out in the woods at this hour of the night! We can hear the wind rustling through the trees and there must be a river nearby, because we can hear it flowing. Our own voices seem to belong to someone else, more profound and mature. What a shame that at two o'clock in the morning we'll have to abandon these stones that give comfort to our bodies! We look at the sky and feel happy, and we see what we never see from our homes; we've exchanged lamps and light bulbs for the earth and the mountains; curtains, decorations, and walls for infinity. Why don't I ever spend the night outside in a garden, or at least on our balcony? Why don't they build houses with glass roofs and sliding blinds? Why are there layers and layers of cement between the bright light and the beds where we sleep? Why extend the distance between them and us even more?

Did you know, little stars, that you'll be fixed in our eyes for the rest of our lives? Do you realize that? Your distant but powerful light will endure in me for many years.

We hear voices.

"Why are you guys so quiet? Okay, gotcha, you were asleep!"

It's two-thirty in the morning and they wake us up to change the guard.

"Yep! We couldn't even hear you breathing. You guys were sound asleep."

"We were not. We were talking. We were feeling everything around us."

Then we looked at each other and smiled. We don't say anything. They wouldn't have believed us. We returned to our tents; inside, we broke our pact with the stars.

◇　◇　◇

Hebrew is easy, charming, and uncomplicated; it's written like it sounds, like Spanish. But it looks kind of funny. You might think it's more difficult than English, because the letters are different, but it's easier. I taught Irene, the maid's daughter who lives across the hall, a few words in Hebrew. She thought I was immortal. I had to laugh.

She believes that since it is written backwards and the books begin at the end, it has to be from another planet. We spend a lot of time with our teacher, Luvesky, conjugating verbs in the present and the past tenses. I like the dictations the best, because even though I don't understand what it means, I can still write it. I have fun making those who don't know Hebrew look foolish. I'm good at writing words; sometimes I don't even know what I'm writing, I just put a bunch of letters together that really don't mean anything. I put the dots underneath to signify the vowels, then more letters and more dots, and since they can't prove I'm wrong, they have no idea the tricks I play on them, and believe it or not, they think I know everything, absolutely everything. Ah, yes, I also write very fast, right in front of their eyes.

Now it's popular to play "Sirenita"—whoever can grab you while your fingers aren't crossed has the right to give a punishment. At first I didn't want to do the kissing thing, but even the more serious girls do it. And I've discovered that it's a lot of fun. Before I was so embarrassed, but with the thousands I've had to give, I'm used to it now. Yesterday I was putting my modeling things away when . . . "Sirenita!"

"Oh, no, you caught me again! What luck! Okay, I'm caught."

"What should I punish you with?"

"I don't know."

"Do you do kisses?"

"Yes."

"Good, give Benito twenty."

"Why so many? . . . Well, okay, let me add them up: ten to Jaime, five to Semy, fifteen to Benito. . . . Man! With twenty more, I'll owe you fifty in all; I'll never ever uncross my fingers again."

At the school entrance Benito told me there was no one in Room 100. We closed the door behind us and I paid off my debt. The last ones seemed so long and we had to stop—even though I owed him five more—because the bus was leaving; we ran all the way to the corner to catch it. I didn't really like the kisses; in the movies it all seems so romantic that it makes you want to kiss. I only felt his tight lips pressing against mine, which were even more closed than his. And you can't breathe until it's over. Really, I don't think kissing is any fun.

At school they showed us some beautiful slides of kibbutzim—young people like us carrying baskets of fruit, wearing shorts, and with their skin tanned, which made them look healthy and happy; young Jewish boys picking huge juicy apples, trees loaded with bunches of bananas, happy faces that invited us to go and live like them. But they're not up on the mambo that's currently in style, and they don't know that the *danzón* requires the couple to dance tightly together and stay within a small square space. I'd rather be there dancing a Jewish folk dance in a circle around a bonfire and holding hands and getting hot and singing into the night. Our teachers have taught me to love Israel.

When I finish high school, I would like to go to Israel for a year, like so many young people from around the world; in Mexico, the majority of those who go are from the Yiddish community; maybe a few boys from our community will go. They're so lucky! It doesn't even cost anything, all you have to do is sign a contract to work in a kibbutz on the border for a year and they will pay your way; but once you've accepted you have to stay the full time; you can't come back sooner, and sometimes that's a problem.

Trembling with fear, I told my parents that I was dying to go, that even my grandfather's brothers live there, and finally, why does everyone tell us all those beautiful things about Israel when they know we can't even go? I got the answer.

"Women leave home with their husbands; you can go wherever you want with him!"

◇ ◇ ◇

I can't believe it! Sofia has grown up so fast! She looked absolutely beautiful wearing that coat with the white leather collar, her hair done up at the beauty shop and wearing makeup. She didn't seem like one of us, and to think that just last year we were together in the same school. They wouldn't let her finish high school and now she has a fiancé who takes her out dancing and to dinner at elegant places. How can she go out with a guy who is so much older than she is? I wonder what they talk about? I'd much rather go to our bazaar that we're planning so we can raise money for our graduation. But I must admit that she was really pretty! After all, she's already fifteen years old. I've heard that his parents bought her some pretty clothes and that she's really happy.

It was still daylight out, about five thirty in the afternoon, and I looked up at the sky and suddenly, a flash! I looked everywhere to see if there was another; unfortunately, there was nothing else. Hoping to see another one, I quickly closed my eyes and made three wishes: first, as always, I hoped that my parents would stay healthy, and my brothers and sisters, well, the whole family. Then I could ask for something for myself: I wished that the biography I wrote and sent to the television program *Who am I?* would win first prize. I sent the biography on Koch, who developed tuberculin, which I took out of my biology text. That Tuesday I was really nervous, especially when they started giving little bits of information on the person they had chosen to identify, and suddenly I realized they had chosen my entry. I was so happy. They're going to send me ten pesos in the mail. Wouldn't you know it: that boring biology class was good for something! And we're going to have biology again next year.

Benito is great at the broad jump, the high jump, and sprints. When he competes, our school takes all the medals; when he doesn't, we do lousy. Every year there are competitions among five Jewish schools in the country in swimming, track and field, diving, and volleyball. Sunday was horrible because we got into a huge fight with another school. A bunch of snobbish girls started rooting for their team and, of course, we rooted even more for ours. Then they began shouting insults at us. Next there was a fistfight, and I charged head-on, throwing punches. It became a battlefield, and I don't know how they managed to separate us.

What made me the happiest is that we beat up pretty good on those prissy, stuck-up girls. But we all went to the infirmary with bloody noses. I hate those girls from that school! Just because their parents are the founders, they think they own the club. Only a few of our parents are members.

Ramón Aguilar is short, dark-skinned, and has straight hair. We have no idea why his "mommy"—that's what he calls her—decided to stick him in a Jewish school, but he's happy. He looks like Benito Juárez, that's why we call him Benito. And he's hopelessly in love with Dori; she is his dream-come-true. And even though he's homely-looking and she's one of the most popular girls in my class, she seems to like him, too. All the guys chase after her.

I feel so badly, and I'm so stupid. I guess they have all the right to be mad at me.

"Next time, don't say anything to her," I overheard Dori saying.

But it was really just my bad luck. Recently, Pepe had been smooth-talking the principal's secretary so he could somehow snatch the history test. With just dates and more dates on it, we knew it was going to be super hard; even if we were brilliant, we wouldn't have been able to remember everything! And yesterday, who knows how, he managed to get the exam. Although he was nervous, he just walked out of the main office and said, "I've got it, follow me." Trying not to call any attention to ourselves, and making sure no one saw us, we casually walked out. About half a block down the street in front of the Mayorazgo School, where we thought it would be safe, we began to jump up and down with joy, kiss each other, and hug Pepe. I saw Becky and Rina coming to school, but they were still at the corner. Since they didn't know anything, I screamed out, "We got the test!" Of course, they started running toward us, and we went around the corner to a park in Coyoacán in order to answer it together.

In the meantime, we didn't even notice a guy who worked at the school passing by on his motorbike. He looked at us and kept on going.

A few days later we were all smiles when it was time to take the test.

"Did you study?" asked David.

"Yeah, I studied a little bit today. If I can finish quickly, I'll give you the answers. Sit next to me."

The history teacher entered the classroom with the principal, who was smiling. We smiled back. We didn't sense anything was wrong. He informed us that the test had been changed because a group of students in the class thought they were being smart by stealing it. All of my efforts to memorize the sequence of letters for the answers, A, A, B, B, C, C, A, A, B, B, went up in smoke; even the cheat sheet I had with me was worthless.

Stupid, that's what we were. What a disaster, so I just shrugged my shoulders at the ones I had promised to help, especially since I didn't even have any dates written down anywhere. And that jerk David was laughing at me the whole time. I can't stand him!

"No, I really hadn't met him yet, they just came and proposed marriage; we went out, we talked, we liked each other, and now we're getting married. I'm happy. Look at my ring!"

"How did he propose?"

"Well," said Sofia, "I went to the synagogue on New Year's; his mother was sitting next to my aunt, and she was watching me. I guess she thought I would be good for her son, so she talked about me, and they came to propose marriage. My parents didn't force me, they just said, 'Give it a try.' And, suddenly, I'll be married in two months."

"But you just turned fifteen and he's thirty."

"Yeah, but I really like him. Besides, the man should always be older than the woman, then he'll always know that his wife will be young and beautiful; besides, the woman always goes downhill first. Ever since we started going out, they've bought me lots of nice clothes. Do you think I would ever go back to wearing the clothes and socks that I wore to school? He's really nice; every Friday he sends me a bouquet of flowers and one to my mother. Everyone in the family likes him. Now that I go out so much, I don't even want to go to school anymore. What's the use? I'm better off taking English and cooking classes, you know, something worthwhile."

There's no getting around it, I can't stop time: I've just turned fourteen. Heck, I don't want to grow any more. I want to be around my brothers and sisters for a long time, but the trousseau that my mom is fixing for me for my wedding day is getting bigger every day. When I saw it today, it was so enormous that I guess my mother will have to start another one for my next sister. While it's true that my mom always manages to be prepared, she's worried about the expense of marrying off her first daughter—me.

"After all," she says, "the men have to finish their studies and they're not always in such a hurry, but the mothers-in-law have to hurry it up."

I can hear my mother talking while she stands on a chair in order to pull down a leather suitcase from the shelf in the closet. She was going to show her friend Paula the clothes she had made for my wedding.

"Oshi doesn't have any idea how much we've sacrificed to get her dowry going," she said.

I just knew it: my mom never wore any of those special blouses. And we've never used those embroidered tablecloths at home either, not even the imported ones from China.

I can't even imagine trading my warm pajamas for those lacy, transparent garments. I know when it's cold I'm going to wear a robe on top. And one of these days I'm going to get that suitcase down from the shelf in the closet—I know where the key is hidden—and quickly try on those blouses to make sure they fit.

The school's board of trustees rented an old colonial house so that our organization—the Sephardic Zionist Youth Group—could have a place to meet. We went today to see it for the first time. It has gardens and large trees everywhere. There's a large room in the basement that looks like it could be full of ghosts. We'll use it for our Saturday activities so we can get into long lines and circles for our Hebrew dances.

They split us up into different age groups and gave each one its own room for meetings. Then we cleaned and decorated them. I'll be in charge of the social events for my group, and I'll be able to organize things that I like to do, especially for our Saturday programs and excursions. This Saturday will be our first meeting, and we're going to invite a lot of new people to come. The Hebrew dances are the best part because I don't have to get nervous waiting for some guy to think he's doing me a favor by asking me to dance; I don't like the anguish. But here it's great. I don't feel that anyone is staring at me like, for instance, in other types of parties where I would have to ask a boy to dance. Here, while we dance the hora, there are more chances to meet people in the middle of clasping hands and jumping up and down, and I can dance in the middle of the circle as much as I want to—and I always do. As we go around exchanging partners, I begin to feel limber, and throwing my head back, I smile. I enjoy moving my feet, my hands, and my shoulders. I crouch down, I jump, I grow. Sometimes I feel like I'm out in the countryside feeling the wind in my face; other times I imagine that I'm in Israel sitting in front of a bonfire that throws light on our faces as we look at each other. The flickering flames dance—continuously—across our faces. We hold hands. I love them and they love me. And I love all the folk dances—Kol Doodí, Sherele, Crakovia—which I could dance all night long. We form a circle with a man behind each woman, and we clap to the rhythm of our voices and the accordion. It's amazing how that instrument creates the right mood! After holding onto each other's waists and going around in a circle, each dancer grabs another partner, and each couple dances in pairs. Then the first couple begins to form a new circle and everyone dances behind the other, holding onto the person's waist in front of them. They go around in a circle two or three times and then repeat the steps all over again, forming couples by making a sign with their fingers. And then they sing:

Once upon a time Esther went on an excursion
and on that excursion she met a friend
Hey, say, da la la
Da, da, da la la
Hey, friend, come over here
Da, da, da la la
Oh, oh, poor me, there she goes
lo, lo, lo
come, come, come
no, no, no
don't say no
let us dance.

We take each other by the arm and swing around, each time with a different partner. That's the part I like the best; it's the perfect moment for jumping and laughing. I wish we could have a bonfire and dance every Saturday.

That's why I like Israeli dances the best. I don't feel the same way when we go to regular dances, where the boys and the girls are feeling very insecure and trying to hide their fear. Anxious, I have to look around to see if anyone seems interested in me, and when they come toward us and ask the one next to me to dance, I feel betrayed. Then I start worrying that all the girls will get invited to dance but me, and they'll look at me and think I'm weird, or boring, or dumb, or offensive, or whatever; no matter what, I feel sad.

◇ ◇ ◇

Today our teacher gave us copies of the latest news from Israel.

Dear Friends:

I have noticed that in Jewish Mexico there are sharp differences among the three predominant groups. That is a real pity, although it seems natural for them to exist, because your parents grew up in different parts of the world, and upon arriving on the new continent, they wanted to continue their own way of living, eating, marrying, educating their children, and burying their dead. The different groups believe their customs are better.

But later generations, that is, their children, have grown up in Mexico, speak Spanish, have experienced the same basic culture, participated in the same Israeli Sports Club, and shared the same history and the same past. And the differences will tend to disappear. But in some Jewish schools there has been a preference for Yiddish over Hebrew, especially since in Israel they decided to adopt Hebrew as the official language, and schools in Mexico have done the same, after Spanish. Students, let's not postpone unifying the three groups—we have been victims of racism; please, let's not encourage it, especially among ourselves.

We should let this natural process develop on its own; let's not stop it. Remember: the Russian language is no less attractive than Arabic, and Indian music is no less important than Turkish music. They are *distinct*. Let's stop and consider the word *distinct*.

We listen to our relatives talk about the lands of their origin as if there were no other places on earth. They have memories that tie them intimately to the countries where they were born, and they will never stop feeling melancholy when they think about their nations. We should listen to them with love and try to understand them, but when they feel superior to people from other places, at that moment we should stop believing—just as we did when we were children–that what they say is the truth. We should develop a critical perspective and reach our own conclusions. Can we really say that Arab food is better than Yiddish or Turkish food? All of them are wonderful, and we should learn to appreciate their distinctiveness and enjoy a *gefiltefish* as much as some *zambuces* or *bulemas.*

How can each group have its own school, synagogue, and cemetery? We are all Jews, and that's that. We all chose Mexico, which has taken us in lovingly, so that we could live out our lives and our children could live theirs. The youth organizations, along with the sports endeavors, as well as the kibbutzim in Israel, are producing this union with much success.

Whew! I'm so happy the biology class is over. Boring as ever: the teacher opens his book and, walking from one side of the room to the other, reads straight out of it; he doesn't explain anything, he only recites. If that's all it takes to be a teacher, anyone can do it. What a stupid, boring old man!

Since this is the last year of high school, we are going to learn about the development of the male and female bodies and how children are born. Man, that's a touchy subject.

But it's so exciting!

There are only two more chapters until we get to the good parts. I've spent a lot of time looking at the pictures, but I don't understand anything. I think I'll wait for the teacher to explain it, and at the rate he's going, it'll take two more classes.

We made it! Today we were super quiet . . . but the teacher just continued reading from the book without missing a beat, not even raising an eyebrow, as if he were talking about any old thing. What a joke! We can read it by ourselves at home. Even though we were excited to get to those chapters, that didn't make the class any better. At least at the end of class he said, "Are there any questions or doubts?"

Some asked questions, but I didn't say a word.

"For the next class," he said, "we'll form two groups, one for the guys and one for the girls, so that no one will feel inhibited."

I'm going to write down some questions so I won't forget them. Do I dare ask them?

1) Is there any other way to have children? (With a vaccination? You know, some other way?)

2) Is it true that a daughter can have her father's children? (Someone told me that one night after a father peed in the toilet so did his daughter, and since he hadn't flushed it while she was sitting down, a sperm got inside her and she became pregnant. Could this happen, teacher? Now I get really nervous when my dad goes to the bathroom; I wait at least two hours and sometimes I can't hold it.)

3) I heard that a young girl had a baby because she was in a swimming pool. (What happened was that first the father took a pee in the swimming pool, then the girl got in, and since she liked to swim frog-style she spread her legs and a sperm entered her through one side of her bathing suit, and just like that she became pregnant. Now I don't swim frog-style.)

The teacher said repeatedly we shouldn't be afraid to ask questions: "I don't want anyone to have any doubts."

It was obvious that Mr. Biologist became a little abrupt when I asked him a question. Since one of his answers wasn't really clear to me, I finally decided to press him: "Professor, are you sure that is the only way to have children?"

"Yes. It's the only way. There is no other."

"I see . . ." but I didn't start squirming, although I felt embarrassed. I just couldn't stop thinking about it. So, my parents . . . them, too? No, I don't believe it. I'll bet that teacher only follows what's in the book.

✡ MOSHÓN'S BAR MITZVAH.

That was the first time I'd ever seen my grandfather carry the holy book and the rolls that contain the Torah, which is covered in velvet with gold lace around the edges. Some have a carved wooden cover with inlaid colored stones. There is no object more sacred. My mother and grandmother, who were sitting in the front row, were crying. When a boy reaches thirteen years old, he becomes a man and joins the community, with rights and obligations. Even though he was nervous, his presentation came off well. After having heard him recite it so many times, I also knew it by heart. Well, I think he skipped a line, but no one noticed:

"Dear rabbis, dear parents, dear grandparents, it is an honor for me . . ." and he went straight through it without taking a breath except at the end.

"I want to thank my parents who have made sacrifices for my education, and I promise to take care of them and my brothers and sisters for the rest of my life." (I liked that part the best because it's good to have a brother who'll take of me when I become a spinster.)

Even though my grandfather would deny it, I saw him crying; so was my dad. Assisted by the rabbis, Moshón read from the Torah, and then he walked up and down the central aisle carrying the sacred book. It made him happy that everyone went up to him to touch and kiss the book while he held it. Perhaps he'll never have the opportunity to do it again, but we knew how he felt. I was so proud of my brother because he was the most important person that day, and the ceremony was in his honor. And he's so handsome, too! He's the best looking of all of us; at least my friends think so.

My father almost laughs to hear him read Hebrew. He even acts like a child in first grade, because he's forgotten it. After it was my brother's turn to read from the Torah, I could tell he did it better than any of them, and no one laughed at him like they did at home. When they called upon him to carry the sacred book, I got emotional because my family never manages to do anything for the synagogue. My dad isn't rich, so he doesn't donate much or even volunteer in the community. He pays his dues, and he's a good Jew.

It was one of the few times that my grandpa's face lit up: every few moments he'd ask Moshón proudly: "Tell me, son, what makes a good man?"

"The three P's: plain, potent, and proper!" my brother responded with grit. He's lucky he doesn't have to be good-looking. That's where I have to shine. The good thing is that I'm pretty attractive, especially if I push up my nose with my finger. But if I had blue eyes, I'd *really* be good-looking. And straight hair doesn't help.

The invitations to Moshón's bar mitzvah were beautiful: they even included a full-length black-and-white picture of him wearing his tallith with Zion in the background. The words were in Spanish on one side and Hebrew on the other. I don't know why they did it like that, because no one around here can read Hebrew. It was great to see his picture on a hundred invitations; now he's famous.

My mom invited almost everyone who came; she has lots of friends who care about her because she always helps them with their problems. Her two best friends came, along with members of the mother's club at school because she helps out there, too. Games were set up everywhere, even in the bedrooms. The guests brought lots of presents. Everyone on my father's side came: his sister and her husband and my grandparents. No one from Lagunilla Market or Chapultepec came.

I went to get a washbowl and a pitcher of water while my sister got a towel. We took them to the dining room for the men to wash their hands. The eldest of the family, my grandfather, was first. I set the bowl down, and when he stretched out his hands, I poured water over them; then my sister quickly handed him the towel. Each man took his turn, starting with the eldest and going down in age, according to our law. Moshón had always insisted on being included in the ritual and every year we would chide him, saying no, not you! And we'd leave him standing there with his hands sticking out; but this year my grandfather wouldn't let us ignore him.

"Eugenia, why do you do that to your brother? He is a man now, for he just turned thirteen years old," exclaimed my grandfather.

I was furious. While I poured, letting the water barely trickle over his hands, my proud brother just laughed. We got settled around the table, and the prayers continued. They prayed and prayed. No wonder we seem boring, it just went on and on.

We're hungry!

Oh, God, Moshón really irritates me!

"The wine, Luna! Bring on the wine!"

I think they're about to finish; they usually end with wine. The silver goblet with a star and the Hebrew letters engraved on it sat next to my grandfather. He has used it at celebrations ever since I was born. Swaying back and forth, he ends with an "Amen!"

His squeaky voice and the frown on his face are his way of scolding us for fighting over who gets to sit next to him. But, with respect, we watch him slowly fill up the goblet and then slowly put it to his mouth, scrutinizing our every move. He takes a sip, pauses, and then passes it to my dad, who follows him in age, but since he's sitting at the other end of the table, we pass the goblet along from one to the other. After he takes a sip, he gives it to my uncle and then to my grandmother, but just when she raises the goblet to her lips, my grandfather says, "No, wait, it's Moshón's turn."

Then it goes from my grandmother to my mother, from my mother to my aunt, from my aunt to me, and finally to my sisters, who are at the tail end of the line. Then he cuts up the bread that's next to his plate, sprinkles a little salt on it, and gives a piece to each one of us without stopping his prayers. When he finally takes off his cap and cracks a smile, we can begin talking. And that is the moment when Uba knows she should give my grandfather a bowl of soup and put the plates of rice and avocado on the table. Since I'm sitting next to him, we share a piece of avocado. Then he jokes with me, and everyone has to listen; no one else is allowed to talk.

All the women must get up to help, because the table belongs to the men.

"Moshón, you can't have my place. See, Mommy, that's why I don't like to serve."

"Luna, sit down, tell us the story about when we first came to Mexico," exhorted my grandfather. "Come to the table and talk to your grandchildren. Sit down, Oshinica, listen to your grandmother."

"No? Okay . . . the first one to come to this continent was my cousin Isaac," said my grandfather. "He wrote to us and said there was electricity, lights, and money by the shovelful. In Jerusalem, people were poor, and then there were the Turks. So, we bought two tickets—second class—on a boat, and we came here."

"And I boiled eggs and potatoes," interrupted my grandmother, "and I packed some cans of sardines and fruit to last us several days. We couldn't eat just anything, you see, it had to be kosher."

"The ship took us to Veracruz," my grandfather continued, "and we had made arrangements to meet with Isaac in Mexico City. So we took the train, but when we arrived, he wasn't at the station. We waited until night came on, and when we saw that he wasn't coming, we managed to communicate with a taxi driver, thanks be to God. We asked him to take us to the Jewish neighborhood. He asked someone who told him it was La Lagunilla, so he took us there. We drove around until we saw a man on the road changing a tire. The taxi driver said, 'Hey, friend, I think they're from your country, they don't know anyone here, what should I do with them?' The man wiped his brow, looked at us, and said he was Jewish. He offered to take us to his home. We stayed with his family for about a month, and then we found a room in the neighborhood where the store is today. Did you know, Moshón, that we lived in Number 3?"

"And do you know who that man is? Why, it's Mr. Behar," said my grandmother, smiling. "He's your grandfather's best friend; he had the store next to ours, and now his grandson looks after it."

"And that's how we got here," my grandfather concluded. "Then we opened a stall at the market, and my son and I started selling dresses."

"It's true, isn't it, Mother, that after we arrived you sent me to school wearing my white tunic?" asked my father. "In Israel they didn't wear pants, and we had brought only clothes that we had worn back there. We didn't know what else to bring. I attended a school that was on República de Chile, and at first I only spoke Hebrew. They made fun of me until one day I hit one kid so hard that no one ever bothered me again. That's why I always say you have to defend yourself or else they'll walk all over you. But I made some really good friends, and even today some still come around and say hello. Efrén—the guy who sells kosher chickens on Medellín Street—well, he studied with me."

"Do you remember, Mom," I said, "the day Dad left me in charge of the stand? I wanted to go home, and when he didn't come back soon, I did it in my pants."

"That's the breaks, child, because there was no way you could have left the business unattended," he said with a laugh.

Ever since the talking to we got from our professor, I've been feeling uneasy, even upset. It makes me mad to do things that I hate to see other people do; I get mad when I see wrongdoing and then pretend not to do it myself. I'm equally to blame. I don't know what to do about it. I know I'm not happy about things. My stomach hurts. I feel like having a fight with someone.

Oh, my God, I felt the strangest things when I locked myself in my room and tried on the nightshirts: the blue one, the yellow one, and the dressy white one for my wedding night. When I looked at myself in the mirror, I was almost naked and I felt something different about me, so I quickly got dressed.

Oh, Mom, listen to me. Why in the world do you think I'm going to wear these things? I prefer my flannel pajamas, even if they don't have any sleeves and I always get cold. It must be embarrassing to walk around half nude in front of the man who marries me!

But I put the suitcase back on the shelf just like it was. I hope my mom doesn't find out. Even now I can't forget what I saw in the mirror—my breasts and everything else. And how my body felt so different. It's really intriguing!

"Grandfather, let me carry the sacred book, too."

"Listen, women aren't allowed to."

"Why?"

"Get your aunt to explain it, I'm going to my room. . . ."

"But Grandfather, it's just that I . . ."

"Come here, Oshinica, darling," said my aunt.

In the kitchen, she said in a low voice, "I'm going to explain it to you; it's that women . . . every month . . . you know, don't you? We are impure, that's why we . . . it's an honor that they don't have . . . it's not possible for us because each time they ask us or examine us . . . get it, my little darling?" she said, hugging me.

Isn't that strange? We're impure.

My mom told me today that the tablecloth that I embroidered for her for Mother's Day—the one I made in home economics class—is for my wedding. I don't know why she's so obsessed with all this, saving everything for that dreadful day. It just frightens me.

And her friends are just like her: they spend all their time watching TV, sewing, knitting, and embroidering. Since I've learned how to use knitting needles, I'm going to make something different with my mother's leftover yarn. I know, I'll make a patchwork blanket. And Andrés's mother is just like them. They show off their stitches, describe their designs, and then praise each other. They gossip about who got married, who went on a trip, what their husbands have given them, their mothers-in-law, and their children—always portraying them the way they'd like them to be, and smiling about some of the silly things they've done. All the while, they're having pastries and coffee.

What am I going to do with so many tablecloths? And I won't be lacking for doilies either; that leather trunk is going to burst from so much stuff. And I'm so scared to get married and have to swim like a frog in bed. No, I only want to *dress* like a bride. And if I don't get married, what will happen to the stuff in the trunk?

Becky annoys me: she's late again. We agreed to meet at the corner of Insurgentes and San Luis Potosí, right in front of Sears. But then my heart skipped a few beats when I saw our art teacher approaching. He's the really handsome one. I wonder what he's doing around here?

"Hi, Oshi, how have you been?"

(Oh, my God, this isn't happening. Mexico is so big and I have to run into my teacher right here.)

"I'm fine, how are you?"

"Well . . . I don't know for sure. I'm supposed to meet Becky Cohen here; we're going to a soccer match: Polytechnic plays against University today."

"Ah, that sounds like fun, professor! So, you're coming with us, then," I said in a forced manner.

"I hope you don't mind."

"What do you mean? I think it's great."

(And now what do we talk about? For sure not about the assignment that's due on Tuesday. Wow! Is he good-looking or what? Becky's done well. She's hit the jackpot! And what if she doesn't show up? What am I going to do? I can't just go alone with him; he's a lot older than me. He must be at least twenty-three, he already has his degree in engineering . . . well, maybe he's twenty-one.)

"Professor Sánchez . . . !"

"Oshinica, don't call me that, my name is Rubén."

"I don't think I should use your first name, do you?"

"Yes, of course; it's Rubén. Becky calls me by my first name."

(He smiled at me so flirtingly that I wondered if he had come to go with Becky or with me. No, it had to be Becky, she's so wild, everyone in class says she is, and the ladies in the mothers' group at school look down on her because she wears pants; and with that large butt of hers, all the guys follow her around everywhere.)

"Rub . . . er . . . Professor Rubén, what time did Becky say she would come?"

"At three o'clock. The game starts at four and we still have to buy tickets."

(Man! We've been standing here ten minutes, or maybe ten hours, already. I hope none of my friends sees me with this older man. And he's a Gentile. At least he's fairly white. And he's really handsome in those casual clothes. Oh, God, he's looking at me with that smile again. Help! I can't stand it anymore; if she doesn't come soon, I don't know what I'll do. I know I'm not daring enough to go alone with him. It would be my luck to be seen with him. I think I'd better try to cover my face or look in the store window. She's so well known for her escapades that she doesn't even care what people think.)

"Professor Rubén, is it true that the algebra teacher is your cousin?"

"Yes, my first cousin no less. He might even come today; we agreed to meet. And you know we have to root for the University team."

(Geez, I'll bet that little devil Becky told him that I like his cousin. No, she wouldn't do that; he's really mean to me. As soon as he sees me coming into class, he humiliates me by throwing me out, and then I feel worthless. I don't know anything about algebra! If I never got it from the very beginning, how would I understand it now? It sounds like a foreign language to me. My hands are still trembling; I can't believe I'm still talking with him. She's crazy, even landed the art teacher . . . naturally. And she didn't tell me anything because she knew I wouldn't go with her. C'mon, please, just hurry up!)

"Is something wrong, Oshinica?"

"No, it's nothing; I'm just a little worried about Becky. All she has to do is catch the train on Alvaro Obregón Street; she's even closer than I am. But it's no big deal, really."

(Ah, there she comes; I don't know what I would've done if she hadn't. Anyway, I wouldn't have said anything bad to the teacher; after all, he is my art teacher and he treats me nicely. But, Mr. Teacher, your cousin is dreadful and he has pimples! In addition, he has a bad temper, but I like him.)

"Oh, oh, please forgive me. The trains were packed and two of them didn't even stop. Let's go."

"Yes," said Rubén. "Let's get a taxi."

(My glances of disgust didn't even faze Becky; she's just full of laughs, ha, ha, ha. She walks arrogantly, and she knows that when she doesn't wear her school uniform over her pants, she looks great, but if she only knew what they say about her at school. Each time we cross a street, Rubén shows his attentiveness and takes us by the arm. He makes me nervous, those things seem so phony to me. At each corner I want to get ahead of them or walk on the curb to avoid his help, even if I might fall. It's better to walk alongside Becky instead. I won't get into a taxi next to him; it's too dangerous. I'm going to suggest that we walk all the way, even though it's as far as the bullring. We cross the bridge at Insurgentes and passed by Las Chalupas and Los Guajolotes. And when we arrive, it's pure chaos: some are happy they have tickets in their hands; others are desperate to get them. If it's really true your cousin is here some-where, I'll go with him since my friend Becky here already has you as her date. And we'll be the talk of the school if we're seen sitting in the stands with the two young teachers.)

"You know what," I said, "you try to get tickets at this window and I'm going to try at No. 8 . . ."

I didn't give them time to answer, and I didn't even look back at my friend's face: I just went home.

Everyone in the class was running around with their class year-books.

"Sign mine!"

"Sign mine!"

"Professor, please sign mine."

"Let's ask the principal to sign them, too."

Oshi: If the dust in the road

manages to erase me from your memory,

keep a picture of me if I live, and a tear

if I die.

Rebecca

For my dear friend, who I
like more than a friend.
Yours, Jaime K.

A handkerchief embroidered
with black silk fell from the

sky, ask your mommy if she
wants to be my mother-in-law.
(David)

(Geez, I can't believe that David would write that)

> Two violets in a vase won't
> die; two friends who care
> won't forget each other.
> *Dori*

The only memory I'll have is this yearbook with pictures of everyone from school. Lots of people have signed it with some little sad or happy poem. We were together for six years, some were together even longer because they met in kindergarten. So many years, so many days! Why did it have to end so quickly? You mean we're ready to choose our careers? To get married?

To the most beautiful and attractive flower
of junior year. You are the most beautiful flower
of the whole school. Don't forget me, I hope that
the memory of those happy days will always be
on your mind and that your memories be glorious.
Pepe

> Oshi:
> You're a dumb tech school jerk.
> Go Poli!
> *Your enemy No. 1,*
> *Becky (Poli)*

They say they're going to open up a University Preparatory School at our school next year; too bad I graduated too soon. We'll have to go somewhere else. But where? David, where are we going to meet? Probably in the Morelia movie theater, or the Gloria, or the Balmori; at least they never throw us out. And there won't be any graduation or good-byes.

For the nicest, most well developed girl in the class.
Rafael Cohen, the Arab
(The Rat)

For Oshinica with affection
From your best buddy. The day
You read these words, you'll
Know how much I . . . respect you
And . . . you for me?
Rafael G. M.
Note: autograph is patented

These are fantastic! I never get tired of reading them; I like to have written proof that people care about me, they think I'm pretty, they wish me the best, and they want my mother to be their mother-in-law.

Oshinica:
With his sword, Napoleon conquered
many places, and you and your tenderness
will always conquer hearts.
Rina

For the most well-built and
prettiest of all my friends
(not girlfriend).
Jaime

(The dummy.) (He's a jerk even with what he writes.)

Eugenia:
The restlessness of the spirit
manifests itself at any moment;
try to pay attention to it in order to be happy.

(I think the physics teacher signed it.) (What a signature! One
of these days I'll remember his name.)

Oshinica:
Keep that zeal to learn as
you expand your knowledge; virtue and
wisdom will even gain
the respect of men.
Leonora

Oshi:
Butterflies with their large
proboscis bound from flower
to flower, and at twelve o'clock
a terrifying scream, Mommy, my
little chamber pot, please.
A friend who thinks
a lot of you and will
never forget you.
Semy L.

I hope you get rid of
those silly shoes
and get a more
serious
perspective on
life.
Signed
(The biologist)

(Geez, what a jerk.)

Today was our graduation in a beautiful ballroom in the Italian Club on Eugenia Street. We descended the majestic staircase to the music of Aída. It was like in the movies, as if we were princesses. At the end of the line, the six girls without a partner went on either side of a guy. The dumb conductor was more nervous than ever, but we had practiced the songs so many times that we were ready to give it to him.

Luckily, I danced with David and neither of us got bored, even dance after dance together; so, I guess I would've preferred to keep practicing all day long.

These are the last times we'll be together. After today, who knows where or when we'll see each other again. David is holding me tight around my waist; he would like to have arms six feet long to wrap them around me several times. Me too.

For part of the waltz, the girls dance with their fathers. Darn it, I just couldn't get the step right; it wouldn't come to me. I don't know, maybe it's because he kind of jumps from one side to the other, so when I was going one way he was going the other; it looked pretty bad. But I was happy because he had a big smile on his face. I smiled too, hoping that no one would realize I was out of step with him. What a relief when it was over! That was the only one we danced together. The only one!

Later, the school rings were handed out. It was the first ring I've ever had in my whole life. I still can't stop looking at my hand because it looks so much prettier with a gold ring that has the school insignia on it. What a fantastic ring!

Andrés's sister Reina invited me to eat dinner at her house. I was really happy, and I think he was the one who told her to invite me because afterward he walked me home. Every time we'd get to my building, he'd say, "Want to walk back a block?" So we would walk back and forth for about two hours. And he always looks at me with those squinting eyes. I like it when he looks at me that way! I can't believe he's the same little snot from the park. He read me some poems; I'm going to ask him for them so I can copy them.

He's really cute, and he looks so shy. I can tell he wants to hold my hand; he turned red and couldn't do it.

Fortuna, who is an elegant dresser, gave my mother the clothes she doesn't wear anymore. She travels so much that she has to empty her closet from time to time in order to make room for the new things she brings back. Among the things she sent over, there was a black velvet dress. I was lucky: my mom gave it to me. It has a straight skirt, and the jacket fits closely around the waist, like a bullfighter's; it even has black arabesque embroidery around the lapel. The blouse is white, and it's light and airy, with long sleeves.

I tried on the outfit, and I thought I was dreaming; I've never looked as good as this before.

The sixth anniversary of the independence of Israel is on Saturday. There's going to be a dance in a large ballroom behind the Mexico movie theater. I'm going because I've been asked to collect donations for the Keren Kayemet and Biker Olim Foundations, to help poor Jewish kids in Mexico.

"I don't want you to go, you're not even fifteen years old yet. Be reasonable, don't be foolish, and stay home. Why do you want everyone talking about you afterward?"

"Please, Mom, what do you think is going to happen? Besides, I'm not going to dance."

"You'll get branded, and they'll think you're much older than you are. Piedad's girls go to this dance, and we know what they say about them."

🕎 saturday: yom hatzamaut, independence day.

Just about the entire Sephardic community went to the dance, including the Israeli ambassador. The ballroom was decorated with little flags both from Israel and Mexico. After the two national anthems, the place became unglued, as if it were a New Year's party.

Since I was supposed to collect money, I stood at the door with a small tray, smiling at the people. I waved to some, recognized others, and was so happy that I didn't have to sit down and wait for someone to invite me to dance. Then everyone there would have noticed me.

To get donations, we had to stop the men, and they always acted like they didn't notice me; but once I got them cornered, I pinned a donor's recognition on their lapel and thanked them. The whole thing was really awkward, but it was the only way to get them to donate anything. One supposes that they come to the dance feeling good about things. They're there to take advantage of the presence of important people who are in attendance, so they fake a smile and take out a bill, all of which is observed indirectly by somebody from the community who is standing by the door near me. Besides, asking for donations gives me the chance to flirt a little. And that's how everyone who came in, absolutely everyone, saw me in my little velvet outfit. When the ceremonies began, we turned in the money and went off to dance. I saw several guys arrive: Harry, Rosi's brother, Beto Cohen, Rafael Levy, David, and Salomón. And they all said to me, "Let's dance later." I used any pretext to cross the large ballroom and let my friends know I was free to dance. The first one to ask me was an imbecile whom I didn't even know. I accepted because my friends hadn't arrived yet. So, I danced with the guy, but I cringed from the very beginning. That's always the difficult part. At the end of the dance, I had no idea what was going to happen. Was he going to say thank you and take me back to my table? Or perhaps he liked me and we'd continue testing each other, trying to find the right words, searching desperately for someone we know, or looking for something that's happening, anything to ease the tension and let us smile at each other. I was at his mercy, until I took the initiative and said bluntly, "Well, excuse me, I'm going to the bathroom." Then I took off in the opposite direction.

It was a fun night. It lasted until four o'clock in the morning. I had never gone to sleep so late. I stayed with Rosi, who is Mrs. Rashelica's daughter.

I think my new outfit brought me good luck: I danced with Rosi's brother, who is thirty-two, but he doesn't look that old, and he's a likable guy; frankly, I was really taken by him. I love my new outfit! I hope Fortuna keeps giving my mom a lot more clothes. When would I ever have the chance to buy something like that for myself?

✡ MAY 15: I TURNED fifteen today.

I put on my socks and my dark blue and white penny loafers, which are in style now. I put on some lipstick and went to the Tiferet Zion youth organization meeting; we were going to have council elections.

My mother begged me to dress up a little more: "You're old enough now to wear stockings."

But I refused. It gave me great pleasure to put on my old socks, just like every day. The younger girls in my class were counting the days to their fifteenth birthday because then they would be allowed to wear stockings and makeup. I don't want to look like a young woman who is ready to get married.

At the corner I ran into Andrés and his nice smile. He's so tall and skinny! His face is thin, too, but I like his eyes the best: when he looks at me he seems to say, "You enchant me." He walked me to the meeting, but he wouldn't come inside. He doesn't agree with their beliefs. He liked the simple way I was dressed on my fifteenth birthday; he said I didn't need to dress up to look pretty. It was so gratifying to know that today he still saw me as the same person I was yesterday, before my fifteenth.

✡ ONE MONTH LATER.

Finally, I'm home. I can't stand this garter belt. What a relief to be able to take it off! Today was the first time I've worn one, and I thought it was horrendous; besides, it's a real pain making sure the seam in the hose stays straight. And I could feel those metal snaps pressing against me. I can't believe it! What a stupid invention; this skirt is so tight that you can see the straps underneath and when I sit down they dig into my leg and leave a mark.

Fortunately, I got a ride in Grandfather's car and I ate dinner at his house; afterward, I just walked home. As I crossed the park, I ran into Andrés, so we walked back together, talking the whole way. He looks different now. He joined the Shomer Atzair youth organization and he was wearing his uniform and special neckerchief. That means he was accepted into the group. My mom says it's the most radical organization of all; in fact, it's communist. And Andrés has really gotten involved; after a rigorous program, he's going to make his Aliyá, which means to live on a collective farm over there. He says there's nothing better than living in a kibbutz. I like listening to him; I want to go too.

David called and said he misses me and wants to see me; but it wouldn't be right to see him outside the school grounds. Where could we go? Benito told me that he's been taking pictures of our group, and whenever I'm in one he enlarges it. When I saw one, I couldn't believe it: I hadn't ever seen a picture that had been enlarged, and I was wearing a bathing suit as well. I don't know what to think, but I feel good that someone in this life cares about me. My mom said, "I'm so happy you've finished high school; now you can stop seeing those young little brats; now you can make some older friends."

We went to the women's vocational college, and the secretary gave us some brochures about the different professional programs they offer; I can't decide which one I like the best. My mom says that anyone who knows shorthand and typing can get a job as a secretary, and they earn good money, too. Why spend a lot of time studying, because I'll just get married and never finish?

Now that I'm fifteen, if I enroll in a three-year program, I can get married when I'm eighteen. That's a good plan. We're lucky there are vocational schools for women. That's the only reason my parents will let me enroll.

Which career should I choose? A tough choice! The one that teaches shorthand and typing? Either journalism or medical secretary. The only thing I know is that I do not want to be a secretary, but . . . why would I want to be a journalist, they'd never let me do it anyway. It's really hard to decide. I'll do whatever, but one thing's for sure; I'm not staying at home.

Manuel Becerra Acosta, who is the editor of the newspaper *Excélsior,* is also the director of the program in journalism at the school. It's easy to tell that he's a nice old man because the students greet him with hugs and kisses; not me, teachers frighten me, although gym teachers aren't so bad. Today he asked us why we thought we wanted to be journalists. My classmates gave some reasons that ran a cold shiver down my spine: they want to be able to express themselves; it's a vocation, they say, and ever since they were little girls they've wanted to do it. They want to become someone. So, how was I going to admit that I'm there only because I'm trying to learn shorthand and typing?

I don't know what this old lady is doing here. Her name is Alicia, and she's a grandmother—and my classmate! It seems so strange that someone her age would still be studying!

Today I began embroidering another tablecloth. It's pretty. My mom had the design put on beige cloth; there are clusters of flowers in each corner, and I'm using lots of colors in a chain stitch, which is easier.

Since my classes at the vocational school are in the afternoon, I don't get to watch the soaps anymore, but my mother watches them with her friends, who still come over and sew together. One of them teaches the rest all kinds of different stitches. She says she has blessed hands. When I get closer to her to look, she asks me, "Which one do you like, my *janum?*" I just love the way she talks to me: *janum* means something like "queen." With so many children, it never occurred to my mom to call me that. And that woman never had any children. I ask her questions, and she says over and over, "Speak more slowly, my precious one. I can hear you, but when you use those new words, I don't understand."

So she teaches them what she learned in Turkey: you must first begin with a short piece of fine beige thread to mark the beginning and then ball up a very long piece for the outline of the embroidery. Each woman is holding her tablecloth that already has a design printed on it. With their thread and needle, they follow the outline of the leaves, the flowers, and other designs. As they begin to finish the outline, the thread gets used up; then they fill up each leaf with different stitches until they've filled the space surrounded by the outline. Once they're finished, a beautiful pattern has appeared on the tablecloth. Actually, it takes months to finish a tablecloth, but the day finally arrives when they proudly open it up and spread it out over the shiny dining room table.

"I'll ask my husband, but I think tomorrow he doesn't come home for lunch," said my mother.

"So I'll come early in the morning and stay all day. We'll be done in no time."

"Ah, the luck of a daughter whose mother will have her ready when the time comes," they chimed in.

Today, when I was leaving home like I do every day, I ran into Andrés at the corner of Juanacatlán and Cholula. Classes start at three o'clock in the afternoon, and since the bus was late, we walked along the bus route in case it came along; it didn't, but I still made it on time for my first class.

I can't believe that Señora Alicia who studies with us. She's crazy! What's a woman her age doing here? And it seems strange that everyone likes her so much. Sometimes she eats in the cafeteria with my class. When I see she's with them, I avoid them; I just can't stand her talking and laughing with them. Frankly, older women are boring, and I couldn't even imagine being a classmate with my grandmother or my mother. I'd rather die first. Why do they even sit with her? I'd rather spend my time studying in the library. I'll bet my classmates are probably uneasy about saying nasty things in front of an old woman. Somehow, though, she manages to complete her homework for the journalism teacher and for Miss Gooding, who assigns thousands of grammar exercises in addition to typing work. But that lady won't give up. I know she won't last long.

I've never had non-Jewish girlfriends before. I want to be friends with them, at least Monday through Friday, because on Saturdays and Sundays I'll be with the Sephardic group. And I'll be with those girls for sports events, but I'll never be able to go to their school parties. So what? We'll be friends at school and that's that.

I've been running into Andrés a lot recently. When I don't see him I get sad. But he always comes around, lanky figure and all, looking at me with those piercing eyes. Wearing his khaki uniform, he comes up to me slowly, like always, and then walks next to me to school.

I'm liking this profession more and more every day, but the writing classes are a lot of work, mainly because I can't think of anything to write about. The professor wants us to learn to be observant: if a person passes by, be able to say what we remember about her—what she was wearing, if she looked happy or sad, what her eyes looked like, the way she walked, how she was dressed, if she said anything. I can't create stuff like that, and that's why I only get so-so grades. Well, sometimes I get a good one, but at least I'm passing.

Next week is María Elena's birthday, and she said I have to go this time. They all know that I never go to their parties, and I usually give some pretext just like the way my father does at his store in La Lagunilla. If I'm such a good friend of hers, maybe I should go this time. I can always tell my mother that I'm studying; I don't have to tell her the whole truth.

Sometimes I wear my socks and blue and white loafers; everyone wears them, they're really popular. But sometimes I'll put on stockings and high heels. When I dress up, I try to avoid seeing Andrés; I feel strange. When I finally get to our youth organization meeting, I feel more comfortable about it since everyone else dresses like that; well, not exactly everyone, a lot of them dress up even more because that's the place to meet more serious young men who are not just out of high school. I met one who asked for my telephone number. He's a doctor.

I told myself I wouldn't dance with anyone. I absolutely was not going to. Maybe I'll change the records, serve the drinks, put sandwiches on the table, but then what?

"Oshi, I would like you to meet my cousin."

"So, you study journalism too? I didn't know that Mali had such good-looking friends. Where do we get a drink?"

"Ah, I'll bring you one if you like," I said, happy to have a pretext to escape.

"No, just tell me where I get one."

(Oops, now what do I do? And the bad part is that he's really handsome; for sure I won't dance with him.)

"What did you say your name was?"

"Eugenia, but my friends call me Oshi, from Oshinica."

"Are you Mexican?"

"Of course I am."

"It's just that your name . . ."

"My parents aren't Mexican, but I am. I was born here."

"Would you like to dance?"

"I can't. My foot hurts. I twisted it."

My shoes seemed to be nailed to the floor. I couldn't move them. I don't know how much time went by. Then he asked me again. I was embarrassed and couldn't look at him, so I just smiled and said, "No thanks. I don't dance."

Then I went running into the kitchen looking for María Elena.

Fortunately, I was in charge of changing the records. I put on "Frenesí." I used to listen to it in high school. It was easier then: I could dance with anyone. I'm not going to any more of these parties. Who are these guys and their families anyway? Are they decent people? There's no reason to wonder about these things at parties in our community, where all the children are sons and daughters or cousins of people we know. Will they go out and get drunk afterward? What if I happen to like one of them? Oh, please, no, dear God. That would be terrifying.

Ever since Dori went to a wedding with her father and met an older guy, I hardly ever see her. "He's no dummy," said my mom, "and who knows how long he's had his eye on her. And, of course, he wouldn't let a girl like her get away. There's always money involved."

"But, Mom, she's barely going to be sixteen, and I don't feel comfortable around him. He's grown up and in his twenties."

Dori says that he's the owner of a huge store downtown and he has a bunch of employees. I don't know what I would talk about with him. Yesterday, he stopped by to pick up Dori, so I asked them for a ride. Once we were in the car, they started kissing. It was bizarre—sitting next to them while they whispered to each other.

I should have gone with Becky. What are you supposed to do when they're kissing right in front of you? After a few moments, they remembered—who knows why—that I was with them. I began to cry. Then he looked at me and asked why I was crying. I said it was because they were kissing in front of me. He told me to get out of the car. Fortunately, we were on Amsterdam Street, which isn't far from my house.

I pray that she won't marry him.

Miss Gooding's face doesn't look real; if you were to see it in a store that sells masks, you'd think it was one of them. When she speaks, not even an eyelash moves. Long, wrinkled, and flat, her face is covered with makeup that still doesn't cover her pockmarked skin. Her cheeks are limp and droopy, like her breasts, I imagine, and she wears thick glasses. The waves of her painted blond hair are held in place with grease and hairpins, with a bottle-bottom on top to catch any rebellious strands. And she pins a flower next to her ear. She walks slowly and wears straight tan skirts, thick socks, and orthopedic shoes. She stands upright, rigid. She doesn't smile, but sometimes it looks like she's going to.

Miss Gooding is our shorthand and typing teacher, and most of the time she's much more fussy and demanding than the others. Today, she brought all the exercises for the whole month, and there are about ten per class. I like doing them; Frida doesn't. Even though she's much better in the other subjects than I am, she won't pass this course.

Miss Gooding is a good teacher, but they treat her as if she were some ancient relic; that's what my mom thought after she met her. One thing for sure, I know I'll never forget those exercises. The best part is when we copy poems in order to practice on the typewriters. Some of them are so beautiful, and I probably wouldn't have ever known about them.

Photography is really cool. The hours fly by in the laboratory: we spend whole afternoons preparing solutions for developing pictures.

"Oshinica, why aren't you better friends with the other girls in the class? They're always together."

"They've probably been friends forever. I haven't been."

"Well, don't all Jews in Mexico know each other?"

"Not really. I've never seen them before, not even at sports events, even though they don't live far from my house. They're from another synagogue and another school."

"What do you mean?"

"Look, Frida, I'm going to tell you what our teacher, Luvesky, explained to us, because I really don't know that much about it. She told us the Yiddish community is from Germany, Russia, you know, those places, and they're blond with blue eyes. I belong to the Sephardic community and my synagogue is on Monterrey Street. Our prayers—and the songs—are different. You wonder what the connection is between those people who come from Germany, Vienna, and Russia; who grew up listening to Beethoven and Mozart, and reading Pushkin, and us, the Sephardics and the Arab Jews from Syria, Lebanon, and Egypt? There isn't one, there's nothing in the language, the music, the dances, the food, our ways of life, the way we speak or dress. Each group has absorbed the customs of the countries they were living in. They live like they used to, back there. When the teacher explained it to us, she cried. She said most people miss their countries."

"Pillita, do you think the pictures are developed yet? We look great, don't you think? And we don't look fat either, do we? I love enlarging these pictures. And Chapultepec Park is pretty, too. Did you think the picture would turn out that nicely? Hey, take them out of the developer already! We need to rinse and dry them; it's getting dark outside, and we're not even finished yet."

Maybe we've let our other classes slide, but we know what we're doing in this one.

"I don't get it, tell me more. Are you're saying there are three groups?"

"Yeah. But don't you remember when our history teacher told us that the same year the Americas were discovered, they ran the Jews out of Spain? Look, I'll get my notes out. I think that was the day you missed class. The teacher talked about how the Jews went everywhere: Bulgaria, Greece, Italy, and Turkey. The most erudite went to Holland, because it wasn't far away. My mom was born in Turkey, and she speaks an archaic Spanish, Judezmo, that most Sephardics still speak today. You've heard, haven't you, how pretty my mom speaks at home, and even more so when she's among her friends?"

"Are these pictures going to take long to dry? If I get home late, my mom will go through the roof. You know how she is."

"What worries me is how I'm going to replace the scholarship money that I've used to buy paper and chemicals. The secretary already told me to pay by Monday or they won't let me into class anymore. It occurred to me to take one of my father's pistols and sell it; he has so many he'd never know the difference. But where?"

"Frida, don't even think about it. Doesn't he have something else? Do you want to hear some more? I think I told you that in the Sephardic school half of the students are from the Arab community? Just about all of them live in the Roma neighborhood. They don't let their daughters even finish high school because they have to help their mothers at home; the boys go straight to work after high school. We Turkish girls ran the school; we all went to the same synagogue and were friends, mainly because our mothers spoke the same language and thought the same way. They let us do some things and forbid us to do others. But the girls here speak Yiddish, and they think they're better than us. Did you notice that they dress up every day as if they were going to a party? Well, sure, I'd love to have the clothes they have, but I'm really more envious for another reason: they're allowed to keep studying. For instance, did you notice that even though several of them are in journalism, there are a lot more of them taking the morning classes, which are for college prep? And they also have boyfriends; I guess their mothers don't care if they get into trouble. They seem like they're easier, and that's why Sephardic boys go out with them. But I've heard that when it's time to get married, they prefer us over them."

"Frida, how long will the hock shop keep it? Aren't you afraid someone at home will realize that you aren't wearing your necklace? You're so daring! Our class picture is really expensive! Who will help us sell the pistol?"

"What about asking Andrés? He might know someone. I'll bring it tomorrow, and we can stick it in your portfolio, which is bigger."

"Oshini, who was that guy talking to you all afternoon?"

"Which one? You mean Leon?"

"Ah, he must be the one. Isn't he a doctor? Didn't his father raise him because his mother had died? That guy will make a good catch, absolutely the best, you can tell. Ah, I'm so happy he's a decent guy. And what did he talk about? What does he do?"

"Ah, yes, you're right. He's a doctor. He's okay."

Leon's moustache is the ugliest one I've ever seen; it's wide and extends from one side of his mouth to the other, and it's so prickly. I'm almost tempted to ask him to shave it off to see how he would look without it, or at least to trim it, even though it probably wouldn't change much. And he has big ears that stick out too much. When I look at him from behind, all you see are his ears, and he combs his hair like a little boy. But he's a nice person; in fact, he's so nice he's boring. For instance, we go shopping on Saturdays because he says he's run out of things, or he wants to fix a light switch or repair some wire. After we go to the supermarket, we eat with his dad. But he's got a nice physique, and I like his voice.

I told Andrés that I had to go out with Leon because my mother says he's a good catch and that I should be nice to him; if I don't, she won't leave me alone. It'll work out, because Leon comes to Mexico City only on the weekends, which leaves the rest of the week to have a good time with Andrés. He didn't make any comments about it. What should I do?

I ran into Andrés's friend yesterday, and she told me that she hadn't known that Andrés had just been circumcised. He didn't mention anything to me; it must have been painful for him. I did notice, though, that he walked a little funny, with his legs apart. It's unbelievable someone would do that at nineteen. Ever since he joined the youth group, his efforts to convert to Judaism must have been more intense than anyone can imagine.

I'm so in love with him!

When Leon dropped me off at home today, Andrés called to say that my parents were over at his house playing cards, that he really wanted to see me, and that our parents are going to be getting together every Sunday. We sat on the stairwell in my building. I never get tired of talking to him; and he reads important things to me. I don't know where he gets the stuff, but it makes me shudder. It sounds like the group he belongs to is communist, or that's what I've heard anyway. It's the only group that my mom won't let me join, but it's the one that's the nearest to where we live. She says the girls who attend are brainwashed; their heads are filled with strange ideas, and they shun wearing makeup or stockings. She says they're plain sloppy. The group leaders make them think they have to go to Israel. My mom doesn't want them to fill my head with those ideas.

Not unlike them, I guess, Andrés is idealistic: he wants a more equal world, without conflicting social classes. He says that we should live our lives through mutual help, that there's less hypocrisy and competition in the kibbutz, and that no one is exploited there either. Here, he says, the law is on the side of the one who has the most possessions. The kibbutz, he adds, is going to create a new society. Two friends from his youth group are going to marry girls from over there, and then live there. They're leaving everything behind: school, friends, and family.

He read a text to me that left me trembling. He's going to give me a copy tomorrow. When he finished, we both felt inspired. We fell silent, took a dry swallow, and hugged each other.

THE FUTILE LIFE OF PITO PEREZ: LAST WILL AND TESTAMENT

To Humanity, I bequeath every bit of my bitterness; to the rich, in search of gold, I leave the most repulsive part of my life.

To the poor, who are nothing but cowards and fail to rise up and seize the moment in the name of justice, my contempt. You are wretched slaves to a church that preaches resignation and to a government that takes everything and gives nothing in return!

I believed in no one! I respected no one. And why? Because no one believed in me or respected me. Only fools and lovers demand nothing.

Liberty! Equality! Brotherhood!

What a ridiculous farce! Power murders liberty, money destroys equality, and our egoism crushes brotherhood.

If you have a breath of hope left in you, wretched slaves, listen to the Apostles: no matter what happens, do not falter. If Jesus did not want to refuse to be God, what can we expect of man?

As a child you prevented me from going to school so that my brothers could educate themselves; as a young man you deprived me of love; as a man you destroyed my self-confidence. You even took my name away from me and turned it into an outlandish and wretched nickname: Whimper.

When I spoke, the words were taken from my mouth; when I did well, others reaped the benefits. Many times I suffered the punishment for crimes committed by others.

I had friends whom I fed when they were hungry, but in times of plenty they turned their backs on me.

As if I were a clown, people would gather around me in order to make them laugh at my misadventures. But no one ever dried one of my tears!

Humanity, I stole money from you, made fun of you—and my sins ridiculed you. I do not repent, and when I die I want to have enough strength to spit my scorn in your face. Pito Perez was just a shadow of himself who went around hungry from jail to jail, a whimper made happy with the ringing of bells. I was a drunk, a nobody. A walking truism. This is crazy, but that's me. And walking on the other side of the street in front of me was Honesty, showing decorum, and Wisdom, exuding prudence.

The struggle has not been equal, and this I understand; but the courage of the poor will rise again, and like an earthquake, nothing will be left standing.

"HUMANITY, I WILL SOON REDEEM WHAT YOU OWN ME"

Jesús Pérez Gaona

Now we are seeing each other on Sunday evenings; at least they're not going to catch us alone. Leon has been bringing me home at nine o'clock, so Andrés and I can be together until my parents get home from playing cards.

Today Leon's kisses nauseated me—he's so slow. And he's always telling jokes, but none of them is funny. Apparently, he wants to marry me, and if I say no my mother is liable to kill me. The best part of all this is that since they see Leon and me together on the weekends, they have no idea that I'm still seeing Andrés.

But today it had to happen. We were sitting on the stairs chatting away like always—about Pito Pérez, Israel, Zionism, how marvelous it is that Eretz Israel exists, living on a kibbutz, the superficiality of life in our community, that here women only play cards or go to the beauty salon and the department store. Of course, you have to marry rich in order to do that. Men have to do the same.

There we were, when suddenly we heard my parents coming up the stairs. I think they had already reached the first landing, so we had just enough time to hide: as I ran into the house, I told Andrés to go up to the terrace and after they went in, he could go back down the stairs and leave. I can't believe how fast my heart was beating as I jumped into bed with my shoes on, holding back my breathing so they wouldn't realize that I was awake, dressed, and trembling with fear, imagining all the while that my mother could have come to my bed, pulled the blanket back, and discovered what had happened!

I can't stop thinking about how I should be helping poor people; the injustices in the world really make me mad. But what can I do to prevent them? Darn it, what can I do? I have to find a way. Will I be able to sleep tonight? How can I calm down with all of these thoughts churning around in my head?

My dad, who always comes in to check on us, peeked in at three in the morning, went to my brother's room, and then went to his own room. Later on, when I was sure that they were asleep, I got undressed under the sheets without making any noise. I wonder what Andrés did?

I couldn't have ever imagined what happened to Andrés last night. He said he went up to the terrace, and when he heard my father finally lock the door, he went down the five flights of stairs, only to find that the main door to the building was locked with a key. He sat down and waited to see if someone might come in. After an hour, still nothing. Then he thought he should go back to the terrace, find our maid, and ask her to let him out. Juanita got scared when she heard a man was knocking on her door at that hour of the night. When she realized who it was, she put on her robe and went down to let him out. Poor guy, and here I was frightened to death in my own bed! Juanita is so nice!

Leon wants to formalize our relationship. My mom is happy. What I find strange is that when I was younger, she never asked for explanations, like when I would be coming home; now, when I get home, even if it's late, she's still up waiting for me so we can talk. I say hi to her and escape to my room because I have nothing to talk about, but she's all ears: "Oshinica, how was it? Where did you go? How did it go at Leon's house? Did his father treat you well?"

Geez, what dumb questions!

On Saturday, his family is coming to ask for my hand. My

mom has already begun to spread the news among her friends, saying it should be announced in the *Israeli Journal*. When they see me they say, "Good luck!"

What a hubbub! They're getting ready for a feast; my mother called my aunt in Monterrey to ask her to come and help prepare some things the way my grandmother used to for such occasions in Turkey. Empanadas with spinach and cheese. The two women have taken over the entire kitchen table in order to roll out the dough: it has to be as thin as a sheet of paper. They add the filling, roll it up like long snakes, and arrange them in a circular pan. The whole building begins to smell like our oven. They even hung the raw spinach leaves on the balcony railing to dry. I don't know why it was such a big deal, but they really got into it. And they made a dip out of nuts, cheese, and eggplant. I can't stand it when they make all this food and then put it away without letting us try a little; it even happens on my birthday. Ah, what's the use! All I want to do is go back to when I was younger, but now things are moving so fast that I don't even dare try to upset anything.

"No, they're not going to ask for a red cent," I remember my mother saying on the phone. "He's a good kid, a doctor. Are we happy? Of course we are. Well, yes, she is too. After they get married, they're going to live in Toluca. He works in the hospital there. But they're not that far away, and they'll only be there two years."

🕊 saturday, two weeks later.

Leon was really cheap at the drive-in. I wanted another hot dog, and he wouldn't buy it for me. I can't stand him anymore; if he's like this now, what's he going to be like when we're married? Something similar happened last week as well. And now, with everything else he's done, I can't take it any longer. They had already told me that his father is like that, but I didn't think it would be this bad. Next time, I'm going to take money with me, and if he won't buy me another hot dog, I'll buy it myself.

SUNDAY.

As we were leaving the theater, I gave it to him: "Leon, I don't want to be engaged to you anymore. I don't even love you. I'm going to give everything back to you. Here's your shawl, your handbag, and, ah yes, your picture: I'm going to take it out of my wallet . . . hold on a sec, here it is, take it!"

How could I dare do that? When my mom found out, she started to cry:

"Why did you do it? You're a bad girl. You don't even deserve him; just see if you find another like him. I've already talked to him, and even if you change your mind, he won't take you back. He won't take you back! He's had it with you."

◇ ◇ ◇

My Aunt Chela had a baby boy. Now her husband isn't as upset as the last time. He went to the hospital with a large bouquet of flowers and a big smile on his face. The ceremony for the circumcision will take place in eight days, if the child has gained enough weight and is in good health; the rabbi will determine that. My aunt's mother-in-law is making all the arrangements; since she is originally from Damascus, the ceremony will be according to her culture, with Arab music, mandolins, drums, and singers. For a few hours, they will recreate the other side of the world.

I'm happy now because I don't have to put up with those unending kisses and that prickly moustache. Poor guy! I'll never forget his face when I gave his things back to him.

"The picture is for you," he said, "but if you don't want it, tear it up."

Right then and there, I instantly tore it up into little pieces and threw them on the ground.

That afternoon, Andrés's mother came by the house. She's also embroidering tablecloths for her daughters; even she, who isn't Jewish, got caught up with the embroidery thing. Andrés looks just like her! She's attractive, dark, has distinctive features, and is even prettier than Dolores del Río. Why wouldn't Señor Mataraso want to fall in love with her and then marry her? She talked about him all the time. Once, he came to get her in the evening, and while everyone was finishing, he came to the kitchen where we were eating. My mom would make signs whenever she could, as if to say, "Don't let me catch you spying on them."

She keeps thinking that Andrés is a not a Jew. I can't convince her otherwise.

When they had gone, I asked her: "Uh, Mom, is it true he just got circumcised?"

"Yes, his mother told me about it. Still, just remember that things are never they way seem to be . . . so don't get too friendly. Understand?"

Today was my new cousin's circumcision ceremony. He's still bald, but my Aunt Chela doesn't seem to care. She watches him in his crib, smiles, and shrugs her shoulders: isn't he cute? Her daughter was pretty when she was born, but this guy looks like a monkey.

My Uncle Isaac is different altogether: it's the first time I've ever seen him drunk. But he couldn't have been more attentive to my grandfather, saying "father-in-law" all the time, and he wouldn't call my aunt by her name, which is Chela, but Chelujele instead. He would go around attending to everyone and greeting the guests: "Now I'm a complete man," he said with satisfaction, while he puffed out his chest.

Everyone in the living room was singing, dancing, and drinking anisette with the musicians. The older women started dancing spontaneously, moving their bodies in undulating waves, revealing their figures. It embarrassed me to watch them, mainly because their eyes became shiny; then some men got up and started dancing with them. Colors are flying: they swirl about like radiant dragonflies—red, pink, yellow, and blue. Their faces are hidden behind almost transparent scarves, their turbans fly around among the guests. Some guests who are standing around clap to the music, others move rhythmically in their seats. Arab food is everywhere. There's no more room for anyone, yet more and more people keep arriving and congratulating my uncle: Your luck is good! Happy father! Good luck! May he be a groom some day!

When the musicians finished playing and were starting to leave, everyone got rowdy. They quickly began to pull money from their pockets and purses to pay the musicians to stay. One by one, my cousins, who are single, began to dance. They were wearing bracelets with tiny bells, holding castanets, and wearing thin scarves . . . and more scarves, and even more bracelets. The large, heavy ladies who were sitting down or cooking in the kitchen suddenly became transformed, and despite their age, they suddenly knew how to move their shoulders and hips, swaying provocatively; meanwhile, the men became dazzled by it all and began making some sounds that were supposed to be words to a song. I was taken by the sounds of the drum; the guy who played it must have been under a spell. I wanted to look at the drum when they took a break.

Oh, I don't know, I don't really like those songs; I'm better off in my aunt's room, where she's wearing a robe while she's feeding my cousin.

"Poor little guy," she'd say to him. "What have they done to you? My poor little soul."

Something seems wrong. I'm stretched out on the back seat of the car and I don't see any of the usual advertisements. My grandfather has taken a different route home, he didn't go down Balderas, so I didn't even get to see the H. Steele clock or the Real Theater like I've done forever and ever, it seems; and, like always, he turns on the radio to listen to his Arab music, which sounds like somebody wailing. It sounds like the guy doing the singing must have a stomachache. Today we gave the store owner next door a ride home. And what luck! My grandfather was so absorbed in the conversation that he forgot to turn on his music. Poor guy! My grandfather always gives him a hard time because all the man has are daughters. When he gets out of the car, my grandfather says to him: "Take care of that ulcer, you've got six daughters and you'll have to save a lot for all those dowries. And your store will only provide enough for the first one . . ."

"Go to hell," the man responds.

🦂 Later that night.

I wonder why Jews aren't happy when girls are born into a family? I can't figure it out. Could it be because they have to spend so much money on them when they get married? I think I heard that the Biker Olim organization can help poor girls with wedding dresses and dowries. And when women get married, they lose their surnames, so that must have something to do with it. Their names are not passed on to their children.

And if their parents are rich, no problem; like Dori, soon it'll be her turn. I really don't like the guy she's going out with. But if a woman isn't rich and there's no dowry, the guy really has to be in love in order to get married.

At our house, we have to be careful to make sure the money goes around. When we go shopping, we're always looking for the best deals, and we just got a car three months ago. I'd prefer to become an old maid before my dad has to pay for a dowry or, worse, get a loan to pay for it. On the other hand, it frightens me to think I might never get married; it must be really lonely ... and not even have any kids? Dad told me there wouldn't be any money for a dowry, and that my brothers won't ask for one when they become engaged either.

"She should be a good girl from our community, nothing more."

Just by the way a house is decorated, I can tell if the people are Jewish; I don't need to see the owners or anything. They don't have any old furniture, because they didn't have any relatives leave anything to them.

I like my grandfather's bedroom set, but how can I say it?

"Will you give it to me when you die?"

And there aren't any statues of a Virgin, a Christ or other Saints, candlestick holders, potted plants, or animals—well, I'm referring to chickens or pigs, but there are dogs, sometimes cats, but usually not many.

The houses of our friends in the community all look alike: the furniture is modern looking, and there aren't many decorations because the mothers keep everything super tidy.

"Why have so much clutter around? It just has to be cleaned all the time," they say. Basically, their houses are just different; for instance, at my house there is a wooden folding door between the living room and the dining area, which is to keep us out. Ever since they put that door in, my mother has been able to show off her porcelain dolls that she had in the dining room under lock and key, just waiting for the day when we had grown up and wouldn't break anything. Before, when her friends would come to visit, she would get them out and then put them right back again. They're precious. I love them.

At our house, everything is locked up: there's a lock on the television, on the telephone, on the folding door, on all the windows (well, that's so my brothers won't fall out), and my mother locks her closet; funny, she never lets us see what's inside.

Sometimes our journalism assignments can be fun: today we had to write about the airport. Fortunately, the local newspaper provided us with a letter of introduction, and Frida and I got to see everything. In the control tower, we put on the headsets and could hear conversations with the pilots. It's a room with lots of people, electronic gadgets, and levers, and everything seemed to be in constant motion. Two pilots invited us to go for a ride with them. What an experience! We were the only ones getting on! We left through gate no. 3 and felt very important walking to a private plane as a group of passengers nearby were getting on an airliner.

Our plane had only two seats, so we sat on the floor behind the pilots. But there was a window and we could take pictures. We were jumping out of our skins from the excitement.

"Let's see if we can get one good roll of pictures," I told the pilot.

When we were airborne, I got into the pilot's seat and put on the headphones. I could hear them giving instructions on where other planes were supposed to land; almost everything's done in English and who knows what other languages. Then, just to scare us, he pushed down on the joystick and the plane took a sharp, horrible nosedive. We both screamed like crazy while they just burst out laughing. We were really high up! All of a sudden, we could see the pyramids at Teotihuacán; even though I'd never been to them, I could easily recognize them. We went as far as Cuernavaca and Toluca, and then we circled the city.

"If only my mom could see me now! I wonder if I can spot my house from here; after all, it *is* a five-story building."

"Calling the tower, calling the tower, we would like clearance for runway no. 6."

"Okay, girls, get on the floor behind us; we've got clearance to land."

"No, I want to steer a little more."

"Little girl, either you get to the back or I'll give you another surprise."

"Ay, no, that's being mean! Uh-oh, Frida! The pictures! The photography instructor is going to get mad at us. Get close to the window; take some pictures. And then we'll have to see how they come out."

"But this window is filthy. Nothing's going to come out. Young man, how long has it been since you've cleaned these windows— or the whole plane, for that matter?"

"So what should I do? I can't see a thing."

"It doesn't matter, we've got no choice, whatever comes out, comes out."

"Well, we can't get clearance for another fifteen or twenty minutes. We'll take you to see the pyramids again, and if you like, we can even land near them."

"Not 'even,' young man, we've already been by them."

"But we can go back, ha, ha."

"Okay, then, let me steer a little more."

"Sure, come sit up here. Pancho, sit in the back, okay? Now, you come up here, put the headphones on, and grab the joystick tightly."

"Wow, what's my mom going to say when I tell her about this?"

My Aunt Rosica arrived yesterday from Monterrey. She's my mother's sister-in-law, and I haven't seen her in a long time. She's very pretty, but she's pretty big, too. While she put us to bed, she told the story about how she married my mom's brother.

"He sent a picture of himself and he looked rather good. Since my mother—May she rest in Heaven—had died recently, I came to America with your mother and your grandma. They used to live right next door to me. I'll probably die in some distant land, I thought then, and my father was worried I might marry some undesirable man. And that's why I left. Actually, they made me get married right on the boat, tied up at the dock in Veracruz; they wouldn't let me off otherwise, and when I saw this kid who was to become your uncle—well, he was so young—I just burst out crying. I was to become his? But it was all for the good. And then he asked me, 'Rosa, is that your name? May I take you for mine?'

"Thinking I was doomed, I swear to you, Oshinica, I wanted to run away right then and there, but how could I go back home? I was already alone and getting older. And I was frightened. Just think: I was fifteen years old and on a ship with all those sailors. So, we got married, and from then on, we did everything together. But I have to tell you that I never could have loved him. He wanted me to be happy and content, and he would always say, 'we're going to dance from morning 'til night; we're going to really enjoy ourselves. Uh-oh, what's wrong, Rosica? You're supposed to have a smiling face, my mother told me so.'

"Oh, how your uncle cared for me. He would work from early morning until very late at night, more than twelve hours a day. It hurt me to see him work so hard. But that's all in the past now. After some time, he began to travel far away, but no sooner than he'd return, he'd go away again, spending weeks and weeks in those god-forsaken towns. But he liked it; so much so that I thought some day he'd probably forget to come back. That was twenty years ago, and that's why when he doesn't travel, I do. How else should it have been? Just sit around and stare at each other all the time? Donna and Levy, Levy and Donna. Am I going to die like this, I thought? But now I'm happy when I'm with my daughter and my son, and I've got many friends here in Mexico City. I don't want to move here, because I'm used to Monterrey now, and to tell you the truth, I like it better there, even though it's always the same old thing. Well, good night, Oshinica, be healthy, because nothing else matters. It's getting late now, and your mother will be upset if I keep you up.

"I guess I'm still a regular old chatterbox. Anyway, I'll be staying for two weeks, so I'll tell you more another time. You should come to Monterrey when school is out. You'd have fun there, and you might even find a boyfriend. Let's open the window a bit, I'm feeling dizzy. Oshinica, where are you going? It's time to go to sleep."

After all that, I'm sad. My poor uncle, she never loved him. That's not right. I listen to her and I don't know what to think. Even though she's adorable, I don't really care for her.

After January 6, everything gets back to normal around our house. Right now, we're selling lots of children's coats for the holidays. That's how we survive, because we could never—ever—depend on my grandfather for help.

Today, my grandfather bought another shipment of goods, and the store is full once again. What we don't know is when he will be able to get rid of the three hundred princess dresses made out of a special, dark-colored material. Another problem: one size fits all—small. Over the next two years we'll have to lure all the skinny girls into the store and try to sell . . . no, not coats, because we'll have to convince them that they are going to need one of those princess dresses made out of special material in elegant, dark colors. There's even another problem: this type of dress really accentuates one's figure, and it only fits someone who has a narrow waistline; they'll look great in it, but not me, I won't even try one on.

A girl who would fit perfectly into one of these dresses just walked by. Whenever my father is feeling pretty good, like today, he always puts on a show that usually produces results. So, he stops her, and as if to whisper in her ear, he makes some gestures; then she turns to look inside the store.

"Allow me to say a few words, Miss: we just got in a specially-made dress that will make you look glamorous. And there's no obligation. Please, I really don't want you to buy it, but just try it on."

And taking her by the arm, he leads her into the store—with her mother and everything else they have with them.

"First of all, Miss, let me have the pleasure of offering a chair to your mother. . . . See how striking you are! Examine the jacket and note how the princess dress fits your waist. You look stunning! Am I not right, ma'am? Doesn't your daughter look precious?"

"Yes, she's pretty, but to tell you the truth, we came to buy some chairs."

"Oh, please don't buy the dress, I only wanted her to try it on. See? It fits her perfectly. It's incredible. The dress usually costs forty pesos, but I'm asking you to make me an offer I can't refuse. You'll be the only one: this is the first princess dress we've sold. Please, just make an offer."

"But really, Mom, we don't want it, do we?"

"Miss, did you see yourself in the mirror? Just look at that fit. This style is really becoming to you. Put it on layaway for twenty pesos and you can come back to pick it up whenever you want."

Then he calls over to his employee, "Bring us a bag, please; wrap it up, the lady is going to leave it on layaway."

And in caravan fashion, he walks them to the door: "I'm sure you'll enjoy it."

Man, what a disappointment! Apparently, some of my dad's friends, who come to visit him almost every Sunday, are city inspectors. One day, they came to fine him for having the store open on Sundays. After they had left, my dad said I was an idiot for telling them that if they were looking for my dad, they could just come in. Even though my dad usually isn't very nice when he's in the store anyway, this time he really bawled me out—and in front of Goyita and the store employees, no less. I cried, but I was determined to continue to be nice to people because I see the way he is with them. But why am I such an idiot?

"If no one else would open up, no problem," said my dad, "but even though it's against the law, everyone stays open. When I arrive, I take a look down Honduras Street to see who's there and if any customers are around. Then I check to see if any of the other stores are open, because, you know, we've got to keep trying; if we don't, they'll just take all the customers away from us; and besides, they usually come to buy from *me* on Sundays. Let's face it, that's the way these wolves are."

There's no problem at my grandfather's store because there's a colored crystal glass partition with grapes engraved on it that no one can see through. So what he does is he brings the client inside and shuts the partition; then he can always say, "I just came to the store to do the books, the store is closed." When the partition is open, you can see my grandfather's desk. That's where he sits to read the newspaper. All he has to do is look up once in a while to know what's going on in the whole place. At the back of the store there's a storage room with a bamboo top where he stores fur coats. There's a strong camphor smell everywhere. Some of the coats are mink; others are white, gray, or spotted rabbit. And he has some that are fox, chinchilla, and gray squirrel. Some are long-haired and white. The silver fox is the most expensive. And can you believe that for some of the coats he even invents names of animals.

"What kind is this?" they ask him, and sometimes it's obvious: silver fox. But when it's just plain rabbit, he's likely to say, "It's chinardina," and the customer leaves happy with a fine fur coat in her bag. The most popular cheap item is the waist-length rabbit-fur bolero jacket. A lot of people like ones that have pockets in them. That's the only fur you can buy in children's sizes. I wouldn't mind having one, but Mom says that only hick girls wear them; anyway, that's what she says, and given the gesture she makes when she says it, I wouldn't dare wear one to a party.

An army general came to buy bolero jackets for his two daughters. The older girl chose a gray one with pockets, and the younger girl bought a white one. They were happy. You could tell the jackets didn't seem ridiculous to their father, because he didn't haggle over the price; he paid whatever my grandfather asked. Many parents, like the general, buy those things for their daughters for their coming-out parties or for some other festive occasion.

It's a real sight to see my grandfather taking care of a customer: he's all smiles. Then he cracks a joke to break the ice, and makes friendly gestures. When the customer finally tries something on, he lets go with a bunch of flattering remarks that force me to leave the store because I can't contain myself from laughing. He's such a cynic, and I can't stand to be around when he uses lies to sell his stuff. I don't believe that anything goes when you're trying to sell something. Nevertheless, he puts on that seller's face; his wide smile reveals his gold teeth. On the other hand, those are the moments when he is really nice, and the worst thing about it is that he can be so convincing.

"We weren't going to buy a thing, but your grandfather was so gracious," a man told me one day.

I almost fainted.

The good part about Sundays is that we close up by three o'clock in the afternoon and then we go to eat at my grandparents' house. And poor Ubaldina is such a good cook! Even though it's always the same, we love it anyway: stuffed chicken with meat and rice, and guacamole, artichokes, or squash—one or the other, but it's always the same.

One thing is for sure; no one is going to find a husband for me. I can do that by myself. There'll be no introducing me to anyone. When women have to be introduced, they're usually over twenty years old (and I'm barely fifteen), or she's not all that nice or attractive. Or they could be so crazy that they've already burned their bridges, or they've gone out with so many guys that no one wants to marry them. The guys have fun with them and even take advantage of them, but they don't marry them. At least that's what my mother says. And that's why I'm going to be careful.

"If they want to fool around with someone, let them do it with their mothers," said my father. Sometimes I overhear my mom and her friends talking about introducing some boy to a girl, like a friend of the family living in Guadalajara or Veracruz who is coming to town; and if there are any girls over twenty still around, they try to get something going between them. They plan it so the two of them meet each other, and then they organize a party.

"Enough of this, Mom, just stay out of it."

"What's wrong with it? Maybe they'll get lucky. That's how we all got married—Max and Fortuna, Ilana Peretz and her good-for-nothing husband, Uncle Isaac and Chela . . . even your dad and me. Listen, there are so many examples that maybe it'll work out for them, too."

"And, to top it off, they're all very happy and love each other, too. Love, you know, comes later. Also, you should learn how to cook: the way to a man's heart is through his stomach," adds my father.

But they're not going to choose anyone for me; if they ever try to suggest some guy, I'll reject him as soon as they mention his name. First of all, he'll be dumb as all get out, just because of the outmoded way he has to find a bride—especially in this day and time. They're probably afraid I won't get married. Well, I guess I'm a little worried too. What would they do with me?

◇ ◇ ◇

There's a lot happening in Lagunilla Market these days. It's a madhouse: everyone's yelling, giving orders, throwing buckets of water into the streets, and piling up cases of soft drinks, piñatas, and boxes of fruit on the sidewalks. Cata comes and goes carrying a hammer and rope, Chucho and his kids are inflating balloons; others are hanging strings of flowers across the street. Lighted lanterns are everywhere.

With all the guys that are checking me out, I could dance up a storm, but what's our chance of participating in the traditional *posadas* Christmas party? Everyone's talking about how it's going to be this year, about the ones in the past, and the ones in the future, five years from now, or even seven, but I've never gone to one. Using the pretext of going to the bathroom, I've been walking around our area of the market. I heard there's going to be two orchestras, and they'll play lots of *danzones*. Every time people from the neighborhood pass by the shop, they call out to my dad, "Hey, Don Samuel, stick around to dance a *danzón* with us; you'll be able to hold your babe real tight," and then they pretend to do a few steps and grab their stomachs and hold them in, which is exactly where the couples rub up against each other.

But my dad? No way. He won't have anything to do with it; he's afraid everyone will get drunk.

"The Jewish people don't get drunk," he said.

"Oshi, can you come to our Christmas party?" asked some guys.

"I'm not sure. I asked my dad about it, and he says there are always shootings and then the police show up. Is that right?"

"Ask him again, okay?"

"For the life of me, Rashel, believe me, the food's delicious. Don't be so annoying. I don't know how to convince you to come up and have a little something to eat with me. If you go slowly up the stairs, you won't get tired. I'm making some meat sandwiches, and you should see what's left over from yesterday. Yep, meat loaf. It's so good you'll end up licking your fingers. Sorry there's no fried fish left, because I know you like it. I haven't been able to find the type that you used to like when you lived in that other neighborhood and would get it fresh every morning. I remember you always complained about having to go and get it, but you always went.

"Last night we were remembering your brother. I've never laughed so hard. Fortuna found some pictures of the time when we had just arrived in Mexico, and there was one of you—a recent immigrant from 'stanbul. You were dressed up like a Mexican country girl, and he was a *charro,* the Mexican cowboy. You were out on Lake Xochimilco in a boat. And where did you get those dark braids? Come over and join me for a while. Tell me about your loves and your losses. I can tell you that mine have to be the worst. So, here's what you do: put on a dress and come over before it starts raining. Zelda and I got soaked when we took my husband's lunch to him, and then the thankless man made us mind the store while he went to get some more merchandise somewhere. By the time we got back home, we were incensed, so I took a hot bath and splashed myself with some rubbing alcohol.

"So, what am I supposed to do, Rashelica? You know I can't go over there; I don't have a servant. I got upset at her on Monday, so I sent her packing. She was just plain dumb: anything she did, absolutely anything, she did it all wrong. She even broke my dolls that I had stored away for all these years. And, to top it off, all she did was talk on the telephone; ever since we got one, every call was for her, something about her father being sick. A liar, an outright liar! And since she was deaf, too—I don't even want to think about it—she just yelled all the time! And she didn't even realize it. So, I lost my temper and fired her. Enough was enough! And now, so long as I'm still up to it, I actually wake up early feeling relieved, and in no time, I'm finished cleaning the house and it's never been cleaner.

"Those lazy kids, they don't want to do anything. One thing's for sure, before they leave for school, they have to make their own beds. And Heaven help them if they don't make it right. I give 'em a good swat, and they learn real fast. And so, Rashel, how many times do you swat yours? I've already taped a Help Wanted sign on the window, but my darn neighbors just keep ripping it off. What can I do? You know, I think they must enjoy seeing us suffer not having a maid. Three came by inquiring today. Worthless filth! One stank to high heaven. Another came with a child. One seemed to be pretty good, but she didn't have any references. Yeah, you're right, they'll steal you blind when you're not looking. What rotten luck! Just before the one you had recommended ran away on me, I talked to Micaela. Do you remember her? She was the little fat one who wore those embroidered dresses. Well, she said she'd help out on Sundays, which was her day off. But I'm going to entice her to come work for me permanently. So, Rashel, are you coming over? If you're tired, you can rest here. Look, if you want to play cards, I'll call Fortuna and my sister-in-law, and we can play a few hands. It's better with four of us; six is too boring. When you get here, you'll see that I have the green tablecloth out. I know, it's your favorite."

When we arrived at our grandparents' house, they were looking through their photo album: on the first page, there was a woman wearing a white tunic with long, flowing hair and a water jug on her shoulder. It looked like it was straight out of the

Bible—I think it was when Ruth goes to the well for water—but my proud grandma said it was her mother.

"That strange lady was my great-grandmother?"

On the next page, another woman, but she was even older: "My mother-in-law," she said. And she kept turning the pages, from one curious person to another: uncles, cousins, and great-grandparents. What a parade of strange people! Farther on, a picture of my grandfather just after he had arrived in Mexico. There he was—young, handsome, standing tall—and proudly dressed as a Mexican *charro*. Holding that sombrero in his hand, he looked like an exotic Jorge Negrete.

"As soon as I arrived, I went to the flea market to have my picture taken because I had promised to send a picture to my mother," he said with a big smile.

Then more pages of men with beards and little old men, who were also smiling. They were all a part of my family, and if I go to Israel someday, I might even meet some of them.

After the holidays, my dad always took us to Acapulco. Nowadays, just us older kids go with him, and we always have fun. My mother hasn't come for the past three years. The last time she came, she said, all she did was brush our long straight hair, and she just got tired of it. All she wants my dad to do is buy something for the house with the money that, according to her, he throws away in Acapulco anyway.

We left at midnight. Soon the bus grew quiet and you could hear low voices, some coughing, and then snoring. When the driver turned off the lights inside the bus, we could see the stars outside the window. They followed us all the way to the beach, even though the light of day finally erased them from the sky when we arrived at the steamy Acapulco bus station a little before six o'clock in the morning. While we were all piled on top of our luggage in the corner of the station, trying to sleep, my dad went to find a room at Señora Sultana's hotel.

Before breakfast every morning, we go the beach. The ocean is calmer, and it looks cleaner, too. After we eat breakfast, usually at Flor de Acapulco, we head for the docks, and while our food is digesting, we rent a boat and row out to Roqueta Beach, where there's a hidden cove. Standing at the helm, my dad takes charge, and we row and row and row—and we get burned from the sun. Finally, we reach the transparent waters at the cove.

🛩 BACK AT SEÑORA SULTANA'S HOTEL.

I don't know why my dad brought us to this hotel. I guess he likes it, or he feels more comfortable here. It's not really a hotel but a boarding house; at least that's what the sign says outside. Señora Sultana has several children who must be quite famous because a lot of people stop by to see them. They're all water-skiers and own businesses around town. The hotel is located on a narrow street just off the main plaza. Ever since we arrived, the Señora has taken a liking to me, and now they're even giving us special attention. This time we got a room with an air conditioner, but it doesn't have a view of the ocean.

Man, they're really taking care of us. One of her sons, Goyo, has stopped by our table several times; he's even been flirting with me. Then he asked my dad if he could take me out one evening. Take me out? He's kind of sad looking. What would we talk about? To make matters worse, he keeps on trying. I'm glad Dad told him that I'm just fifteen and I'm still too young.

When we got back from the beach, an old gray-haired man with a large moustache was showing some embroidered blouses to a group of ladies. My father always says hello to everyone, so they called him over to talk for a while. It wasn't long before the old man told my dad that he wanted to give me one of his blouses, and he insisted that I take it. I guess there was something about the man that my dad didn't like, so in a friendly way, he said no, thanks, and we went to our room.

Back in the room, he became furious: "If these dirty old men keep this up, we're leaving! Can you believe it?"

Around five o'clock we go to another beach called Hornos. Even though the sun is still strong, it's great. There's music coming from a jukebox in a restaurant on the beach. Somewhere else, people are playing guitars, while others are playing in the sand. They build canals between piles of sand and float little boats in them. The waves are a lot bigger there, so it's more fun. At Caleta Beach the waves are so puny you can't even ride them. What a joke!

I'm not swimming today, because I want to walk along the beach with the shorts I made in sewing class. They fit me perfectly.

At the hotel, I met a girl who is two years older than me. She has two brothers, and they like to go to Hornos Beach too. One of them is really handsome; he's twenty. I even went for a walk with him along the beach. I was barefoot. Then he kissed me. I really liked it! If there hadn't been so many people around, we might have kissed some more. Like in the movies, he could have thrown me down on the sand and put his arms around me. I would love to have that dream come true some day!

The history exam was very difficult, and the worst part of it was that they put us in a large hall so we couldn't copy from each other. I've never been able to learn anything about history, but I've never worried about it either because Frida would always give me the answers. Now, in that big hall, however, I was sitting far away from her. Then I got scared to death when I saw her finish the exam and leave. At the door she turned to look at me and laughed. I guess I must have looked pretty stupid. She's a little snot!

So, there I was–the wall on one side of me and Ingrid on the other. And I can't even stand her. I couldn't copy from anyone. Then I heard something: "Hey, listen up, I told you number one was Catherine the Great." I couldn't figure out where that voice was coming from, although I knew that it had to be Frida who was whispering to me.

"Number two is England," she said, now in a stronger voice. "Dummy, can't you hear me? Number two is England."

Then everyone in the room heard her, and I think the teacher was the first one to figure it out. I looked down at my feet and saw a hole in the wall next to me. Then it dawned on me.

"You nitwit, what else do you need? Write them down on a piece of paper. Number three is 1848."

Frida's voice started to get even louder. Then the teacher stood up from his desk, and the other students started looking at each other. She didn't realize it, but by then she was shouting. The correct answers were floating in the air like sacred chants, making a fool out of the teacher.

"Eugenia, number five is Spain."

Then the teacher started to catch on, so he left the room and found my friend outside on the patio kneeling on all fours next to the wall where the plumbers had made a hole to fix something.

"Oshi, can't you hear me?" she continued to yell.

I was kicking the wall so she'd stop yelling, but like a maniac, she just kept going. The teacher approached her, tapped her on the shoulder, and said, "You're just a little too loud, don't you think?"

I almost fell out of my chair when I heard that Miss Gooding was studying Arab literature and that she greatly admires the language and the culture. She said that she even has some Arab music, and that each letter in the alphabet is like a little drawing, which is why writing is used to decorate paintings. She showed us some slides that she took recently of Aleppo and Damascus. To go to Damascus and not visit an ancient synagogue, she said, is like going to Mexico City and not visiting the pyramids at Teotihuacán. She was excited about the abundant green pistachio trees and even the marriage rituals and traditions. She also said that it's rich with jewels, gardens, rivers, mosques, and imposing domes and spires.

"Oshi, could I go to Israel with you, even if I'm not Jewish?" asked Frida.

"Sure, we can go together."

"Just like you want to go to Jalapa where the weather is misty, I want to go to Israel. I told my parents everything about life on a kibbutz, and they said if you're going, so can I."

"Lots of people have gone there and come back to tell wonderful stories about their experiences; it's not like visiting just any place. I'm sure we'll love it. Let's go to the Jewish travel agency tomorrow and see how much it costs to go there. After all, they need young people to work the land on the kibbutz; we only have to sign a contract to stay a year. Hey, can we handle that? But what if we get killed there? For sure they'll put us in a kibbutz along the border."

"I'm so happy we don't have wars in Mexico. We really live well here."

One of Andrés's friends came by my house after a youth meeting; she was wearing her uniform, scarf, and a big smile.

"I just had to meet you," she said, "I'm tired of hearing about you, so I've come to see if all the wonderful things they say about you are true."

What was I supposed to do? How could I be so wonderful? She had just left Andrés at his house; they had attended a meeting on the Diaspora.

"And what is the Diaspora?" I asked. She just smiled.

"What? Andrés's great friend has never heard of the Diaspora?" She took out some photocopied sheets of paper from her notebook that one of her group leaders had given her. As she read them to me, she explained the idea. I stared into her clear eyes that were barely perceptible in that long, narrow face; her voice was raspy, and her deep laugh ended as fast as it began. She sounded like Andrés. She said she's proud that she doesn't wear makeup or hose, even though she's already seventeen years old. Just as well my mother didn't hear her say that; she'd have a fit. This girl knows everything, and what she knows is the truth. Here's what she read to me:

The Diaspora is the dispersion of the Jews over four continents. The Jews have created diverse communities all over the world, and the Diaspora has generated new Jewish cultures every-where—in North America, Mexico, Ethiopia, Italy, Uruguay. The center of global Judaism is in the United States. Jews went there because they were offered freedom and the right to develop and grow. Before immigrating to places where life will be hard and the environment and weather are hostile, they prefer to remain where they were born or where they are accepted. They go as tourists, or live somewhere for a year or so, and then they return home. Jews always adapt to their surroundings, but they remain distinct; that is, they identify with their surroundings, but they don't lose their identity.

During four thousand years, my friends, we did not have a nation of our own, but our history continues through today, because the concept of Judaism is more important than the concept of nation. "Medinat Yisrael," which means the State of Israel in Hebrew, was created out of the Diaspora. The Diaspora is indispensable. Do you realize how important all of you are to Israel? Jews have the right to immigrate there, and if they so desire, they automatically become citizens as soon as they set foot on Israeli soil. In reality, however, most Jews are happy in their own countries and choose not to live in Israel; but wherever they are, they cooperate and help maintain the integrity of the Jewish state.

It will not be long before Israel becomes a museum of the history of how and from where the Jews came, how they lived, what their synagogues and their lives were like, how large their communities grew to be, what their relation was with the country that took them in, if they assimilated, and in what numbers.

Now, that's interesting! After she read that, I knew I would like Tzivia. We might even become close friends. She doesn't live far from here; it's on Amsterdam Street.

Here, in Lagunilla Market, I've been working harder than in school or in sports. The guy selling suitcases on the street in front spends most of his time just staring at me; when he sees me arrive with lunch, he starts to follow me, darting in and out of the stalls and saying things to me that I don't understand. But I can tell from his expression that it must be something like "Hey, baby" . . . or "Big Mama" . . . or whatever the guys around here say to women.

When I finally go inside our store, he stops at Goyita's stall and continues to hawk his wares, still staring at me all the while; then he leaves, only to return a little later, schlepping his suitcases back and forth. If these guys like me so much, why don't they nominate me for Miss Lagunilla? I wish *someone* would. The girl who got it last year sings country songs and wears wide skirts that are really pretty. She is Jacob's girlfriend; he works in the store next to ours. I'm dying to be the queen of anything! Or the lady-in-waiting at some wedding. Even the sons of the guy who sells flowers—Chucho—like me. They come around selling flowers made out of crepe paper. And the colors are beautiful! Since they make them in their own stall somewhere else, they're always passing by our store; so, they come and go, they see me, I see them.

At six o'clock, the lady who sells cooked corn-on-the-cob sets up her stand at the corner. The aroma makes its way up the street and, once it reaches our store, there's no way to avoid buying some. Chucho, the youngest son, must smell it at the same time I do, because we always see each other at her stand, but we never speak; we just stand at the corner until we're finished eating. Then we look at each other.

"Why did you come?" I asked Moshón.

"To eat some corn."

"To eat some corn my foot! You're spying on me. Let's go, you jerk. Get a move on."

When our employees sell something, they always give the money to Moshón because he has the keys to the box where my dad keeps his secrets. He takes the money, puts it in the box, closes it, locks it, and sticks his hands back in his pockets. He does it really fast so I won't have time to see what else is in the box. I don't know why he's like that; it's not that I'm trying to snoop around. Him and his secrets. Moshón only discusses money matters with my dad, and he makes sure I don't hear them talking, as if I were some stranger.

"Dad, why do you give the keys only to him? Let's take turns, okay?"

"Some other day. I give them to Moshón because he's a man."

"But I'm older than he is."

My stupid brother smiles vainly and says, "Fix your skirt! Get inside! Dad, what is she doing outside? Everyone who passes by just stares at her."

"I'm not going inside, you jerk. I'm staying right here. Go inside yourself!"

I saw Señora Paula leaving our house. She told me that Andrés was sobbing all night while he listened to the record I had given him for his birthday, the one by María Grever that Libertad Lamarque sang.

"Oh, Andrés, don't cry," I wanted to tell him. "I can see the way you're walking, with your legs spread apart. But you never complain. Andrés, why didn't you tell me about your circumcision? Tell me . . . why?"

I guess there'll never be anything between Andrés and me. My parents say that he's only two years older than me. Since he's just starting out, he wouldn't be able to support me. But his mom doesn't mind if we get married, and she says we could live in her house for two years or until he finishes school. Now that would be crazy! No way. I know I couldn't do it. So, we'll just be friends, no—really good friends, even though sooner or later I'll have to get married.

Besides, he wants to go to Israel, so long as I'll go with him, but my parents won't let me. Just last week I mentioned it again, but there's no way they'll let me go.

"God didn't bring you into the world to marry a Gentile. Going over there before you get married isn't the right thing for a woman to do. First, you get married; then you can go wherever you want—with him. Then you'll be a horse of a different color."

So, does that mean when I get married I'll belong to another family? My dad is always using this saying about the horse of a different color with my mother. Is she now a horse of a different color and doesn't have to worry about being a part of her real family?

Becky's so lucky! She got accepted to UNAM, the national university. My dad gets upset at me because I go around saying she's so lucky. I'll try not to say it in front of him anymore. Only two girls from high school are going to college. Becky, the crazy one from my class, is going to be a psychologist. I recently ate at her house. They had a party, and her two married brothers went. They like Arab food; it's amazing, they love it. They fixed some special dishes with squash and rice. I agree, the food is really good!

Since I don't have any classes at my school right now, I went with Becky to the university. What an amazing place: gardens, trees, a swimming pool with a diving board, lagoons, coffee shops all over the place, a ton of classrooms, and hundreds of students, male and female. Is this what college is all about? Well, it's worth it. I'd probably never get accepted.

She's so lucky! Not only does she get to study for a real degree for four years, but also her parents bought her a VW to get back and forth to school. So, what do you call that? If that isn't luck, I don't what it is.

One of her classes was held in a small auditorium in which there was a one-way mirror to the side of the room so the students could observe the doctor without the patient being embarrassed with a bunch of students watching. When the class was over, the professor reminded the students that they would be meeting the next day in La Castañeda, like the week before.

"If you want to," Becky said, "why don't you come along?"

The professor's office was next to the observation room; he walked in quickly, dodging the sick people who quickly surrounded him with friendly greetings and endless requests. After the doctor had managed to escape from them, the patients stopped me instead: "Doctor, please call my daughter; Doctor, take this message and give it to my husband who works in a warehouse near our house." And so it went, "Please Doctor" this and "Please Doctor" that.

While the professor hid in his office, I took down phone numbers. I promised to bring them an answer another day.

"My family doesn't even know I'm here; please tell them where I am. May God bless you!"

When I got home I started making calls, but no one who answered knew who these people were. The next day more patients, but none of the ones from the previous day stopped me.

"Doctor, please do me a favor." I took down more numbers. Maybe this time I can help someone. But it's useless, the numbers are all wrong. After a few days, they forgot to ask me to make more calls; or perhaps it's just that I was running away, like the professor. Becky and her other classmates teach them knitting and embroidery. It's great therapy for them, and we have a lot of fun too—we gab, they laugh, no one argues.

Sometimes I accompany the doctor on his rounds (since he sees me around there every day, he thinks I belong to the class), or I sit in on an individual consultation. I hear a litany of incoherent responses that seem so disconnected. One woman assured us that it was 1990 and that we were in France. Each day I spend here, I have less and less desire to go back to my own classes, even though I only have to write my thesis in order to get my degree in journalism. But I'm not interested in that anymore. I would love to be in Becky's shoes and go to school at UNAM. Out of curiosity, I went to the insane asylum here, and I discovered that I'm really curious about it all, and suddenly I've been going there every morning for the last six months. I learn something new every day, and every time I go home I see and feel the pain of life more and more intensely. Andrés had talked to me about misery, but if you don't see it, you don't even know it's there.

A woman with transparent eyes, rather chunky, with unkempt long, blond hair, had been following me around for several days; then one day she stopped me and pleaded: "Did you talk to my daughter? You promised . . ." Once again, she gave me a piece of paper, and when I went into the doctor's office, I threw it in the trash. Every morning, as soon as she sees me coming, she gets up off the floor, wearing those loose blue overalls with no buttons that reveal her breasts.

"Doctor, what did my daughter say?"

"I lost the number."

"Please call her on your way out," she said, handing me the same number as before. I didn't throw it away that time, but it wasn't my intention to call, either. At home, the piece of paper mysteriously appeared in my hand as I was taking something out of my purse. I dialed the number.

"Is Señora Saíde there? I have a message from her mother . . ."

"From my mother? What's happened? Where is she? She disappeared two weeks ago. Please, tell me where she is," she said, trying not to cry.

I tried to explain the situation as simply as possible.

"I'll take you to the hospital, but I can't go on Saturdays, so let me work on a way to get you in," I said to her finally.

She offered to pick me up.

We walked through several buildings that were surrounded by beautiful gardens. Assistants in worn-out uniforms were pushing carts with large aluminum pots full of some soupy mixture from the kitchens. I could recognize the smell of the contents. I held my breath so I wouldn't be smelling it for the rest of the day.

The smells—that was the most unpleasant part of my visits. I knocked on the door, and the custodian looked surprised when she opened it.

"Where is she, Saíde?" Then I saw her, sitting on the floor at the end of the hall. She recognized me immediately and quickly stood up. When they recognized each other, they ran to hug each other.

"Mom, why are you here? What happened to you? How could this have happened?"

Mother Saíde told us that the police found her drunk at an intersection trying to direct traffic and, instead of taking her to the police station, they sent her to the insane asylum for creating a public scandal.

I felt proud of myself. Thanks to a dumb little teenager, a mother and daughter were reunited. I feel important.

The women in the asylum wait every day for us to return. While they knit and embroider, we all talk. They explain to us who their friends are and who are not their friends. They really like to gossip, and they have their own little groups. Some of them even think they're important, and they don't make friends with just anybody. At least that's what they say. And others beg us to leave their knitting and embroidery with them when we leave, but we can't: if a fight were to break out, they might use the needles to attack someone; that's why every day we bring their work with us and we take it out when we leave.

Irene is seventeen years old. She's pretty, friendly, and healthy. I wondered why she was in there.

"Hey, Becky, Irene seems pretty normal to me, just like us; do you think they made a mistake?"

"I don't know, but I agree with you. I've heard that her parents brought her here. If it was because they couldn't afford to take care of her, I'll ask for permission to take her to work at my house."

Then we looked through her papers: it said she was a lesbian, and at certain times during the night, she'd try to climb on top of other girls next to her. Also, there was a big hubbub the night before last because she kept molesting Chabela. Two custodians had to intervene, and they sedated her with a shot.

"It's a miracle they didn't give her the electric shock treatment because they're just looking for excuses to practice it on as many people as possible."

✹ some Days Later.

I don't know how she did it, but Becky devised a way to sneak Irene into her car and take her out of the hospital. She told her to get down on the floor behind the front seat. In his friendly way, the guard at the gate just waved to us. We took her to Chapultepec Park; rode on the little train; bought her ice cream, candy, popcorn, or whatever she wanted; and then went to the zoo. The custodians didn't even realize what we had done. Our only problem was trying to take her back at two o'clock in the afternoon, because she wouldn't get out of the car. Becky promised to talk to the hospital director about the possibility of Irene going to live at her house.

Since we had only been in the observation room, we decided to visit some of the other buildings. We ended up in one that housed those who were severely mentally deficient. Now, that was a trip if I ever saw one! People with old bodies and infantile minds, some with beards who sat around begging. But the second floor was even worse: in some cribs there were just shapeless forms with hands and feet. As we entered the room, a nurse was changing the diaper on one of them; when I got closer I could see that the tiny body had the face of a grown person, with a beard and all. His voice was unintelligible, but he was an adult man. His body—except for his head—had never developed. They told me he was twenty years old.

"For twenty years they've been changing his diapers and giving a bottle to this thing . . . a baby or a child . . . or whatever. Twenty years? Why? Why haven't they put him out of his misery?"

"How could we do such a thing? It would be a crime."

"So what! And letting him live like this? And to think there isn't enough help to take care of the children downstairs. Why don't they give them something to put them to sleep?"

"The administration won't allow it. That would be like killing someone."

"For the love of humanity, let them die."

"These aren't the only ones, there's more. Follow me."

We heard the slow, rasping voice of a child; he was asking the attendant for something. She brought a diaper, saying, "Here I am, here I am," and she changed him.

He understood.

"I think we should go now, Becky. Let's go back to our building, this is too much for me; I would have let them die fifteen years ago. Just think of all that suffering!"

As we went down the stairs, the smell of urine penetrated the air while the hands of those beggars grasped anxiously for some change. The custodians hurriedly closed the iron grates behind us so that none of them would get out. They pushed up against the bars, stuck their hands through, and repeated in hoarse voices: "Give me, give me."

We felt like running away. I faced straight ahead, looked up, and suddenly found solace in the trees outside that seemed so unrelated to the suffering of those people inside. The trees will continue to live in order to make the grounds beautiful, and their leaves will descend once again in the fall, because they are assured of coming to life again in the spring. This little forest left me feeling secure again. Like Sara, however, I looked back—which I shouldn't have done—and the image of the old people behind the bars, hands extended, touched me deeply.

Whenever Becky's friend Jorge, who attends the university, comes back from the asylum with us, she drops me off first. I'm suspicious.

"So, do you like him?" I asked her. And she blew her cool.

"I'm fed up with *our* way of doing things. Do you know what it's like to come to the university and find yourself in a totally different world? And it's different only because that's what our parents told us to believe. Look at all the cute guys here! Wouldn't you know it: the ones I like the best are those who aren't like us, and they're the ones who like me the best. How do you explain that? It's like going to buy ice cream and you see all the different flavors and colors, but you always end up asking for the one you learned to eat at home. I'm fed up with asking for the same flavor. I want to experiment, and with Jorge, I can try other flavors. Do you know how many guys here want to go out with me? When I go to our clubs, there's no one to hook up with; there aren't any guys around anywhere, or if there are some who are worth knowing, they don't go to those clubs anymore. At least I don't run into them.

"It's a drag being Jewish. A thousandth part of this country—no, it's worse, a ten-thousandth part of the people who live here—is Jewish. We were born in a place where the majority isn't Jewish, and being able to choose only from among what's out there, you're limited. And that's not all: if you don't get married early, they make you feel like you're an old maid at twenty; then they start looking for some old man, usually from Los Angeles or wherever, for you to marry.

"Besides, when you say to these guys, 'Yes, I'm Jewish,' they shrug their shoulders, and then you don't know if they'll ever speak to you again. One thing's for sure, the Jews aren't that popular in this world: just ask these guys what they've heard about Jews."

I wonder what's going to happen to Becky. I can't picture it. Can anything be done about this clash of cultures? Anything at all? No wonder they want us to get married so soon!

🏃 the dentist's office.

What's going to happen when my mom finds out that I've quit going to school? I haven't gone back since I started going to the insane asylum. I've already finished two terms in journalism. All that's left is the thesis. It must be neat to get a degree. I can just imagine my schoolmates: they're all probably getting close to finishing; maybe some of them already have. I'm going to the school in the morning to see how they're doing, who's finished, what they're writing about, who's going to examine them. I hope my mom doesn't find out what I've done, or find this diary and read it; she's so curious she's almost perver . . . oops, I shouldn't write it, but nothing will change.

Coming back in the jail truck, no matter how much I waved my arms or banged on the window, my mother and her friends didn't see me. But it looked like they were turning our way.

"Frida, there's my mom." "Mom!" "Look at her face. Is she feeling sick? What's wrong with her? There's Señora Rashel and her friends. They must have been playing cards. Señor, por favor, stop right there at that pink building. Those ladies with the surprised faces are friends of my mom's. Yes, you can park in front. Oh, thank you so much. That saved us from having to take a bus. The director is so nice, isn't she?"

"Heaven help us! What have I done? My daughter . . . what's happened?" she said, terrified.

"My God," said another.

"Mom, before the truck leaves, look how neat it is inside. It has a row of seats on each side; the only problem is that the driver can't hear us because of the glass."

"Poor child! What were you doing in jail?"

"Oh, Mom, it was so much fun. Frida is doing her thesis about the women's jail, and I went with her. In fact, we're going back. We ate some of the most delicious bread that they make themselves. In their sewing classes, they make the uniforms for the guards and the other inmates. We visited the nursery; some women go to jail while they're pregnant, and they have their children there. They raise them there. They even have certain privileges, and the children seem to be happy. There are cribs, playpens, walkers, and toys. The walls are decorated for children. They don't even realize they're in jail.

"There was even a theater group there. We were so lucky to get a ride. We didn't have to change buses, and the one that says 'Women's Penitentiary' on it takes forever.

"What a great day! Right, Frida? Ok, Mom, I'll tell you all about it later. I'm going to walk Frida to the bus stop. Are your friends leaving already?"

Dori is getting married. Yep, she's doing it. Plain and simple. Even though her boyfriend seems friendly enough, I'm not convinced. I'm too shy to talk to him, and he's always in a hurry. I went with her to see the apartment her father had bought for her. How strange that an apartment would be yours; she says that soon it'll be like that in many buildings. I don't believe it; who's going to buy air? From her window on the third floor, I could see something shining like the sun. When I looked out I could see a golden angel standing above the treetops. I sat on the end of her bed and continued to look at it; from any angle I chose, I could see the Angel of Independence monument. It's amazing to think she has an apartment in the middle of trees, shag-pile rugs, paintings, carved wood, an antique telephone on the wall, and so many, many other things. I looked at Dori. I can't imagine her being a Señora, even though she's lived in better houses, like the one in Campos Eliseos that had a staircase, majestic banisters, stained glass windows, a large room upstairs, and nannies and nurses for the half-sisters who arrived there. In her house there was a piece of furniture that was a stereo tape recorder. No one else had one. We had so much fun, making up and taping our own little plays of mystery and terror.

My dad is upset with my mom because she just decided to have plastic surgery done on my sister Zelda's nose.

"But if her nose looks just like mine, what's wrong with that?"

On our way home from the store, my dad tells me about what my mom's doing to him. I always agree with him, except when it comes to my sister's nose. I'm so lucky not to have gotten such a hook-shaped nose like them. My poor sister, she really inherited it. My dad never imagined the wonders of plastic surgery.

It's true that my mom is well liked among her friends. When they are together, they seem to enjoy each other. Today, I cracked a joke and one of them said, "You see, you're just like your mother." My dad was in the bathroom and my mom's friends were talking.

"Poor Dad," I said, "he's furious because of what they did to Zelda's nose."

"Oh, come on. Did you think I was going to let my daughter look like that? Now she's pretty. Let him get mad, it doesn't bother me. I want your sister to look appealing and to be lucky; and I'm going to do everything in my power to make sure it happens, despite your father's wishes. I'm not like your grandmother, who has to ask permission for everything, even to go take a pee. Don't get involved, you say? If it had been you who were born with that nose, you'd be very happy to have it fixed. Am I not right, my darling?"

In order to be successful at selling in Lagunilla Market, you have to do the following:

1) No matter what, get the client inside. If need be, grab her and pull her in.
2) She should like what we're selling, or you should convince her that she likes what she sees.
3) It should fit her well (well, that's not hard to do because we can easily change the size on the label. We take her to our other store while we change the label; she tries it on again and feels good about it).
4) The hardest part is the bartering, which can last five minutes or the entire day. There are clients who already have their own systems. They offer low, and if we don't accept it, they leave, but only for a little while: they keep coming back every half hour and offer a little more each time, until finally, after several trips back and forth, they strike up a deal with my dad.

I don't want to work in our store during vacation; I would rather work in a classier place, with different people, and more importantly, in a place with fixed prices. I would love to work in Sears or some other big department store, but my mom says I should work with my people. My dad contacted Max and Benny, who sell costume jewelry.

"Why, of course, Samuel, send her to our store downtown on Monday; that's where we'll be, and we'll be glad to keep an eye on her. Now that it's December, we've got lots of business. She can be our secretary; she's already learned dictation and typing, and I know she'll be happy at it. Vicky works with us too; she's one of us, a good kid. I'll bet your daughter knows her; she's a little older, but she studied at the same school."

❖ ❖ ❖

There's no comparison with my dad's store! This is really a swanky place: earrings, necklaces, brooches, rings, bracelets, compacts, purses, and chains. Everything is so shiny. I would love to buy it all. Fortuna and Anita are so lucky to own the store. And to think they can come down here and take whatever they want for free. The best part is that bartering doesn't even occur to anyone; that only happens in Lagunilla Market. The employees think I'm someone important because I know the owners so well. In fact, they're upset about it.

"You should call them Señor Max and Señor Benny, don't try to be on their level."

But I can't help myself, because I've always spoken to them on a more personal basis. Nevertheless, at this store Max seems like another person; I'm even afraid to talk to him.

I don't know anything about being a secretary, but Vicky is patient with me, and I'm learning how to answer the phone and pick up the mail and the balance sheets from the other stores. Everybody is so easygoing, we're always laughing at something, but we do have to work. At noon we go upstairs to eat in a lunchroom for the employees of the building. There's nothing fancy—soup, meat, rice, and beans. It's served up fast and everyone gets the same. I like learning about these kinds of restaurants; here, I've met girls who work at different department stores nearby: Liverpool, Boker, Palacio de Hierro, and others. Frankly, I'm really happy here. Since the stores close later on Wednesdays and Saturdays, we have time to eat a more leisurely lunch and to walk around downtown afterward.

Yesterday marked two weeks that I've been working for them, and they actually paid me. Now I'm wondering how I can spend it. But we work so much that there's hardly any time left to go out and buy anything. When I get to work, the jewelry store isn't open yet, and when I go home it's already closed. I'm saving my money.

At this store, Benny and Max are really important. Are they the same guys? Their wives are so admired, so high class, and so different that I don't even recognize them . . . especially when I hear the employees talking about them. I can't even believe those women are my mom's friends and so close to me. My mom says that Fortunita is somewhat inattentive. Down here, they think they are something extraordinary.

When Max is near our desks, we hardly breathe, we're trying to work so hard. I'm afraid he might find out that I have been asking Vicky how to do everything. Sometimes, when there are a lot of customers, he tells me, "Go work the till." He's always overseeing things, and the employees don't even dare look at each other. If the store closes early, I usually go home by myself. Last night when it was almost ten o'clock, Max said to me, "Oshinica, call your dad and tell him you're going home now; you need to be here early in the morning. December is our busiest month." I didn't say anything. I probably won't even be able to sleep a wink tonight; I hope I don't pee the bed.

On the 24th, it's customary to have an office party. Max orders roasted chickens, appetizers, French fries, desserts, and cider. He turns up the radio full blast, and the owners dance with the female employees. There's no way my dad would've done something like that at his store.

The managers of the branch stores come to the main store downtown to turn in sales receipts and money, and to pick up more jewelry. They turn over the dirty but brimming moneybags to us, the secretaries. The other day, the manager of the store that's almost next to my dad's in Lagunilla winked at me. He's so handsome! He's got green eyes, a thin moustache, black hair, and a good body. He looks like James Dean. And his butt is cute. Wow, does he know how to wink!

Nowadays, I'm the one who is usually waiting around for them to bring the money, especially the guy who winks at me. I hope he'll come when we're closing. His name is Lalo, and he's the son of Señor Eliezer, one of Max and Benny's uncles. I'm glad that he's one of us. I've already met his dad; I used to see him in Lagunilla talking to everyone, but I had no idea that he had children, much less such handsome boys.

I've decided to work until January 6th because I'm going to Acapulco; Lalo will have to wait. Vicky said that he likes me, but I don't believe it. The dummy, he doesn't even say anything to me. The other day we were going to ask him for a ride, and today he came with his mother. I don't like that lady much, she's so big and wide, with deep eyes, and she dyes her hair black. We ate lunch with Vicky's brother-in-law. He's really ugly and speaks with a twang. I can hardly understand him. He told her that he knows a guy who wants to meet her, but he's a bit older. Vicky is two years older than me: she's nineteen, and this guy is forty. But just like he said to her, "Look, Vicky, he'll give you everything: a house, a wedding dress, and he'll pay for the wedding, banquet, and even a dowry. Give him a try; you just might like him. Don't you see, the young guys are only going after the women with money; it's that simple. I'll bring him by tomorrow, and we can pretend we're just stopping by to say hello, and then we can have lunch together. And dress up, eh? We'll come for you at three o'clock. Look at your face! I'm not forcing you to do anything."

We finally got up the nerve to ask Lalo for a ride, and he invited us for an ice cream cone. Then we dropped Vicky off. As we arrived at my house, I saw Mom waiting for me in the middle of the street, and she was furious. I slouched down in the seat and said to Lalo, "Keep driving, and don't stop!" He got scared and parked around the corner.

"My God, what should I do now? What am I going to tell her? She's going to kill me. Did you see her? She must have talked with Max and Benny and all my friends . . . I know! Here's what we'll do: I'll get in the back seat like I was coming in a taxi; I'll be real serious, pay you, and get out. She already warned me that she was against me coming home with you. Ah, heck. She's not going to believe this. Quick! Got any ideas? Say something! Okay, so she won't believe the taxi bit, but I can't think of anything else. Please, do your best to look like a taxi driver."

I was pushed and shoved all the way up the stairs and into my bedroom. I guess I'm not going to work there anymore. My sister Clarita is so frightened from the beating I got, and all the screaming, that she doesn't even talk to me. She never talked to me much anyway.

When my mother's friends came to watch the soaps, I got my little sewing basket out with my knitting and sat down with them. I looked at the small squares that I've finished, some with yellow in the middle, others with red, wondering when I'll have enough to sew them together for a quilt. I told them that I was going to continue my education when I get married; there are lots of women that age who go back to school. I wanted to see if any of them supported my idea.

"They'll say yes at first, but once you're married they won't give a rat's ass."

"And where do you think you'll find a guy who would care, my precious one?"

"When do you think you're going to get involved in it all?"

"There's no getting around it," said another one, "they'll say you can do whatever you want, then they'll do whatever *they* want."

And they went around the room, giving advice.

I wonder why my mom plays cards? I leave them sitting

around the table with the green tablecloth and go to school. I talk with Frida, and then go to Miss Gooding's class. I discover that lots of things are not necessarily true, that I'll have to erase them from my mind and start over. I want to travel and to love the trees, the ocean, the rivers, and men. I want to be a stowaway on a ship and go to Egypt and India—no, just Israel. And when I return home, they'll still be dealing cards. Can't they think of anything better to do? Well, it's true, they eat and eat, mainly those little pastries with eggplant, with cheese and nuts inside, which, by the way, my mother makes only when they come over. They roar and shout and laugh and argue. They dress up to the hilt only to show off to each other. If Anita gets all dolled up on Monday, then it's Fortuna's turn on Tuesday. Each day it's a different person. They play hearts, canasta, and poker. They say that the woman who doesn't play cards doesn't have any friends. Every time one of them wins the pot, they scream to high heaven. Last Saturday, I was doing my homework and I thought something serious had happened, with all the screaming; but no, it was just that Fortuna, who they say is absent-minded and doesn't like to play cards, had won the pot. They almost killed her; they chided her so much that she began to cry. She even wanted to go home.

"It's just that you're not taking the game seriously, you need to pay attention, look at the cards that are being dealt. If everyone was getting rid of their fives, why didn't you, and here I am praying and praying for a five, and you're just holding on to yours."

"We didn't come just to talk or daydream, we came to play," said her sister-in-law.

Poor Fortuna; being the wife of a jewelry store owner doesn't count for anything at this table.

◇ ◇ ◇

To celebrate Teacher's Day, Miss Gooding wanted us to take her to an Arab restaurant. She has become so enthralled with the music that she doesn't act as stiff as usual. Or maybe she's changing, even if it's slowly. For example, she wasn't wearing her hairnet and some of her hair had fallen out of place. Wow, her hair moves like normal people's hair! I wonder what's going on with that Miss Spunky.

Since I'm taking off for Acapulco tomorrow, I thought I'd better talk to Lalo. But what if he snubs me and says, "Have a good trip," and that's it? He said he could see me. I told him to meet me two blocks away. We were sitting in his car when he caressed my cheek, put his arms around me, and kissed me.

"Darling, sweetheart, honey," he said to me, "I'm falling in love with you."

I'm going to send him the prettiest card I can find.

I traveled all night on a bus, looking out the window at the stars and savoring his kiss. I remembered, "Darling, sweetheart, honey." No one has ever spoken to me like that before—it sounded straight out of the soaps—especially from someone with green eyes. Those green eyes—what a feeling of serenity!

✈ acapulco. the oviedo bungalows.

My dad didn't want to go back to Señora Sultana's hotel this time.

"It's for old men," he said, "and they won't leave well enough alone."

Today, finally, I was able to buy a card for Lalo. It was one of those with foldout pictures of Acapulco and, at the end, a rose and a heart. Even though I wrote and wrote, there was still space left over. I told him that I was happy, and that I wished he was with me now. While I waited for my dad to take his afternoon nap, and instead of trying to fish off the dock, I managed to escape from the watchful eye of my brother and run to the post office across the street. I think I made a mistake not sending it inside an envelope: now everyone is going to know about my new love. How embarrassing if his secretaries at the store read it first! I'm so stupid! Why didn't I think about this before?

There's outright chaos at home. My mother has been crying all afternoon. Moshón wants to quit school. He barely started prep school, and now he's bored. He wants to work at our store and make money.

"So, what's this all about?" said my father. "You can't do that. Think for a minute, son, why do you want to work? We'll provide you with everything you need until you get your degree. We want you to be successful, a professional. I don't want you to spend the rest of your life buried away in Lagunilla Market like me. The world is big and I'm in a little space inside a store. If it's a car you want, you don't have to quit studying to get one. As soon as you turn eighteen, I promise to buy you one."

"That's not it; I'm just bored. How many more years of school is it? I want to buy my own car. You don't have a lot of money, and you don't even want to spend what you have."

"What do you mean I don't have much money? I'll buy you one, wait and see. And what a car it will be, too!"

Now, if *I* wanted to quit studying, they'd have a party to celebrate it. I'm furious.

Lalo didn't really know about our sports club. How strange! He didn't even know they existed. He seemed so out of place; he felt uneasy going there. This place has been the center of my life for years now. My only connection with the outside world has been this club. I've even been a gymnastics teacher for little girls; the real instructor, who gives the classes, likes me a lot, and I like him even more. He gave me a group to teach on Saturday mornings. I'm his pet, and I almost have the entire class to myself. I'm really good at forward and backward somersaults on the trampoline. On Sundays, they put it near the swimming pool, and it seems like the whole world stops by to watch us jump. On holidays, like today, which is the only time my dad can work out because it's forbidden to be open for business, he too will stop playing tennis and come over to watch me.

Lalo and his friend were talking with my dad while he was on the tennis court. Jacob is the grandson of Señor Behar, the man who took in my grandparents when they had just arrived in Mexico. We had never talked to each other before. He seems either too serious or stuck up. Our dads would go out together when they were single. They both sell overcoats, but each one tries to sell a different style. Looking partially embarrassed but almost snickering, Jacob told the story about the times when my father would nap on a chair on the sidewalk in front of the store after lunch, and they would sneak up behind him and light a firecracker under his chair. When it went off, he would jump up, petrified. He wouldn't get mad because they were old friends. He would just laugh. They won't be friends after my dad finds out that I've been going out with Lalo almost every day. I think my dad suspected that Lalo had come on his own just to see me. I'm so happy that I was wearing the red outfit that I made for myself; the shorts fit nice and tight and they're real short shorts. Lalo said I have pretty legs.

◇ ◇ ◇

Since my mother says that she made a mistake letting me go to high school, and that it was a waste of time, she's decided not to make the same mistake with my younger sisters. So, once they've finished middle school, they're going to study to be English-Spanish bilingual secretaries. According to her and her friends, that's the program to be in these days: it doesn't take long, it brings in a lot of money, and it's great for women who want to work a few years and make money before getting married. Even if it just helps to buy some clothes and other little things, it's better than running around poorly dressed like me. No matter what, they're not going to study anything that takes a long time to finish; it's no use to barely finish the first year of something and have to stop.

"Women shouldn't do any of that, which is fine. We don't want you to be an intellectual or a wise person," said my mom, making that gesture of hers: lifting her head up and wrinkling her nose.

It's not boring anymore to take my dad's lunch to him, because now I get to go by Lalo's store on the way. What a coincidence! The two stores are almost side by side; only Jacob's store is in between them. Lalo has been there for almost a year, and I never noticed him. I must have been blind. I am, because I walk without looking at anyone, but how am I going to look at anyone while I'm walking? Then they'll start saying that I like this one and that one and so on. That's why I don't stop to look at anyone, and even when I sense that someone is looking at me, I never turn around to look. Besides, I haven't been going all that much to Lagunilla because ever since they prohibited us from opening up on Sundays, my father has been going to the sports club with us. He's really happy; it's the first time in his life that he's got a full day off to do whatever he wants. He's not even tempted to open up;

LIKE A BRIDE —

169

everyone has to obey the law. So, we get up early before the tennis courts fill up. We play in pairs: my dad, Moshón, me, and anyone else who is around. Then he puts on a bathing suit and spends most of the time sunbathing. He likes to be tanned. If we didn't have to take my grandparents out for a while, we'd probably stay the whole afternoon.

Finally, we bought a car.

"One of these Sundays we'll go out and visit the pyramids, right, Dad?"

"There's no reason to; let's just go to the sports club."

"But, Dad, I've only been to Caútla and Acapulco."

It's really nice having a boyfriend who has a car and will take you wherever you want, and buy whatever you want; who thinks you are the ultimate; who never says no to anything; and who always brings you presents. There's no comparison to that cheapskate Leon, no way, and I was so fortunate to have gotten out of that relationship when I did. Lalo doesn't care how many hot dogs I eat. He wants to marry me, but I don't think it's going to be easy. The other day my mom saw him outside the store talking to someone, so she kept me inside. And she's already checked up on his brothers, who haven't been good husbands; neither has his father, who never did amount to much either. That's why they say, "Like father, like son." But he's not to blame for what his brothers have or haven't done. What a big deal they make out of it. My mother inquired everywhere, and they all told her the same thing. And here I am the oldest in my family, serving as an example of how to behave.

Whenever Lalo sees me leave the store, he always catches up with me and we walk around together for a while. I can't take my eyes off him. He's not tall, but he's taller than me, and since he plays football he's got nice muscular legs. He's five years older than me, and I don't get embarrassed talking to him like I do with the guys my mom wants me to go out with. Lalo has been helping to support his family ever since he was a kid, so he's not educated. If he hadn't told me, I wouldn't have guessed. I'm going to help him study for the entrance exams; he's really intelligent. I proposed it to him, and he seemed enthusiastic. He doesn't have the slightest idea why they won't let me go out with him. I'm certainly not going to tell him that my mom doesn't like what she's heard about his family.

I ran into Andrés and told him the truth: I'm in love with Lalo. I felt happy telling him what Lalo's like.

"I'll never be able to marry you, and if it's not with him, it'll be someone else."

And that was that. I didn't dare to look at his face. He said goodbye, without saying anything. He walked away slowly.

I went to my school today. My friends were so excited about having finished their theses that I wanted to finish mine, too. I went to the insane asylum so many times that I could do an investigative report: describe the hospital, mention each one of the buildings, how many patients there are, what diseases they have, how they live, and how they got there. Three weeks are left to have the thesis edited and sent to the printer.

This past Sunday, Becky and I went to Chapultepec Park. They say you can get really sunburned there. We went anyway. And we had a great time. We went in her blue VW, drove around, looked at everyone, laughed, and parked at a kiosk in order to talk to some friends of hers. They invited us to a marvelous place called Los Csardas, where the musician Elías Briskin plays the violin. I was avoiding them like the plague because they were all older: Jack, a French doctor who has just arrived in Mexico, is a cousin of Dr. Maya, who is very famous. He explained to us that in order to practice in Mexico, he has to revalidate his title and take some exams. In the meantime, he and his cousin are going to open a laboratory for clinical analysis.

"Do you know any young person who might like to work as a secretary?" he asked.

"No. I'll let you know if I hear of someone. But I would like to work," my voice was hardly audible, "and I know dictation and typing."

"Come by the laboratory."

"I doubt if I'll be able to."

"Give it a try."

"I'm going to ask my mother for permission."

"I'll give you a call and you can let me know. We open in two weeks. We're on Insurgentes Street, in front of Sears."

When I told my mother, she was happy.

"Don't you see, you didn't even finish dictation and typing, and who says we parents don't know what's best for our children? The new owner's mother is a cultured person; I've already been talking to her in French, and we discovered that we're related: a cousin of mine in Istanbul is her niece."

Now my mother was really beaming.

No doubt about it, conflict rules in my house. My mom is going crazy. The telephone rings and then they hang up. I'm here with my knitting, working on a red square this time, and the phone rings again. My mom answers but they hang up again. The next time I put down my knitting and answer the phone.

"I want to see you," said Lalo, "I need to see you, honey, I'm going to make a pile of money for you."

My mom grabs the receiver from me and starts yelling at him, telling him to leave me alone and that he doesn't understand Spanish. She doesn't want to let me go out with my girlfriends or answer the telephone; and she said that if she sees me with him she'll take me out of school and make life hard on me. I spoke with Lalo, and even though he was sad, I won't be seeing him anymore. What am I supposed to do? This is too much!

I finished my short project. I don't know what else to write to make it longer; I can't think of anything to add. I'm just dense. But I did write the minimum. And it's done! I made it by adding some dedications at the beginning and adding extra blank pages in between the chapters. The important thing is to produce a little book with my name on the front. I wanted to dedicate it not only to my parents but also to Andrés; but my mother would have killed me.

I ran into Andrés, and we saw each for only about ten minutes. His little loving eyes just looked at me, but he didn't say he missed me. He showed me a letter and some pictures that his friends—a couple from our group here—sent from Israel. How neat! The guy was hanging from a banana tree and she was milking a cow. They looked happy. They told him to join them there, that she is pregnant, that they only speak Hebrew because they want to revive the language, that soon the whole world will be speaking it. And that their child's mother tongue will be Hebrew. Andrés is getting ready to go.

What a luxurious laboratory! The waiting room has some beautiful curtains with colorful designs on them. I've never seen anything like them. When I get married, I want to have the same thing. I never get tired of looking at them. As you enter, there's a new, shiny desk for the secretary: that's me. The typewriter can be stored away underneath the top of the desk. I'm happy I have a place to put my diary, Lalo's cards, and Frida's letters. Finally, my mom can't go through my personal things. This is the first time in my life that I've had a little secret place where I can hide my things because my mom's mania for cleaning reaches every corner of the house.

Behind my desk is Jack's office, which is full of marvelous books and magazines about medicine that aren't hard to understand. There is a small cubicle for taking blood and vaginal samples. At the back of the lab are the microscopes, lab tables, refrigerators, centrifuges, glass tubes, flasks, beakers, and Bunsen burners. At the far end is another room for analyzing urine and feces cultures.

Jack doesn't want receipts for money spent from petty cash, but I keep a record anyway. I buy everything we need, and I don't even ask his permission. I'm really happy that he trusts me so much. I adore him.

I have a telephone on my desk that I'll use to inform Jack that a client has arrived. I've been typing a list of prices of the different types of analysis. Their names are real tongue twisters, but by the afternoon I was able to pronounce them easily. Now all we have to do is mail the list to a bunch of doctors and wait for the customers to roll in. It will be exciting when the first one comes through the door!

Starting Monday, Rita will join us. She's a young, beautiful girl, who was alone with Jack in his office for the interview. I thought she was his lover. She's going to be the head pharmacologist. She has a long red braid and a long thin body. She seems to walk fast wherever she goes. She's pretty in her white smock.

Finally, Rita and I welcomed our first clients. I had put on my smock and my best smile, because I was really nervous.

I opened the door and sat down at my desk to take care of the first customer. He showed me the doctor's orders. I looked for the price of the analysis on the list, took out my receipt book, and asked him how much he was going to give for a down payment. Then I asked him to take a seat in the waiting room where he could admire, like me, the curtains. I took the doctor's orders to Rita, prepared some other documents, and then asked him to go into the cubicle and roll up his sleeve in order to take a blood sample.

I stayed around to watch. I couldn't pass up waiting for this moment; it's been two weeks. I'm fascinated with Rita's professionalism. I never tire of watching her do her work, peer into the microscope, get excited about what she sees inside, and then call me over to look at the red and white cells.

Before going to work, I dropped by the school to pick up my project, which had already been graded. I couldn't believe all the red marks! There is more red than black; you can hardly see my writing. I'll take it to the printer tomorrow.

Amazing! I did it!

Now I'm a full-fledged journalist.

I miss Lalo and I want to think that he probably misses me even more. He was so happy to have a girlfriend. He had said that if he can't marry me he won't get married at all. He said he thinks about me wherever he goes. My dad says he doesn't hang around the tennis court to talk anymore.

Our school graduation is going to be held at El Patio, and they've hired the comedian Beto El Boticario. I'm not as excited as I was when I graduated from high school. The best part is wearing the robe and hat like the students who graduate in Law.

I just found this poem, and I've already learned it by heart:
I can write the saddest verses tonight.
To write, for example: The night is starred,
And the cosmos seems to be twinkling from afar.
I wanted her and sometimes she also wanted me.
In nights such as these I had her in my arms.
I kissed so many times under the infinite sky.
She wanted me and at times I also wanted her.
How not to have loved her lovingly intense stare.

That's a powerful poem. It makes me want to cry. I can't believe what poetry does to me. I'm so happy that Miss Gooding stopped having us copy letters and more letters that said the same old thing, and instead had us type poems. I really like them, especially the poetry dedicated to the trees, traveling, and mankind.

Enough already! I'm not going to spend the entire day on this poem. I have lots of other reasons to be happy. I've just finished my first month at work, and I've learned many new things. Now, whenever someone calls for instructions on having an analysis done, I can do it with ease; it's like I've been doing it for years. When a woman comes in for a vaginal analysis, I go into the cubicle with her, and in a friendly but serious way, tell her to get on the examination table and remove her panties. I guess this white smock looks important because they do exactly as I say. I would feel pretty embarrassed if I had to get on that table myself. I'll never do it. It's such a humiliating position to be in—you're at the mercy of the doctor and the nurses, lying there half naked while they're formally dressed.

If we don't have a lot of customers, I run back to watch Rita do her work. After seeing so many urine analyses, I know exactly how it's done. I type up the remarks that she makes in a notebook.

I always make an extra copy for myself, even though there are three for urine tests and three different ones for feces. One of these days I'm going to do an analysis and compare it to hers; I bet they turn out the same.

They're so easy to do!

"Are you okay, Princess?" Jack asked me. And that was enough for me to break down crying. I'm not used to being treated so nicely or knowing that they care so much.

"What's wrong?" he said, hugging me.

"I miss Lalo."

He didn't say another word; he just kept hugging me while I cried.

When I got home, I took out my knitting and calmed down; this time I combined purple and yellow with a different-colored border. Now I'm making little squares every night. My mom likes what she sees.

What I don't know is when she's going to let me sew the squares together.

They offer a program that certifies you as a lab technician at my school. They have an afternoon schedule, and it takes three years.

"Find a friend who'll work half-time for you, and you can study; but you'll have to split your salary with her," Jack told me.

He's cool! What a guy! I'm going to look around for someone to work here. I would love to hug and kiss him. Classes begin in two weeks. I know I'll find someone. Who wouldn't want to work in such a delightful atmosphere? The hard part will be telling my parents that I'm starting a new degree program. My mom is going to have a fit.

"Lab technician? Oh, my God, this young lady will never give up. Are you crazy? Why do you want to do this, and why now? I've been praying and praying for you to finish. Are we ever going to be done with that damn school? Please, tell me: why? To hang your certificate in the bathroom? That's all it will be good for. You've gone off the deep end. Okay, answer this: do you have any friends who are doing such a silly thing? Dori never finished anything; she got married. She doesn't have a certificate, and she's happy. I saw her the other day with her baby; I felt so happy for her. Her daughter is beautiful. And here you are, just when—thanks be to God—you got your certificate in journalism and your father finished paying for your studies, you come up with the idea to get *another* certificate. And when will we be able to sit back and tell everyone that our daughter is earning her way a bit? But no, barely two months go by in your new job and you invent something new: now you want to be a chemist. Dear God, why did you give us an intelligent daughter? Why? Where does so much studying get you? And you, Shamuel, why don't you say something? Why don't you tell her what you told me last night? Why do I always have to be the one?"

I turn to him and see that he's in agreement. Well, then, why do I want to keep studying? I've already got one certificate, why shouldn't I be happy with that? I've been thinking about Alicia, the woman who was studying journalism although she was already a grandmother. And what if I get married and my husband lets me study like her? Will I find a man who won't think I'm crazy just because I want to continue studying after I get married?

I'm so happy that I finished knitting my sweater with red, white, and blue stripes (they're my favorite colors) in time to wear it last night when I went out with Maurice, who is Jack's younger brother. My mother is pleased that he invited me out; so am I, because he's a handsome brute. I hope he doesn't notice how nervous I get around him. He took me to a restaurant called the Swiss Chalet. The waiter made a big fuss about everything, and recommended several dishes that only Maurice knew about. He asked for wine and cheese. I'm so dumb about those things that I waited for him to serve himself to see how he did it; I was intrigued with the melted cheese, and it tasted great. I didn't try the wine, because I really don't like the taste of alcohol.

I was really worn out by the time I got home! He may be really handsome and cultured, but I prefer to go out with Lalo.

When my father arrived home from the store, he told me that Lalo had gone to see him. He had told my dad that if he can't marry me, he's going to kill himself, and me as well.

"If that's what you want, go ahead and kill yourself," my father told him with anger.

Now he says that Lalo has gone crazy, and how could he ever allow me to marry a madman.

Lalo, I feel so sorry for you. I'm sorry that my family doesn't think much of you. You'll see, things will get better and no one will trouble you ever again. I'll always feel guilty for not having the courage to marry you.

I feel happy whenever someone comes to the lab with their vial in hand; and the bigger the better, because there'll be some urine left over for me. I use what's left over to practice and compare the results. Today, I did three experiments, using different procedures for each one. My results were correct, except that I sucked too hard on the tube and I drank a sip. The last few times I've been scared that I'll do it again. It really tasted horrible, but more than anything, I just got nauseated from it all. And what if the patient has an infection?

Now I've seen how they do every analysis that's on our price list. On Saturday, they cleaned out a man's stomach, and stuck a probe down his throat all the way to his stomach. At first he felt like vomiting, but they had to keep it going down. Then the gastric juices came out. I can still see it happening as I watched this guy's face full of resignation and fear at the same time; he was doing everything possible to control his nausea.

Poor guy.

One of our clients came in for a sperm analysis. Since I had never been involved in that, I talked to Jack about it. Using the intercom, he explained what had to be done. Then he gave me a flat vial with a glass top for making the cultures, and told me that the patient will want to find out if the amount of sperm he produces is enough to fertilize a woman, and if his sperm lives long enough. Oh, so that's what it's all about, eh? That man who's sitting over there reading a magazine is going to deposit his semen in this jar right now?

"Oshi, send the gentleman in, please."

Oh, dear, how do I tell him to go into Jack's office? Once inside, Jack told him something in a low voice and gave him the jar. Then the man went into the restroom. After a while, he came out and gave Jack the jar; then Jack walked him to the door. I was sitting at my desk acting busy, but I was watching everything out of the corner of my eye. He left in a hurry, and I think he was embarrassed, like me.

Now, you feeble little sperms, I'm going to find out what you really look like!

I was walking through Mexico Park and they started whistling at me. I saw a really handsome guy wearing a red sweater, in a fancy car no less. It was Lalo. Unbelievable! He looked like James Dean. He's changed so much in the three months we haven't seen each other. As always, he winked at me, got out of his brand new car, and walked me to the lab. He told me that he loves me, and that he can't live without me.

"Marry me, I swear you won't be sorry. I will make you happy."

"I don't want to get married yet. I'm happy right now. I've been learning new things. I'm studying to become a lab technician; in fact, I'm going to quit as secretary, and soon I'll be doing the analysis all by myself."

"Marry me, and you can continue your studies."

My mouth fell open and my eyes popped out.

"Do you really mean it wouldn't matter to you if I continued studying? Are you sure?"

"Why should it matter to me?"

"I can't believe it. You must be joking with me. My mother's friends say, 'They'll always tell you yes, but after you get married they say no.' If you don't like it, what do you do about it? Liar, that's what you are. But now I've got to get back to work. I'll talk to you later. Hey, you really look handsome in that sweater. Is it new?"

No, this isn't happening. I love him; I adore him. He loves me. I don't know what's happening. I can't even sit at my desk. Of course, I will get married, but Lalo's so handsome! And after not having seen him for a time, I feel like I love him even more.

A few days ago, I saw some sperm under the microscope. I still remember the movements; they're oval-shaped with little tails that whip around really fast; they move so fast, they don't even stop. They're in such a hurry to get to where they're going; they seem like little fish or eels. Stop running around so much; quit working so hard and enjoy the fact that I got someone to work for me. It's a girl corked up in a small but well-formed body. She loved the laboratory. I'll be with her for a week while she learns what to do. I'll use the rest of my salary to pay for buses and the school tuition; that way my mom won't be able to use the cost of going to school against me. I'm going to pay for my schooling. Oh, dear, my head is spinning with thoughts about Lalo, wearing that red sweater and driving his car. It's over. I'm crazy to continue thinking about him. Why do I want to cause myself so many problems, now that I have these convenient plans?

What a joke! In high school the two subjects that I detested were physics and chemistry, and now, every day, they envelop me, and I love what I'm doing. I'm sure Rita is going to let me help her, but I wasn't counting on the fact that on Saturdays we have laboratory exercises. I'm going to have to work something out, like go every other Saturday.

I hate to have to tell Jack that I have classes on Saturdays as well; it seems like I'm always coming up with a new twist. Oh, dear, I shouldn't tell him, I'll just miss the classes. But I won't learn much either.

My mom doesn't buy any of this: she gets upset because I'm spending every cent that I earn; I had to pay for lab materials and she got upset. But it's not her money! I bought a little flask, two pipettes, a Bunsen burner for heating alcohol, and several glass tubes. Next month I'll buy the rest of what I need.

I'm so happy with my flask; it's cute.

Lalo serenaded me. First, he sang "Muñequita Linda," but instead of saying "muñequita" he used my name; then he sang "Novia Mía," "Oshinica Linda," "Novia Mía" again, and all night long he just sang those songs. He said he was crying because I wouldn't go to the window. I didn't even know that I was supposed to go to the window. I was trying to remember what they did in the old movies, but I couldn't. Besides, I didn't want my parents to know that the serenade was for me; but the dummy kept repeating "Oshi," and of course, that gave it away. And when my parents did take a look out the window, they saw him with Jacob standing next to the mariachi band. They were singing so loudly that I could hear them clearly from my bedroom, which is in the back of the apartment and on the fifth floor. Even though I didn't go to the window, I was happy. The serenade was for me. What a great feeling when someone sings to you at midnight with a band that's half-plastered!

After last night, I'm afraid to talk to my dad. What will he think about his daughter who is serenaded at night? They must be livid with anger. I would have been crazy to get out of bed. My mom might have thrown me out the window.

Lalo locked up his store at four o'clock in order to meet me at school, but my cagey father began to wonder why he would be closing so early, so he called my mom to pick me up: "Just in case," he said. Lalo parked on Constituyentes, and I saw him arrive from the classroom window.

"He has green eyes," I told my classmates.

Around five o'clock I was able to sneak away, and I was so thrilled that I had pulled it off. No one had ever come by to pick me up in a car. Just when I was getting in, my mother appeared from nowhere, and she went into a rage: "And where are you going? So this is why you are going to school, eh? It's certainly not to study, like you've been saying! Because of this, I'm taking you out of school; this is your last day. So, go upstairs and say good-bye. Now, my princess, school is really over. From now on out, you'll go everywhere with me."

I couldn't wait until that evening when my dad would come home. I met him at the door crying, and I accused my mother of wrecking everything.

"Okay, then, just go ahead and marry him. If that's what you want, get married."

"He's not a bad kid, I see him working every day in Lagunilla with me. Before these two met, I used to talk to him all the time. Woman, please calm down; after all, we're from the same place."

"No, I can't stand him, I was hoping for something better for my daughter," said my mother, who started to cry. "All those years trying to raise her, all that embroidery, all that studying. But if she wants to get married, she should get married. And quickly, too. In two months. I don't want that guy going in and out of our house. One thing's for sure, no one is going to force me to be around him day in and day out."

"Yesterday, after he had gone to the school looking for her, he came to my store to talk to me. He was pretty upset. He said they loved each other, and he wanted my approval for them to get married."

"She can do whatever she wants; just let us live our lives. We still have five children left, and we're not going to kill ourselves over her. Am I going to my grave for this? Ha. The first daughter, and so many problems; but we have to go on. Think about it, here's the choice: either you get married right away or you agree to never see him again. Ah, yes, and I don't want to hear anymore about school because it's all a lie. You say you want to study but it's only an excuse to get into trouble."

"You are the first child we must marry off to someone, and we're not going to go broke over it," my parents had warned me.

"If your family demands a dowry, I'm not getting married," I told Lalo.

"I'm not going to ask for anything. My cousins are going to raise my salary. We're going to have a nice house. Soon I'll have my own business. You'll never be hurting for anything."

His family is coming tonight to ask for my hand in marriage. They'll decide on a date for the engagement, which is when Lalo will give me a ring. The groom's parents have said they will provide a dowry. They'll also talk about where the newlyweds are going to live, if the groom will make enough money to support them, who will provide furniture, who will arrange for the wedding and the honeymoon, if there will be a banquet, etc.

I'm scared, I mean really scared. I just found out that future newlyweds are supposed to go out for a walk while the families reach an agreement on everything. I hope that's true. Anyway, I wonder what's going to happen.

"I'm amazed by the way Lalo worships you," Vicky said to me. "He jumps through hoops to make you happy. No one had better say anything negative about you in front of him. I heard that he yelled at his mother when she told him that she didn't understand what he saw in you, and that he was too handsome for you."

Vicky is about to marry that older guy.

"I would love to go skating with my fiancé, or ride bikes together, do things young people do. All I do now is meet with the wives of his friends, and they're all older. Yes, I really would like to do that. Otherwise, I'm pretty well satisfied with everything else. He is well mannered and good-looking; so is his family. This must be my destiny," she said, with that typical smile of hers.

My mom just told me I could go ahead and sew the patches together for the quilt.

Lalo's father had always lived in Veracruz. When he arrived from Istanbul, he stayed there because his brother was already living there. The city had a small Jewish community, but there were easily ten people who would get together on festive occasions. They would even bring a rabbi from Mexico City just to give more formality to their celebrations. They say my father-in-law was a confirmed bachelor. Since he was tall, thin, good-looking, and could easily go astray, he always ran the risk of marrying someone from Veracruz. They told him they would introduce him to a good Jewish girl and, if they liked each other, she would be willing to move to Veracruz. Señor Vitali ended up liking her because she had flirted with him when she put a flower behind her ear. "She's a simple country girl," he thought.

"That was how it worked out for me," he said convincingly.

While she was neither a country bumpkin nor a woman of the world, after living for three years in Veracruz, she almost went crazy, and they had to move to Mexico City with a child in hand and another one on the way. My father-in-law was a traveling salesman for fifteen years, and she lived alone most of the time, taking care of the children.

My good father-in-law has two vices: gambling and dancing. He's capable of betting on anything, like which ant will win out over the other one. And he loves to dance. He immediately learns every new dance that comes along, and then he teaches his daughters the new steps. They're always dancing together at parties. He taught them to feel the music and dance with the rhythms at an early age. He would take them to any and every festive event there was. They're exactly the same as me, except that I was always put to bed early, which is why, says my mom, one day I walked outside and was surprised to see so many lights in the sky; I didn't even know stars existed.

I'm getting married in November. Is that good or bad?

I've only danced to our Jewish folk music, but Lalo likes other types of music. At five o'clock on Sundays, he listens religiously to the radio because he likes to hear live music by Arturo Núñez being transmitted directly from the California Dancing Club. It's obvious he liked to go there, but he says it wouldn't be appropriate for me to go. When they play "La Sitierita," his face lights up, and he sings it to me while he looks at my eyes and dances around like Tin Tan. I had never heard of that orchestra before, or who José Antonio Méndez was; but they fascinate Lalo. When they play "Novia Mía," Lalo is deeply affected by it because I'm his first girlfriend. And when he hears Olga Guillot sing, he almost breaks down and cries. I still prefer Hebrew music, and he said it never even occurred to him to dance in a circle holding hands. He thinks it's funny.

Oh, yes, there's another singer he likes a lot: a Cuban named Beny Moré.

When my sister-in-law was single, her father used to take her and her friends out to dance. My father-in-law could easily spend his entire salary in one evening, even though there wouldn't be anything to eat the next day. Lalo said they used to have a lot of fun. I feel strange when I see my fiancé dancing with his mother, but I get furious when I see him with his sister, who is really pretty. They seem to melt together; I can't stand it. They must get along well just because they never see each other anymore. Man, is it hard to hide my anger and smile at her! How could they suspect that I would be jealous of his sister? I can't imagine they would ever detect it. But I can't stand it when she says, "Come here, precious," and then she takes him away.

Lalo knows a lot of places for dancing, restaurants as well, and he always knows what he's doing, like ordering drinks, placing our orders, giving tips. He's not timid at all, unlike when he's at the sports club.

"They aren't a normal family," said my mother. "They're all crazy. Who would live like them? We've never taken our children to a restaurant, but we've never gone hungry at home and we've always paid the school tuition on time. And our house always looks good. Jews don't live like they do."

So, what is the best way to live? Like we do, without ever experiencing one crazy day in which you spend a lot of money and feel like a millionaire, or like them, one day a rich person and the other days making it as best as you can? No doubt about it: like we do. I shouldn't even question it.

"No, it's not because I'm an Arab; if I were rich, your parents would accept me," said Lalo sadly.

I haven't been able to stop thinking about it.

His family's strange, no doubt about it. His sister married an Arab Catholic. Apparently it caused quite a scandal. His mother had to go to Acapulco to get them, because they had eloped. My future brother-in-law, Roberto, lived in the same building, and under the pretext that he didn't have a telephone, he would come and go, and they fell in love. She was fifteen and he was eighteen. That was a long time ago. They would never have let them get married otherwise. Now they live in San Luis Potosí. I guess they have images of saints in their house, and their children even took first communion.

"How could that have happened?" I asked Lalo.

"I don't know, but all kinds of things could have happened in your family if your brother and sisters weren't still so young. They haven't lived their lives yet. I'm the youngest in the family. For instance, my sister Emilia brings her children over to the house all the time, and then she returns to her husband. So, she comes and goes. What can I say? We have to stand behind her. Your parents would do the same."

Our apartment isn't going to be cheap. It's really pretty, and there's lots of light. We'll put a TV in the little room facing the street. But there isn't an entryway. Fortunita and Anita went with me to the furniture store where they always shop; they'll make a special design for our furniture. And Rufina is already living there; after I'm married she'll work for me as my maid, and she'll only take orders from me. It will be great to have a house with no mother living in it, even though I really didn't want to get married this soon. Why the rush? And what happens if one night I pee the bed? It happened to me not more than a month ago. And I won't be able to stay awake or sit up all night like on the excursions.

Recently, my father-in-law came into some money, so he invited the family out for dancing at the Prado Floresta. My sisters-in-law and their husbands went too; Regina's husband was on a trip. My father-in-law ordered two bottles of whiskey and a bunch of soft drinks that covered the whole table. They played the type of tropical music that the family likes so much. My mother-in-law became a different person; she loves the music, and she can dance, too, but she is better dancing the Arab dances. My father-in-law is very agile, and he looks young on the dance floor; he dances every number, almost all of them with his daughters as if they were his fiancées, looking into each other's eyes. They love to dance with him, especially the daughter whose husband didn't come with us. Everyone says she's beautiful, but I think she's just all dolled up. I was scared my father-in-law would ask me to dance. I don't feel right if I can't dance with my fiancé; with him, I can more or less follow along. I asked Lalo to tell his dad not to ask me to dance. Everybody drank and drank, even the daughters. Then they brought out a huge platter of seafood, and my father-in-law called over the musicians and asked them to play all the songs he could think of.

What a way to throw money away!

The other day, I was talking with Fortunita, and she says my father-in-law is a likable guy, even though he's indulgent, and he always says he's traveling to make sales when he doesn't even look the type, and he pines to return to the slow-paced, happy life in Veracruz, meeting with his friends at La Parroquia and playing dominos at five o'clock every afternoon. She said I should educate Lalo to be a better husband than his father. After all that, I realized she had come to see me as some kind of emissary: my mom had sent her to talk to me about the first night of my honeymoon.

"At first, you're not going to like it, but little by little you'll change; now, even I like it," she said, and then she gave me one of those little towels like the ones I always see hanging on our clothesline that, according to my mom, were for washing the face. It seemed strange to me that in order to set the date for my wedding I had to reveal when I had my period. These things are only my business. It's none of their business, the damn busybodies.

✻ JULY 1957.

Lalo dropped me off at home at one o'clock in the morning. Then everything began to shake. My parents were playing cards with the neighbors next door. As always with earth tremors, everyone always stands in a door frame; Clari, who had a temperature, was kind of groggy and started holding onto a doorknob, while the rest of us fanned out through the house to stand in the door sills. When it seemed like it was going to subside, it started up again, but stronger. A piece of furniture fell over on the floor, and then there was a loud noise from the street below. Our neighbor wanted to go downstairs to see her children before the shaking had stopped.

"Stay still, nothing is going to happen. Don't go down now," yelled my dad.

The shaking started to die down little by little, but you could still feel the swaying.

"Clarita, let go of the door, you're supposed to hold onto the frame of the door. Come over here!"

"Be calm, it's starting to let up," repeated my dad.

Even though there was no light and you could smell gas in the air, our neighbor still went downstairs. Fortunately, the building had stopped swaying. The noises subsided and we could hear our voices in the darkness.

"Nothing's happened. Go back to bed."

The lights came back on and we gathered in the living room. The TV was on the floor. The doorbell rang: our neighbor told my father that we should get out of the building.

"She's crazy. It's over. Off to bed!" he ordered again.

"Samuel, please come down for a few minutes."

"Okay, I'm going. If I don't, the old woman isn't going to let us get back to sleep."

There are sirens, lots of them. I look out the window in the hallway and I can't see the building that was under construction across the way.

"Mom, that horrible sound came from the building on the corner."

We looked again and we saw that the top floor had collapsed; the rest was still intact.

"Get dressed, we're going down to the street," said my father, coming back up.

The neighbor is terrified; her son's crib is full of bricks.

"He was sleeping with his sister; if not, he would have been crushed by the bricks."

Out on the street, other neighbors showed us how our building had separated from the one next to it, leaving a space so big that my father got inside. We got our car out of the parking garage from the building next door. There were lots of people with their clothes on, and all of them were terrified. Ambulances kept coming by, their sirens blasting. Who knows what the damage must have been, but the shaking was strong. All of a sudden, Lalo showed up. He really came over fast! He was all over me, hugging me as if he had found me in paradise.

"I'm so happy that you're all right. I called your house, but no one answered."

He didn't let go of me; he acted like he had resurrected me from the dead.

"Did you see our building? Look how it separated from the one next to it!"

"And the one in front of my house, where I keep my car, also fell. The whole building came down, and my car was inside. Lots of my friends live there: Pepe and Danny, Beto Cohen, and several other families. Let's go and see what happened."

It was three o'clock in the morning. We listened to the radio on the way and heard that the Angel of Independence statue had just fallen to the ground. They said other buildings had done the same, the one at Obregón and Frontera and another at Insurgentes and Coahuila.

We parked the car some friends had loaned Lalo as close as possible to his house. Ambulances, rescue workers, and firemen surrounded the collapsed building. Families stood around praying to God that their loved ones—fathers, mothers, brothers and sisters, children—would be found alive in the rubble. On the bottom floor of the building where Lalo lives is a post office. We would be able to see from there, so we went to the rooftop, remembering the faces of so many friends who weren't sure if their relatives were still alive. We heard that Señor Cohen, when he saw that the building was coming down around him, ran out onto his balcony without getting a scratch. The mother and brothers of some of our classmates at school who were already married also lived there. They hadn't heard anything either. Then I saw some of Beto Cohen's friends arrive to find out if he was still alive.

"We're praying he comes out alive," they said, sobbing. "Shema Israel."

Large spotlights were involved in the search—bed sheets half-buried under bricks and rubble; clothes still pinned to a clothesline; family pictures with the glass broken out of the frames; people, moaning, pinned under brick walls. Hypnotized by the horror, we watched the sun come up. Then the bodies started to appear everywhere. They found Beto with a wooden beam driven through his body. I couldn't take it anymore. Now I wonder where I found the strength to murmur, "I want to go now." I have no idea.

I got to my grandparents' house at eight o'clock in the morning. My brother and sisters were sleeping on the floor in a bedroom. I had to go to work at nine o'clock. Mexico Park is only three blocks away from the lab. Walking along Sonora Avenue, I saw people waiting for the bus, others getting on the train. The same man as always was selling newspapers. The guy selling juices, as usual, had his three or four large glass jugs brimming to the top and ready to go. The stoplights were working; some cars went and others waited. The employees at Sears were scurrying inside to punch the time clock. What if this were nothing but a dream? I'm not sure what's real. Was it last night or this morning? I greeted the doorman to our building, took the elevator, opened the door, and talked to Jack about how I felt. He was surprised to see me cry like that. He gave me a sedative. Little by little, I grew calmer, and his eyes seemed to be listening to me.

"I didn't feel anything. No one in my house felt anything. I got up so late that I didn't have time to listen to the news on the radio. Is it really true?"

My dear God, thanks for those pills that make me fall asleep and forget for a while about the horror of what's happened. I fell asleep in the lab.

Ever since the day of the earthquake, we've been staying at my grandparents' house, piled up in the bedrooms, improvising beds, and trying to get comfortable however possible. The specialists examined our building; they would only let us take out the furniture.

Now I'm even more in love with Lalo; just thinking about the way he lit up when he saw me that night was enough. And how he hugged me! It really feels great to know that someone cares about you! Maybe he loves me more than Andrés did.

I was watching the light fixtures, just waiting for them to start swaying again, waiting for the walls to begin to thunder, listening for the people to start screaming, ready to get down on my knees and pray. I wish that I had never gone to that building that had collapsed. Will it happen to us sometime? The images of that night have become absorbed into my dreams: my friends were crying and staring at the piles of rubble, desperately waiting for any news and confident that God would save those who were still buried underneath. Beto's sisters waited and waited. The scene passes through my head over and over again with no mercy, like reels and reels of the most horrible movie that I have ever seen. Unending images of clothing, bodies, pictures ground into the rubble, clothes ripped from the clothesline, a picture of a bride amid broken glass and a twisted frame half-buried in the destruction.

As the movie continued, I saw piles of bricks and dust, and more dust, and then . . . pots, plates, spoons full of dirt instead of soup. I wanted to flee from that movie because I felt trapped in a place from which I couldn't escape; it was the same as when I was a child and I saw movies about W.W. II: the planes fell to the ground like dead birds. At the Royal Theater, I would get down underneath the seats and crawl along through people's legs while I listened to the bombing and the moaning. My cousin would bend over looking for me to see where I had gone.

"The bad part is over," he shouted at me, and then he laughed. "Tell me the truth!"

"It's true: there's the young guy; nothing happened to him. Look, he's already back in his room; he's safe."

Completely dirty, I would crawl back to my seat. Then I would hide behind my cousin just in case he had lied to me. I would barely cock one eye to look. Fortunately, it was over: the dead and the wounded had disappeared and, in their place, groups of soldiers sat around a fire singing and drinking.

I wanted to make all that destruction of clothes and life disappear, but the movie had stopped on me and it was torturing me. I could see Beto with that beam running through him and the weight of the entire seven-story building on top of him. I took another sleeping pill. All I wanted to do was sleep, just sleep, and quickly. And I was afraid to wake up.

❖ ❖ ❖

I don't like it when Lalo leaves me alone with his mother. Her face tells me things that she can't hide because of the fear she has of her son. Lalo says to me, "My life, my love, you choose something, whatever you want," but he scolds his mother every so often. Señora Estrella wants things done like the way she used to do them in her hometown. Since she is the mother of the groom, she thinks she can do whatever she wants; then there are parties to celebrate anything you want. We, on the other hand, my father and I that is, don't like parties. I could just imagine the weddings of the era of the *One Thousand and One Nights* that lasted eight days. I really don't like all that pomp and ceremony; instead, I want to be more modern and get rid of some of those outdated customs, like the dowry, and others that I don't even know about but, apparently, still exist. If I accept these traditions from the beginning, then I'll have to follow them forever. I'll have to give my daughter his name or something like Yemile, or Secoye, which aren't Mexican. No, I'll die if I have to name my son Pinjas, Vedríe, or Latife. I could accept some customs, but not the one where you have to take a ritual bath before the wedding in order to purify yourself. I'm not going to bathe with anyone, much less my mother-in-law; I would be so embarrassed if they saw me naked.

Last Sunday, when we went by Lalo's house because he wanted to change his clothes, his mother became excited, like it was all just casual, as if she were talking about an episode in a soap opera, and told me that she wants to walk down the aisle at the wedding holding her son's arm. I want only him to be waiting at the altar and my father to accompany me. Lalo must have suspected, even from his room, that something was about to explode because he came out half-dressed, scowled at his mother, and yanked me out of the house. But his mother had already spoken and she probably had more things to tell me.

I'm so happy I had told her that I was against a dowry. But she still kept telling everyone that the reason there would be no dowry wasn't because her son was dumb or ugly.

Last night I met some of Lalo's cousins. Marcos, who was skinny and half-bald with droopy eyes, was with his wife; she was beautiful but quiet, and she paced the floor a lot. I couldn't take my eyes off them.

"How could this young child marry this older man?" I asked my sister-in-law. She said that Linda is not only Marcos's wife but also his brother's daughter. He was thirty-three and she was fifteen when they got married. Marcos was afraid to get involved with another family; with this one he knew what he was getting, because he had known her since her birth and had seen her grow up. Obviously, she is one of the few women who did not lose her last name. Her brother became her father-in-law. Everything was guaranteed.

"They are happy, and they love each other," she told me. "See that blond baby, it's her child; it looks just like her."

Astonished, I couldn't stop staring at them.

I wonder if she knows that she is beautiful? We finished dinner and I couldn't stop thinking about them. She probably doesn't say "uncle" to him, does she? I tried to catch Linda's eye, but she always looked away. Her gorgeous blue eyes fail to smile—ever.

By the time I had arrived, everyone was preparing something for the meal: a sister-in-law was mixing the meat with the rice, and another was stuffing the squash. I really didn't want to participate. If it never occurred to us to help out at my grandmother's, why should I peel potatoes when I'm just a visitor here? How boring! I went crazy over the string beans. I didn't understand why there was so much food.

Celebrating the New Year in Mexico is lots of fun. What a

difference! You can feel the excitement in the air; it's everywhere, on street corners, you name it—balloons, streamers, and whistles. They play "Son de la Negra" and "Cielito Lindo," and shout "Viva Mexico!" No one shouts "Viva Israel" around here; there are just hugs and congratulations and several days of eating and praying. I do like to celebrate, but in this house food is celebrated. And the desserts are still to come. They really can make you fat; they have dates, almonds, pine nuts, and everything else. And then, the pastries!

"What do you mean the New Year, it's only September," said my mother-in-law's maid when she saw that every time someone arrived, there was a round of congratulations. Well, the New Year for Jews is almost always during this month, which is determined by the lunar calendar, not the sun calendar that is used in Mexico. There are two days of festivities: the first night, plus a meal the next day, is spent with the husband's family; the second night, which some people don't observe, is spent with the wife's family.

In this family the women spend all of their time buying and preparing the food for eight consecutive days. Lalo is making his mom go all out. They prepare crisp pork rinds with meat, mushrooms, fish, rice and pasta, green beans, beets, olives, salads, lamb (I had never tried it, but I loved it), pasta soups, lima beans, spinach, and rice wrapped in grape leaves. My mother-in-law oversees all of it.

"The daughters of the lady across the street, with the help of their daughters-in-law, have been working since early this morning. They don't let her get too tired. They take ten minutes to eat something and then they continue. Their refrigerator is full," said my mother-in-law, "and then the next day they get up at six o'clock in the morning and go to the beauty parlor.

"In the afternoon, they rinse off the vegetables for the salads, set the table, and go to the synagogue. Everything has to be ready when they come back. They're tired from praying. That's our way of doing it."

"The way our people do it . . ." says my mother-in-law, and my mother says, "Our people do it differently because . . ." Well, if there are differences among the Jewish people, they must really be great between Jews and non-Jews.

Dear Andrés:

I'm getting married. I could never marry you—you're barely beginning your career and I can't wait for you to finish. Don't you see, ever since I turned fifteen I've had a steady boyfriend. How many others could I go through? Lalo loves me a lot and I love him. He says that even though I'll be married, I can continue studying. He says yes to everything. He's almost your age. You even met him once. You said he seemed like a nice guy. He works, and he can provide for me. Even though he's Jewish, my mother hates him. She said that if I was going to go out with him, we'd have to get married in a hurry because she doesn't want him to come near our house.

I'm going to give you my graduation ring; it's the one thing that I love the most in my life. You had asked for it several times, and I just couldn't give it up. But you are the only person who should have it as a reminder of the love we had and still have for each other. I still remember all the times we spent together. I'll never forget how I would walk with you and you would walk with me back home after school. We spent a lot of time walking together.

The ring is for your love of Israel and justice, for the life on a kibbutz—its simplicity—for the respect you have for what you believe, because I had never heard of the things you told me about, because now I think like you do. That's why I'm giving it to you.

I love you,
Oshinica

"Oshinica, what kind of wedding dress would you like?"

"I don't know. White, long, with a train, a veil, the works."

"No, not that. What kind of cloth? Smooth? Organdy? Do you want it fluffy, draping, narrow, wide?"

"Oh, I don't know, whatever."

"What time will the wedding be? Setting the hour is very important for a wedding. Everything really stands out better at night. But now that there's no banquet, it would be better during the day; people don't like to dress up at night only to go back home and go to sleep."

"Well, let's have it during the day."

"That lady really knows how to sew. She's an expert, you'll see. She made a dress for Estherica, my sister-in-law's daughter in Guadalajara, and the bridesmaids. They're all coming with her. Now, then, my dear, while we're waiting for the lady to take care of us, keep looking at the magazines for models of something you would like for yourself and the bridesmaids."

"Let them come dressed however they want. I don't want them to have to spend money. Look, Mom, this dress is pretty, isn't it? Hey, Fortuna, do you like it?"

"No, that doesn't go. It's still November and it's chilly outside. This type of cloth isn't suitable. You need to find something in a fine satin. Look at these dresses, they seem like the latest style; they have embroidery on them. Let me ask them if this is something new that's come out recently. Yes, it came out this month. Well, of course, a seamstress like her would have only the latest magazines. Check out the embroidery, around the collar, the train, wherever, but it's all embroidered."

"Mom, look at this one made of satin with flowered embroidery, do you like it? I want them to make this one for me, just like the picture. I don't know anything about being a bride. I like whatever you like."

One day, in a guarded way, without making anything out of it, Lalo complained. He said my family wasn't recognizing his role as a fiancé enough. It seemed he'd gotten the idea from his mother. I think they were expecting the same treatment that my grandfather gave his son-in-law. They treat him with kid gloves; they don't want him to get mad and abuse my aunt. My brother and sisters like Lalo—they adore him—and my father is his best friend. They've been playing tennis together for the last few Sundays because Lalo just became a member of the club. It's been hard for my mother to accept this situation, but slowly and surely, she's coming around. Still, ever since we announced our engagement, she has treated him as if he were any other friend of mine who would drop by to visit. On the other hand, Lalo is a likable person and he stumbles all over himself to be attentive.

Today, however, Lalo said it outright: "Your family has never opened a box of chocolates in my honor."

His complaint seemed a bit strange. No, they've never opened one, neither for him nor anyone else. We keep them for presents when we have an invitation to go somewhere.

Whenever my friends get married, they usually go to San Antonio to buy their wardrobe. Of course, I won't be going, but

I am getting some clothes. I have to be well dressed. I already have several different-colored pairs of shoes and purses, and I have lots of undergarments. I've never had so much nor have they been as pretty. Everywhere we've gone, we've had to run, literally, because my mother takes such long strides like my father; and she's always scolding me for no reason at all. Of course, she bought for me what she preferred, and she got after me for wanting to buy such tacky stuff, and then she got tired just talking about it.

"So, Lalo, are you going to give me an allowance to run the house?"

"I'm going to give you fifty pesos a week. Does that seem okay?"

"Really, fifty? And I'll be able to spend it the way I want? All of a sudden I go from the ten they gave me every Sunday to fifty a week! That's cool!

"And you won't get upset if I buy things to make some exotic food that my mom refused to make for us?"

They had pillowcases and sheets embroidered for us. They have our initials on them. They feel great. They're made of satin and are pink on one side and blue on the other. I can't wait to use them.

My mom said there are still many things that we have to buy because her insistence on a dowry includes curtains for all the windows, throw rugs, and towels. She already bought the cloth for the curtains. I told her it was pretty, and so was the color. But for the study I want some curtains like the ones we had at the lab.

"The stuffed chair you bought for the living room is silly; it looks like a bed. Only an idiot would sit in it."

"Say whatever you want, I like it. Lalo said that if I like it, I can buy it. Mom, may I try on one of these dresses?"

"After you're married."

"I'll just try it on today and put it on layaway. They're so pretty. Please?"

"Arab husbands are friendly and loving at first, then they abuse you for no reason at all," continued my mom.

"But Lalo is only half Arab, Ma."

"Hey, Dad, can you give me fifty pesos for my trip to Acapulco?"

"What are you going to do with it?"

"Nothing. Just have it with me."

"Ask your husband for whatever you need in Acapulco."

"I know I can already, I just want to have some money on me. I might find something I like."

"You don't need anything."

Even though I won't have any money, then, if he tries to hit me I will sell my watch in order to get a bus ticket back home.

My mother sent me to a woman called Toña, who did the makeup for her friend's daughters when they got married. On my wedding day, she'll show up at eight o'clock in the morning to do my hair and paint my face. I can't imagine what she'll do with all my straight hair; oh well, they say she's really good.

One evening, my mother-in-law and my fiancé took me around to five different houses in order to invite members of their family to our wedding; in reality, they were taking me around to introduce me to everyone. I was livid when she told me to put on something prettier. Did I look so bad? She said that the fiancée has to wear pretty clothes.

"They bought me a lot of nice stuff," I told her, "but it's for after the wedding."

My father-in-law refused to come along; he can't stand those things, so he marched off in a bad mood to the coffee shop.

The relatives, surprised when they opened the doors, usher us into the living room, and the wife runs for the kitchen; meanwhile, we tell the husband when we are getting married and that sort of thing, for which they probably have no interest whatsoever. Then the wife comes out with her keys to open the dining room cabinet door and takes out Turkish plates, fills them with pistachio nuts, and arranges everything on a serving tray. I'm happy because I like those nuts; we never eat them because they are so expensive. When I finish what I have, they give me a little more and tell me to dump them into my purse.

"May you have good luck! Happy bride! Happy groom!"

Then they ask me if I'm from the Jálabi or Shami clan. My mother-in-law breaks in and says Turkish; they don't ask any more questions. Then they offer coffee. I wonder why they serve the same thing to everyone and in the same way? I don't like their coffee; it tastes like dirt. They wouldn't even think of offering me the other kind.

They put the coffee pot in the middle of a large plate with the cups around it; the saucers are stacked next to it. It seems strange that they don't use a tray with a doily in the middle, with the cups on each saucer, like you do when you have guests.

Every last one of them welcomed us and said good-bye with the same words and courtesy, all of which seemed exaggerated.

"Why are you leaving; stay a while longer," they would say. "*Alamac.*"

"That means 'God go with you,'" said Lalo, who begrudgingly translated the phrase for me.

"My family knows very well how to receive visitors," said my mother-in-law.

◇ ◇ ◇

I enjoyed dancing with Lalo tonight because they played slow music and we danced together tightly; since it was dark inside, I could close my eyes without anyone seeing me. Besides, all the other couples were doing the same thing. At least I think so. It's beautiful to feel like you're not being watched, to forget about everyone else around you. Lalo's not embarrassed; he just closes his eyes like a love struck movie star. I love it when he sings in my ear, kisses me, looks at me, strokes my chin, and winks at me.

Now I've learned to kiss and breathe at the same time. It's great not to have to hold my breath! I can breathe and we continue kissing. Lalo was so close to me that I could feel every part of his body, but I didn't get scared or back away. Maybe this horrible fear I have of the wedding night might start to go away. The good thing is that it's almost a given that I'll be having my period then, and we're not going to be able to do it. And he has to be respectful; well, it's not my fault.

I'm feeling better, so now let's see if I don't have to be so afraid.

Once the children who are getting married leave their parents' house, dressed for the wedding, they can't return, even to change their clothes. It brings bad luck. That means we'll go to our apartment after the wedding. Lalo has the camera ready with film and flashbulbs. He's going to take pictures of me wearing my wedding dress in the bathroom, the kitchen, the bedroom, and the study, which now has curtains with beautifully hand-painted diamonds on them. We left our suitcases ready to be put in the car.

"Here you are getting married tomorrow, and you seem so calm about it."

"What's there to do? My mom has done everything, and besides, I'm enjoying sewing the squares together for the patchwork quilt; it's taken me years and many, many squares, but look at how it's coming out! Especially this side that I've stitched together. It's for our bed. Do you want to come with me to Insurgentes Street to see if we can find a small pillow for the rings? We can get some ice cream, too. Okay?

"Becky, do you think some of my friends from high school will go to the wedding?"

"Everybody's going. I'm glad I came over. I thought you might be busy and wouldn't have time to see me."

"Becky, how are you doing? And psychology, Jorge, our friends who used to go to La Castañeda?" While I asked her, I noticed that every day she is prettier than ever and her hair is more tousled than ever.

"My studies are going great, I love it more every day; Jorge switched to medicine. We continue to see each other, but it's not the same anymore. I invited him over to eat the other day, since he was coming to study anyway. And my mother likes him too. But, of course, she has no clue that I like him. And I'm on the board of directors of the Zionist Sephardic Youth Organization. I enjoy it. I'm head of the Cultural Committee, which gives me the opportunity to meet more people—lecturers, sculptors, and painters—and invite them to give talks. That's about it: I'm happy and feeling no stress."

"Look at these giant balloons that I bought to throw at people we encounter on the street after the wedding. It's going to be fun! And look at the way I sign my name now: with a big O. And I've got a new name now. I like Lalo's last name; my old one goes on to my brothers and their wives. That's good enough, isn't it?"

Just my Aunt Matí and her children are coming from Monterrey for my wedding. She's so pretty! And she has taken to Lalo quickly. As always, all she talks about are books. She's still a member of the Book-of-the-Month Club, and she receives new books all the time. I think it's all a farce. I look her straight in the face and I say to myself, yes, I look like her, that's the way I'll be at her age, even though they say I look just like my Aunt Chelita.

"I brought you some poetry for your wedding ceremony. When your mother, well, my grandmother, who died before I was born, was going to get married, they gave the poetry to her the night before her wedding in order to take advantage of that day on which the bride and groom can't see each other."

She wrote on a special card and dedicated it to us: "For Oshi, who really appreciates Ladino, the language of honey; for my little niece with dark eyes and a sweet face, who deserves these verses."

"Where's the future little wife who's getting married?"

"I haven't seen her all day long. She must be getting ready. This morning I wanted to go with my daughter, and I was waiting for you. I napped, got up, took a bath, put on a red dress with a green scarf on my head. I dressed up like you do."

And then finally, the verses:

I saw them coming through the window
the face of the bride, like the moon
next to her three nieces,
the tall one, the shorter one, and the really short one
And to the three sisters, I say:
enjoy your youth
enjoy the changes in life
that later on will pass,
thanks to God who lets us live.

My wedding dress covers the whole bedroom. The hair stylist opens up her large case of cosmetics with creams, eye shadows, eyeliners, cotton balls, lipsticks, brushes, powders, foundation, and mascara. Little by little, she starts to put things on my face and then take them off: first, some type of cream, which she removes with a small towel; next, a cooling lotion; then she paints a series of lines underneath my eyes, on my chin, and on my forehead; I looked like a white-feathered chief.

"Don't get worried, this is only the undercoat; when we put the makeup on, you won't see those lines."

She applies shadow, both light and dark, then some rouge.

"You look pretty, don't you think?"

"Yes," said my mother, entering the room, "she looks beautiful."

And she continues adding, taking off, lightening, and evening out with a little sponge. I've had rollers on since last night, so she removes them and begins to comb my hair. And just when I feel I'm not quite the way I want, she says that I'm ready. Only the perfume is lacking—behind the ears, on the wrists, on the inside of the knees, between the breasts. She hides the fine aromas everywhere and, at the same time, mine as well.

"Toña, put my diamond earrings on her, she'll look better with them on her than on me."

Finally, I was transformed into a modern bride: my mother and the groom will be satisfied. I take a quick look in the mirror because I don't want to see just how different I am. . . . Those who had seen me say that I looked pretty, and I believed them. With so many people saying the same thing, they can't all be wrong.

I wanted to be one of those who arrive on time, but they told me I had to wait so that more people could arrive. We stopped at the corner of Medellín and Coahuila, and at that very moment, a good friend from the sports club whom I had forgotten to invite drove up next to us. I crouched down in the seat so she wouldn't see me, but of course, when you see that the car is going to a wedding, everyone stares to see if they're really happy. We looked at each other. What rotten luck!

With the agility of a man who's been doing exercises for the last twenty years, my dad scampers down the steps of the synagogue to help his first daughter, who is getting married, out of the car. He helped Andrés, too. I felt uneasy when he saw me dressed as a bride. I smiled at him fleetingly. I grabbed my dad's arm. The ladies in waiting were Max and Fortunita's daughter, my two sisters, and one of Andrés's friends. The choir was finishing a Hebrew song in order to entertain the guests while waiting for the ceremony to begin.

The organ player announced the arrival of the bride; finally, she had arrived. The guests stood up. The first ones to enter were Lalo and the rabbi, who was dressed in white with gold trim, like always. They walked down the aisle, reached the altar, and turned around to look at the entourage. While the choir was singing, the ladies-in-waiting walked up the aisle. Then, with the wedding march playing, I walked up with my dad. Behind me, I heard my mother-in-law saying to her husband that she had wanted Lalo to go with them.

"I'm giving away my son too, you know."

Arm in arm, my dad and I looked straight ahead, but we heard her. Knowing we had no alternative but to listen to her, my dad said in a low voice, "My dear, you should have made your mother-in-law happy; changing things a little doesn't ruin everything."

"No, it doesn't change things that much, but in this case it does. This is my wedding. She already had hers."

My father-in-law, who constantly tries to avoid any problems, tried to calm her down but it only made things worse.

When my dad and I got halfway up the aisle, which was covered with a white rug, we stopped. Smiling, Lalo walked slowly toward us, covered my face with the veil after looking at me and making sure that I was who I was supposed to be, and took me by the hand. We started walking together. I finished the second part of the walk up the aisle on the arm of the man to whom I had just been promised: my husband, and his transparent loving eyes. My dad followed after Mom, then my Moshón.

The rabbi had a sweet, melancholy voice! With him, each wedding and any prayer becomes a concert. No wonder the synagogue is full during Kipur and Rosh Hashana. Our hands became entwined, and when I squeezed his, I was telling him that I loved him, and that I appreciated how much he had supported me.

I could see the choir seated above us and the guests in the pews. I smiled at my Aunt Matí, who threw me a kiss. My sister Clarita was crying, and Moshón was biting his lip, and his arms were crossed on his stomach—his normal position. The poems that my aunt read to me last night floated through my mind:

And let her luck shine
and shine and shine
like the sun when it comes up,
like this bride shines
inside this holy place.

I love that synagogue, with its stained glass windows and crystal chandeliers. The rabbi sang songs that I knew by heart, and they were for us. The way the rabbi twists his mouth in order to sing made me laugh; I shouldn't have looked at him. Lalo turned to look at me and we smiled at each other. The tallith draped over us symbolized the roof under which we would live together. He asked my mom and my mother-in-law to stretch the ends of the tallith over us.

I felt like my husband really cared for me. Lalo lifted my veil, and we drank wine from a silver chalice and he broke a crystal wine glass with his foot. At that moment we could consider ourselves man and wife; our lives as single persons had ended. If those fragments of glass were ever to come together again, only then could we be separated from each other. The rabbi put his hands on our heads and blessed us in Hebrew and in Spanish. He asked that we be a happy couple, that we love each other, and that we support each other. Then he gave my mom the wedding certificate. She was to keep it for us.

> The streets are made of stone
> I want to shower them with roses
> For the bride to glide over them.
> The streets are made of bricks
> I want to shower them with lilies
> For the groom to glide over them.

The ceremony came to an end, and we were the first to walk down the carpeted aisle underneath a canopy of white gladiolas. We received congratulations in the vestibule. I wanted to keep looking at Lalo, who was smiling with all his teeth and was calling me *Chapis*. I winked and wrinkled my nose. He was right when he said that a wink is more effective than words.

> May they always have bread and wine
> And the bride her groom.

My dad was really happy. I caught my mom's forced smile out of the corner of my eye while she was thanking everyone who was congratulating her.

"We pray to God that we will see our children, one by one, get married. Amen!" said Señora Rashelica. "For the next one hundred and twenty years."

I didn't like having our families together. I wanted everything to be over so we could leave on our honeymoon. But there was still the banquet that Lalo's father had organized. He even brought mariachis. He wanted a party with dancing.

And kiss her and hug her
And take her for yours
And maintain a deep love
For both to cherish.

It seemed strange that they were letting me go to Acapulco with Lalo, with no chaperon or anyone to watch over us.

Not for one hundred ships, not for another thousand
To have a night like this—which is not for sleeping.

Then I saw someone with a cane making her way through the crowd. It was Señora Magriso, sporting a big smile, but she was such a tiny woman, always wearing that same gray overcoat. Her gums were as pink and false as ever. How could she have made it through this large crowd?

"May you have good luck, my precious one!" she said as she grasped me tightly. She raised her eyes up to Lalo's and looked him straight in the eyes: "You've made a fine catch, she's adorable," and planted kisses on each cheek. "And you look happy, with your radiant face. Goodness, what a surprise when I saw that you were the bride getting married today!" Then she gave me a big hug and said, "May you soon be like a mother!"

like a mother

Like a

Mother

ROSA NISSÁN

TRANSLATED BY DICK GERDES

This novel is a continuation of *Like a Bride*.

To the memory of my father, who
died at 67 but who never grew old.
To his eucalyptus trees, a reminder
of his presence and absence.

acknowledgments

I would like to thank Alicia Trueba, Concha Creel,
and Carlos Olivares Baró for their time in reading
this manuscript.

And to Eugenia Behar, Daniel Motol and Nena,
his wife, who helped me perfect my *Ladino*.

And to Paula Haro Poniatowska, Bill Landau,
and Elena Cordera for their encouragement.

. . . I begin married life with the fear that once I lose my virginity, I won't be able to go home to my family again.

"That's the only thing men want," Marga López used to say in her movies. It's important to keep everything from happening so fast, because when my hymen breaks, I'll belong to him.

I was fraught over the possibility that I had made a mistake.

I want to make this ride in the car to Acapulco last forever. I'm afraid of getting to the hotel and being alone with Lalo. What's the first night going to be like?

I have five bags with one hundred balloons in each one. We're supposed to throw them out of the car at anyone we see along the way.

ONE

"Hey, doesn't that girl standing next to that car look like Jenny? I heard she got married last night. Yeah, that's her. Pull over, let's see what's up. We can throw some balloons at them. There's her husband, Mario; he's Lebanese. We used to play tennis together at the club. Come on, I'll introduce you. He's a nice guy, even if he's a loudmouth."

"Have you met Jenny?" asked Mario proudly. "She's fifteen," he added, as if she were a movie star.

"Of course, we went to the same school."

"And she's only fifteen!"

"Yes, I know, she's two years younger than I am. You say it as if I were an old lady."

"Jenny, tell them it's true that you're only fifteen."

"Yes, my love," she said with a sparkle in her eyes. "Could you guys give us a ride? Our car broke down, and we've been baking in the sun for over two hours trying to fix it. What a honeymoon! Do you mind if we put our things in your car?"

"All of these dresses are yours? Not even María Félix travels with so much stuff."

"Don't be so mean. For over a year now my mother has been making clothes for my dowry and the honeymoon. She never imagined that I would end up only going to Acapulco. Didn't your mom make a dowry for you?"

"Yes, but I didn't bring it with me."

"You know, Oshinica, my mom said that we should exchange gifts: it's bad luck if two recently married couples meet up with each other on their honeymoon, because one of them might not get pregnant. But if we give each other something, everything will be fine. Here, take my scarf. Wow! That's a beautiful engagement ring you have on."

Lalo felt proud that they had mentioned the ring. He had worked so hard to buy it for me. My new young husband is really a good driver, and it's such a bright day. I've never gone on a trip without my dad. It seems strange that they would let me go alone with him; but he's my husband, and he's handsome, too. He even looks like James Dean. I loved that day after I had broken up with him, when he went looking for me in that red sweater and the car he had just bought.

We were walking around downtown, and I saw a bathing suit that I liked. Even though it was expensive, Lalo insisted on buying it; he thought it was cheap. After putting it on, I covered myself with a low-cut shirt. I looked good, even with my legs and straight hair, which was cut short. I just love wearing all these new clothes.

This is the third hotel we've gone to, lugging our belongings along the way, as well as Jenny's forty dresses on hangers. We left the Majestic, which is on Hornos Beach and which, when it's lit up at night, looks like a thousand lighthouses. The Yacht Club is beautiful, simply divine. The hotels in the center of town where we used to go when I was single don't even compare. The dining room has a great view of the ocean, and there's always a nice breeze. What's more, the food is delicious! The bread at breakfast time is great! I don't think there's anything better than this. And our friends act as if they own the place. Every time Mario goes into one of those hotels, he yells for the manager.

"Look here, Señor, we are married . . . *recently* married, that is, and we want king-size beds. Do you understand? *Big,* you know, giant size."

Then he pats the manager on the back and finagles a big bed. But this is it, no more looking for hotels. If they don't want to stay here, they can keep looking themselves. Last night, we were beat from carrying so many dresses. It was a joke to bring everything on hangers just because her mother didn't want her clothes to get wrinkled!

I wanted to rent a boat, so we could row from Caleta to Roqueta, but they just about fainted; they said there are strong currents that could carry us out to sea.

"Don't worry, I'll row. The hardest part isn't far, and it's easy for me; we always did it when we went there with my dad."

After a lot of insisting, we rented a boat, and I showed them some private beaches nearby. I rowed furiously, just like when I used to jump with all my might on the trampoline at the club. Lalo joked with Mario and Jenny: "This woman is going to do me in; she never gets tired. Okay, Chapis, okay, take it easy."

It's three in the morning. I can't sleep, because our friends are making so much noise in the room next to ours. The guy must be horny.

"Jenny, I love you! Jenny, I love you!" he screams.

Those Arabs are scandalous.

◇ ◇ ◇

Lalo spends his time lying around in shorts and reading comics; as for me, I'm having my period, so we put off the first night. It's a good way to gain a little time and to make sure he acts right as a husband. I don't think it's the case here, like it is in Oriental countries, that the bride has to show him a bloodied handkerchief that proves she was pure at the time of marriage. How embarrassing! It's horrible to think that even today some Mexican families still use that form of humiliation.

The first night frightens me to death! I just want to wear my regular white nightshirt, and maybe some other night I'll put on that delicate "baby doll" lingerie.

 tHIRD Day.

Well, there was no way to avoid it: Yes, I was frightened to death, but we did what had to be done. And Fortunita, my mother's emissary, was right: There was nothing great about it. End of discussion.

In fact, it was horrible. It seems so shameful to have to spread your legs. And here we spend our lives trying to keep them crossed. Frankly, I had no idea it was going to be like that. If I had been forced to produce a bloodied handkerchief, my relation to his family would have been a problem from the very beginning. Maybe I'm strange, but there must be other women who feel the same way.

How horrible! Jenny was already worried.

"I know my husband wouldn't have waited. No way!" she assured me.

We are going to spend the whole honeymoon together. It's great that we ran into each other at the beginning. We've had a good time together. We've gone to the best places to eat and dance.

Now I'm feeling better about things; we are returning tomorrow, and nothing really happened to me. He didn't treat me badly, so I guess I didn't need that $10 in case I had to escape from him. To the contrary, Lalo told me that if I needed money, all I had to do was ask for it.

"Don't feel strange about it, I'm your husband. I'm going to make money for you."

We left Acapulco at the same time our friends did. Our car worked perfectly.

When we got to Mexico City, I stopped by Rufina's house; she's going to be my maid. She's been waiting a month for me to get married, but she's also been helping out at my mother's house. Once we got home, we made the bed using those beautiful, feather-soft blankets that my mother had ordered, the ones with pink and blue designs. We put them inside the sheets that had been embroidered with our initials on them. Our bed looked very elegant.

✿ the properly equipped kitchen

Double saucepan, round saucepan with steamer, deep trays, copper ladles, flour sifter, potato masher, different-sized sieves, wooden spoons, a varied selection of regular knives, stainless steel knives, large spoon with holes for draining, regular spoons, casserole dishes for the oven, funnels, measuring cups for one liter and half a liter and a quarter of a liter, molds for Jell-O and pastries and flan, grills for roasting, fish knife, plates, chinaware, heat-resistant dishes, rolling pin, frying pans, cutting boards, dish towels.

Lalo leaves for work at nine o'clock. He doesn't work in the store next to my dad's anymore, but at the one on 5 de Febrero Street. It's a larger store, where he earns more money. He no sooner leaves than I begin to cry. What am I going to do here alone all day long? Go to the market, fix lunch, and then what? It takes forever for him to come home, and then he's here for only half an hour, because every night he goes to visit his mother. I really can't stand it, but he promised her he would. His brothers also visit her after work every day, and then she invites him to play cards, or whatever. He's never home before eleven or twelve o'clock at night.

My sister-in-law doesn't like her either.

"Oh, my poor son," says my mother-in-law, "he has to do this and do that for her."

Is my sister-in-law that bad? Who's telling the truth? I don't know, but ever since I've known her, she badmouths her daughters-in-law. She probably says the same about me.

I'm sad. I want to see my brothers and sisters. Fortunately, they live only ten blocks away. I can take a bus at the corner and get off at Elizondo. And they can get off on Xochicalco, at the corner of our house. They promised me they'd never tell Lalo that not that long ago I would suddenly wet the bed. That would be the worst thing they could do to me.

An aunt and an uncle are moving to Israel, so my grandparents are going to make the trip with them. Lalo took them to the station in the company truck. They took a typewriter and even a pressure cooker. Poor Lalo, they made him carry everything.

Speaking of which, I'm dying to get a sewing machine. I guess we're going to buy one on credit, and Lalo said to be sure and get the most modern model available. I'm happy! There are some machines that do embroidery, sew buttons, make buttonholes, and do zigzag stitches. I'm going to get one of those. Finally, all of my sewing classes will pay off. I've been making my own clothes since I was thirteen years old. What a dress I made for my fifteenth birthday! It was covered in sequins, and the skirt was made out of a turquoise-colored fine sheer net. It was beautiful! My mother will be so surprised when she sees the new sewing machine. At least maybe she'll start to believe that Lalo isn't such a bad husband after all. But if he ever turns bad, I'll get a divorce. I'll never forget something my mother told me: "The Arabs take their pots of food to the living room and eat on the floor." That's the way it is in Arabia, and it's supposed to be that way . . . nevertheless, every time I go to my mother-in-law's house, it never happens. I expected something else.

BAKED EGGPLANT

Cook the eggplant the same way as for *empanadas* (my mom's going to give me the recipe, but she says I have to watch how it's done), add an egg and a little extra cheese. Put the sliced eggplant in a greased Pyrex dish, sprinkle grated Parmesan on top, and place in the oven.

CHICKEN BROTH

Wash the chicken and boil it in water, onion, and garlic. The result is chicken broth.

◇ ◇ ◇

What? These are my wedding pictures? That's not me. I look so ugly. But it has to be me, that's my wedding dress and veil. My hairdo looks horrible, those curls on my forehead are dumb, and they put too much makeup on me. How am I going to choose which pictures I like? At least from the side I look more natural, or maybe that's because you can't see much of me: the veil is in the way.

I took the proofs with me, and before going to the studio, I stopped to look at the photographs displayed in the window. I saw one of a bride that was taken from the side, and of course I didn't see that it was me until the photographer himself came up to me: "Did you notice that I have one of your wedding pictures in the window?"

I didn't say anything, but I like the pictures they took in the synagogue a whole lot more. The place was decorated to the hilt. The main aisle was so full of gladiolas that you could hardly see anyone in the pews. It seemed like we were in the middle of a field of flowers.

Lalo and I looked beautiful together, holding hands as we left. I was looking at the line of men and Lalo at the women.

I'm going to get a copy of at least one photograph for Señora Magriso, the one in which she's landing a kiss on Lalo's cheek while she congratulates me, saying, "This is a magnificent groom you have here, he's very handsome." I wish the pictures had been in color, because in black and white you can't see how red her gums are.

My period started today.

I'm happy, because I'm afraid to get pregnant; if we have problems, and so long as there aren't any children involved, I can get a divorce. Free for one more month, that makes three. Like

Jack, my ex-boss at the laboratory, advised me, I try to take my temperature before I get up. I'm afraid to take these precautions, because God might punish me for not having any children. And that would be a disaster; there isn't a man around who wants a woman who can't bear children. After ten years without children, our religion supports the husband, allowing him to leave his wife. There's a saying in the Bible, and I think Sara said it: "If I don't have any children, I'm a dead woman."

That's it . . . I don't want to be a dead woman.

Before, I never got along with my siblings; now I want them to come over as much as they can. And the good part is that they *like* to come over. We usually end up going to the market together, buying mustard, ketchup, and all the hot dogs and potato chips we want, and whatever else looks good. Here, no one scolds us for making a mess: I'm the one in charge. I don't like the idea of littering, so I tell Rufina to pick up everything. She obeys.

And I really like to cook with my siblings. We make all kinds of bad food, according to my mom, nothing that is supposed to be good for us. But it's great being married and the boss in my kitchen. And there's a large closet that's all mine. I can put anything I want in it and lock it. I'm the only one who has a key.

I don't want to grow up and become bored like the old people who pretend to have fun while they're playing bridge.

two o'clock.

I'm afraid everything's going to start moving again. You can hear a thousand noises in this building. The walls reverberate, promoting a rebellion of bricks, reinforcing rods, and beams. If there's a tremor, I'll pull Lalo over to me and we'll crawl underneath the dining room table; it's big and sturdy. Now my heart is pounding. I keep thinking that everything is about to begin anew; and then I remember that in July they found my friends—embracing each other in their bed with fear on their faces—in the building on Frontera Street. Oh, dear God, please make things stay still.

Our Father, who art in Heaven . . .

Shema Israel.

Before I got married, I had my own piggy bank, but Lalo wasn't to be outdone: he brought his along too. It's a wooden box about eighteen inches tall. He says we're going to put all of our spare change in it, but we have to do it every day. He could barely carry it up the stairs; it's almost full.

No period yet this month.

I've barely been married three months, and every time I run into Rashelica la Puntuda she asks me with a smile that reveals her illusions: "Are you pregnant yet?"

I tell her no, and she provides some solace.

"Don't get worried, dear, all in good time."

Am I supposed to be having anxiety attacks? Maybe I'm not normal. And anyway, why is it such a big deal to have to get pregnant so soon? When it's time for her to go, she doesn't say the regular goodbye to me, but rather, "May you be a mother. A happy mother."

My mother just left.

She came over to measure the tablecloth my Aunt Cler had crocheted for me. She didn't want it to be too short, so she made it too big. It took three years and much laughter to finish it. Since my dining room table is oval-shaped, however, there's about three feet too much on the sides, so several squares have to be unstitched from the sides and added to the ends. As always, nothing goes to waste: whatever is left over can be turned into doilies for the coffee table. The tablecloth is magnificent; it makes our house look so elegant, but now that she's taken it to fix it, the house looks ugly, as if it were naked.

Since my brothers and sisters don't come around now that they're taking final exams, I've become friends with the kids living in Apt. 4. Their mother works, and they spend a lot of time alone, so they agreed to help Rufina and me scrub the kitchen. We took everything out of the cabinets and put the table and chairs in the bathtub. Since they're made of chrome and Formica, we could scrub and rinse them all over, and then underneath and on top again. The kids got their bathing suits, and we ended up washing ourselves off along with the furniture. Afterwards, the kitchen looked brand spanking new, just like the ones in the soap ads on TV: "Tide gives you pride." Not even my mom's kitchen is ever this clean. We've decided we'll do this little number every month. The kids said they'd always be willing to help. We had fun, and when we were done, we ate tons of French fries with ketchup.

I cried when we had to sell the car; it was so nice, but the truck is better. With the money we got for the car, we bought some savings certificates, which means we have to add money every month in order to make it grow. That's the only way to create enough capital so that Lalo can start up his own business.

I need to make some friends.

I loaned fifty cents to Rufina. I like lending her money because later I can take it off her pay and make my own savings.

I vomited, and I even threw up the roasted pork rind that I always buy on the street at the corner. I must be pregnant. Do I have to put up with this for nine months?

Lalo shaved off his moustache. He looks ugly; it must be his mouth. Something's different.

We went to the club, ate lunch at my grandparents' house, and brought my brother Rafael home with us. It's the first time anyone besides us has slept at our house. My brother was pleased to be able to sleep by himself in our study. I put sheets on the sofa bed. When I turned off the light, he had a big smile on his face. No one said to him, "It's late, get to bed. You're going to miss the bus in the morning." He watched TV until he fell asleep. The next morning we made a delicious Mexican breakfast, and of course, I vomited again, even though I'm taking medicine to prevent it. Throwing up really tired me out; it was green in color, and there was nothing left in my stomach.

No more tennis or swimming for me. Now what am I going to do on Sundays? How come Lalo, who is also going to be a parent, gets to lead a normal life? I can't decide whether to go to the club and sit in the sun, or stay at home and knit. I don't feel good when I can't exercise, and to make things worse, Lalo has become obsessed with it. I can't believe it: nine months! When I'm at the club, I feel even worse because everyone sees that I'm pregnant. Then I see some guys whom I liked, or who liked me, and I feel so strange that they see me getting larger. Pregnancy carries the following announcement: I'm not available. If there ever was a hope of developing a relationship with someone, or getting to know each other better, it's gone now. It's beautiful to be pregnant, but this tummy, well, it's hard carrying it around everywhere.

What do you mean I'm married! Is it forever? Once I was so taken by that cute guy over there, but I never dared to say anything to him, or even try to look at him. Today, it was obvious that he was going to come over to me, and I wanted to disappear, but I couldn't leave; he just looked at me, and I knew exactly what he was thinking. I hadn't wanted to get pregnant so fast, but at least nothing happened for the first four months. Then everyone started asking questions. And what if I can't have children?

After lunch, Lalo takes me to my sewing lesson, where, sitting among different colored skeins of worsted yarn, I talk to other ladies. Afterwards, I go home and take a nap. Time goes by faster until Lalo gets home; the only problem then is that I want to go out, and he's always too tired. That's what I do all day long: just sit and wait for him. We never go out; we only watch TV. But sometimes even that's fun; then we go to bed.

For several days now, Lalo has been coming home even later.

"Mom fixed my favorite dish and she makes it just for me. Poor thing, I miss her so much. She sacrificed her whole life for us."

It makes me mad to have set the dinner table, and it's not

worth trying to make anything good.

When he gets home, I'm already asleep, but as soon as I hear him come in, I check the time. Last night he came home at ten o'clock. I can't stand it anymore. Let's see, what could he have been doing after they close at seven o'clock? He gave me the story that when he and his mother got to her house, his brothers and an aunt showed up, and they stayed to play cards. At that house, someone is always carrying around a deck of cards.

Once again, the jerk came home at ten o'clock. If he thinks he can show up any time he pleases and find me with a big smile on my face, he's got it all wrong. Next time he won't find me here, and believe me, I've got lots of places where I can go.

Where will I go? To my mother's house? That's out. I don't want them to find out that his mother is having such a big influence on him.

On Sunday, he promised he'd stay at home with me, and all he did was make my whole day miserable. He was here, but he was in such a rotten mood that it would have been better if he'd gone out for the day. What can I do on Sundays if I can't go to the club? I've never done anything else.

I've locked myself in the closet of the spare room. I brought two pillows and a book, along with this swollen belly. Let him sweat it out for a while. Of course, he knows that all I can do is wait for him. I said goodbye to Rufina with an "I'll be back," and I closed the door behind me. Instead of going out, though, I turned around and went back inside.

Well, it's almost ten o'clock again, and I've been in here since eight. He has to come home sometime.

Ring! The doorbell! Now let's see what happens!

"The Señora isn't at home," Rufina informed him.

"Where'd she go? Call her mother's house and tell her I'm home. She shouldn't be out on the street at this hour."

He continues: "What do you mean she isn't here? What time did she go out? Did she say where she was going?"

Then he goes to the kitchen, opens the refrigerator, goes to the study, changes channels on the TV, opens the drapes to the balcony, and looks out.

"Did she speak to anyone? It's almost eleven o'clock. Where could she have gone? No, that's all right; I'm not going to eat dinner. Go to your room. She should be coming back any time now."

When he went to the bathroom, I came out of the closet, crossed the living room, and opened and shut the door so it would sound like I was coming in. He came out with his pants unzipped.

"Where have you been?"

"I went out for a while."

I asked Lalo to pick up a piece of flannel cloth for me. I'm going to embroider the edges of the diapers. It's crazy, I know, but I'm nervous and it keeps me occupied. The doctor said my baby is now eleven centimeters long; I weigh fifty-nine kilos.

I don't know what to do, because Lalo seems totally bored with the monotony of our lives; he acts like a caged animal. Does he want to keep going out with his friends? I can't figure it out, because it seems like it's really hard for him to leave it all behind and dedicate his time to me. But isn't that the way marriages are supposed to be? My dad, Benny, Max, and all of their friends leave work and go straight home. That's what marriage is all about. He has to get used to it; he has to be a good husband like them.

Before our marriage, Fortunita and Anita advised me to train him to be like our family, because if he were to follow his dad's ways, that is, go out dancing or play cards without his wife, I was in for trouble. That's why I like to go out with my parents and their friends, so that Lalo will learn from them. I get nervous watching him pace back and forth in the house, as if he had nothing to do. It's obvious that he's upset; he even switches the TV channels with difficulty.

"What's wrong?" I ask.

"Nothing," he responds sarcastically.

That afternoon, la señora from Apt. 7 came by to visit me. I liked her; she has a beautiful little boy. I'm going to copy the sweater she's making for him. I think I'll go back to my sewing classes.

Lalo's friends have been coming over to play poker; I'm glad he'll have something to do. After serving them some pastries and Jell-O, I'll go to bed in order to stay out of their way. I get so frightened when Lalo loses, hoping it won't be a lot. I go to the bedroom, but around two o'clock in the morning, I go out to serve them coffee and dessert, which is when I check to see who has more chips.

"Go to bed, honey, don't worry about us," my husband murmurs.

What he doesn't want me to see is the list of money he's been loaned. From my bed, I can hear him ask for more in a low voice. Repeatedly they reshuffle the cards to see if their luck will change.

With all our efforts to save money . . . when will we have our own store? We've barely saved a few hundred pesos, and we never touch last year's Christmas bonus.

"How did you do?" I ask, barely opening my eyes.

"I won."

He gives me the good news with a kiss and he's off to work. But while I'm cleaning up the mountain of cigarette butts, I spy the sheet of paper with the list of loans. Lalo had the most. I wonder how they play? They can lose a lot, that I know. Who knows how late they played. I woke up at five o'clock in the morning and they were still at it.

Lalo doesn't like Olga Guillot or Juan Antonio Méndez, who sing "Novia Mía," the Andalusian song that is so reminiscent of Arab music. His mother says it's "the sweetest thing there is," and it makes her cry.

Today we went to the wedding of one of Lalo's cousins. My sister-in-law from San Luis was with me. We get along fine, so long as I don't see her flirting with my husband; otherwise, I get nasty. She and Lalo could have danced the whole night together, and I got jealous that he might even like her. I want him to love only me. But there's something between them that excludes me. I'm so happy she doesn't live in Mexico City! I want him to be mine only.

My mother-in-law decided to fix dinner for Sabbath. She made all kinds of delicious food that takes days to prepare. No matter how good it is, she just winks her eye. Even before we've finished the meal, she takes away the plates and the tablecloth, exposing the green flannel cloth underneath. Once the table is cleared, everyone gets excited about playing cards and the hand they've been dealt. When the women take a card from the deck, they rub it against their chest before looking at it. I thought it meant they wanted to warm it up, but no, it's so that they'll continue to have milk. Little by little, they go around the table. I try to sit behind one of them to watch, but I really can't see much, except when they go out and put their cards face down, expressionless. Sometimes they team up to win . . . or lose. If they win, they hug each other. They really become involved in the game. I just stare at them.

Lalo was watching me, and from time to time he would throw me a wistful smile, or a little kiss like the ones only he knows how to give. Even though I smile back, I'm still in a bad mood. They play dominos, *pula,* poker, or whatever. All kinds of people come to her house—cousins, neighbors, sisters-in-law, mothers and fathers-in-law, daughters-in-law, and more cousins—all of whom gather around the table and put their money down. They fight, they argue, they laugh, they hate each other, they love each other, they eat, they drink coffee, and they eat pistachio nuts and sweets.

As if by magic, at nine o'clock on the dot there is total silence; everyone grows mute. The men, looking hopeful, open their wallets, and the women reach into their brassieres: they pull out their lottery tickets. The winning number is always announced between two TV programs, *Las Estrellas y Usted* and *Estudio de Pedro Vargas.* At my grandmother's house on Friday nights, we'd all be dozing on the couch, and my grandfather would be saying, "Damn them." It's what he says all day long, just like my father, who says, "Darn it." Darn what? I ask him. For him, it's just automatic.

"Shh, shh, hold it, be quiet . . . Shut up!"

The big moment arrives.

"I barely missed it!" yells my father-in-law. "We could've been millionaires, honey."

He always barely misses it.

"At least I've got the right numbers to play again," others exclaim.

"Okay, whose turn is it?" asks my sister-in-law.

And the game continues. Everyone quickly forgets that no one got rich that night.

"I've got a good hand. Anyone want to team up with me?" says my mother-in-law. "I've got good cards this time."

Lalo approaches the sofa chair where I'm dozing and kisses me. "Let's go, woman."

On the way home he told me about how on Sundays he used to play poker with his buddies. He always had fun. Instead, I used to go to the movies, to Chapultepec Park, to *Majané,* to meetings where they talked about the marvels of Communism and the desire to create a better world. On the other hand, there they were, young twenty-year-olds, crammed into an apartment on Calzada de la Piedad, wasting their time and money. I don't understand it; in fact, I hate it.

🦅 SUNDAY.

For the first time, I just tried on a maternity dress. I look strange; better yet, horrendous. I don't want anyone to see me. We went to the park, but before long Lalo wanted to go to my parents' house, and that's where I really felt uncomfortable: I was embarrassed in front of my dad. It'll take me a long time to accept the idea that I still look pretty and that I should be proud like him.

Why is it that every time we go out somewhere, we end up

going to my parents' house? My mom still can't stand Lalo, even though she tries to fake it.

I need to remember that tomorrow is Monday, which is when we change the sheets. I've embroidered the edges of a green flannel tablecloth—for playing cards—just like I've been doing with the diapers. I'll show off this exquisite piece of work the next time Lalo's friends come over to play. I gave my mother-in-law another one just like it. Her old one has cigarette burns all over it. What's hard to take is that she never says "thank you" for anything, and she's never been nice to me. When I gave it to her, she just said, "Good." Then she put it away and that was that.

I don't know why, but for some days now I've been in a bad mood. I think I need to attend a lecture, like the ones at the college or the ones that those of us who were too "feminine" didn't attend. Where could there be a lecture? How in the heck can I find out? I'll look in the newspaper.

My waist hurts. Darn it, why doesn't he hurt somewhere, too? His body is the same as always—perfect . . . firm muscles in his legs and not an ounce of fat on his stomach. I don't like it that you can't tell he's going to be a parent too. And all those new dresses that I can't use! Why wouldn't they have let me wear them while I was engaged, at least? Fact: they'll just hang there until I can fit into them again.

🤸 may 15.

Lalo wasn't feeling good, so he left work and came home. His parents, brothers, cousins, and sisters-in-law showed up immediately. His mother's face indicated that her son was next to dying, and only she was capable of saving him. Lalo put his head in her lap while she hummed a lullaby.

"My little Lalito," she would say, "my only youngest son."

I was about to throw up again; she's more theatrical than Bertha Singerman. And, of course, he's lapping it up while he watches TV. She applied some rubbing alcohol and put a newspaper against his stomach and his back.

"That's the way I've cured my son ever since he was a little boy," she said, giving me that sick smile of hers.

"If you want, I'll stay the night with you," she announces, turning directly to her son.

These self-sacrificing mothers are something else. I can't stand them. *My* parents came by to give me well wishes. They gave me a robe, six pairs of hose, and a pretty serving tray.

I think I forgot to write it down: I turned eighteen today.

I attended a lecture at the synagogue. The rabbi, who talked about Judaism, said the mother is the one who carries the religion. If it's a mixed marriage and the mother is Jewish, the children will be Jewish; if the mother isn't, they won't be either. Could it be that we don't have much faith, and that it's not always a sure bet that the son is from that father?

"There you have the importance of women in religion," he said. "The mother is the pillar of the family; she is the one who transmits Jewish values and traditions."

Nevertheless, I think he says all that just to pacify us, because the importance of the woman in the religion to which he is referring is false. In my family, the women are the least important. No matter, we'll end up doing whatever we believe anyway. Then he taught us the prayer for lighting the candles on the Sabbath. He also explained how to be a virtuous woman, adding that a man is complete only upon getting married. I'm going to tell Lalo about it so that he'll feel proud of himself.

While I was there, I ran into Fortunita, who is always pretty with her blue eyes and red lips.

"And how are you doing?" she asked affectionately.

"I'm fine," I responded, "and I'm still following your advice about keeping Lalo on a short leash."

"Don't get worked up over it, Oshiní, Lalo isn't the same as his Uncle Vitali. Lalo loves you; he worships you. Don't worry about it."

"But, Fortunita, you know my mother very well, and if Lalo doesn't work out, she'll say to me: 'Didn't I tell you, Lalo learned that at home, and everything you've saved for will be lost at the card table in a single night. It's then that he will have forgotten about his children.'"

I'm happy.

They bought me about twenty yards of nainsook cloth. I unfolded it all over the dining room table. It's all mine! This is cool! Mom isn't going to keep checking on how I use it, not even if I waste a little. She won't be able to put it away in her closet, either. I can do whatever I want with it, and if some of it doesn't get used, it doesn't matter.

I spent the entire day at home. I think I'm going to explode; since I don't have any friends, I don't know to whom to turn. I called Jenny, but she's in bed, suffering from a difficult pregnancy. Dori's at the university, and Becky's taking care of her daughter.

Tomorrow is Saturday, the day to clean the kitchen again. I wonder how my grandparents are doing? Are they still on that ship? I'll bet my grandmother's got a piece of *matzá* bread in her purse, waiting to see if it's true that in rough seas you can throw a piece overboard and everything will calm down. What will they bring back for me?

I just received a letter from Frida, which makes me really happy. She's just about the last friend I have. I'm going to glue it into my diary.

The Daily Xalapeño
Xalapa, Veracruz

Dear Eugenia:

You don't know how pleased I am to know that nothing has changed between us. I've never been able to tell you that, but now I can. I don't know why I find it so unpleasant to talk to some Jewish women I know; ever since I was young, it seemed to me that their friendships were always so false and superficial. I can't really define it or explain it. But with the passing of time, I don't want our relationship to end up like that, because I think you care about me. I have proof of it. I care about you, too, and that's why I get sad when I don't hear from you. Maybe that's why I think that way. No matter what, just forget it. I regret having said that to you. Just remember, I'm your friend; in fact, I feel like your sister. I don't think our friendship will ever end.

I miss going to school with you, the articles we wrote, the jail, the insane asylum, even Miss Gooding; but this is my home, and my father's newspaper is here.

I love you,

Frida

We just did the *corte de fashadura*. It's the first time I've had so many people at our house: sisters-in-law, mother-in law, Fortunita, Anita, Rashelica la Puntuda, and other friends of my mother's. I was proud of my house. *El corte* is when a single or married girl, but who isn't pregnant, has to sew part of the baby's shirt and stick some things signifying good luck inside: "May a son be born to you!" "To a happy, healthy mother!" Then we cut the cloth for the diapers. The one who cuts it has to put some sweets inside and sews everything by hand.

Then they sit down to play cards.

"For the sake of God, *Dio,* please don't let there be another earthquake like the one in 1957," screams Rashelica, becoming dizzy.

When she finally calms down, I ask her: "Señora, I've been wanting to ask you for a long time now, why do you say *Dio* instead of *Dios* for God?"

"You mean you really don't know why, my dear? You say *Dio* because *Dios* is plural, and our religion has only one God. The word *Dios* is for those people who have several Gods."

At six months, you're supposed to make your reservation for a bed at the clinic. I was at the French hospital when they operated on my grandfather; now they'll be visiting me there and bringing gifts. I'll take walks in the garden, wearing an elegant robe.

I've been so sick that I haven't even wanted to go out. But where would I go, anyway? I've seen all the movies they've been showing on TV. I still like the ones starring Joaquín Pardavé, Pedro Infante, and Rosita Quintana, even though I know them by heart.

MONDAY.

Whenever it's not too cold outside, I like to take walks. I used to take them with Andrés, from my house to the park and then back again. We'd walk slowly, observing everything around us, and then stare at each other. We usually walked too fast, so we'd start over, filling our path with ideas, ideals, plans, illusions, flowers, smiles, tender expressions, holding hands, showing a love for everything and everyone. I wonder if he misses me? Would he still be a member of that Jewish scout group, the Hashomer?

◇ ◇ ◇

"Lalo, I want to go for a walk; let's go to my parents' house."

"We might get mugged."

"Oh, Eduardo, where do you get those ideas? It's beautiful outside; the night's cool. C'mon, put on your sweater. There aren't many things I like to do, but this is one of them. It's not that you're going to spoil me."

"I'm not going."

"But who's going to attack us? There are thousands of people out on the street."

I'll probably never go out for an evening walk again.

◇ ◇ ◇

This afternoon I went with my mother to see our Aunt Cler. Her eyes give me the shivers; she has that overpowering, cold look about her. I told her that I was pregnant, and she didn't even smile. She just continued her knitting, but once in a while she'd look up with her penetrating black eyes and then continue what she was doing. We talked about the soap operas, stitching, and yarn. She remained in her wheelchair while she served us her own sweetened orange rinds. It's the only dessert she makes in her little apartment whose windows look out onto La Piedad Avenue.

"What's it going to be? I want a boy, and Lalo even more, because his brothers only have daughters. He wants to beat them at this as well."

"Mom, what would you prefer, a boy or a girl?" I asked her.

"I wouldn't care which, it's all the same to me."

"Couldn't you be a little more specific and say a boy or a girl?"

"I'm just being honest."

"Oh, Mom, you know that Dad is worn out from telling you that you don't have to be so sincere. Who wants all that sincere stuff?"

I flipped through a copy of *La Familia,* looking for embroidery patterns for the baby's sheets. I'm making some for the stroller and for the crib.

This pregnancy seems like it'll never end. Everyone says I'm going to have a baby girl, because when you're carrying a girl, all you do is sleep. I'm so happy that I sleep all the time; it makes the time go by faster.

My mom and I are going to buy some baby clothes; well, you know, bedding, pajamas, and undershirts.

"Not until the seventh month," she said.

"Why is that?"

"You just can't," she answered back.

That's the way she would answer me when I asked her about our religion. It bores her to have to explain anything, even though she knows everything backwards and forwards . . .

But then, maybe she doesn't.

I've knitted twenty-four little nightshirts. I know that's too much, but I don't have anything else to do. And three blankets. And the mattress cover for the crib. And a blanket for the stroller.

Dori's mom is still a member of the ladies auxiliary of some volunteer group, and each year they organize a bazaar. Now that I'm a woman—eighteen years old and pregnant—I'll go and be just like all the other ladies. I've become important, too, because I'm allowed to sign for things that I buy; my husband receives the bill later.

Bored to no end, I stop with Dori at the cosmetics stand. I'm more anxious to move on to some other tables where they're selling handmade items for the kitchen or the bathroom. They always ask my mother to donate a couple of her own hand-knitted blankets. Most of the women who attend make something or other that they donate to the bazaar. And here I am looking at face creams; I don't like this stuff—it's useless, and it just makes more people spend money.

"Señora," says one of the ladies to Dori, "you've got very porous skin, and if you don't take care of it starting now, you'll pay for it dearly later. Now, this cream will seal off your skin and keep it humid all day long. At night, use this one, it contains vitamins. And you, Ma'am?"

"And me?"

"Yes, of course, you have such a pretty face, but it's obvious you don't take care of it. That's foolish! If only I had taken care of my skin when I was your age! Take a look at this—and there's no obligation, of course—it's a fabulous treatment, and you'll end up being grateful to me for the rest of your life."

Dori looked interested, and I also need some creams.

"This is it, honey; before going to bed at night you should wash your face with cleansing cream. What do you wash it with? Soap? No, Señora, stop doing that right now! Soap dries your skin out, and at your age it's not noticeable, but soon it will be. After wiping your face with a cotton ball—and don't use Kleenex because it's too rough—thoroughly cleanse your face with an astringent lotion. It will feel like you're rubbing your face with flower petals, because they're the basic ingredient. Finally, apply a night cream that you'll leave on all night. That way, your skin will get a chance to recuperate from the brusque changes in the temperature, the light, and the air. The rest of the treatment is done the following morning. When you get up, apply the astringent lotion again, followed by a hydrating cream and, finally, a base cream. Señora, what kind of makeup cream do you use now?"

"I don't use makeup," I said with embarrassment.

"But Señora, how can you go outside with no protection? No wonder I can see so many little blackheads! Those are open pores that have gotten dirty. They're hard to get clean later on, and your face will eventually take on a withered look."

"But, Miss, do I really look that bad? I wasn't even aware of it. May I sign for it? Good, I want everything, just show me how to do it again. I'll write it down."

That made me happy; I couldn't wait to get home to start the treatment. The Palmolive soap company guarantees noticeable changes within thirty days, so just imagine how beautiful I'll be. I'm not going to tell my brothers or sisters. I'll bet they notice the difference.

"Lalo, thanks for letting me sign for this stuff. I bought these three serving tables so we can eat in the study. And some face creams. Soon you'll be able to show off a beautiful wife. Do you see all these blackheads I have on my nose? No, get closer! Take a good look, because I'm going to get rid of them. I bought the full treatment. If you had seen the lady's face who was giving demonstrations, you wouldn't have believed it. And to top it off, she's at least forty. Imagine, forty!"

"What? You're already in bed? I'm coming; it won't take me long. I just need to finish putting on these creams. This is marvelous! Lalo, please smell my face, no, touch it. Didn't I tell you it feels great? Don't go to sleep on me; all that's left is the night cream."

"Hey, my handsome ol' man! How'd you sleep? I'll get breakfast going in just a minute; all I have to do is take off this night cream, because now it's daytime . . . I'm hurrying. By the time you're dressed, breakfast will be ready."

"I'm coming! Be patient! You got ready faster than you usually do. Don't yell at me. I have to read the instructions, and as soon as I get up I start with the cleansing cream, then the lotion, and finally the makeup cream. I'm not going outside without covering up my pores. The cleansing cream opened them up and the makeup cream closes them, so don't be in such a rush, Okay? Lalo? Lalo, where are you?"

I feel like I'm getting prettier every day. I need to buy more skin cream so I won't run out. I've been following the instructions to a T for twenty days, and as soon as I wake up every morning, I look in the mirror to see if I can notice any change.

What makes everything harder is that I sleep so much. Being swollen like this makes me lethargic. My skin is stretching; does that mean it'll become like a baby's? My child will be like the baby that comes out of a rose on the Mennen Talcum bottle. It's not easy to be beautiful, but women shouldn't ever let their skin go, not even to have children.

My husband goes to the club every Sunday. This time he signed up to play in a tennis tournament. Clarita came by with Fortuna and Anita, so I showed them the pictures in which they're wearing their bridesmaids' dresses. They're twelve years old, just like my sister. They're knitting little blankets for me, too. I love them a lot, but they don't know how to knit worth beans; they're always missing stitches, and even though I try to help them keep it even, they always leave unsightly holes. Sometimes their stitches are too loose, sometimes too tight, and they invariably get everything dirty. Nevertheless, it's heartening to see them knit something for me. Then we play games. We have fun, and it helps me to forget how mad I get when Lalo abandons me. I really feel like swimming and running—everything I'm not supposed to do.

I'm so bloated, it's getting harder and harder to sleep comfortably. I'm counting the days. I want this child to be born now, so I can go wherever I want without lugging this huge belly along. I want to leave this bundle in the crib. As it is, I don't want to go anywhere. It makes me sad to have to say that it feels horrible to be pregnant. I shouldn't feel this way. Everyone says it looks beautiful to be pregnant, that they are complete women now, and who knows what else. Well, it would be horrible to be abnormal! I guess I'd better drop the subject.

What I do like, though, is to feel my child move around inside me. Yes, that's nice! I'm going to miss it afterwards.

Yesterday, I went to buy bras and underwear. I've grown so much that I had to buy a size thirty-eight.

Where did I hide my diary? I don't want anyone to read it. Now it's become the same here as at my mom's place; before, it was she who would poke around everywhere in her obsession to clean everything; now it's Lalo who might find it. I don't know why I'm afraid that someone might read it. I know, I'll hide these loose pages in a book that he never reads.

Why do I write? I'm just blathering away uselessly. So, if I've already written something, why not just rip it up and quit worrying about somebody finding it? But it's true: I write when I feel all bottled up or because I'm bullheaded. I'm not going to write anymore. What's the purpose? Why do I do it?

We had a fight, and there wasn't any particular reason. What can I say? He's bored. I want him to be happy, have some kind of hobby. Maybe when the baby's born he'll take an interest in something.

This was the worst Rosh Hashanah ever; we neither went to the synagogue nor exchanged gifts. There was no chance to do that at my parents' house either. I took out a pair of new stockings; it felt horrible to wear all the old clothes. Also, they say that however you spend New Year's will determine how you spend the rest of the year. Basically, then, there are two times during which I have the chance to determine how things will go for me for the next twelve months.

Last night I woke up at three A.M. And to my horror, the bed was wet. I looked over at Lalo; he was dead to the world. My God, what should I do? This is so embarrassing! I was worried this might happen. I thought of changing the sheets; no, that wouldn't work. After agonizing over it for half an hour, the only thing that occurred to me was to try to sleep near the dry part by nudging Lalo a little closer to the accident. Every time he turned over, I gained a little more ground. I turned off the light and lay there in the dark, terrified, curled up next to him, until I finally went to sleep. Then Lalo woke me up, also embarrassed.

"Oshi, I wet the bed. I wet the bed. I swear this has never happened to me before."

"Oh, don't worry, dear, it can happen to anyone. Don't get upset," I said, giving him a kiss of sympathy.

Once again, I've been in a bad mood. Arguments with Mom. If I don't do what she wants, she gets mad at me. When she came near me, I stepped aside and she just walked past me. Lalo doesn't irritate them, because at my parents' house, they hardly even acknowledge his presence. According to his mother, they should do a lot more for him. He's convinced, finally, that it's going to be difficult for my mother to be the way his mother says she should be with him. At least they're not impolite to him.

I finished knitting a sweater for Lalo. The embroidered edges are simply divine (every time I write the word "divine" I remember being told at school that only God is divine).

I'm so happy that Frida is still writing to me. I'm putting her letters in my diary so I won't lose them, and I can easily reread them, too.

Oshi:
It's raining here, and even though it's half past six now, there's still a certain clarity of light outside. At the same time, the lights from stores are reflected in the puddles of water on the streets. People walk by; I don't know if they're happy, but they're alive.

(I sense that my friend, who is from Xalapa, the land of eternal mist, is sad.)

It's strange, but like everyone else, I also long for something that I know doesn't exist. Happiness. I don't understand why some people have to live in such horrible conditions. Why is there so much poverty? You don't know how much I suffer to see such enormous disparities in our society. I don't know what else to tell you. I guess there isn't anything I can do.

What a pity that you never came to Xalapa while you were still single. It's still not too late. I want to walk with you on our land, enjoy the rain, and feel the nostalgia of the mist that makes one sad. But I still prefer the light of the sun, because the humidity seems less friendly. I want to take you to Emir's café to meet my friends and then over to the newspaper office, where my dad works. He wants to see you again. He said our friendship won't last, and I don't know why he believes that.

Oshi, don't change, just continue being who you are. I beg you. This is all I can write.
Adiós,
Frida

I don't like going to the club to do nothing but knit. I want to play volleyball, and I feel like wearing shorts. Lalo is still obsessed with playing sports. My God, time goes by so slowly, and I feel like no one should be looking at me. I'm a señora now. It would be my luck for Andrés to show up right now.

My sister-in-law just had her fifth daughter; they're worried that their surname is going to disappear. My mother-in-law wants a grandson, who will be called Jacobo or Vitali, like my father-in-law. He's likable enough, so long as he doesn't invite me to dance at one of his parties.

If mine's a girl, I won't hold her back. I won't stifle her, like they did to me. I won't stop her from going on field trips, and I'll teach her how to face life's dangers. I won't make distinctions between her and her brothers; I'll say nothing like "I'll let you go if your brother goes along." She'll study whatever she wants. If I have a girl, no one will dare to ask me what's the point of getting married; if I have a girl, she'll study at the university. I'll make her strong.

On the fifth of each month I have an appointment with the gynecologist. This time Mom couldn't go with me, so Lalo had to go along. The doctor recommended that I take walks, and that's why Eduardo agreed to get out a bit; but every time we do go out, I can't figure out what happens to him: about half way through our walk he begins saying that some guy has been watching us since we left the house. One time, we got to the point of almost running back, but I couldn't do it; and my arm was hurting because he squeezed it so tightly, mumbling something like, "Don't turn around, don't turn around."

We jumped into the first taxi that came along.

For Yom Kippur, women who are pregnant and people who are sick are allowed to break fasting. It's always hard to go twenty-four hours without even a little water. We left the synagogue at noon so I could eat. We ended the fast at Lalo's parents' house, and it seemed strange that we drank only orange juice. I missed that delicious rice pudding that Uba used to make. On my mom's side, the first thing they eat is bread with some oil on top.

Everybody has their own customs according to where they're from.

The contractions could start any time. My suitcase is ready. After eight more days of nothing happening, my mom went with me to the clinic, where I had to get onto that awkward examination table. After working in that laboratory, I promised myself I'd never do that in my life. The doctor stuck something inside me and there was a big gush of water. I thought a faucet had been turned on, but all that liquid was coming from me.

"Don't be frightened, my dear," said Dr. Castelazo with his usual calm voice. "Go to the hospital and get ready; I'll be there right away."

"But how am I supposed to walk in this condition?"

"You're fine."

They put some cotton padding between my legs; since the hospital is nearby, we walked down Alvaro Obregón like nothing was happening. Here I was going to the hospital and no one around me was even aware of it. I asked my mom for some change to make a phone call.

"Lalo! My water broke! A lot of water came out. We're on our way to the hospital. Come right away."

When the contractions were starting to get painful, the doctor arrived. He said hello in his usual way and turned on the radio.

That was the last I remember.

TWO

There's some light coming into the room through the blinds, but it's still dark outside.

"Oshi, Oshi, you had a baby girl. She's beautiful, simply precious," I heard my mom telling me.

I can't believe it. I touch my stomach and I get frightened. It's true, then, my stomach is gone, but in its place there's a heavy bag of sand.

They told me that several doctors had pulled hard on the baby so it would come out, because I wasn't helping at all. How embarrassing! I wonder how many saw me with my legs spread apart. I'm glad I didn't see them. Since they gave me a few stitches, it hurts to sit down, but it's not as bad if I use the little inner tube. The bag of sand is to keep me from having a protruding stomach, or perhaps it's supposed to make me feel like I haven't lost my whole stomach so quickly.

I met my daughter.

She's so precious! She's round like a ball and constantly moves her tiny little mouth. But I'm livid with anger: I have to name her after my mother-in-law, who already has five granddaughters with her name—as if there were no other name in the world. I don't want to have to think of her every time I use my daughter's name. I'm going to suggest to Lalo that we use the English version of her name; that way it won't sound so bad. Let's see what he says, and her as well. A man is coming through the rooms to register the babies' names. I'm going to use his ink pad to put my daughter's finger and footprints in the album that Frida brought for me.

I woke up feeling like I had been beaten up; everything hurts, probably because of all the pulling the doctors did. I'm ready to go home; all I do is spend my time staring at the high green ceiling in this room. I'm going to ask Lalo to bring a radio. I just love the doctor; he came by today with that sweet smile of his.

A priest, who went from room to room, just left. It took me a while to find a way to tell him that I wasn't Catholic. He apologized for not having looked at my name. I felt uncomfortable with him. Fortunately, he didn't stay long. I hear that at night he visits all the new mothers and wishes them a good night. He means well, but I prefer that he not come around. I don't know what we would talk about.

After four days, I was able to leave the hospital. It was bright and sunny outside, but Lalo picked me up inside the parking garage so that I wouldn't have to walk very far. Wrapping my new little package in a pink blanket, I said goodbye to the nurses, and we left. Back at home, there was a surprise: Lalo had bought a light green coffee table cover for the living room, and Rufina had put yellow flowers everywhere. The room seemed like a garden.

The baby cried all night long. I breast-feed her, but I'm still not producing much milk, so I top it off with a bottle of milk, just like they showed me to do in the hospital. What a night! She was due to feed at eleven o'clock sharp, and she did, but then she cried continuously until three A.M., which was the hour the pediatrician said we could start over, because from the outset we needed to establish a schedule. We had no choice, so we let her cry for three hours. Conveniently, at midnight, Lalo had to go to his mother's house for something.

"Mom! What am I supposed to do now? What should I do with this child who just stares at me? How do I know that I love her? Why has everyone left me alone with her?"

We picked her up carefully, hoping she wouldn't break into two pieces. My mother-in-law tried to make her sit up so she could play with her. I quickly took the baby back into my arms.

My stitches still hurt, and her umbilical cord just fell off. Now we can bathe her. That black piece of intestine was ugly. I had never seen one before, because it was always covered with a bandage. But when I saw it, I got scared. How could I have had something like that inside me?

When I was born, my Mom, Sarica, was almost sixteen; she had lost her mother, and her family lived in Monterrey. I was the first born, and Max's mother was the first person to bathe me. And now, for the first time, they bathed Jessy. Yes, Jessy . . . Jessy? I still can't get used to that name. My mother-in-law came up with the idea that the translation of her name was Jessy. At least it sounds different from the other granddaughters' names.

In the afternoon, my grandparents came by to see their first granddaughter, and as usual, Granddad came in with his hands in his pockets. I was breast-feeding and I felt embarrassed in his presence. He didn't think a thing about it: "Let her suck, little mommy, cover your legs, put some heavy socks on, be careful of drafts."

And so he sat right next to me and watched my baby get fed. Why doesn't he understand that it's not easy for me to expose my breasts from one moment to the next? Although he was there quite a while, he didn't take off his hat. He doesn't know how to act on a visit. I'm glad, and I hope he never learns.

Every day at the crack of dawn, my mom comes over to bathe the baby. Sometimes my brothers and sisters come along too; they enjoy playing with Jessy. We bathe her in her little nightgown because my mom thinks she will slip out of her hands. But she says she just forgets to take it off. Startled, Jessy stretches open her little hands. I wonder why she gets frightened like that? It seems like they're born with that mistrust.

Later on, I'll take her out in the stroller. I just look at her, and look at her, and look at her.

Today is our first wedding anniversary. We couldn't go out dancing like I wanted to, but it's better to celebrate a first wedding anniversary with a child than to be alone; also, our bedroom is a lot nicer, now that it's adorned with that fine sheer net and Duchess lace.

My family has been coming over to visit more regularly these days. While they've forgotten that they didn't like Lalo much, my brothers adore him. I'm lucky, they love me because of Jessy, and I'm so proud to be the mother of such a cute baby. She has so many dresses that we won't need to buy anything until she's three years old.

Jessy gets really excited when she eats: she moves around, kicks her feet, makes strange sounds, and generally has a good time whenever I stick a spoon of food into her mouth. Both of us laugh and laugh. Sometimes she doesn't like the taste of something, so she makes all kinds of faces.

She's happy.

Today my neighbor from upstairs came down, looking thin and acting conceited. She always brings her son along, and his face seemed humongous, as if I were looking at him with a magnifying glass. If he seemed so precious before, why doesn't he now?

For the first time, I went out by myself . . . well, to the supermarket. I left her asleep with the maid. I was walking along the street when I was sure I heard her cry. What a horrible feeling to leave her! In the afternoon, Mom's friends who play cards together came over. They brought some gifts. I felt uncomfortable. I didn't know what to talk about, and I didn't want Mom to leave me alone with them. If she'd go to the kitchen, I'd be right behind her, like a baby duck following its mother.

"Do you remember, honey," said Fortunita, with a bit of irony, "when you said you wanted to study? Look here, darling, men shouldn't feel like they're inferior to women. Instead, they have to feel superior; if not, they're unhappy. You were smart to clear your head of those ideas."

"You are going to have fun with your daughter," added Anita, "and now she is the most important part of your life. You are indebted to the beautiful little thing."

Oh, it's nice to be thin again. I put on my blue fitted polkadotted dress, the one that I looked good in on my honeymoon. Without that large belly, I'm attractive.

My little tike was born exactly forty days ago. I went to the gynecologist. If there's anything that strikes panic in me, it's having a ton of kids, like my sisters-in-law. How can these accidents keep happening? If I get pregnant when Jessy is three months old, I'll do anything to have an abortion. The doctor took measurements and sent me to Sanborn's on Madero to buy a diaphragm. Of course, I was embarrassed to go in, so I just adopted the expression of one who is used to doing these things and a lot more, displaying confidence in myself, without looking at the salesperson in the eye. I was so happy she was a woman, so I made the purchase. I thanked her and left in a hurry. I wear a size seventy-five.

Following the doctor's instructions, I put the diaphragm on, but now that I want to remove it, I can't find it. I haven't been able to go out, because I've been trying to retrieve it. The piece of plastic for inserting and removing it that came in the box doesn't work. I try and try . . . no luck. It's ten o'clock at night, and I still can't find it.

"Doctor, I'm desperate."

"Don't worry, dear, you'll locate it. If you can't get it out by tomorrow, call me. Just go to sleep; it's in there somewhere."

Ever since Jessy was born, I haven't been bored at all; she's so lovable. Becky came by with her son. It's amazing that he's so big, even though he was a seven-month baby. I remember that day when we went to the soccer game with our high school teachers. I was frightened to death that someone might see us together. I still can't believe it! She had more fun than I did. She always had a ton of boyfriends, and despite all that, she still got married. Wasn't it true that no one would marry a girl who had messed around a lot before getting married? There were so many years in which I made sure that no one would be able to gossip about me. And there she is: landed a good husband who is from the same community and has a good profession. She still wears those same pants that brought her so much success and so many problems in high school. And she's so thin. I'm just the opposite.

"You're fat and benevolent," Mom says.

I neither exercise nor go with my father to Chapultepec Park; I just cook and taste all kinds of food that I like to make, and cookies—lots of them—for visitors. Yesterday, for instance, Rashelica la Puntuda and my mom came by and watched the soaps. Rashelica's as irritating as ever, always asking for more and more things to eat: "Would you please bring me something to snack on before lunch, like some pickles, or whatever you have in the icebox? All I saw were some deviled eggs."

My sister went with me to the pediatrician. I can't do it alone . . . the baby, the diaper bag, the taxi, the bus . . .

My neighbor came down again, astonished: "You mean you don't wear a girdle? You're going to get flabby. I even began to wear one in the hospital; that's why I look so good."

My mother-in-law's sister died yesterday. Now the poor thing is going to have sit on the floor for seven days. It's the first time I've ever experienced mourning up close. The first day I saw them—brothers, sisters, husbands, wives, children—all sitting like that, I felt horrible. I couldn't even look at them, much less console them. I had no idea what to do. Little by little I got used to it. The good part is that they get up from time to time, talk, and even laugh, usually in another room like the kitchen. My mother-in-law says that, out of respect, we shouldn't turn on the radio or the TV for a month. And we can't listen to music either, because that would signify we were happy.

"My sister really liked Lalo," I was assured.

The women attended to the visitors who came to pay their respects or to those who participated in the weeklong mourning. In the kitchen, they prepare Arabic food, including meat or cheese empanadas. My sister-in-law also helps, hangs out in the kitchen, and invites me to eat something too. But I refuse.

"I don't really like these customs; they seem like parties," I confessed.

"It's not like that," she replies. "This week has a purpose: the family stays together; it's not like the way Christians do it. Yesterday, for instance, an uncle talked to his brother after four years. A lot of things can happen. Our religion is wise."

Señora Estrella pointed out to her son, my husband, that we should stay there all day, because she's participating in the seven-day mourning. Lalo told her that the Sephardics on my side of the family don't have such customs, but I'll go with him in the evenings. They're lucky they have one of those large older homes in the Roma neighborhood; they can accommodate a large crowd. They even rented chairs.

My mother-in-law looks at me disgustedly, but she doesn't dare get mad in front of her son.

"Our ways aren't so dull and tiresome; we are more flexible," my mom has said before.

My mother-in-law is furious; since her son is the husband, I'm obligated to do things the way they do. In the Arab community, the husband's mother has a lot of authority over her daughter-in-law. Maybe the women hope to become mothers-in-law so that they can get revenge.

Before getting married, I remember that Lalo tried to bring up the ritual for the bride that requires a purifying bath with the future mother-in-law and the sisters-in-law, chanting, blessings, prayers, and sweets. That would've killed me! I'm not interested in those medieval rituals. They're not so marvelous. Anyway, she's still peeved at me for standing up for what I believe and not giving in to what they do. The funny thing is that my mother-in-law's husband is Sephardic, but that doesn't matter to her . . . or me, for that matter.

🏃 ten days later.

We were going to attend my brother's high school graduation ceremony, but since we're still in mourning, we couldn't go. And I'm tired; my baby eats at eleven o'clock, and by the time she burps, I change her, and we giggle together, it's already midnight. Then I have to get up early to feed her again the next morning. We haven't gone to the movies once since she was born. My dad says my eyes look swollen, but I don't notice it; it must be because I haven't slept enough. I'm really fatigued.

"When she sleeps, you sleep," he advises, a little upset.

Of course, he's a man. He doesn't know that when she's asleep, I take baths, cook, clean, and prepare bottles.

Mom came over to the house to see Jessy. When she kissed me, she thought I felt hot. I took my temperature: it was 103 degrees. I wasn't even aware of it. She took me to the doctor immediately. On our way back, we went to her house, with her saying she could only take care of me there. With that temperature, there was no way I could take care of a three-month-old baby. I was ordered to have all kinds of tests done, so we called the laboratory and Jack came by to draw some blood. He must have been worried, because he came back with an ophthalmologist and a cardiologist. Neither one charged a cent, but neither knows what I've got. It's probably a virus. I guess I'm pretty sick if that many doctors have to examine me.

𝓧 the next day.

I look like a mess. My face is puffy. Whenever my mom has a few free moments, which isn't often, she sounds like a broken record on the phone with her friends.

"My poor daughter, she's so sick. She has everything—salmonella, leprosy, mange, measles."

Then she goes into great detail to explain each type of medicine that I'm taking. She's completely in charge of Jessy, and she even took her to the pediatrician for me. They bandaged my breasts and gave me shots to stop my milk.

It's been like this for several days, and my breasts really hurt: I still have milk. My brothers and sisters are fascinated with Jessy. They fight over her, because each one wants to hold her. And I want to go home, but I still have a temperature in the afternoons.

Rufina and Lalo's eyes were also swollen.

𝓧 saturday, december 6th.

Lalo didn't go to work today either, but he feels better. I'm still running a temperature, but I removed the bandages. It seems like I don't have any more milk.

What's a virus, anyway?

tuesday.

We came home, and my in-laws stayed for dinner. Lalo didn't take care of me while I was sick. He was busy running errands for my mom; they would even talk and laugh together. It looks like my mother has finally accepted him. Funny, but now I don't feel the same way about him as they do. I can't be all that friendly; I do what he asks, but sometimes he infuriates me.

Month after month, I take Jessy to the pediatrician. I cook her vegetables, and then I put them in the blender. She loves it.

"Loosen up, don't be so regimented," says my mother. "You can start giving her what we eat, too."

But I don't dare do that.

◇   ◇   ◇

I go to the park with Jessy every day at eleven in the morning. We hang out there for an hour, and then I take her back home to eat lunch. About the same time I'm trying to put her down for a nap, my husband is usually arriving for lunch; or I'll put her in the playpen with her toys. We spend a lot of time together while I'm sewing, cooking, or getting food ready for the next day's meals, so we can get to the park early and meet other mothers who go there. My daughter is the prettiest of all the children I've seen.

The stroller fits into the trunk of the car, so I can take Jessy with me and my mother and brothers and sisters to the club. Today, I put a swimming suit on her for the first time. It was great seeing Dori again; I hadn't seen her since she got married. Her baby is already two months old, and she puts her in the pool and dunks her. How mean! Debora doesn't realize yet that she has a friend; Jessy is excited to swim with her.

All I hear nowadays is that I should have another baby, that my daughter needs someone to play with, that a pair . . . so I went to see Dr. Castelazo and he removed the diaphragm.

In the afternoons, I watch the comedy series with Marycruz Olivier. I can't wait for Jessy to get older so we can go to the movies together.

As for Lalo, he's always tired.

I'm pregnant again. When I told my parents and grandparents together, they spoke in unison: "You're so lucky! May you bear a son!"

We're going to have to move, so Dori and I went looking for an apartment. We want to live near each other; when we were single, we fantasized about it. After a hectic afternoon, she ate dinner at our house. We talked about that humiliating custom, the dowry.

"Honey, isn't it true you didn't ask for money when we got married? You see, Dori, he got married because he wanted to. He provided the house, paid for the wedding, took care of everything. He did it all, and that's why I love my little cherub so much," I said proudly.

THREE

Lalo knows a good business opportunity when he sees one, and he's even helped his cousins get established. He'll watch a business that's in trouble—who knows how he does it—and then he'll buy it for the price he wants. Of course, the ones who make out on it are Max and Benny. Lalo is patient; that's the way he got me, despite my mother. We're saving up, so just wait, it won't be long before one of those businesses will be ours. I went to see one of them today; it's on Corregidora Street. My husband is really proud of it. The carpenters are working day and night to finish it; they're completely redoing the store.

I still enjoy going downtown to shop, and I'm always looking for different kinds of lace, embroidery, garlands, and scallops. I like to collect ribbons, small beads, and buttons to adorn trays, boxes, and small jars. It's fun to decorate just about anything. I use little flowers, lace, and ribbons. Nothing goes undecorated in my house, not even the fly swatter, the soap dish, the telephone, or pens and pencils. I look through foreign magazines in search of ideas for

things to decorate. I can't stand people's houses where you open a
closet and find everything a mess; some women are so disorgan-
ized . . .

Yesterday we ate dinner at one of Lalo's cousins'. When they
opened the china cabinet and pulled out "one of their very best
tablecloths," I could have died. Can you imagine! They had lined
the drawer with newspaper instead of self-adhesive plastic, not
even that cheap stuff they sell at the market. Lalo saw that I was
appalled. He felt proud that I'm so meticulous; then he went to the
kitchen, said something to his cousin, and slipped her some money.

"The poor girl doesn't have any money," he said after we left.
"You've had more chances. You've never been wanting for
anything."

We found a new apartment building on a cul-de-sac in the Valle
neighborhood, only three blocks from my parents' place. Nine
floors, two apartments on each floor, eighteen in all. Dori took Apt.
301, and I got 602. Even though mine doesn't have a view of the
street, it seems to have lots of light, and it's bigger. We quickly discovered that there are three recently married couples in the building. Chely and Marica are cousins, and they started renting their
places two months before they got married. Their mothers helped
them decorate their apartments. When they got back from their
honeymoons, they even found Jell-O ready to eat in their refrigerators. One of them will be my neighbor and the other will be
Dori's. Reizela, a tall woman with a good-looking body and two
girls, lives on the fifth floor. A woman from Costa Rica who has a
young child lives on the first floor. All of them have husbands . . .
as it should be.

All of the apartments, whether they face in or out, share the common shaft of light that connects all the kitchens in the middle, the small balcony off the dining room, and an interior bedroom. Life in the building takes place in those areas; in a way, we are joined together when we cook; when we eat breakfast, lunch, and dinner; and whenever we have guests.

The newlyweds usually get up late and, wearing sexy robes, sleepily say goodbye to their husbands as they give them kisses in the doorway.

The cousins invited us to look at the pictures they took on their weddings and honeymoons. Mari's husband is a travel agent, which is why she spends a lot of time at home alone.

Dori and I are going to the San Juan market, where she knows the best places to buy food. I stand behind her while she bargains for something; then we buy together. She and her husband like to eat well, so every day is a culinary feast for them. Sometimes, when she doesn't have any ideas about what to fix for dinner, she'll come up to my place, and as if she were in her own apartment, whether I'm at home or not, she'll open the lid to the pot on the stove, taste a little bit, and tell me it would be better with more cilantro or a dash of sugar. My neighbors make fun of me, because they think she's overstepping her bounds. Not me. I like her just the way she is.

What with her manner of laughing and dirty jokes, out of all my neighbors Susan is the shameless one. She's only eighteen years old. Her mother, who isn't Sephardic, isn't the matronly type like the others; since she doesn't have a husband, she works. And she didn't have the Jell-O waiting when Susan returned from her honeymoon. Susan's mother is an interesting woman and really beautiful, too, probably more than her daughter. Susan is in the process of furnishing her apartment, and the dining room set that she bought turned out to be so large that her neighbors who have apartments facing the street offered to let the delivery guys bring it through their apartments. Later in the afternoon, we had coffee together while we waited for our husbands to come home, so we could introduce them.

It wasn't long before all of us were communicating with each other at breakfast time through the interior shaft.

"C'mon down."

The building echoed with shouting and laughter. Those who weren't in on the commotion stuck their heads out to look, too.

"You come too, the more the merrier."

That way, I'll know if Mari is fixing lemonade or something. I'll know if she has company, if her husband has come home to eat, what time she gets up, and if she eats breakfast in her robe. Susan asked me to come over again on Friday. How nice! Finally, I have friends here. There are eighteen apartments in the building, and all of us are recently married; only Dori and I have babies. Some are Sephardic, Ashkenazi, half Arabic, or half Sephardic; however, there's not a lot of difference among us because almost all of us were born in Mexico. The differences can be seen in our parents; they speak different languages and were educated in different countries.

About a month ago, two of us got pregnant, and my gynecologist took on the other girl as a patient. We vomited together, got fat together, and made maternity dresses together. But we didn't copy each other, because Susan doesn't like to wear the same dress as someone else. Incidentally, she's obsessed with knowing how we behave in bed. As for myself, I don't like to talk about it.

Even though she's pregnant, Susan still goes to her gymnastics lessons. I went for two months, and then they started calling me tubby. I was offended, but they like her. Chela prefers to watch the soap operas in the afternoons; the other day she even watched the reruns. We get together just about any time of the day, whether we have an excuse or not. I'm always concerned about the vegetables I'm going to fix, so I go up and down from one apartment to another with a couple of bowls, one for the peeled vegetables and the other for the peels. Some of my friends play canasta while they watch the soaps.

The bedrooms are large here, so we can do just about anything we want. When we get together in the mornings, we usually stay in our robes and slippers; later on we'll take our baths, or as Mari says, "Wash our tutus." We laugh and laugh, because none of us wants to be the last one to leave the elevator. Dressed like this, we get embarrassed when we run into the milkman or the bread man. One day I laughed so hard I peed my pants.

Chilly likes to buy porcelain figurines; she took me with her cousin to a place that sells them. I bought five little angels: three blue ones and two naked ones.

It won't be long now. My bag is packed—hospital admittance card, magazines, books, two nightgowns, slippers, three shirts, and a fancy robe that my mom bought for me in San Antonio. I even baked two big boxes of cookies to take with me. I learned that I should have these things with me in the hospital. If nothing happens between now and Friday, we'll go to the doctor. Lalo has become really nervous; I'm even worse.

"Look, if it's another girl, don't feel sorry for me. And don't say, 'One more time.'"

When they anesthetized me, I was crying. And what if I die? When I had Jessy, I had no idea there was any danger. Now I'm really scared.

When I cracked open one eye, there was Lalo smiling sweetly at me.

"It's another girl and she's really cute."

He sent me an orchid with a bouquet of flowers and a nice note that said, "A kiss for my love. Congratulations."

My sister-in-law and her daughter came to see my new daughter.

"May she marry some day!" they said. They had bought her an ugly dress that they had found hurriedly in Loganville.

"It's amazing, Susan, that we had our kids within six hours of each other." She sneaked out of the British hospital and came to see me at the French hospital. She didn't have any problems; Sergio weighed 4.55 kilos.

The very first night home, little Esther was already demanding her milk.

"Don't bother breast-feeding," said Dr. Gonad, "just use a bottle. There are some really good formulas nowadays."

What a relief! Breast-feeding is messy. If my grandfather or dad comes by, I don't have to spend hours in my bedroom feeding the baby. That's it, no more walking around with wet bras; I like that.

Since she's my second child, I can give her my mother's name, but given that she doesn't have an exact name, I can use whatever name I want. I'm happy that I have two daughters.

It seems like she's actually going to have blue eyes. What I liked best about Lalo were his green eyes, and . . . the way he closed them, too.

"Petra, look, come close to the window. Don't you think she's going to have blue eyes?"

Now, finally, we've all had our children: Esther had a boy; Chela, a girl; Dori, a boy; and Mari, a boy.

I just realized that my apartment doesn't have a lot of light, so around ten o'clock, when she finishes eating, I've been taking her outside with Susan's son, Sergio. Susan turned her over for me when she started to get red (she's so white!), so I rushed her back upstairs. I can't believe that I wasn't paying attention to how much sun she was getting. Her room has a dollhouse and a swing.

The owner of Apartment 302, who is leaving, agreed to let us have it.

Every morning, at eleven o'clock, we're sitting outside in the stairwell of the building, each one of us with our stroller. Sergio is down to eating three times a day; mine still needs five. Susan laughs at her son's tiny penis, comparing it to the other babies' in the building:

"Your kid is well endowed," she says to Mari, "he'll surely make his wife happy."

"Oh, Susan, how can you say those things? Men's penises are ugly."

"Okay, girls, we're having a card game at my place. I feel like playing. See you around four o'clock."

"I can't. I have to feed Sergio at six."

"Don't be a wet blanket, Susan. You know you can feed him at my place."

"No. You guys always get mad at me for feeding him while we're playing, and it takes at least twenty minutes for each breast and then I have to burp him."

"That's not true. No one gets upset. We all have to do the same thing."

Sergio was also born with a bad cough, and he always vomits after he eats. Susan has such beautiful dresses but they get dirty all the time.

There's no doubt about it, my little Esther is going to have blue eyes.

"She has eyes the color of the sky," says my mom happily.

Her eyes aren't going to change. She's obstinate. I'm not as hard on her as I was with Jessy.

"Go on, don't worry, I'll take care of one of them," Petra tells me.

That's what I prefer, because taking both of them out together is just too much. And there're a thousand things to take along. I would rather drive.

Today I switched the study to the room that looks out to the inside air shaft that joins the apartments. I want the best for my baby. When the window's open, I can hear what's going on throughout the building: dishes being washed, Radio Sinfonola, Radio Variedades.

"Sergio, if you don't eat, you don't know what I'm going to do to you!" yells Susan.

Bam! Then screaming and crying. She must have smacked him good! Now she's hysterical.

"Don't vomit! I'm telling you, don't vomit! Why do you have to vomit every time? Margaritaaaaa! Bring something to wipe this up!"

Everything in this building—cooking smells, laughter, and anger—is seasoned and prepared in communal fashion.

Before long, we were all sharing, and whenever an apartment became available, one of our relatives would get it. That's how Lucilla came to live here. She's about thirty, has two girls, and is about four months pregnant. She likes to do anything, just so long as it's cards. She gets so involved that it's contagious. I had even forgotten that I promised myself that I wouldn't play cards anymore. She plays with five different groups of women. Even in the early morning, she's calling to us from her kitchen: "Chela! Dori! Mari! Oshi! Let's get together this afternoon and play a few hands. I've already put something in the oven, can't you smell it?" she yells happily.

Before she came to live here, we played cards, but not as much as now.

Of course, some time later we're all sitting around the green tablecloth. I check on my kids every so often, or the men check on us to see what the "moms" are up to. If Lalo calls, they all hiss at me. Now that we're friends, we go everywhere together: to the theater, to the movies, and out to eat; but more than anything, we play cards together.

When we play at Lucilla's, her mother, sisters, and Señora Bulizú join us; at first, I didn't like it, because I felt like I was playing with my mom's friends. But they won me over; they're a lot of fun. I love the way they speak Ladino.

"Honey, I'll eventually give you a card that you'll never find anywhere else in the world. Go ahead, play. I'm going to keep this one for a while."

And she saves it; but if she has to get rid of it, she'll always say, "Oh, for God's sake, I messed up. Heaven forbid!"

"Play, Bulizú, why open the window? We're just fine," says her aunt.

"Yes, close it. When I arrived I was feeling cold."

"My dear, when you want to hear more of this drivel, come one afternoon and join my group at La Piedad. You'll have a great time."

Yesterday, the card game never seemed to end. There was lots of arguing, and it got late. Just about all of our husbands had gotten home, and the doorbell started to ring off the wall.

"Señora, the Señor just got home."

"Just a few more minutes. Tell him I'll be right up. We're almost finished."

The doorbell rings again.

"Damn, I'll bet my husband's already home, and he gets really upset if I'm not there waiting for him. Okay, girls, please, let's stop now. We can continue tomorrow."

"You're joking. You want to leave just because you're winning. If we keep going, I'll recoup my losses. If anyone wants to quit, you lose."

"Okay, okay. Let's keep going. Deal the cards. Give everyone ten each so we can finish quickly."

"Oh no, not that way. The one who throws the highest, wins."

"All right, fine. But let's make sure everyone gets a chance to throw a card."

Once again, the doorbell.

"Oops! I'll bet Lalo's home. We're having dinner at his mother's house."

"Finish the hand and let's go, Eugenia," says a voice on the intercom.

"Oh, this is fantastic. The last round is always the most exciting. Susan, please send your maid up to tell him that we're just about done, that I'm still losing. Hey, I'm back in the running. One more hand. No, we've got to stop. Our husbands are waiting."

"No. We've got to finish this. I'm going for it. This will be the last round."

"Is Señora Chela there?" calls out a masculine voice. "Tell her that if she doesn't come now, her Señor is leaving."

"No! I'm going now. Let's finish this tomorrow. Come to my place. I'll fix breakfast and we can continue the game then."

"Let's finish it now, while we're hot. Someone should play."

"You just want me to go because I'm ahead. No way, I'm on a roll now. I'm gonna win, I can feel it in my bones. I'm going to the bathroom while you're dealing another round. No one look at my cards; it'll bring you bad luck."

"Don't linger; we're in a hurry."

"All right already. I'm back. Just let me zip up."

"One, two, three . . . ten."

"I won. I'm taking the pot. I've got the whole suit. All I needed was the ace of clubs. I'll draw another, and . . . bam! Ace of clubs. I'm invincible. What a draw!"

"Why, of course, the deck wasn't shuffled right. You didn't have to do a thing."

"It's the luck of the draw. You could have gotten it."

"That's it. No more."

"Quickly, tally our points."

"How much do I owe? Damn, I was really off today, and I ended up bitching the most," said Susan. "Girls, I'm not playing tomorrow. I'll pay my debt later, even though I haven't a cent to my name. But I'll ask Jaime to cough up some money."

"It's my turn to have you over next time. Just so we won't be in such a hurry tomorrow, tell your husbands to come straight to my place and we'll have dinner together."

Only one couple came that day, but we had a good time together. The only problem was that when our husbands play, they take too long to decide what to play. They act like they're going to lose their entire savings and even their houses. They take a card, study it, and end up keeping it.

Today, as I was leaving the building, I realized that I hadn't seen the front door in a long time. I was trying to remember . . . I haven't left the building in over a week. That's strange, am I a prisoner there? Oh, I know! Even though I had left my apartment several times, I was just going from card game to card game, from one neighbor to another, but always inside the building.

We organized a costume party. I painted Susan black and wrapped her head in a red bandanna with white polka dots. We peed our pants laughing as we fixed each other up. I took her around to show everyone in the entire building. Not recognizing us, Dori barely opened her door.

"Look at Susan! Isn't she darling?"

"Um . . . yes, she looks great," she said dryly.

"Is Miguel home?" I asked, as we pushed our way inside. "Come look at Susan," I yelled down the hallway.

We caught a glimpse of him scurrying to his desk and making like he had been sitting there all the time.

"Did you see Susan? . . ." I said, looking at him, then at Dori, whose hair was a mess, standing at the end of the hall. "Let's go, Susan . . . to Mari's. Excuse us. Sorry," I said, embarrassed, smiling as we scurried out.

"You and your giggling. You never catch on, do you?" she said, as if to reprimand me.

When Lalo arrived, he began hugging and kissing me and hold-ing the kids, promising them trips, outings, dolls, and bicycles. He was bubbling with happiness.

"We're going to open a store by the main post office. My brother and I are going to be partners. Oshinica, the sky's the limit, and I promise you that within a year we'll have another store, then another, and before you know it, you'll be driving around in a fancy car. You'll see how much your old hubby spoils you. Since you'll have to wait a few months for the new car, my brother will pick me up and you can use my car for the time being. If he can't pick me up, you can run me to work. I want you to see the store. We got a loan to buy it. I've already told my cousins that I won't be working for them after January. I took Max to see it, and he hugged me and said the time had come. Soon I'll be rich."

"If you like, I can help out too."

"Oh no, you take care of the kids. I'm the one who's going to make the money."

It was hard to believe. I'm pleased that we had saved some money.

My Dear Oshinica,

I was so happy to see your parents here in Los Angeles. I felt like I had seen you too. I'm enclosing our wedding invitation. I heard that you have two little girls, both with blue eyes. You're so lucky, because you always wanted kids with light eyes. Your mom told me that Lalo is handsome, works hard, and is a good husband. Well, I'm twenty-three years old now, and I'm getting married. Harry, my fiancé, is really a nice guy. I've included a picture. He's not all that handsome, is he? But that's not important. He loves me, and he's made me feel like I'm important to him. He's an engineer and very indulging, as our moms would say. He can even fix our TV; and he's just about bought everything for our house. I love him so much that I told him that I was from Mexico. Of course, he couldn't believe it.

We've been living here seven years already. It was difficult at first. I suffered a lot; there were many nights, too many to count, that I had nightmares about reaching thirty and never getting married. One morning I woke up choking, because I saw myself as an old maid. Can you imagine how horrible it was?

When I turned twenty-one, I became an accountant and had my nose fixed. Here, no one gets married when they're fifteen, but it's still a custom to have a dowry. I wasn't worried about it, because all of a sudden one day I felt young, not like a soon-to-be spinster. Do you remember Rashelica la Puntuda? The one who was nasty through and through? Well, she introduced my sister to a guy who limps. Whenever I would see your mom's friends here, they said they were going to introduce me to a nice guy, but that I had to lose some weight. They seemed so worried about it that I became panicky about being single. I had already lost weight; it's just that, well, you know me, I have a broad back, and that's the way I am. The pressure in Mexico was terrible. I can still remember the dances for Yom Hatzamaut in that ballroom around the corner from the movie theater. It probably doesn't even exist anymore. Our moms would spy on us while we danced: if we danced too much with one guy, we were considered loose, and we'd probably get dumped; if we didn't dance, we'd never get anywhere with anyone. Everyone talked about us. I was so worried about it that

I almost got sick. If I had stayed in Mexico, I would have been
destroyed.

Leaving Mexico was the best decision my dad ever made.
Do you remember Fortuné Roditi? She lives here too. She
confessed to me that she went through the same thing; when
she turned eighteen, she married whoever was around. It would
have been a disgrace if no one had asked her to get married.

Getting married was a matter of life or death.

Oshinica, please write to me, and send some pictures of
your kids and Lalo. You are welcome to come and visit anytime.
I'm going to have a great guest bedroom waiting for you.
With love,
Leonor

I had already forgotten how nervous we used to get about becoming old maids. The best part about being married is that I'll have a
husband for the rest of my life. No more fear, no more having to
go to those dances, no more worry that I might not be asked to
dance, for now I have a man at my side. And it's beautiful. I'm really
happy that Leonor is getting married. I wonder what she looks like
with a new nose. We spent a lot of time together when we were
younger. We played tiddly winks and pick-up-sticks for hours on
end. We went wild over cutout dolls, and we'd dress them up to go
to parties, shopping, or as brides. Her mom was really great; she
never got upset whenever I would show up at their house with my
brother and sisters. It was embarrassing, but either I took them
along or I didn't go. They had a pretty house on Cholula Street. It
had a garden and a piano. I still remember the day when they loaded
up the car and left the country. That changed their lives forever.

I really missed her, and I mean big time.

When Lalo came home, I hugged and kissed him intensely.

"Hey? What's going on with you?"

"I have a surprise. An Arab dish: rice and meat turnovers that I bought from that woman in the Roma neighborhood. I ordered a bunch for freezing."

Despite Lalo's assertion that his mother makes them better, they were delicious, finger-licking good.

I didn't know what else I had to do to express to him how much I appreciated being married to him. There's no doubt in my mind that marriage is the perfect relationship for a man and a woman.

I got up early. While Lalo was getting dressed, I went to the market to buy some eggs. As I was parking the car and getting ready to go up the stairs, the doorman screamed at me: "Stop! The ground is shaking!"

In effect, everything was shaking, even the electric lines were swaying back and forth. The first person down was the woman from Costa Rica, who lives on the first floor. Then came Eduardo, his hair wet from the shower; he was wearing a robe, and he was carrying one of my daughters.

"Give her to me. Where's Jessy? This isn't her!"

"I slipped on the stairs and set her down. Since everyone was in a hurry, I must have picked up someone else. I'll go back for her. Jessy! Jessy! Petra, bring little Esther with you."

"Susan, your nightshirt is all bloody."

"Oh, no. How embarrassing! What could I do? I was asleep. Has it stopped shaking yet? I'm going back up. Hey, do you think anyone has seen me like this?"

I saw Andrés at the club. He's so handsome! He's got that same cute smile that makes him so irresistible. I was wearing my bathing suit. I sat down with the children not far away from him. Being so close was unnerving. I couldn't read, talk, or even play with my kids. We glanced at each other all morning long, and when he said hello to me, I answered him as if I were in a hurry.

I was shaking all over. How dumb of me! We could have talked. When he was my boyfriend, we'd sneak around behind the club, and my mother went crazy trying to find us. I wonder why he hasn't gotten married yet? Maybe he's still in love with me. Could it be true? It's been six years.

My sisters are going to graduate as bilingual secretaries. My mother is so proud, mainly because this time she didn't make any mistakes. During high school, they took the right courses. When they finish the program, they'll get good jobs with good salaries. They're happy, because just about all of their friends, including Beatriz and Annette, did the same thing. Clarita is going to get married, but she's going to keep working; she's had the same boyfriend for years. They get along well.

Whenever I'm out walking down the street, if some guy whistles or honks his horn at me, I don't turn to look, unless I think I'm going to get run over. If he's just trying to catch my attention, I make myself look serious and walk faster. I'm not even curious to see who it might be. What if it's my husband trying to test me? That's why I don't turn around to look. A married woman isn't supposed to return a glance to look at just any flirt on the street.

Little Esther walks now, and she's become more demanding. What really makes me happy is that for two weeks now she's been waking up in a dry bed. My kids aren't going to have to live with the fear of wetting their beds. Today we played while she ate in her high chair that her father bought for her. I made her a little laced cloth for the tray. Lalo didn't come home, but we used the tea service anyway, and then we ate a piece of his birthday cake in the evening. He turned twenty-nine.

This week I made two dresses, one out of white batiste and the other out of pink cloth with white squares and a narrow fringe. I made similar ones for my girls. Lalo took a picture of us. He gave me a beautiful ring in the shape of a flower with coral and lapis lazuli stones.

My Aunt Zafira's son is getting married, and it promises to be an elegant affair. All the señoras will be decked out in their wedding attire, wearing their beige, gray, dark or light mink stoles. For the first time in my life, I'll be wearing one too. It's my mother's. She's not going, because they operated on my dad for varicose veins. The bad part is that it's been so cold lately. Frankly, my fur-collared overcoat would have been warmer, but a stole looks better with a long dress. Also, I don't want to lose the opportunity to borrow something. No matter how hard I try, it doesn't cover me enough. They always seemed so nice and warm, but this one is more like a bikini. I have no idea how much my dad paid for this thing; naturally, it's not one of those that my grandfather sells. My mom wasn't happy until she had one of her own. One fine day, after combining five birthdays, three wedding anniversaries, and two Mother's Days, he finally bought her one made of fancy mink. It's a champagne color, and it's in style. It's the prettiest one around, so my mother proudly declares.

And Lalo is proud of my elegance too. He likes the touch of mink; it's so sensual, and he caressed me all night long without even being aware of it. The problem is that he was caressing the stole, or himself, but not me. He runs his hand back and forth, but I'm freezing to death; the lining is like an iceberg. But the fur is warm, and Lalo keeps stroking it to keep his hand warm.

Another couple that are friends of Lucilla's moved into 201. They have four sons, and the last batch were twins.

"Now that must be hard," I said, terrified.

"You're wrong. It's beautiful," she said, seemingly offended.

From the beginning, Miriam became our resident radio gossiper; she knows everything and everybody, and it seems like she always wants to be the first one to tell everyone what's going on. Now that we play cards together, of course, she knows everything, but it's probably better to keep her at bay; in addition, our husbands have already become fast friends. She invited us to play cards with them on Sunday.

FOUR

Three years later, there was another round of pregnancies: first Susan, then Chela, me, and almost Mari; but now she's included. Poor thing, she was in such a hurry; we went to Susan's to talk about it. She took a while to answer the door. She was straightening her dress and buckling her belt.

"What are you up to?" I asked.

"Nothing much, just had a quickie. Come to the kitchen, let's eat something. Ah, here's Jaime, he's got to be at work early."

I really like her, even if she does talk a lot about sex. It embarrasses me. To me, it should be something personal and private. She just laughs and says that I'm a prude. If I'm like that in bed, she says, poor Lalo.

Now Lalo is dying to have a boy. We agreed to have another baby, but on one condition: if it's another girl, no making faces. She'll be accepted into the world just like the first one. I'm older now, and I'm sure my stubbornness about having a boy must be hard on him. Now I'm more aware of what it is to be a mother.

By the time I give birth again, little Esther will already be four years old. If it's another girl, I'll make a photo album for her, too. They say that the first one always gets royal treatment and the last one gets nothing. No, no, no, and no. That's not going to happen here.

It was a girl!

No one made me feel badly about it. She's simply a beautiful little girl.

I had barely arrived at the hospital when she popped right out. But there was no way to stop her diarrhea, so they took her to the baby ward. Who knows how she got salmonella. She must have contracted the germs in the hospital; everybody was touching her little hands. We found a donor with the right blood type, so they gave her a transfusion, and then sent us home. It wasn't easy giving serum to a seven-day-old baby. The veins in her hands and feet wouldn't hold up. Either I'll tell my visitors not to touch her or I'll wrap her up like a tamale.

My neighbors were quick to give me presents and to help take care of the older kids. One afternoon, Mari, Miriam, and Hanna, who is everyone's friend, sat with me while they sewed. My little child almost choked on her bottle, so I stood up to burp her. I patted her on the back.

"What should I do?" I screamed. In a fit of desperation, I handed her to Hanna. "Here, hold her, I'm going to call the doctor."

"Nurse, give me the doctor. Thank God he's there. It's my little girl! She's choking! Doctor! What should I do?"

Hanna passed her to Miriam, who, in turn, gave her to Mari. The baby was having a hard time breathing. While I continued asking for help from the doctor, I was terrified as I watched my little girl, feeling the force of each second ticking away. Then I remembered that when babies seem faint you must put them in cold water. While the doctor was on the other end asking without success for more information, I dropped the receiver and ran to the bathroom.

"I've turned the water on! Bring her in here!"

"I'll get a doctor from the Children's Hospital," said Miriam, leaving hurriedly.

Hanna rocked her back and forth, while everyone else cried. The minutes kept ticking away. Then I heard Miriam coming up the stairs. I didn't leave the bathroom. I just kept the water running. A doctor arrived and took my baby, who was by now turning purple, into his arms. I turned off the faucet. While I looked at Daniela's darkened fingernails, I thought there was hope. The naked little baby, looking dark like a giant bruise, whimpered meekly. Then there was total silence, followed by a faint sound. Little by little, but barely, she took a breath and regained her color, even in her fingertips. I took her into my arms, wrapped her up, and laid her gently in the crib. The baby was exhausted.

"The milk got into her windpipe," explained the doctor, who was sitting on the bed. "In these cases, you need to hold the baby by her feet, and if necessary, shake her. She's fine now."

I don't want to be alone anymore when I feed her. I called my mother to come over and spend the night.

While I'm bathing the baby, Miriam sweeps up for me. Then I take a seat in the rocker to feed her. Finally, when she's about to fall asleep and her eyes meet mine, she allays my fears with a delightful smile. What is she laughing at? Is she laughing with me?

"Leave the talcum and the cotton balls here," Miriam commands. "Take her out of the baby carriage and put her on her stomach in her crib; she needs to get used to sleeping that way."

"No. I don't want to move her from my bedroom yet. She's still too young," I responded daringly.

"Well, finally, we're done," she says proudly. "Go ahead and fix lunch while I do the same. We'll see each other at three thirty. There'll be six of us to play canasta. Hanna might come as well. You can play your hand while you feed the baby, or I'll give her the bottle."

Taking care of three children isn't the same as taking care of two. I remembered that someone, about the time I was excited again to try to have a boy, made that statement as if it were no big deal.

They were lying.

Ever since that frightening afternoon, I prefer to have my neighbors come to my place. By four o'clock, everything's ready: the card table, pastries, candy, and coffee. The apartment is impeccably clean. Miriam takes charge, sending Jessy to play at her place, little Esther to 301 or 402, or wherever . . . The women are ready to play, but they'll breast-feed whenever they have to. While one of them is feeding her baby, the others keep playing until everyone gets her turn. It goes like that well into the night, especially if the husbands want to get involved.

I hadn't realized it, but I'm becoming attracted to Miriam's way of looking at life and her unquestionable belief in her own steadfast confidence. She's great. She knows about the best doctors, clothing styles, and cakes. It's never occurred to her that she might be wrong. People who speak without hesitation make me feel stupid.

There's no doubt that a good wife must be a great house-keeper during the day and a fantastic whore at night, meaning that she needs to stay in shape and always be made up. I began to go with my friend to the beauty salon at six o'clock in the morning on Saturdays. We were always first. We'd get all dolled up, even wear wigs sometimes, and put on a ton of hair spray. If we were careful when we went to sleep, we could make the hairdo last an entire week.

Miriam is short, but she's got a great body. She believes the correct thing to do is always visit a friend after she's had a baby or if she's in mourning, or make a dress for some party and others for those special festive occasions.

If Miriam believes, for instance, that Susan's friend is dumb, I'll believe her without taking the time to find out for myself; I'll believe her just like I'll believe whatever they print in the newspaper or whatever you hear on the radio. We do something together every day: whether it's shopping at the Juarez market or buying cloth at the large fabric stores, she always knows where things are cheaper. We leave while my littlest one is sleeping, and we leave the others with friends. In a way, it's too bad, because my daughter isn't learning how to play by herself. Miriam always finds someone to play with her children so that she can take off without feeling guilty, which leaves us free to do whatever we want.

"You must be happy with three daughters; you'll never be alone. And look at me: I'm going to have four daughters-in-law!"

Yesterday, while I was jotting down who won the last round, I looked at the pencil in my hand and thought to myself: All those years learning how to read and write, and now all I do is write down who's winning and who plays next. What a waste of all that schooling!

My Aunt Mati's here. Lalo likes her so much that he insisted she stay with us a few days. I bought some black olives and a special *cashcavá* cheese. By the time I got up, she already had her "little something" prepared. Fortunately, I had already cooked some meat in the pressure cooker, and so she put it into a skillet with some oil, cracked some eggs on top, and cooked it all together, Turkish style. I wouldn't have ever thought of it. Lalo devoured it.

"You're a saint," he told her.

My youngest daughter captivates me. She's growing up fast. I just love her. She's easygoing, and she seems to be happy spending hours just sucking her thumb and smiling at me. She looks more like she's staring at me. Her little chin quivers and then she laughs with her finger stuck in her mouth. I enjoy having her next to me. Even when she's hungry, she still doesn't get mad. I just give her a bottle whenever I want. And I don't have to put up with any coughing, like Susan does.

I really don't know why I'm so delighted with this daughter; maybe it's because I'm older now, or that Jessy is eight and little Esther is already five. With a blink of an eye, they've already grown up. Time goes by fast, and they'll never be the same. Now it's becoming difficult to hold her in my arms. She's so chubby that the bracelet she wears is covered with little rolls of fat.

I feel like I'm just frittering away my time if I'm not spending it with her.

Miriam is helping me more and more, and I'm becoming more and more under her control. I'm almost helpless without her. How in the hell have I ended up like this? Of course, the one aspect about my parents that makes them proud is to be so obliging.

My youngest one just turned seven months. I'm not afraid to

feed her by myself anymore. Soon I'll start relying on Miriam less and less.

My mother-in-law misses her children. Just hearing her say "my kids" turns my stomach. When one of them, like my husband, doesn't visit her, she treats the others as if they were kings returning from a victorious battle. She remembers the hour and the minute when they last visited her. I wonder if she's not brain-dead during the interval.

"Look here," says my father with a worried look on his face, "you've got to treat your mother-in-law nicely, make her feel important, and look the other way if she does something you don't like."

I must admit that my children are my favorite topic too. There's nothing more important. When I hear her say she misses her children, I realize that if I don't catch myself, I'll end up doing the same thing.

My sister-in-law's daughter Tania came to see me. She's a knockout! She's sixteen and her eyes are the same color as my husband's. How could she become more independent? If she only knew how to do something like sewing or hair styling . . . we'll have to find some place where they don't require a high school diploma. We looked up a school in the phone book that's located in Las Lomas, so we'll find out what they teach there. She's got to learn something and then find a job. We'll go tomorrow, or after I get back from Acapulco.

Last night, I finished reading a book of poetry, *The Old Man and the Broken Violin,* by León Felipe. At the same time, I gave thanks to God to have allowed me to hear the silence throughout the house. I had managed to turn off the TV without waking up Lalo, so I wrote a letter to the poet. I told him that I was dying to meet him and that he should meet me. While I wrote, my heart was pounding, and I cried and cried for no apparent reason. I was pleased that he had dedicated a part of the book to the Jews. One of his poems, "Auschwitz," has this dedication: "To all of the Jews of the world, my friends, my brothers." But he also wrote this: "When Moses came down the mountain with the stone tablets, many of you turned them into multiplication tables. I cannot relate to that part, because you sell everything, you negotiate everything, you are incorrigible. . . ."

It's fine for him not to admire everyone. And yes, everything means business to them . . . but they're not the only ones.

I got tired of writing what I was feeling. I'm so afraid that he'll die before I can speak to him. He's over eighty-four years old. I hope my kids don't wake up. Otherwise, I won't be able to take advantage of this precious moment.

"Mommy, is it true that my grandfather left his family?" asks Jessy.

"Who said that?"

"Your brother Rafael."

"Well, you children! Yes, it's true, but he's coming back. He only did it to scare your grandma."

"Where is he?"

"In a hotel. It's like he was on a vacation."

"Which one? Take us to see him."

"On Saturday. You children are such busybodies. Get to bed."

"Tell us which hotel he's at."

"The Diplomatic. Now get into bed."

Just as I was parking my car in front of my grandfather's house, I saw things being thrown out of a window: cashmere suits, ties, and clothes brushes that I had given him on Father's Day. Uba, their servant, came running outside wearing a wet apron and was trying to pick up everything.

"Uba, what's going on? Tell me, what's this all about?"

"Not much, my dear," she says, wheezing, as she picks up things. "You know how your grandfather is. He's upset, and he started throwing things that everyone had given him out the window. He says it's all junk. Didn't you give him the brushes?"

"Yes. Aren't they nice? I liked them because they had little old cars painted on them, and you know how much he likes cars."

"Well, your grandfather said those cars are for kids, so you're better off giving them to your kids."

"And what are my kids going to do with clothes brushes? No way, he's crazy."

"But see how he is, my dear. He doesn't like anything."

"Well, I'll never give him anything again."

"Oshinica, take the suits too; they were given to him by your father and your brother. Return them, please . . . and you'd better come back some other day. Don't come inside, just go home."

Getting some sun makes me look better; I like to feel the rays on my face. I'm going to look better when I'm tanned all over. I've done the hardest part: nice hairdo, depilation of underarms and legs, removal of moustache hairs (but not with wax, no way, I did that one day and it made me cry). This suntan lotion will give me a darker Mexican look, and my hands will be beautiful.

I can just imagine the style show I'll get when my card group gets back from Miami. And me, poor thing, I'll just go to the Palacio de Hierro department store and see what styles they have for beachwear, most of which don't cover me properly. I'll have to wear one of those wrap-around scarves that women are using these days; and for breakfast, one of those lace robes—no, better yet, one of those see-throughs, because I'm not buying one of those that they sell on the beach.

How dumb of me!! I had forgotten that none of my evening shoes are appropriate for Acapulco; instead, I need some silver sandals with jewel inlay for New Year's Eve. And, if I have enough money—well, if I'm that lucky—I'll get a beach towel to match my bag. I wonder when I should go to the store, because we'll want to take along potato chips, fruit, drinks, and sandwiches.

"Felipa, fix some pancakes with nuts and chocolate. You know how much the Señor likes them. Oh, no, the trip is really long, but if we take something to eat, we'll make it okay. Honey, don't forget the inflatable mattress and the pump, and the umbrella. Don't we have a bathing suit for Felipa somewhere? She's going to want to go for a dip, too, even though it's going to be difficult at that beach; and since we're staying at the Hilton, we won't even think about going to Hornos Beach. I think we've got everything."

My kids still have last year's bathing suits, but I'm going to buy them some like the ones Mari bought for her kids. Whew! It's more work to get ready for a vacation than to go on one. It's taken the entire week; I'm tired from it all, simply worn out, I swear to God, and I still have to get my hair done; but I'll do that just before we leave. No matter how much I try, it won't last more than three or four days. Then it'll be the rollers and the dryer again, or I can just wear beach hats, one for each color of my bathing suits.

"Jessy, put the hotel reservations in the suitcase and then help me pack for your dad. If we forget something, our vacation will be ruined, and we'll never live it down. Do you remember what happened at Easter, when we forgot his shorts? We almost turned around and came home; life was miserable."

"Have a safe trip," said my mother as we were leaving. "Lalo, would you like some Turkish coffee? I know you like it when you wake up. You know what they say about Turkish coffee: it should be black as hell, strong as death, and as sweet as love."

"Too bad you can't come with us, but being December, your religious obligations come first," said Lalo.

"That's life, but it's all good. Have a wonderful trip," she added.

We took the kids to La Quebrada Beach to see the sunset. When that huge ball of fire finally disappeared beyond the horizon, little Esther began to cry.

"What's wrong, honey?"

"The sun doesn't even have eyes or a mouth," she said, sobbing.

We took some great pictures, and I'm going to put them in an album. Little Esther's and Daniela's albums are up-to-date. They include a month-by-month report indicating how much they weigh, how much they've grown, their first teeth, their first friends with their names and pictures, and a short poem under each one. I reread one poem, "The Crescent Moon," by Rabindranath Tagore, that I loved when I was single. Now, I love it even more.

Back in Mexico City, Tania checked on the classes. All she does is take care of a herd of siblings. That girl has to get a better start in life. To keep from going crazy with so many children, her mother plays cards.

FIVE

At the Institute, we met a man who gave us a list of school supplies. He was so talkative that we didn't understand a thing.

"Why don't you go one week at first? We begin on Monday, and we can talk again on Friday. The classes are in the morning, and all the students are women."

That sounded good, because we didn't even understand what they actually study there. After listening a while, I asked him a question: "What's your name?"

"Alfredo. Why?"

"I thought I recognized you from somewhere."

"We have several types of courses: cultural history; Meso-American art; contemporary Mexican, European, Chinese, Japanese, and even Medieval."

"What did you say your name was?"

"Alfredo."

"You weren't called something else before, were you?"

"Simja."

"Of course, Simja! You're Andrés's friend from the youth organization. I'm Oshinica. Do you remember me?"

"I sure do. Andrés talked a lot about you."

"Weren't you going to go to Israel? What are you doing here?"

"I was there for a year, then I came back. I studied engineering, but I don't practice it. I started this school with two other professors. We're doing well, and I'm happy."

"What subjects did you say you offer?"

He repeated the whole list, but he didn't mention typing, physical education, journalism, painting, or photography, so none of it meant much to me.

"Come inside and take a look at the classes. When you decide, you can sign up. And you, too, if you like."

"Thanks," I said. "I'm married and have children. I brought my niece, but she doesn't have her application with her."

"But *you* can study here; it's just that you won't receive a diploma. Why don't you sign up too?"

"I don't think so. How would *I* be able to come?"

NINE O'CLOCK, MONDAY MORNING.

I had come to the Instituto de Cultura Superior to meet Tania in order to help her get started. Simja came down the stairs as I was looking for her, and he opened the door behind me.

"Father, the Señora here is going to join your class today."

"Welcome. Please come in."

By that point I really couldn't back out, so I went straight to the back of the room. It took me a while to raise my head and look around the room. Did he say "Father" or was I dreaming? He wasn't wearing a priest's robe. I'm not going to be able to leave the room. This is horrible. I'm embarrassed to even breathe. I want to become invisible like when I was a child.

The music appreciation class lasted two hours. Just before it was over, I realized that I was feeling at ease; I had lost my fear, and I became interested in studying again. And Tania? Did Simja stick her into another class? If he's the one running this school, there should be decent people studying here. Maybe he's still Andrés's friend, and maybe he told him that I was coming here . . . and just maybe . . . The only bad part is that Daniela is still pretty young. It would be hard to leave her with the maid, now that she's beginning to walk. And she's become more attached to me than the others. But at least Estela is there . . . and it's only once a week.

I'm so thankful to be here. I just loved Beethoven's *Pastoral,* and feeling his presence, his emotions. We were imagining the countryside, we could smell it, and the teacher spoke of storms, then peace, and birds. I don't know, it doesn't make sense, but I could never imagine that birds could be flutes. But they were! They really were! I thanked him and ran out.

I waited impatiently for Monday to come around so I could go to the Institute. If I hadn't taken so many pills, my nerves would've been shot. I'm going to invite my sister Clarita, Beatriz, and all my friends; maybe they'll enroll with me. I returned home feeling exhilarated, ready to cook dinner, take the kids to the park, give them baths, tell them stories.

I love Lalo, my daughters, Estela and Felipa—the maids I care about very much—my brother and sisters, the priest, Beethoven . . . well, I love everyone.

"Hey, how come so much love?" asks Lalo, surprised at all my hugs and kisses.

◇ ◇ ◇

Every Monday, from eleven to one, there's a party going on; I'm comfortably seated on a warm padded chair, facing a forest of trees overlooking a ravine, and I hear another symphony. Half of the women who are here are married and spend the mornings together. Little by little, I get to know the other women; one of them is the wife of my grandmother's cardiologist, another is the wife of the architect of the building in which we live. When they come into class with the priest, they're always talking about the last class, given by a psychoanalyst; maybe one of these days I'll join them there too.

Father Recondo is a priest at the Spanish hospital. He lives there and does the baptisms; in the evenings, he visits the patients and the women who have given birth.

"Isn't that true?" he asks one of the women in the group.

"Oh, yes, Father, you stayed to talk to me for over an hour; I wouldn't let you go, I treasured your company."

My next child will be born in the Spanish hospital. Fifteen minutes before the class lets out, he puts on some records, and we listen to each instrument separately in order to learn to recognize their distinct sounds. I would like to go to a concert. Now I buy a record every week at the Sala Margolín; so far, I have ten.

I went to the ten o'clock class and, of course, I enjoyed learning about the psychology of art. I don't know what it's about, but the class was interesting. The bad part is that the class is also on Wednesdays from ten to eleven, and there's no way I can go twice a week. Ab-so-lute-ly not.

"Lalo, can we go to a concert?"

"Are you kidding? There's a soccer match today."

◇ ◇ ◇

Now I'm teaching Tania how to type and take shorthand. She doesn't want to go to the Institute because it's so far away; in fact, she never even went once. She promised to check out the sewing classes near Sears on Insurgentes Avenue. She could possibly start up a fashion boutique, modeling her own creations. But I'm the one who got that idea.

These young people seem to know everything. I don't understand a thing they're saying. They take their classes very seriously. I've spent several years as a full-time mom, and I wasn't even aware of how much things have changed. They talk about so many different things that are foreign to me. One assignment was to see Pasolini's *Teorema,* and I couldn't figure out why they were giving so much importance to the film director. I only paid attention to the actors. We agreed to meet outside after the film. When I saw the teacher sit down with his entourage of wise students on one side, I sat down on the other.

"My God, what's this about? It's such a strange movie."

The next day, the teacher asked those of us who saw the film to raise our hands. Of course, I acted dumb.

Once again, I missed the movie that was showing at the Continental; they run from Thursday to Thursday.

"Lalo, please take me, this is the last day."

He said no. Unfortunately, the movie wasn't for children, so I couldn't take Jessy along. Now I'm wishing they were a little older; when they were babies, I would go to the movies that were for children. As soon as a new movie came, we'd be the first to get in to see it. But now, when there are movies for adults, who can I go with? For sure, I'm not going alone.

Lalo is always tired.

"I have to work," he says. "You just spend the whole day at home."

"There's work to do at home, too," I respond, but he's not listening.

If not the movies, then, he does like to beat my dad and my siblings at tennis. He can play well, and even though he almost kills himself at it, he never hits a bad ball. Rafael and Freddy fight over who gets their uncle for a partner. I wish he would play more on the weekends, but he's lazy and sleeps until late.

The old colonial house where the classes are held really looks its age, but it has a beautiful view, especially now that it has rained and everything seems so green. What am I doing taking these exotic classes that are so alien to my real life—to my card playing, the baby bottles, and the strollers?

The priest's passion for his subject is contagious. Every week I find myself anxiously waiting for Monday to roll around.

Ah, then there's my mother.

"What are you doing wasting your time like that when you should be at home fixing your closets, young lady? Why don't you take more interest in your home? Why are you so messy? A husband wants a wife who is dedicated to her family and house."

I earned that status long ago. I spent years baking tons of cookies, sewing curtains, making blankets and pillows, putting ruffles around the edges of the cloth I used to line the shelves in the closets (frankly, to open one of my closets is to open a garden of silk) . . . and saving money. There's an unspoken challenge among us to see who can be the thriftiest, while having the prettiest apartment, and to see who is the best overall homemaker. We invent dishes, we share recipes . . . well, some of them won't share their recipes because they're secret.

In addition to his beautiful concertos, Beethoven composed nine symphonies. ("Look, stop playing the martyr. Did you change the sheets? How could you let the maids do that, young lady? Can't you stay at home at least one Monday and get the clean sheets out?") The *Ninth Symphony* is the greatest. In the last movement there's a beautiful poem dedicated to the life of Schiller. ("You mean you haven't put away the clothes that the maid ironed? They'll just get wrinkled on you. How much is it going to hurt you to do the little things that God commands?") Each orchestra director does it differently, sometimes fast, sometimes slow; the one we were listening to was a beautiful rendition by Bruno Walter. ("Poor thing, the sun is shining outside and she's cooped up inside; before you used to take her to the park in the mornings. If you don't want to take care of her, I'll stop by to get her. Just let me know when you are going to that stupid class.")

It occurred to my mother, who is really a saint, to come over and visit with my kids. According to her, my house had been turned upside down.

"Whoever owns a store must take care of it himself" is the

family motto, and because of that, my father has spent his life cooped up in that tiny store. What a pity!

My mother found Felipa in the kitchen with her sister. Dishes were still piled in the sink, and it was already noon. Daniela had dirtied her diaper, and it was everywhere, even in her hair.

"When was the last time the servant looked in on her in her crib? The other girls were soaking wet from bathing their dolls, the balcony door was wide open, and Felipa took forever to answer the door. Who does she think she is? The owner of the house?"

Just then, I walked in with balloons in my hand. There was no way I could make her shut up. She was breathing fire, saying I was acting irresponsibly, where had I been all morning, aren't I ashamed for this rotten life I'm leading, this isn't the time to talk about studying. That night my dad called me.

"What you're doing isn't right. Your only responsibility is to take care of those beautiful girls that God gave you. You should be grateful that you have them . . ."

I'm not going to the Institute next Monday, because it's a Jewish holiday. There are no classes in Jewish schools. That's too bad, but that's the way it is. Now I'll have to wait two more weeks.

Lalo and I are leaving for Los Angeles, San Francisco, and Las Vegas tomorrow. We're going with Miriam and Susan and their husbands. It'll be great fun! I'm going to buy some new clothes for the trip. First, though, I must get things ready for my kids to stay with my mother. My siblings are really excited about it.

In Las Vegas, we saw a show with a bunch of naked dancers. I don't know how it happened, but after the show I stumbled upon a lingerie shop in the hotel. I went in, and like an adolescent who's going to buy Kotex for the first time, I tried to hide my embarrassment when I asked to see the black bra in the window. I tried it on in the room before my husband came back. It was made of soft lace, had thin elastic straps, and there were little holes for your nipples to show through. It was very sensual. I got scared that if I were to die, they would find it among my clothes. The erotic images of the show flashed through my mind incessantly, and I wished that Lalo would sense it and touch me with his hands and kiss me. When the sun was coming up, I went downstairs to look for him in the casino. When I found him, he seemed confused about where to place his bets on the green felt. His stupid smile gave him away; he had been losing, and he seemed to say, "Well, I tried." When I put my arm around him to give him good luck, he put one hundred pesos in my hand.

"Here, take this, go play a while."

I asked myself why couldn't he be that generous in Mexico?

When he finally saw me wearing the new bra, his eyes almost popped out.

"Take that off right now. You look like a whore."

I was embarrassed. He had made me feel cheap. I went to bed hating him. I turned my back to him, leaving a space the size of the Grand Canyon between us.

When I first started going to the Institute, I talked a lot with Simja. Well, not anymore; as it turns out, I decided last week to sit in on one of his classes, something about art. I just stared at him; he seemed so tall, the same way his face is long. And he's so sarcastic. I was shocked. Either he knows just about everything, or he just makes it complicated. I'm embarrassed to talk to him, because I'm so ignorant, so now I just avoid him. I just never realized that I was so dumb.

"Lalo, can we go to a concert on Sunday? You said maybe."

"Are you crazy? The soccer finals are on."

"And the Sunday after that?"

"Next Sunday? I could be dead by then."

Miriam is on vacation, and like she does every December, my mom likes to go shopping. It's great. Our trip is in three weeks, so I'm going to get rested. Bored, though, I went out for the heck of it. I always have a lot of free time. In one store, I found a postcard of *Mona Lisa*. I was going to buy it until I realized that she had a fly on her forehead. I thought someone had drawn it on the card, but no, it looked real; and she looked so ugly. I put it down, but then I picked it up again and bought it. I put it on my dresser, and I look at it whenever I walk by.

I'm so happy that no one's coming to help me straighten up the mess here. I've spent my life trying to keep the house neat, and no one seems to want to recognize my work. It's just the opposite. Actually, Estela, Felipa, and I get less done when Miriam's around. I feel much more comfortable moving at a slower pace; but, little by little, we get the beds made, the toys put away, the towels hung to dry and then folded. I'll sit down in the recently vacuumed living room, take the lid off the candy jar, unwrap a candy, and look at the jar again. I'm fed up with cleaning so much and trying to be perfect, which everyone expects from me. I unwrap some candies, and as if I were spraying cleaner everywhere, I throw them all over the place.

"Felipa! I threw these wrappers on the rug. Leave them there until I tell you to pick them up."

"Señora, can I pick up these wrappers? They've been there for over two days. What would your mother say?"

"You can sweep around them; just leave them there."

They must think I've gone crazy. I have to learn to live with the wrappers thrown on the floor, to see *Mona Lisa* with a fly on her forehead, to escape from order.

As usual, I'm surrounded by the jubilation of the birds in the living room, the same ones that sing to Daniela in her crib. While she sucks her thumb with delight, she watches the birds swing back and forth, eat, and sing.

Why do I have them caged up like that?

When January rolls around, the women who demand order in their lives return home from vacation, not having gained an ounce. They're always wearing the latest styles, surrounded by children who are devoted, beautiful, friendly, and educated.

Enough already! Please, Miriam, no more. For more than a month now I've been trying to find a way to pay her back, but as soon as I do one thing for her, she does two more for me; at this rate, we'll never be even. Perhaps she doesn't know how to receive, and I don't want to offend her. Does she really understand friendship?

How can I put an end to this? I still owe her so many favors.

The parks in Coyoacán are full of squirrels. When I give one a peanut she grabs it and runs straight to her home in a nearby tree. They don't say thanks, and they don't feel guilty just because they don't return the favor. I give them peanuts just for the pleasure of seeing them scramble for them and then eat them.

Squirrels, I need to learn a lesson from you.

Susan invited me to play cards at her house.

"How can I go if you don't invite Miriam? She'll think I organized it," I told her.

My brother, who is the most handsome person in my family, I believe, and who's about to become a real architect, is ready to get married: he can actually support a wife, so he's marrying a girl from Monterrey. She's been living barely a year in Mexico City. He says he doesn't know how to ask her to marry him. We can detect that nervous smile of his, like when he has to say a prayer and he hasn't learned how to do it very well. My dad said there's no way he'll ask for a dowry. They say she is pretty. The only thing that bothers me is that ever since he met her he doesn't come around anymore. Before, he used to stop by and ask if the girls needed anything, or he would bring me things from school that I could copy on the typewriter. And now he's about to graduate; I can't figure out how he did it, because ever since grade school he was always a little slow. Her father is the owner of a construction firm, although he isn't an engineer by profession, only by experience. My brother will work with him on his next building project.

Now that she's finished high school, I've been inundating my cousin Lety, who is my Aunt Chela's only daughter, with advice about continuing her studies. But one Saturday night at the synagogue, a señora decided that she wanted my cousin for her son. The next day, a young twenty-seven-year-old arrived at her door and asked her to go out. Her parents encouraged her to go out. The result: wedding plans are already underway.

This made me cry the way I couldn't cry at my own wedding. I was unable to postpone my wedding, and so was she.

I'll keep my distance, because I don't want to say anything to hurt her. Anyway, they say her fiancé is really handsome, has given her lots of gifts, and has taken her out. I should probably leave her alone and spend my time educating my own children, because I'll be able to support them while they finish their studies.

"How can she get married?" I wondered. "She's barely fifteen years old. I thought she was happy because she was going to college to get a degree."

"Her destiny was otherwise."

"But why? She's so young and studious."

"That's the way it is, my child, we all want her to be married. Here's the invitation for all of you. Read well what it says at the bottom: "Please dress appropriately."

"But they just met each other; a three-month courtship isn't long enough. Why are they in such a hurry?"

We came back happy from the Merced market, where we had bought a lot of things. I had someone build a miniature wooden house with a slanted roof that I'm going to cover with animal crackers and chocolate, like the one Hansel and Gretel had. I'll make a little swimming pool out of caramel and use cornmeal for the sand. We put the house on a piece of glass and stood up rows of cookies with wax, and, finally, we'll make a road with some candy.

This year, Jessy's birthday is going to be the best ever; the kids can pick anything they want off the house and eat it. I took a doll to Sanborn's to have them cover it with meringue. It'll be such a beautiful decoration, and so original.

I just heard that my brother Moshón bought a house on Amores Street, but it's going to be torn down in order to build an apartment building. I pass by there every day on my way to take little Esther to kindergarten. What a house! Too bad they're going to tear it down. It's enormous, and only one family had been living there. Now they'll probably divide it up into forty apartments. I asked him if we could at least use it for the birthday party.

"In fact, the kids can destroy it if they want," he said with pleasure.

I bought some paint and brushes. The children can paint whatever they want. That way, they won't be traumatized by never having had the opportunity to paint graffiti on a wall.

We'll be celebrating our tenth wedding anniversary this month. I'm going to tell Lalo that we should have a party. Our wedding wasn't any kind of a party for me; it was hard to deal with a family that was mad at me. My mother felt deceived; who knows what kind of a prince charming she had in mind for her first daughter! But Lalo proved that he's a good husband and a responsible father; in fact, he bends over backwards to make sure we have everything.

Whenever one of the girls gets sick, he can't go to work because he worries too much.

I would love to have a gigantic party—I mean pull out all the stops. Maybe we won't be around to celebrate another one. You just never know.

It was really hard to have to leave Daniela at kindergarten for the first time. She suffered, I suffered. She was scared, and I was scared. Well, I was scared to have to stay at home without a baby around anymore, but I could always get pregnant again. The problem is that something's always happening to her, and it frightens me. I heard her crying for over an hour while I stood outside the school gate this morning. I was devastated. Even our maid Estela gave me a nasty look because I had taken her to school; I mean, they caused a ruckus, and here I was signing her up at one of the best—and closest—schools, the Elena Espinoza on Moreno Street. It's the best school I've ever seen. Jessy and little Esther went there.

I'm still buying a record every week. They're imported, too. Today, I bought *Symphony No. 9, From the New World,* conducted by Rafael Kubelik. It's simply wonderful. These records will be my legacy to my children. The collection just gets bigger every week, just like our book collection. I pay monthly on a set of encyclopedias and a collection of the classics for adolescents.

Susan has to be the coolest person I know. It's her energy that impresses me. I would love to be so easygoing and open. Well, maybe not as much as her . . . like the other day, when we were coming home, and, out of the blue, she asks me if I'm cold or hot.

"Are you cold or hot?"

I literally dropped my books, oranges, and pears in the elevator. I wasn't even sure, and that's what I told her. I had no idea what to say.

Then she just started laughing out loud, always with that strong, likable smile of hers. As I was opening the door to my apartment, I was still dumbfounded. I could still hear her laughing down the hall.

I went up to her apartment today; it was strange to see her mother there. When Dori went downstairs to give her son some medicine, I played her hand. Then Miriam showed up at my apartment, looking for me.

"She's in 501," Jessy told her.

There was no way of getting out of it; she had come up to find me. And there I was, my hands in the cookie jar; that is, I was playing cards.

"Miriam?" I screamed, as if I had been caught in bed with her husband.

"None of my friends appreciates me. There's no friendship anymore," she yelled, stomping down the stairs.

While my friends just stared at her, I quickly put my cards down and ran out after her.

"Darn it, I knew this would happen," I shouted, leaping down the stairs and trying to calm her down. Offended, she slammed her door in my face.

"Miriam, listen to me! Miriam, please," I screamed. "I'm not a bad friend. Wait!"

While I begged her to understand, I tried to explain: "I just went upstairs for a little while. I had no idea they were playing cards." I was frightened to death, so I lied to her.

Susan and her mother came down looking for me. They gave me a hug and took me back upstairs.

"Look, honey, the people who don't believe in friendship don't believe in anything," said Susan's mother. "The problem is that they don't know what to expect from a friend."

While I sobbed, they tried to console me.

"They'll always demand more than they're willing to give. That's the problem. And there are those who never have a friend in their whole lives. Thank God, I have lots of friends, and I know it's important to have them. Ah, don't worry about it. Let's play cards."

Lalo was enthusiastic about having a party. We told Hanna and her husband about it, and they got even more excited about it. He said he'll dress up like a rabbi; he's so funny. As we drew up the marriage vows, we almost peed our pants out of laughter. We ordered a large horseshoe wreath to put over the door, like the ones you see on the boats on Xochimilco Lake. I'll have to let out my wedding dress in the middle, but a long veil will cover the seam in the back. And Lalo looks great in his suit; he hasn't gained an ounce. I'm so envious! Although he's short, he has a good body and athletic legs. And he's handsome. That's why I have such beautiful daughters. I'm going to make the bridesmaids' dresses for them. They can throw rice on us when we get out of the car. We're going to have a full orchestra. Since Miriam won't talk to me, Lalo went downstairs to invite them to the party. I decided to rest. Now I feel liberated. As for the favors I owe her that I don't care if I ever pay back, I'm at peace with myself. I'm a slave to her no more. Everything ended so badly, but at least it's over.

I ran into some of my neighbors downstairs; they were knitting and asked me where I was going with the notebooks. I felt proud to inform them that I was going to a music appreciation class. Like the first day I went to class, they had no idea what the hell I was referring to. Instead, they asked me to join them in a game of cards.

"I only play twice a week; I can't handle any more than that," I answered.

My dad was talking about my cousin, whom I like very much.

"Her husband left her because she had too many friends. She paid more attention to them than to him. It got so bad that he just told her to go straight to hell."

Funny, but I saw Alegre today, and it didn't seem to me that she was burning up. She didn't even look sad; in fact, she had guests coming over, and she was playing some great music. After dinner, her actor friends read poetry, and she read something for her daughters that was quite moving. The big surprise was that my Aunt Mati and her son Aron came into town. She has more fun here than in Monterrey. Artists just fascinate her. It seems like my aunt, who's sweet as honey, is always having fun.

"Oshinica, dear, do you want me to tell you one of those stories that I used to tell you when you were young? Do you remember the one about that crazy guy Ishodotro from Yojá?" she asked, with dreamy eyes.

"Yes, that would be great. But I remember hating it when you and my mom told those Yojá stories. No one knows them in Mexico. And they're dumb stories, anyway."

"But what would you expect, my dear; that's the way we were taught back in our homeland. Tell me, Oshinica, do you still have the poems I gave you when you got married?"

I clutched my aunt's hand and held it for a good while. When just about everyone had left, we talked more intimately, and I learned that my cousin's husband is still looking for her.

My father had told me just the opposite.

While we were in the elevator, we ran into some neighbors whom we hadn't invited to the party. They were surprised to see me dressed up like a bride in the company of a handsome groom wearing a tux. The doorman's eyes popped out, and we broke out laughing. We arrived in our old, but heavily decorated, car. As they played the wedding march, we got caught in a rainstorm of rice. Afterwards, of course, they played a waltz. And Daniela presented the bride and groom with a tiny pillow bearing rings.

The next day, we left for Acapulco for our second "honeymoon." If I get pregnant . . . oh, well, I get pregnant. Perhaps I'll have a boy this time, but I doubt it; they're much more difficult to conceive. Besides, I'm a better mother for girls, and who knows how he and I would get along anyway? For sure, you can't play favorites. But only God knows why we haven't had a boy.

Lalo and my mother have been criticizing me for going to those classes at the Institute.

"Hardly anything gets done around here. It was bad enough that you go on Mondays, but now Wednesdays too?" they have been saying.

This is outlandish. I'm envious of those women whose husbands want their wives to learn more. It's only an hour on Wednesdays, like a quick trip to the supermarket, for Heaven's sake.

I don't care if he gets mad. Lalo knew I wanted to continue studying, and I haven't stopped. The thing I liked best about Lalo is that he swore he wouldn't ever get in my way. My problem is that I got distracted along the way, because I enjoyed playing the role of matron, the mommy, the indispensable one, and I'm always fearing he wouldn't even be aware of it. Well, why doesn't he study some more too? Anyway, then Jessy was born, along came little Esther and Daniela, the apartment, then a friend was about to have a baby, there were the birthdays, I had to go here and there all the time, take Lalo to work, pick him up . . . and the years just went flying by. But I've never forgotten my original plan.

Lalo's yelling was appalling. The slightest thing would set him off. Finally, at three o'clock in the morning, I went down to Susan's apartment. Her husband is always traveling. When she saw me all teary-eyed at her door, in my pajamas and holding my pillow, she laughed.

"Is that what that jerk does to you? And you who look so attractive?"

I didn't want to laugh, but when you're around her, it's hard not to.

That's it! He needs a hobby. I want Lalo to have a hobby. Please, God, help him find one, something to occupy his time besides the kids and his work. I've been suggesting everything: painting, sculpture, film, photography. I must be driving him crazy, because I'm so obsessed with it. I'm sure I'm beginning to pester him, and then he gets mad.

"What's the use of having a video recorder and a camera? Tell me, why did you buy them if you weren't going to use them? The camera has been sitting in the closet for two years."

So, if he's not going to use it, I'll learn how to take pictures. We hardly have any pictures of the girls.

"Why don't you see a psychoanalyst?" I ended up telling him. "Perhaps you'll discover what you'd really like to do."

He started going to group therapy, and he likes it. He goes on Wednesdays. Let's hope he doesn't come home one day and say he's not going anymore.

Darn it! Why does she have to get sick on Monday? I tried calling the doctor, but he hadn't arrived at his office yet. I was going to the drugstore, and to my surprise, who did I run into on the elevator with his doctor's bag and a surprise on his face? Dr. Gonda.

"Doctor! I've been trying to call you for over an hour. It's my daughter. She's . . ."

"Are you getting in?" he asks, looking at his watch.

"Oh, I'm sorry," I said, quickly stepping into the elevator. "She woke up with diarrhea."

He was in a hurry, but he gave me a prescription. Then I got the medicine, fixed her a light lunch, and headed straight for class.

If I had to, I could leave class a little early. My mom can check on her too.

"Mom, here's the deal. Daniela has a little diarrhea. I've already talked to the doctor and given her Kaopectate. Would you please stop by to see her for a few minutes while I'm gone? I don't want to miss an important class at the Institute. What? That's a mean thing to say! Okay, okay. The maid can call you if she needs something. She hasn't had to go to the bathroom in over two hours."

Then she really started yelling and scolding me.

"All right already. I won't go. I guess it's not the end of the world. Anyway, come over if you want. I'll be here."

But when it was time to go, I could neither hold myself back nor help reproaching myself; I was wrong to leave the three of them alone. And what if something happens? And what if I get home and they tell me that Daniela has choked to death on a marble or a coin, or that she fell off the balcony?

I went down to the main office at the Institute to call them three times. I would love to have a direct line, so I wouldn't worry so much. I didn't understand a thing that was said in the class; I could only hear my mom's voice instead of the professor's, who was talking about the meaning of love according to Plato, Saint-Exupéry, and Stendhal. I couldn't enjoy the class; all I could do was write down their names and hope to read them someday.

When I got home, the girls were playing house, and Felipa had served them potato chips, cake, and juice. I sat down with them and my youngest one said, "Yummy." They were happy as could be on the balcony. And I got nothing out of the class. Felipa put on some children's records. When it was time for their nap, I sang them a song: "The three little mice went to sleep/and with their mommy's kisses they stopped counting sheep." I kissed them and then read a story. Daniela, who's always sucking her thumb, got another book and handed it to me, saying "more."

They fell asleep in no time, so I turned out the light and put on some classical music. Father Recondo says it's the best way for them to begin to absorb the music, when you're a baby still in the crib. They're not even aware of what's happening. They'll already know *The Symphony of the Toys* and *The Emperor Concerto*. This way, they'll grow up with it, and they'll find themselves humming it some day when they're older. It's during these moments that I really enjoy being a mother. When Lalo comes home, I turn off the music.

He prefers TV.

One of these days we're going to take the girls to the concert hall at Bellas Artes so that they can become familiar with everything that I'm just beginning to learn about. I will dress them up with their little orange-colored outfits and gloves. They're so pretty when they wear matching clothes. I have fun dressing them up and combing their hair. Well, it's no fun combing Daniela's hair, because she cries when I have to get the tangles out.

I hope I don't forget to stop by the Spanish lady's store and buy those flowered felt hair bands.

I saw Andrés talking to a friend on the escalator at Liverpool's Department Store. I almost tripped, because I wasn't watching where I was walking. He laughed. Keeping my composure as always, I didn't say anything more than a brief hello. I'm so dumb. Why I can't I ever say anything to him?

Professor Espinaza, who took us to see *Teorema,* is one of the school's directors. The students say he's very knowledgeable. He just told us that *8 1/2* was a jewel of a film and that it will be showing Wednesday and Thursday. Since we're going to discuss it in class, Lalo and I went to see it. He almost killed me.

"That's a piece of crap! What kind of professors do you have at that school? I've never seen such a weird movie. I didn't understand one iota."

In class, the film was considered a masterpiece. And there was this scene and that scene, and the ending was unsurpassed. They made so many comments about the film that I'm not sure I saw the same one. I didn't see anything that they mentioned. And me . . . I just kept my mouth shut. During the second hour, they talked about politics, because some of the students had just been in a History of Religions class. The debate was between those who wanted to practice religion without so many limitations and those fundamentalists, who, in addition to the laws of each religion, invent so many obstacles that you can't even sneeze without breaking some rule.

It was the first time I had heard the term "fundamentalist." And, yes, there are Jewish fundamentalists, too. When the professor found out I was Jewish, he commented zestfully that he had lots of friends from our community and that he had attended many of our weddings and bar mitzvahs, always wearing his little cap in the synagogue out of respect.

"And, tell me, when you go to church, do you kneel with everyone else?"

"No, it's against Jewish law. It's a sin. Jews never kneel."

"So why do I have to do what they ask me to do in the synagogue if you, on the other hand, don't show any respect in a church? It won't hurt you. Kneeling is like sitting down and standing up. It's no big deal."

❖ ❖ ❖

I don't know what I was doing back then, when all these women who go to class at the Institute were learning so many new things. Whenever I run into one of the professors, I take off in another direction. It's hard for me to talk to them. Simja is a talented teacher. Good luck to anyone who has to answer one of his questions! We usually get so choked up that he feels bad he ever asked the question.

At a school party, Professors' Day, even the married women danced. I wouldn't ever be crazy enough to stay for the dance, and besides, what would I do if I were asked to dance? It would be even worse if they didn't ask. No matter what, it's stressful for me. I just couldn't let myself be caught standing there, hoping someone would invite me to dance.

Lalo has started to criticize just about everything I do. He says I'm lazy and that my cooking is lousy. So, on Monday, I sent out for tortilla dough. The maid prepared the tortillas with shredded cheese, lettuce, refried beans, sausage, and salsa. The *chilaquiles* were delicious. But when Lalo sat down at the table, he said I was crazy because all of that was too heavy for breakfast. He drank a cup of coffee and left.

We just stood there, dumbfounded. It was hard to believe that he wouldn't at least try it. I was really confused, and it was the day I usually go to the Institute. That's when hardly any meals get fixed.

And he got mad today as well, but I was so happy after my class that when he got home that evening, I just kissed and hugged him. He looked at me so strangely that I suddenly remembered that I was supposed to be mad at him.

◇ ◇ ◇

Lalo asked me if I had ever desired another man. I looked straight at him and thought that a clear, sincere question required a similar answer. One thing's for sure, I'm no hypocrite; besides, it would be absurd for him to think that during all these years I've never had a yearning for another man. I've had so many fantasies, so many sleepless nights, dreaming, that it occurred to me that one afternoon . . . a look, a yes, an adventure, daring to . . . but I'm always too busy and unconcerned about my own feelings, and I'm getting even fatter. He's even jealous of my female friends. Perhaps this came up because we read some chapters from *Open Marriage* together.

Nevertheless, I finally said yes. And when I saw his face scrunch up, I felt even more at ease about telling him:

"Yes, my dear, I'm sure that some time . . . when you didn't love me, when you had been yelling at me, when you didn't take me somewhere, when you didn't come home, yes, I felt that way."

"Why, I didn't think you'd ever be so deceiving. A decent woman would never . . . I could just puke."

By then, his face had become quite distorted, his eyes breathed fury, and I just continued:

"Well, fidelity is not natural; maybe it's possible at first, but what about later on? Just one man forever? It goes against human nature. Forever? When we got married, when you were just twenty and I was barely seventeen, did we have any idea what the word 'forever' meant? Due to my upbringing, I've never been unfaithful to you, but it's not natural."

"Shut up! You should be embarrassed to say those things."

"And, what's more," I insisted, "the women who say they've never desired another man are simply hypocritical. I've asked other women, and they confess that they feel the same way I do. Can love really be forever?"

"If you want to have a lover, go ahead; but just don't tell me about it. You've hurt me; I'm not made of steel. So if I haven't fulfilled you as a man, just leave. Do something else with your life. Get off the train, or I'll push you off. Who knows what kind of people you've been hanging out with!"

Well, well. Sincerity . . . honesty, none of these concepts really applies here. Why did I say anything? Everyone keeps telling me that I run off at the mouth.

You have to be stupid to be honest.

When I went to the dentist, I had my camera in my purse. I keep carrying it around because I want someone to put a new roll of film in it. The dentist is a camera buff, so I asked him. After examining it for a while, he said finally: "Señora, doesn't it seem like this camera is too good for you?"

What a jerk!

I haven't had my period this month. I'll bet I'm pregnant again. And I've started to have those sleepy spells.

SIX

"Lalo, promise you won't get mad at me if it's a girl again?"

For years now, Lalo has liked spending Sundays house hunting. I think it's boring. It's true that he's done well at the store, mainly because he's a masochist for work, and it seems like his brother is always asking him for his opinion on some deal they're making, but it also seems like we'll never buy our own house. We only drive around to see them, mainly because he's been wanting to get something in La Herradura neighborhood. It's quiet there, and the children can ride their bikes and have a dog. He doesn't want to live somewhere downtown over a store with a mechanic's shop on one side and a plumbing store on the other. He's become a suburbanite! That's okay by me. I'd love to have a backyard. The first thing I'd do is hang a hammock and plant a large jacaranda tree to create some shade.

🦅 SUNDAY.

"Hi, Grandpa. How are you?"

"A little better, my dear," he responds, bending over and letting us kiss his flaccid cheek. Upon seeing me, my grandma wipes her mouth with a napkin; lately, she's been having trouble recognizing me. But she kisses me on each cheek.

"I *corbanes* for you."

Who knows what that Persian word means, but ever since I could remember, she's been showing her love with it. Their maid, Uba, winks at me and puts her finger to her lips as if to tell me to not ask. Had I said anything wrong?

"Uba, what does that mean?" I asked her in the kitchen.

"Have you forgotten that your grandfather doesn't want anyone talking during dinner?"

I go back to the table. My father smiles at me with that look of complicity. Then I detect a stern look from my mother. I try a couple of stuffed peppers. We eat in silence. Looking down in unison, everyone takes a bite of their chicken; afterwards, they lick the bones. You only hear the sound of the knives and forks on the plates.

"Well, it's going to be difficult for me to remain quiet until we're finished dinner. Grandad, don't you think that at dinnertime everyone should be talking to each other, just like when you invite a client to eat? That way, you make more friends."

As my grandfather's hands begin to tremble, his spoon drips. He coughs to clear his throat.

"It's written in the sacred book," he states, first in Hebrew, "that when one eats, he doesn't talk."

"That's incredible! It says that, too, huh?"

"Yes," my father assures me, fearing that his father will get

LIKE A MOTHER

327

upset, even though he's already spent his life being upset and upsetting us.

"Our religion respects health and hygiene," he adds.

By pushing back his chair, my grandfather announces that dinner is finished. He jerks his napkin from his collar and retires to the living room. Once the door is closed, we let out a sigh of relief, and everything comes to life. The movie, which was on pause, starts to roll again.

"Don't get upset, my dear," says Uba. "The other day, when your brother Freddy came over and talked so much, your granddad got a stomachache."

Today being Sunday, there's a movie on TV with Emilio Tuero, but the main topic at the table right now is focused on the fact that since it isn't the Sabbath, my mom can find solace in her knitting. My father dozes off and then wakes up with a start. He smiles and then falls asleep again.

"Hey, I didn't even realize the movie was just about over," I said, looking at my granddad, who was peeking over the newspaper at the TV.

"I've brought you tea, as it should be," said Uba, carrying in a tray with cups.

I add a sugar cube to mine. Then, silence.

"What? Emilio Tuero again? What's the deal here?"

Everyone laughs, but my granddad keeps his composure.

"And now he's got remote control," says my mother, who giggles.

Sitting in his green armchair and hiding the remote control, my grandfather has complete domination over his little world. Stone-faced, he sips his coffee. Then, suddenly, he switches channels and Emilio Tuero becomes Angel Fernández, then a singer, then Angélica María and Raúl Velasco, and finally, back to Emilio

Tuero. In neither my dad's face nor my grandma's could anyone detect a grimace—only in my mother's, who is the "outsider," so says my grandfather, who was detecting my displeasure.

Then one of our immortals of the national movie industry sang "Life in the High Rise," which I really like. I shiver to think that with a click that song becomes, "And it's a gooooool for America," narrated by Angel Fernández.

No. I can't take this anymore. Why this compulsion to keep switching the TV channels?

I give my dad a hug. Not even a cup of tea will relieve my stomachache. How could they put this lethal weapon in his hands? I let out a sigh of relief when I see the screen project the image and melodious baritone voice of Angel.

My cousin Lety, who's wearing a bride's dress, walks down the aisle on the white carpet in the synagogue. I don't want to even look at the groom for fear of getting mad, but they do look attractive together. I have to admit that she and her dress look lovely.

"He's a good boy, he'll be a good son," whispers my Aunt Chelita. "He *is* handsome, isn't he," she murmurs playfully.

After the ceremony, everyone goes to the ballroom, where a row of tall potted plants divides the room: on one side are the women; on the other, the men and the orchestra. Arm in arm, the men dance in a circle around the groom; then they lift him up into the air, put him down, and make him dance. They all seem to be having such a good time, which is more than me, because women can't sit with their husbands and brothers.

It's a male wedding. Almost all of them are dressed in black and wearing hats. Many of them have stringy white beards. I'm not the only woman to stand on a chair and watch them dance. Even the groom's mother tries to do it, but she's almost too heavy to get up on a chair. The groom's sisters and sisters-in-law and Lety's friends dance in similar fashion around her on our side of the ballroom. I ask some of the girls who are dancing and two younger girls if the overt division between the sexes doesn't put them out.

"That's the way it is," they concede. And they're certain that's the way it should be.

"If they danced with us, all they would do is just throw us around. Look how fast they swirl and twirl around. They're brutal, like animals," said one of them, who was having fun watching the men dance with such energy.

That's the way it is. It's been that way forever, and they've always said, "That's the way it is."

We could also say, "That's the way it used to be. That's how it was."

A little later, my Aunt Chelita comes over.

"This is Oshinica, my favorite niece."

Lety had already told them about me. I devised a way to talk indirectly about what's bothering me, while everything seems so normal to them.

"When I get married, this is the way I want it. I'm not from an orthodox family, but . . . this is what I want," said the prettiest girl there, who studies at the Ibero School.

"Why? I just don't get it," I said.

"My sensuality is private, I prefer to give it to the man I marry, and only to him. I'm not interested in showing it off to others. Covering my head with a scarf is an indication to men to stay away from me. Judaism covers the precious things, and like bread, we always cover it with a pretty cloth."

"And using a wig is not covering your head either," said

another one of the girls. "I'd never use a wig; that's why we have different types of cloth, which we can wear like the hippies."

"Men need a lot of rules in order to control their surroundings," explained the prettiest girl.

"And that's why they send us to the second floor of our places of worship?" I asked. "Doesn't that bother you?"

"Not in the least. You go to the synagogue to pray, to unite yourself with God, to concentrate. It's not a place to flirt."

In the meantime, my uncle hasn't stopped dancing in the circle around the groom. You'd think he'd forgotten that his daughter is the bride. Are we that invisible? I really can't believe it!

Every time I want to question something and try to justify it, there are others who see it differently. Why do I have to be so antagonistic? I should just enjoy the party on this side and join the circle of women who seem to be radiating happiness as they dance around the bride. But who wouldn't take issue with this? Especially since I'm the daughter of a mother who even fights with my grandfather; it's useless, but she fights just the same.

My Aunt Chelita came running over, grabbed me to dance a hora, and just kept smiling at me. She's beautiful, and I adore her, but her surrender to obedience infuriates me.

"Everything's just fine, Oshinica, just enjoy it. Your cousin is going to be happy; she'll have lots of children. See how handsome the groom is? May God grant that your daughters become brides."

"After today," my mother informed me, "your cousin will cover her hair and use dresses that cover her arms and ankles. Never more will she wear a bathing suit at the beach; and she'll only go swimming with other women."

"Hair excites men," my Aunt Chelita whispers to me, trying to convince me.

Oh, my God, look at the problems caused by men's outlandish and uncontrollable lusts! Once upon a time, women got married and lived happily ever after. And, yes, most likely their plans to do something beyond being a mother . . . ended right there . . . just like mine did when I got married.

I'm going out anyway. . . . I won't dress up, and I hope no one from the community sees me. I'll be back by six. Wearing a long overcoat, I run up the steps to the Continental Theater. Taking advantage of the darkness, I sit down next to the oldest lady I can find. When I see that the movie is about to end, I'll get up and leave.

Perfect. No one saw me. Even at home, no one noticed that I was a little late.

It was a great movie. I'm so happy that I went!

I'll make sure I catch more movies; besides, the theater is just around the corner. Otherwise, I'd probably never get to see a thing.

It's a new school year for me too; instead of Psychology of Art, I'll be taking Literature. I think I'll submit my papers at the end of the course. Since the teacher will be absent the first three weeks, a funny-looking guy will teach classes. He's thin, with long hair and a straggly beard, and he's not very tall. Even though he uses thick glasses, his attractive eyes shine through them. He has thick eyebrows and a soft voice, moves his fingers rapidly while he talks, and always puts his hand on his forehead. He's cute to watch and listen to. He lives in one suit that literally hangs on him. He teaches drama. They're going to read Ibsen's *A Doll's House*. I invited my sister Clarita and her friend Beatriz to come along; then Beatriz invited Annette, her closest friend from grade school.

I guess we're all taken by Gabriel's class, and we've only got five more with him, because on Monday Rosita Presburger is coming back to teach the class. Last year we took classes together, and now I'll be her student. Clarita and her friends want to enroll in the classes, but they'd have to go back and finish high school first. We're all like Nora: we play with our dolls, and we have husbands like hers who take care of us as if we were little girls. We can't swear or talk about sex, but we have to explain life to our children as if we knew all about it. And we have to be sweet to them, careful not to harm them, and teach them to be independent—even though we ourselves are not.

"It's important to train the girls," states Gabriel. "They must be stimulated, pushed. And it's okay for them to think like Sleeping Beauty and hope they'll be rescued by Prince Charming, who will take care of all their problems. But they should stop waiting for that to happen; instead, they should read Virginia Woolf's *A Room of One's Own*. They should have their own room and be in control of their own body. Work is key to this transformation; they must learn how to stand on their own two feet."

"That's it . . . support yourself!"

I still remember the times when my dad used to take Moshón and me to his store in the Market, and his neighbors, who were store owners themselves, would ask: "Don Samuel, did you bring your children to help you in the store?"

The clients were always bartering for everything. Moshón learned the ropes by the time he was ten, and he was always good at selling. My father's friends would listen to the spiel he'd use to keep customers from going away empty-handed. I would always stand toward the back and observe the observer observing: my brother would take a bag and stick the coats he had sold into it.

"See how good a salesman your son is?" a client would say. "I came in to buy only one coat, and I'm leaving with three."

You could see that Moshón was proud of himself as he took the money and gave it to my dad.

"Unbelievable, Samuel!" said the owner next door. "He's even surpassed you. And you, Oshinica, you're probably just as good at selling as your brother. It's in your blood."

I gave him a dirty look and left the store. If anyone would come up to me wanting to look at a coat, I'd get nervous. It was hard for me to talk to the customers. When my dad would see that I didn't invite anyone in to look around, he would jump in and say something like, "It doesn't cost anything to look, Señorita, come in and check out what we have."

If the customer was at all hesitant, he would begin seducing her with his charm. He'd actually mesmerize them, and they'd follow him right inside, as if they were being reeled in on a fishing pole, ever so gently, so as not to lose them. To me, it was a sad sight to see, but I couldn't help laughing at the same time. Many times I just wanted to hide from it all.

"I've just received the latest styles, and I'm sure there's one that you'll adore," he would add, getting ready to haul in his catch. "Oshinica, show a coat to the young lady."

Embarrassed, I would take the coat off the hanger and help her put it on. The customer felt good in the new coat.

"My dear, what's wrong with you? Thanks to me, she bought the coat. If it were up to you, she'd have left without anything. You saw her looking at herself in the mirror, and you just stood there, stone-faced. That's wrong!"

To me, Moshón looked ugly as he enticed another customer

to go inside; I preferred to look for Goyita to see if she had gotten the latest issue of *Pepín* yet.

I can still hear Gabriel, who insisted that so long as women don't learn how to take care of themselves, we'll never be in control of our lives.

Just to think about selling in Lagunilla makes me sick. I don't like it. I hate it.

"Women need to find ways to support themselves that are gratifying," continued Gabriel, "something that makes women happy. If not, they'll be condemned to frustration. Read Simone de Beauvoir's *The Second Sex,* and toward the end of the year, read Samuel Beckett's *Waiting for Godot.* I'll bet none of you wants to wait until the end of your lives to do what you really want. Perhaps whatever you're waiting for may never arrive."

What could I do to support myself that doesn't involve selling something?

Last night, Lalo started an argument because I had dared to disagree with him in front of our neighbors. He says that a wife must stand behind her husband, even if she disagrees with him. The real issue is that he doesn't want me to think for myself. All he wants me to do is remain quiet, and to agree with whatever he says, no matter how embarrassing or stupid it might be. My God, how can I not say what I believe?

"Well, of course, honey," states Lucilla, "your first duty is to your husband. You have to know how to humor him." My neighbor from Costa Rica agreed with her. I've gone to her place several times now, and she still hasn't decided whether or not to put up curtains because she's probably going back home. Just about everyone else would have finished doing theirs by now. So, she waits . . . and waits.

Today I took my youngest child to the pediatrician. He asked about my sister, and I told him that she's still in high school.

"And why aren't you studying?"

"I guess it's because my husband never went on to get a degree of his own, and I don't want to outdo him; but I'm taking a music appreciation class . . . well, I've dared to take two."

"Is that the reason why you don't do what *you* want?"

"Yes, that's the way I want it; if not, I won't feel right later on."

"You shouldn't put yourself through this. If you want to do something else, just do it."

I looked at him, wanting to absorb everything he said. That's exactly what I wanted to hear, but what I'm getting from everyone else is just the opposite: that I'm supposed to take care of my husband, make him happy, be sure that *he's* fulfilled. No one has said that the wife has a right to the same thing.

"I decided to stop going to school," I added, trying to hold back my tears, "but it hurts, doctor."

And I repeated what I had been hearing from the other women: "In order for a husband to feel satisfied, he has to feel superior to his wife."

"That's all wrong," said the doctor. "You shouldn't let this destroy that spark inside you. Marriage means that both husband and wife should grow together and take advantage of the best that each has to offer. Not the opposite."

By the time I got home, I was thoroughly confused.

Rosita Presburger told me that the next time León Felipe has dinner at her house on a Sunday, she'll invite me to join them. He dedicated a poem to her and her husband in his book *Este viejo y roto violín.* I bought all of his books. I learned one of his poems by heart, and it goes like this: "What a pity I don't have a picture of a grandfather who won a war/not even an old leather chair, a table, a sword . . ." I liked the poem so much that I wrote this in the margins: "León Felipe, don't despair over not having a grandfather who won a war; I have one who has a green leather armchair, and he loves me . . . but he's abominable, because he's a tyrant."

Rosita's lucky to have such interesting friends. I hope she invites the poet to her house soon. He might die anytime, because he's getting so old.

Freddy really upsets me. I told him that when he got to Israel, he shouldn't join the army. And that's the first thing he did. And here I am reading Saint-Exupéry's *Night Flight,* in which he talks about peace and the absurdity of dying for some stupid nationalist cause or in wars being fought for others.

"To go to war," he writes, "is to commit suicide. Death surrounds you. Men are sacrificed to squelch anarchy. Nothing makes any sense."

Because he's an idealist, they'll kill him. In-cre-di-ble! What a brainwashing we got from my grandfather, my dad, the school, the Hashomer, and the other youth organizations. When I was single, they wouldn't let me go to Israel, but no one stopped my brother from going. He said he was going to work growing oranges and bananas on a kibbutz. Will I ever see him again? Why would he want to die so young? If he does, I will always miss him greatly. He would have missed me too. I only wish my letter would change his mind.

He had barely arrived when they showed them military films about parachuting, and he got excited about it. I wish he could read this book.

"I sleep only two hours," he says. "My greatest desire is to have a day off, and do nothing; that would be paradise. Basically, I don't know anything, and I shouldn't even know where I am."

And I have no way of sending him some of Cuco Sánchez's records or cans of green chiles. I should probably just copy a few paragraphs, mail them, and hope nothing happens to him. He wrote to me saying that in his kibbutz the Mexican volunteers have given two cross-streets the names "Insurgentes" and "Reforma." They say that those from Mexico are having trouble adapting. Maybe that's why he returned. Over there they call him "the Mexican" and say, "Hey, you, Mecsico!" And here in Mexico, they call him "Jew."

It's a drag being pregnant again. I'll bet it's going to be another girl. That's okay. Daniela is simply precious; she's mild-mannered and easygoing. She doesn't let anything bother her. Whenever I check on her, she's always sucking her thumb . . . and smiling.

Last night at nine, everything started to shake. Even before it had stopped, my mother, who is such a dear person, had already arrived; she knows how frightened I get. It's amazing to think that she must have run all the way over here, from over three blocks away.

"We're going to be destroyed," screamed the neighbors, as everyone pushed and shoved to get down the stairs. I refused to sleep there that night, so we went to my parents' house, which is a single-level home. I can still hear the building reverberate. I'm going to get rid of the chandelier in the living room. As I watched it swing back and forth, I knew that one day it was going to fall and split someone's head open.

Out of the blue, Lalo made the statement that sex is important. He even criticized me about it, so now he wants me to flirt more.

"But don't you remember the sexy bra I bought in Las Vegas? And you called me a whore. How come things have changed all of a sudden?"

He said I should see a psychoanalyst. I can't wait.

I can't believe how much I would like to talk to Andrés. It's been over a week since I last saw him, and I can't forget how he looked at me, with those long eyelashes . . . and that smile! He probably thinks that I'm really happy. He's always had such a high opinion of me that he surely won't ever give me a chance; on the other hand, I don't want him to think I'm uptight either, like the ones who spurn every guy who comes along. But he's never made any advances either. A kiss here, a kiss there, but the innocent kind, and that's all. He told me that some guys at the Shomer had been pawing Ruth and that they had seen her naked. I relished hearing him say that I wasn't like that. How was I, then? Is it really that good to be the decent "other one?"

I saw Ruth at the club the other day. She had married the handsomest, richest, and most important guy around. He was so good-looking that I almost couldn't look him straight in the face.

I dialed Andrés's mother several times until he finally answered, but I was unable to utter a thing. He's always thought I was something very special.

I've been seeing a psychoanalyst for two months now. This lady doctor is dreadful. She came up with the idea that I was dominating Lalo, and that I hate people who dominate others. But what if she's right? It's true that I've wanted Lalo to take up painting or sculpture classes. I just wanted him to be happy.

"But that's not what he wants to do. You see, you don't respect his feelings," she admonished me.

I hate her.

Okay, I'm going to leave him alone. I'm disgusted with myself. I'm so embarrassed to have had him on a short leash.

"You were afraid that his mother was going to control him, and that's exactly what you've been doing yourself," added the imbecile. Now I'm afraid that's what Lalo's going to discover in his sessions.

That's it. I won't say any more. If he decides to go somewhere else after work, let him do it. He's not my prisoner. I feel absolutely despicable: I've been trying to change him, and I didn't respect him for what he is. I've tormented him with trying to make him take classes. Our marriage must be appalling to him. And to think I've been just as authoritative as my grandfather. That's horrendous!

Now I'm not even sure I want a boy. I've grown accustomed to having only girls. I may not even like having a boy around. They're more mischievous, and I wouldn't even know how to deal with him, or change his behavior if I had to. And, on top of that, I've been fostering this anger over the fact that as a woman I was prevented from doing what I wanted in life. And now Beauvoir's book. Yes, I'm afraid I could end up punishing him for it. Maybe it's best.

There he was, like an old monarch, the poet. Several people had already gathered around him; like me, they wanted to meet him, hear him talk, share the moment. Rosita took me over to him, and I was surprised to get a hug from him, and he immediately made me feel at ease.

I could see that he was interested not only in a young architect's work, but also in the musician's ideas, in the Institute, and in the classes we were taking there. As I was listening to him, I couldn't help but compare him to the other older men who were there. He seemed genuinely interested in all the young people who were edging close to him, full of admiration. So, can someone grow old and still be interesting? I don't want to grow old and have no one to talk to me. On the other hand, the old people around me are nothing but that: old. This old man is a wise old man.

🦅 SUNDAY NIGHT.

"Ma'am, you just had a baby boy."

"Oh, now that's a joke," I murmured to myself. "I can't believe it. They're probably just pulling my leg. Excuse me, nurse, please don't leave me alone here. By the way, is it really true I just had a boy?"

I guess having changed hospitals also changed my luck. A boy, no less! I was sure I'd never have a boy. I'm waiting for the priest to stop by my room. If he doesn't come in today, I'll go look for him somewhere in the hospital tomorrow.

I don't like the idea of circumcising my boy. I heard one day that it was like castrating him, and that he loses his sensitivity. I would be stoned to death if I were to repeat that out loud.

It's already past ten, and the priest still hasn't come. What great lectures on music he gave at the Institute. What if something has happened to him? The nurses said that he had to attend to several baptisms, but that they had told him that I wanted to see him. He said he would come. I'm excited.

It seemed like every last person in the world came to the circumcision ceremony. Ever since my mother learned that she had a grandson, she's been preparing all kinds of special food. I've been devouring caviar, which isn't always easy to get. Everyone's happy now.

"Where did all these people come from? Even a crazy guy, a dumb guy, and a basket case came by," commented my Aunt Mati.

"Oh, Auntie dear, you come up with the strangest things," I said, hugging her.

My brother Freddy is going to be very happy that I had a son. There's only two more months before he returns . . . if they don't kill him first.

I'll start little Jacob's album with his toe prints and fingerprints on the first page. I'll keep his first tooth and his first shoe, and I'll write about his first friend, his first time out in the stroller, the age at which he stood up in his crib, his first words, and the second ones as well. Lalo is delighted with his children. He's fascinated.

"Wow! This little tike wants to nurse all the time." Now, after the fourth child, I've finally learned to go to the bedroom when it's time to breast-feed, to say excuse me, leave the room, and take my time to enjoy it. It's good to breast-feed, and it makes me feel good, but only if the baby and I are alone together. It's something intimate.

I've had to forget about classes for a while. Felipa will come back to work for us in six months.

My baby is looking more handsome all the time. His name, however, is something else; it's even hard for me to pronounce. I've never liked Biblical names, but tradition has it that the first son has to take the name of the husband's father. A second son would get my father's name.

And he's a restless baby, too. Just to be able to keep him in my arms a little longer and just a little closer, I have to invent games.

"Wait! I've got to count your freckles to make sure you've still got them all." Then he grows quiet and listens to my voice counting each one. When I get to five thousand, he's had enough and wants down; then I'll try to invent something else, and he'll stay quiet a little bit longer, at least until I say, "Yep, you've still got 'em all." If I didn't have a way of tricking him, he wouldn't stay still for a single moment.

"He's fidgety," says Susan. "He's just like his mother; in fact, your mother says that you've never been able to stay still for anything."

Isn't it strange how each child's character is so different? It's the same with animals. Take the cat someone gave Jessy. It's so skittish. I don't really like it. It would never sleep on the bed next to me like others we've had.

Jessy is already ten years old, and she continues to be the top student in her school. And friends always surround her. I'm so proud of her. She has everything that I ever wanted myself. Little Esther, on the other hand, isn't like that.

Every Saturday, we go to the club to swim; while little Jacob sleeps, I'll usually play a little tennis. I'll take sandwiches and some Gerber's baby food, which he devours instantly. If I take too long to get another spoonful into his mouth, he starts making little noises, as if to tell me to hurry up. Everyone's always amazed at how fast he finishes those little jars of food. He responds to just about any name I give him. Sometimes I'll call him Serafin, but I'll also say serpent, pencil, pen, shark.

My brother arrived back home yesterday. I'm so happy that he decided on his own to get out of there! He got off the plane crying; his handkerchief was soaked from so many tears. He was so anxious to see us . . . and to meet his little nephew. I thought that just maybe the letters I had sent him did some good. To the contrary, they just created problems.

"Just think," he said to Lalo, his brother-in-law and friend, "to tell me those things while I was living in a place where no one ever doubts their future, and where, in fact, it's your duty to serve. You're crazy, Sis! I really didn't appreciate getting your letters."

Now that Serafin is ten months old, I'm attending a class at the Institute once a week. There, Gabriel tells us not to make little machos out of our boys. And he keeps harping on the idea that all women must know how to fend for themselves, which is the first step toward independence.

"My mission is to make you aware," he explains. "That is, wake you up, get you going; and if some of you are unconscious, then show you that you are. To live is to take risks; there's no insurance against every eventuality."

He read one of Elena Jordana's poems: "We can be happy without drapes, a car, or money in the bank; we should feel free, like the butterflies, act crazy, let Spring surprise us, feel the sun, that's the way it should be, Señores and Señoras, boys and girls, my loving flowers."

That's no good. I'm not interested in working. I'm too lazy. But if I have to go to work someday, it has to be something I like to do, because this stuff about waiting on clients and having to smile hypocritically at someone just won't cut it.

Beatriz, Clarita, and Annette are really dazzled by Gabriel's lectures: they're going to finish high school and get jobs. Fortunately, their husbands agree. What a miracle! They received their certificates!

"As soon as you register for college prep, I'll do it too," I assured them.

Their mothers, who are Sephardic women with similar ideas to my mother's, never questioned their daughters' convictions; they, too, believed that the future consisted in becoming a bilingual secretary. So, all of them who finished middle school took Civilization and other classes at the Garsai School. Poor things! They have such a long way to go, but at least they've gotten a start. They haven't had it as bad as the others who had to get married, or should I say were *convinced* that they should get married, at fifteen years of age.

Lalo took little Jacob and me to my parents' house. Freddy is going downtown with Lalo. They're going to look at a store that they're buying together. As I'm getting the stroller out of the car, Freddy leans over to me:

"I'm only going with him to have breakfast at La Blanca; there's no way I want to lock myself up in a store like Dad did."

"Well, why are you going with him, then? What do *you* want to do?" I asked him.

"I just got back five days ago; I still haven't adjusted. I don't know what I want to do. Why is everyone pushing me?"

Dad comes running out with his lunch pail and a bag with plates. He gives me a quick kiss, and laughingly imitates his own father's bad humor.

"My-dad-can't-get-his-car-out-and-he's-fuming. Uba and your grandma are scared to death of the *zar*, so I've got to get over there before he does them in."

I barely enter the house and my mother pulls little Jacob from my arms; then she dances with him. She loves his dark eyes.

"We've never had them before in *our* family."

She hugs and kisses him with such force that the child yelps, trying to get back to my arms. Just then, fortunately, the phone rings. It's Rashelica la Puntuda, and she's curious to find out the latest gossip. She wants to know every little detail: how did Freddy get involved in the first place, and why did he come back from Israel? Whenever she calls, it's better to sit down. She's a meddler, says my mother, and resigns herself to telling the whole story.

"Now it's time for him to settle down. He went, and now he's back. That's fine. And he quit trade school; he didn't want to study. He only wants to work! So I say let him work at our store in

Lagunilla; he can help his father. Thank Heaven, Rashel, things aren't out of control anymore. Ever since Oshinica got married, we haven't had any problems with our kids. Well, one child may turn out better than another, but at least we're at peace right now. The only thing left now is to find a good bride for this young man of ours. Good grief, woman, he's got to have something in this world; he's even without a job. So, I told Moshón, go on, son, get involved with your brother, start a business with him; he'll help you and you'll be earning money in no time. Now Freddy . . . he's crazy. He doesn't want a store, and he doesn't care if he marries a Jewish girl. I wish God would have given him brains. And your daughter, how's she doing? Why don't you come over for a bite to eat at noon, I'm all alone here. And my sister-in-law from Monterrey is coming to play canasta. We'll wait for you to come to start."

My little serpent woke up with a fever this morning, just when I have a class with Gabriel. I gave him some medicine, but the problem is that Lalo got up late, and as much as I tried to get him moving, he just seemed to hang around. Putting on my dark blue cap—my hair was a mess—and a poncho, I was getting ready to leave before he was.

"I won't be long. While you're still here, just peek in on him. His fever's down, he's fine. He's going to sleep now. Faith, don't do anything but sit with him. Thanks."

"You're not going anywhere!" Lalo yelled.

"I'll be back in an hour and a half," I said, bolting out the door and running down the stairs.

He ran to the balcony. His eyes were about to pop out.

"I'm going to tell your mother!"

I arrived at the Institute only to discover that Gabriel wasn't giving his class today. I just about died, and while the other single girls were screaming, "No class, no class," I cried in front of the secretary.

"Why are you crying? Don't get upset; it's not so important."

"If you only knew what it took for me just to get here," I said faintly. "My son woke up with a fever, and my husband just about killed me for leaving home."

"Take it easy. Here, call home and ask how he's doing. And if he's okay, come with me and sit in on another class: it's a fiction-writing class with Elena Poniatowska."

"I can't imagine what the class could be about, but I've certainly heard of her."

I enjoyed the class. I was ever so quiet, very quiet, listening to the other ladies read their texts. Suddenly, feelings of panic disappeared. One of the women, Alicia, read a fragment of her novel. Angélica, who was quite pretty, read something interesting too, but another lady was stuffy and boring. All in all, an interesting experience. Every time Gabriel doesn't show up, which is quite often, they say, I'll sit in on this class.

Freddy is excited that he's is going into business with Moshón on Correo Mayor Street. I talked him into going to the theater to see *Thus Spoke Zarathustra*. When we arrived, I realized that he was wearing sandals. What a scandal! We must have looked like hicks. People were filing in and walking down the aisles to their seats. Then two young people walk through, announcing "First call, first call." I was surprised to see the stage without a curtain, and the actors, as if they were alone, were undressing and dressing in front of us. And there were no stage props. It was strange, to say the least!

"Hello, similar people," the four actors pronounced in unison, mockingly.

"Everyone who applauds will receive a prize: an aspirin," says one of them.

Zarathustra appears onstage without any clothes on, and the other actors, who could have been lawyers, architects, or engineers, are scandalized. They believe he's in a costume.

"We've covered ourselves so much that we don't recognize each other unless we have a costume on."

Zarathustra doesn't want to know about our sins; he only wants our warmth. Actor D enthusiastically proposes a beauty contest based on ears and necks. We're always in contests. Waiting for prizes and punishments.

I had never seen a play like that before. It was incredible; everything seemed so unpretentious. I'm used to the lavish and complicated scenery created by Manolo Fábregas; the wardrobes; the drama; the movie *The Happy Widow* that I liked so much; the actresses at the awards night, with all their smiles, hairdos; the leading men; tuxedos; fancy carpeting; new automobiles—in other words, pure pleasure.

But, here, in the Dance Theater, in the back of the auditorium, I'm speechless, unable to comprehend that they've created a play with such everyday naturalness. That's what I've never seen before, and all of a sudden it seems so distant and strange.

I don't know what's wrong with me, but I begin to tremble, my arms hurt, and my legs stiffen. I have no energy, I'm ready to cry. Suddenly Freddy and I turn to each other, looking frightened.

"Freddy, I'm shivering," I whispered.

"Me too," he answered.

"I love those whose souls are profound," says Carlos Ancira, alias Zarathustra, "even when they're wounded." Actors A, B, C, and D, accuse him of poisoning people's minds. They perform acrobatics in order to divert the audience from Zarathustra, he who is damned, he who is "Everyman."

My legs are killing me; I can't move.

"Who is the superior being?" I asked Freddy.

"He's just someone who manages to defend himself, the one who protects himself from being contaminated, the one who proposes the self against all that prevents him from becoming himself. He's so different that he becomes superior to everyone else," answers the person sitting next to him.

The acrobats keep trying to call attention to themselves by jumping into the air and falling to the ground. The actors, that is, this collection of mortal voices and bodies, are sickened by his destroyed body. They're upset. One of the acrobats should have prevented this moment, the moment when they see him like he truly is.

Zarathustra takes one of them into his arms and carries him to the mountain for burial.

"Your soul was dead long before your body; you lost nothing by dying."

My God, am *I* dead even though I'm still alive? If A, B, C, and D are dead, and I'm the same as they are, then I'm dead too.

Zarathustra wanders about aimlessly, carrying the acrobat's body. On the road, he becomes hungry and asks for food. They give him nothing, explaining what they shouldn't do in order to get what they have. Don't try to live, they said, only sacrifice that which will give you something you can be sure of.

"Whoever feeds the hungry, feeds his own soul," answers Zarathustra.

I'm not a part of the living anymore. I'm dead! I think to myself.

"I want to live again. Be alive!" I pronounce from my seat, brushing off my body with my hands. I need to cleanse myself, remove the dead cells. When did I stop living? I must have died little by little, while I was asleep, slowly, unknowingly. I died a natural death. Zarathustra! Take me with you! Za-ra-thus-tra! My arms and my legs are heavy, they pain me.

Zarathustra walks up to the base of a tree, buries the cadaver, and announces that he is going away: "I don't want to be an undertaker; I need companions who are alive."

I, too, need friends who are alive, and that's why we must resuscitate each other by massaging our hearts, giving mouth-to-mouth respiration. It's urgent! I'm dying! The ones left behind won't want to carry my body, but the dead must be buried.

"I'm tired of being poor," yells one of the actors, and I come out of my trance.

"The less we possess, the less we are possessed," answers Zarathustra, raising his voice. "They are but flies. They envy you because you have grown. Escape to your inner health. Your destiny is not to be a fly swatter. You can't find anyone until you have found yourself."

Zarathustra remains a bit longer on the mountain, because he has to learn, to discover, and to learn again.

"How could I ever hate mediocrity in people?" he says, coming down the mountain. "How could I think they were inferior? I need to meditate more in order to abandon darkness."

I had never seen a play with naked actors before. Seeing them undress didn't really bother me, but I was taken by their revelations that were so profound.

"Learn how to belong to yourself," yells Zarathustra.

I could visualize my notebooks from school that said on the

inside cover, "Belongs to . . ." First, to my mother, then to my husband, and lastly to my children. Will I belong to my children more than to myself for the rest of my life? How can I belong to myself now?

"I'm still alive," I said to my brother after the play.

"Eugenia . . . me too. Well . . . I think I am," he added, touching himself.

As we rushed down the stairs of the theater, we hugged each other and wept, proudly, smiling at his sandals. We started walking. Freddy shared his wet handkerchief with me.

My cousin Lety invited us to her house. My grandpa is proud to have such a religious granddaughter. She has a new hairdo, and frankly, you can hardly tell the difference, but she looks pretty. I still can't hide the fact that I've never forgiven her for not continuing her studies.

"You have to respect my feelings; this is the way I want to live," she implores me, while serving Turkish coffee, pastries, and baklava.

"But religious extremists don't respect those who aren't. They don't help women, they talk about the women's circle as if it were something impure, they forget that they were born from women. Whenever they want to pray, and if there aren't ten men around but there happen to be fifty women instead, we still don't count to make a chorus. Doesn't it make your blood boil that we're only good for having their children and keeping their houses in order? They've totally forgotten the little detail about trying not to make us feel inferior. They're not even conscious of it."

How I can respect them, I say to myself, when this cute, happy cousin of mine not only covers her hair but also now hides her desires, her ability to see; even her smile is constrained. She is totally obsessed with religion.

"It's different for each one of us," says my mom.

And she's always going back and forth from the kitchen, putting out her pretty dishes and then taking them away, making sure there's more milk, more meat, kosher chicken, and more meat. We sit down to eat. The women sit at a separate table. While the men look out of the corner of their eyes, they turn to continue their conversations with the other men. I always have the feeling that we're in their way, and that they'd have more fun if we weren't around. They talk endlessly about business and religion. That's all they talk about at my grandparents' house too. The women don't do that, thank you. After all, what could we contribute? We're just beings who are uninteresting and whose world is taken up with children. Lety, my aunt, and her mother-in-law serve the food.

And I get mad when I see my brothers, my dad, and my grandpa seated so far away. They must get some pleasure from knowing that I'm upset, and that I don't dare complain in someone else's house.

We're disgusting to them. We're disgusting to ourselves.

I try to catch my dad's eye, so he'll come to my rescue. He's the only one who understands me. The men in the family don't care about us. They must love their mothers in an exaggerated way and their daughters a little less, but always just enough.

"You see, they're very orthodox. You've got to try to understand them. Come with me," he says, excusing us and taking me by the hand.

Clarita joins us, and we stand defiantly next to him, next to the "Untouchables." It doesn't take long for my aunt, who speaks for her children, to come over to us:

"Oshinica, come here. If a man is standing between two

women, his ideas will just evaporate. They can't think straight."

"I think it's best for me to leave," I said to my father, almost crying. "It's too hard to fight for a place in this family. I don't want to come to any more of these family gatherings."

I'm also mad at my aunt, who completely brainwashed him.

For our mid-year papers, Rosita told us to choose a work about which we'd like to write something. I chose "The Crescent Moon," by Rabindranath Tagore. I've never read such a beautiful poem. It's dedicated to his son! And he's so sensitive. Like my classmates, I'm going to use transparencies and pictures of my kids; I can't wait for everyone to see them. I look at my older kids, and I can't believe that they've already gotten so big. Childhood is so short! I want to enjoy my younger ones before I find myself without anyone to hold in my arms.

I've just picked out what I'm going to use for the visuals. I took two rolls of film, but there were only four good pictures. How disappointing . . . and expensive, too! I'm depressed, so I've decided to take a photography course on Saturday mornings. Daniela can take something at the same time.

I can't believe it! I noticed that every one of those crazy things that Gabriel Weiss told us in class is starting to appear in songs by Serrat.

"Life's only worth living if you live it."

His latest album just came out.

SUNDAY.

Lalo almost went ballistic waiting in the car almost half an hour for us to go to the club. By the time I was ready, I was wiped out, but I had the food and the kids dressed, and they had their bathing suits, towels, and playthings. Lalo, the jerk, complains about me taking so long, and it doesn't even occur to him that things would go so much faster if he would lend a hand, but he'd never stoop that low.

SEVEN

This family of mine is spaced out: I bring them breakfast, and they eat in a trance, without tasting it; there's no reaction. I wonder if they liked it. My questions irritate them, because they're glued to the television set. I drive over to the lake with my littlest one, just to get out and go somewhere. When I come back, they're still in the same position: in their pajamas, unkempt, surrounded by dirty plates and a full ashtray.

I feed my little Serafín and he goes to sleep. My daughters and their father expect me to get them pillows and blankets, to peel them some fruit, to go out and buy a roasted chicken and some sweet bread at Elizondo's. They want to be comfortable every time someone scores a goal. I'm supposed to pick up everything that gets in their way—that is, clean up after them.

I prefer to read at night when the house is quiet, the phone has stopped ringing, no more ringing doorbells, the kids are snoring, the maid doesn't need any potatoes, milk, or meat, my husband doesn't want any more coffee or fruit, not even an ashtray, no one needs anything. They all go to sleep. No one sees me, no one needs me, no one scolds me, no one judges me. While they sleep, I'm wide awake, alert.

This is when I'm free, so I read, I think, I cover myself up, I uncover myself. I'm my own boss; this is my time. Even the TV has given up the ghost; there's no one around to switch you on. What can you do to me now? Your screen is dark, no one will turn you on and bring you to life. But I'm able to illuminate myself without any help. I have my own inner light. Now that we're alone together, just you and me, who's the one in control now?

The courses at the community center have already started; there are even puppet classes for children outside in the garden. I signed up Jessy, and I take Estela or Felipa to watch little Jacob. One of them will feed him breakfast while he sits next to his big sister, who works at making a puppet.

The first thing we learned was to develop black-and-white pictures; then we critiqued each other's work. There's about forty of us from different social classes and ages, which makes it perfect, because each one of us has something different to offer for the critiques. This allows me to view divergent worlds, to discover new ways of looking at life. Everything seems nicer in photographs; perhaps it's because we remove the subject from its surroundings.

"You have to learn to see," says Lázaro, the teacher.

Since there are so many of us in the class, we develop our pictures every other week. I was assigned to use the photo lab on Thursday afternoons. Now that they won't let cars into Chapultepec Park, the first day I had to walk to the community center, which embarrassed me; but after four or five times, I'm comfortable enough without feeling like I'm looking to get picked up by those guys we used to see when we'd go on those boring rides in my grandparents' car with the family tribe.

I had this idea that to walk through the park when no one else was out for a stroll was a signal to get picked up.

Now my dad prefers to go to Pedregal Park, but it's far away and he only goes on weekends. His friends who used to go to Chapultepec Park also switched. I take my children on Sundays; we get there shortly after daybreak and smell the eucalyptus trees. On those humid outings, we wipe the dew from the rose petals and rub it on our faces. My dad says it's the best skin protection there is, and it makes it soft. Once we're up on the lookout, my dad introduces us to Don Pablo.

"How old do you think he is?" asks my dad.

"He must be your age, Dad."

"No way, he just had his seventy-fifth birthday. It's amazing, don't you think? He's been coming here every day for the last seven years; for him, it's easy, because he lives nearby in San Gerónimo."

We started out near "La Bota." They've given names to all the paths throughout the park. There are long trails and short ones; some of them cut through the zoo and others go around the outside. You either return the way you came, or you take another route that cuts back into the original trail. My dad is determined not to grow old, and he believes the only way to fight off looking old is to exercise. He's frightened of old age, and that's why he rows, swims, or plays tennis almost every day. No matter if it rains or thunders, he doesn't care how he arrives to work in Lagunilla.

While I was walking along, I came upon an enormous, beautiful spider web. It was unbelievable! I saw that a splendid

Monarch butterfly was trapped in the web. Its wings were a mosaic of orange and black. Still alive, it struggled with desperation to free itself.

Why did I just take a picture of it instead of letting it go? Was I afraid of the spider's anger if I did? So I didn't. I went away with a picture of a trapped insect.

The people at the Institute organized a field trip to Palenque and Catemaco. Even though I had no hopes of going, I talked to Lalo about it and told him I wanted to go.

While he didn't respond, he did look at me with hatred. At the park one day, I told my dad about what had happened, even though I knew he'll always say that the wife should obey her husband.

"Go," he responded nonchalantly.

I wasn't sure if the money I had been saving for a rainy day was going to be enough for the trip, and my dad didn't dare offer anything either, probably because he didn't want them to accuse him of being an accomplice. He can't ever openly support me. I didn't ask him for any help either, but his face lit up when I told him that my piggy bank had just enough to cover the cost of the trip.

"By the way, Dad, why do you acquiesce so easily to everything my grandfather orders you to do? Why are you so afraid to tell him that you want to take a trip? For five years now we've been sticking a 50-watt bulb on your birthday cake instead of candles. Don't you think it's time that he showed a little respect for you?"

"Listen, my dear, your grandfather is already too old to change his ways. How long do you think he'll be with us? He's already accustomed to the way I am, and so am I. Frankly, I like being this way."

"You ought to yell back at him sometime. Just say no to him. You're not responsible for taking care of his business. Tell him you are going to Israel and that you've never been back to the place where you were born. Wouldn't you like to see your cousins?"

On the day I was leaving, he came by dressed in his workout clothes and took me to the bus that was taking us to Palenque. He even accompanied me to my seat.

Wow! Our country is so beautiful! And all that tropical jungle is ours, too? How is it possible that I hadn't even heard of that marvelous area? What a closed, small world I've lived in all my life! Club, home, stores, club. I'm really happy that I'll get to see Catemaco and listen to folk music, like the *jarocha,* on this moon-lit night where the waters are sweet and calm.

At daybreak, we were already on a launch listening to the sounds of the lagoon. Several other married women came along, but none from Elena's workshop. They had all been at Angélica's house in Tepoztlán.

At sunset, while we were still walking around the ruins, which were surrounded by that age-old silence, some women from our group played flutes and other pre-Hispanic instruments, all of which allowed us to perceive the magic attached to the place.

I bought handbags, skirts, and pants made out of rough cloth that was embroidered. Lalo and my neighbors are going to think everything is horrible. Our art teacher is really handsome; everyone wants to sit next to him. It's wonderful to see all this happen!

I wrote a postcard to Lalo.

"I want to take this trip again, but with you. I want you to enjoy what I've seen during the last five days. Don't be upset that I made this trip without you. Just think, I was hoping to see a waterfall, and I've seen two already. And what a pair! One is beautiful, the other is breathtaking. Which one is the best? I have enjoyed the trees so much, and I've seen a ton of them. The flowers that we couldn't find in Mexico City are all over the place here; they're everywhere. Also, there are lakes, rivers, oceans, mountains, jungles, ruins, and towns.

"I'll return with a lot of love for you, the kids, and everyone else. Let's get out more, let's learn more about nature. What great medicine life provides for us.

"Just because I came alone doesn't mean I love you less.

"Dearest Lalo, please accept my invitation to come back here."

The writing class is moving to another location; Trueb's wife is adding some space to her new house. Since they're all from the south side, it's closer for many of the participants. Elena is going to teach there. The class will be three hours long, and they'll bring in other writers. They invited me to go with them to the San Miguel Inn, at the corner of Reforma and María Luisa.

I've been having to put up with Easter for years, and one more is coming around. You can't go to the movies, because all they show are boring religious movies; and it's the same on TV. If we hadn't made a reservation to eat somewhere, it would have been impossible. Just about all of our friends go to Disneyland or to their summer places in Cuernavaca. Why is Easter so oppressive?

"Lalo, I want to visit some new places in Mexico. Why do we always have to go to Acapulco?"

"I'm not interested in anywhere else. Go yourself."

"Yeah, sure, typical: 'go yourself,'" I respond, hating every time he says no to me.

"I'm fed up with him," I told Dori, "there's no way I can get him interested in going anywhere in Mexico."

"We're going to take a bus to Mérida, Cozumel, and Isla Mujeres. Why don't you come with us? It's a long trip, so be prepared. Bring lots of books to read."

I spoke to Lalo about it.

"Go ahead, but leave little Jacob with me."

It's a deal, we're going. Jessy, Deborah, and Shai, who is Dori's youngest, are elated. So are we. Her husband is great: he's willing to see other parts of Mexico. They make such a good couple! They're totally together. I wonder how they happened to meet?

We got reservations in a good hotel. The kids swam, jumped off the diving board, and whooped it up. We had gone on vacation with Dori once before, when the kids were really small. After visiting Uxmal, Chichén, and other places, I decided to strike out on our own and discover more places. We agreed to meet in Cozumel afterward. Unfortunately, as soon as we arrived in Mérida—we had arrived first—Jessy came down with paratyphoid fever. We didn't know that the water could be contaminated.

"Is this the first time you're traveling by yourself?" asked our friends. In Mérida, the girls wanted to have not only their own lunch boxes, but some for their cousins as well. We bought six. I was fascinated with the Dutch cheese balls, so I bought four more. From then on I went around carrying this cumbersome bag, but, ah!, my hair dryer, I'm glad I brought it. Still, it's useless, but I thought it would be indispensable for the trip. I never use it. If I weren't such a pack rat, I would have gotten rid of it along the way; I almost couldn't carry everything.

The night we left for the island, the notably second-class bus dropped us off on a deserted beach called Ciudad del Carmen at five o'clock in the morning. The bus driver told us to wait for the boat to arrive. Terrified, we sat down on the sand. Some stray dogs kept us company. At daybreak, we saw a small boat in the distance. With all the stuff I was lugging with me, it was hard as hell to get everything on board. Everyone was amazed at my sense of practicality: I had the girls, a pile of lunch boxes, and the cheese. My God, I was worn out from having to go back and forth, taking my stuff out to the famous little boat.

We got a room in a first-class hotel, because, well, Lalo gave us a ton of money. I told them at the desk that we'd be staying four days, but then I thought to myself, "Why should we have to leave if we're having a good time?"

Then one morning, when I was stretched out on the sand at the beach, someone from the hotel came over to me: "Señora, you'll have to leave the hotel, because we're expecting a large excursion."

Without getting haughty, I replied, "Why, of course. Surely."

Then I began to call around to some of the other better hotels. They were all full. Feeling somewhat less dignified, I spoke with the manager about the possibility of negotiating a price so we could stay. It didn't work. The famous excursion arrived at the hotel, so I decided to rent a small beach taxi and we loaded up: lunch boxes, cheese balls, hair dryer, and our suitcases. Then the girls climbed in. At least we weren't out on the street. The only bad part was Jessy's fever.

When it finally got dark, we got a room in an old hotel in the downtown area. There was no air conditioning, but at least we had a roof over our heads. Since Jessy had to get a shot every twelve hours, we went to the Red Cross, which was three blocks away, at midnight. The other girls whined about having to stay in the room alone, so here I was walking down the street with three girls who were half asleep, whining, upset, and scared. But we had gone on an excursion on a yacht, and you can't just experience this blue paradise without learning about the rest of the island. What I loved the most was driving the little safari buggy around very fast; we went from one end of the island to the other, soaking up the air, the landscape, and the exuberant vegetation.

Some days later, we returned to Mérida and bought some clothes that are native to the area. I fell in love with the embroidery. Lalo had recommended that we go back on a plane, but there was nothing available for two days. Lacking the energy and the desire, we stayed on, only to invent things to do in which we had absolutely no interest.

Our two men were waiting for us at the airport. I was so happy to see my handsome little blond with long, lank hair, but he showed no emotion upon seeing us. He hadn't even missed us.

I admit that I had a difficult time of it after we had left Dori, but it couldn't have been any other way, especially now that I have the opportunity to be free and heed Miguel's admonitions.

"No pain, no gain," they say.

When I go to Lalo's store, I walk down the long corridor past his employees to his office. Now I'm important, like Fortuna and Anita, the wives of the jewelers for whom I worked when I was single. I worked then, it should be noted, not out of necessity, but to have fun and to learn something new.

"My wife has no need to work," states my husband proudly. "Is there anything you could ever need?"

Yes, there is: freedom, I thought, and the time to spend it without feeling guilty, without having to wait for the right moment to mention it, without the fear of being denied my rights, without having to report on everything I do, but I wouldn't dare say that to him. Besides, what's the use? I don't know anything except how to take care of my children. It's easy to live the way I do, and there's no way I can chip away at my husband's sense of pride. Two or three of my friends who work also lie about it: "I have no reason to work," they repeat. "I do it just to have something to do."

While I was there, I decided to check on Freddy at his store nearby. I get knots in my stomach just seeing him trapped in that place. That's the last thing he wanted to do, but there he is, good-humored and all. His friends work close by, so it's not so bad after all. However, he has forgotten that he wanted something else in life. I didn't say anything to him, because I didn't want to upset him. Then for sure he'd end up never knowing what he wants to do.

I'm thinking about taking something to read for the writing class. I wrote about half a page, but I'd be crazy to read it in front of the others. Everyone was happy with the new location. Alicia opened a bottle of wine before the first class began.

I took a chance and read the short letter I had written to León Felipe about the poem he wrote to his grandfather. Elena said something unusual: she thought that *my* grandfather sounded like an interesting character, and that I should write something about him for the next class. They gave me some ideas about things they would like to know about him; they were extremely curious, because he's from a world that's unknown to them. I hadn't realized that I was the only Jewish person in the class. It's funny they would think my grandfather is interesting, when in reality he's the most boring person I've ever known.

If my little Serafin, who's always hungry, gets up and sees me still asleep, he'll go to the kitchen, put a chair next to the stove, climb up on it, crack an egg and put butter in a skillet, and cook it. Quietly, without making any noise, he eats his breakfast. I just love watching this little guy standing on the chair fixing himself something to eat. And I love to take pictures of him!

Finally, we convinced Lalo to go out to the country for the day. It being Sunday, he gets up, takes a shower, and puts on his white pants. When we get there, he won't sit down to eat because he'll get his pants dirty. He stands up to eat. I give him a pillow to sit on, and he blesses us with a few minutes together. He certainly isn't a person in love with the outdoors. We decided that we would come back without him sometime; we could do it just about any day of the week. That way we won't have to be begging him for weeks on end and possibly provoking his ire. No matter what, he's just going to say, "I'm not going." But we need to be loving, and caring, and . . .

Whenever it's warm outside and it's a pretty day, my little Jacob always says, "Let's go to the park and eat oranges without seeds." Then he goes running to the kitchen, gets a basket out of the cupboard and puts in the salt shaker, napkins, plastic dishes, a tablecloth, apples, a bottle opener, and, of course, the oranges. Once that's ready, all we have to do is buy a roasted chicken, French-fried potatoes, and drinks.

On the way, we sing some children's songs. We really have a good time together.

Once we're at the park, we start looking for an empty spot. "Here!"

"No, just a little farther."

"Let's find a place with lots of trees."

Serafin carries the toys and drawing materials, Daniela gets the food, and I bring the drinks.

We spend a lot of time at the park instead of being cooped up inside the apartment; we can hear the birds chirping and look at the white butterflies fluttering around in pairs.

"Daddy is missing something really nice, isn't he?"

Lalo returns late at night, tired and worn out. We eat dinner in front of the TV, talk during the commercials, and then he falls asleep. And when he gets up in the morning, he's hard to deal with; I wish he wouldn't wake up until everyone else has left the house.

So when I get up—and I'm hardly able to move—I cover the telephone with a pillow and I get the kids ready for school, asking them not to wake up their dad. I carefully place some juice and fruit on Lalo's nightstand, hoping he'll see it when he opens his eyes. Then I get dressed, put my purse by the front door, and fix breakfast. When Faith has the radio turned up, I never know when he's getting up. But he's probably in a bad mood anyway.

What will he bitch about today? I hate, simply hate, breakfast time!

"You're going to wake him up."

"I don't care."

Then little Jacob wakes up crying, so I pick him up and hand him to Faith.

"Dress-him-fast-and-take-him-to-buy-something, now!" I bark at her in a low voice, while turning on the record player to drown out the yelling.

"And I don't even want to go to your dad's house for dinner. With that innocent smile of his, you'd think he couldn't kill a fly. Everyone lives to take care of *him*."

He's giving us his litany; I'm glad I'm ready to escape, but I can't prevent my son from hearing it all. At least the others have already left.

"And why didn't you wait for me on Sunday?"

"They were dying of hunger, so they sneaked into the kitchen and grabbed whatever they could—potatoes, bread, avocados. It was already half past five, and you know that we eat at four."

I grab my purse and head running for the stairs, fall down and then pick myself up along the way. I'm already two floors ahead of him, four, three, two, the only way he could get me would be in the elevator. I pray he isn't waiting for me on the ground floor, because I'm furious at him. I don't think he'll do anything while he's wearing his robe.

I finally make it outside, and I can hear him screaming from our balcony on the sixth floor.

"I pity you if you ever come back!"

The doorman is washing cars. At the corner I hear my son yelling, "Mommy, Mommy, go to the Diplomat!" I can see him on the balcony. Then I begin running, and I run all the way to my dad's house; by then he'll have gotten home from rowing, and he'll be eating a big breakfast because he's always so hungry.

Just before getting there, I slow down, so I won't look too upset. My dad, fresh and happy, has just showered after his workout and gives me a cold kiss before putting on his suit coat.

"Dad, you're cold. Couldn't you at least take a hot shower?"

My mother is fixing breakfast: the white serving plate is starting to fill up with food, the eggplant is frying, and she's dipping more in the egg batter. I fix a meat sandwich.

"Put some lemon juice on it," says my mom to him. "Don't you want to try a little of this?" checking to see if it's fried enough. "It's a little sweet."

"Yes, Sarica, but first I'm going to get some bread at Elizondo's. Do you want to come with me, Oshinica?"

"No, I'll stay here. I want to get this recipe from Mom; I just love it. You put in tomato sauce and rice, don't you?"

"Yes, but you have to cook it with a low flame, so that the rice will cook thoroughly. When it's almost done, just add a spoon of sugar at the end."

Little Jacob finally started kindergarten. At thirty-five, with no more kids at home, I feel a terrible emptiness inside. No way I'll have any more; they'll just end up leaving me, too. At noon I get all fixed up to pick him up; then on alternate days I'll take him swimming, to the market, or rowing. I'll go out somewhere with him, but I'll never go alone to the park to get an ice cream cone. And what's going to happen when he goes to grade school, and I don't have to pick him up until later? I've got to find something to do, because by the time I'm fifty years old, I'll be totally bored and all I'll do is talk about my kids, just like the women who are overly proud of their children and grandchildren. Have I already forgotten that I wanted to be an interesting old person like León Felipe? In order to do that, you have to start early in life: if someone's bored at forty, won't she be that way when she gets old?

I still remember that day perfectly, the one when I was still wearing my wedding dress and I understood then that I didn't want to happen to me what had happened to my mother-in-law when the last of her children got married. I quickly understood that I should prepare myself so that when my kids left me, I would have a life beyond just being a mother.

My little boy likes airplanes so much that when I go to pick him up at his school, I tell him the name of an airline and he comes running at me like a plane. I bend down and wait for him with open arms; he grabs me so hard that he almost topples me over, hitting me in the face. It's the right moment to give him a big, comforting hug. He's always on the move, so my airplane hug doesn't last long.

I called Gabriel Weiss, and we went to his house on Sinaloa Street. He met us at the door, holding a miniature dog that was sticking its head out of his jacket pocket. Even though he has long hair, he got flustered the other day because someone had yelled "hippie" at him with such vehemence that it seemed he had done something personal to the guy. He's going overseas to study . . . so there go my classes.

EIGHT

We went to Cuernavaca to see where our friends had bought a house. They go there every Sunday. It's a compound of eight houses, and they share a swimming pool and a clubhouse. At night the adults play cards; if they don't have enough players, they just call over to their neighbors, and all of sudden there's a bunch of people ready to play. During vacation, the wives and the children remain there, so there're always enough players; the husbands come on the weekends. I think we need to make our lives more carefree. We need to escape from the routine of work. Please, let's do something new in life. I hope we can buy something there, even if we have to pay it off with a loan.

"We're better off in Mexico City," suggests Lalo. "Get Cuernavaca out of your head. I'm going to make an offer on that house in Herradura."

It's so beautiful, and the two things I like best are the chimney in the study that looks out to the yard in front, and the complete kitchen that looks out to the back.

"It doesn't have the tree you wanted," says Lalo, "but we'll plant one."

Once he made a down payment, they gave us the keys. As soon as I receive my allowance, I'm going to put in two posts for the hammock. It'll be marvelous! Now we'll have a place to eat breakfast in the garden.

We're already moved in. My mother helped out a lot, but all she wanted to do was throw things away.

"You keep a lot of junk. You need to put things in order."

If I didn't watch her, she would have thrown everything in the garbage.

We bought a bunch of plants in Xochimilco. Lalo planted a tree, and he waters it; all he needs to do now is write a book.

That afternoon my family left me working in the house. They returned later with a Saint Bernard puppy. They say they get really big. What a pain! I'm trying to make friends with our new neighbors. It was hard to leave our apartment building, but how was I not going to be happy in this new house? The kids just love the dog, and they talk to it as if it were a new baby.

"Hey, woman, get up, it's almost nine. I'm hungry."

"But it's Sunday, and there's nothing to do. I'm really sleepy. Just a few more minutes. And turn down the TV, it doesn't have to be that loud."

"Felipa, Felipa! Darn it, they're never around when you need them."

"Sir?"

"Bring me my coffee and the newspaper! Can you believe it? Someone just listened to me."

"Take it easy. You don't have to slam the door."

"I didn't do it on purpose. The door to the bathroom closes by itself."

"Felipa! What are you going to make for breakfast?"

"You mean *you* don't know? You know what I'm hungry for? Some rolled tortillas with beans and some of those pastries that you bought the other day."

"Okay, okay, I'm getting up."

"That-a-girl," he says, looking at the *TV Guide.* "There's a soccer match being played in Los Angeles this afternoon."

"It's eleven o'clock already. Breakfast is getting cold. The tortillas are ready . . ."

"Wait, wait, this program is just about over."

"That's what you said twenty minutes ago."

"Hey, bring everything up here."

"There's not enough room for all of us; besides, we'd have to haul everything upstairs. The table is set and it's sunny outside."

"C'mon, bring it upstairs.

"Hey, you're beautiful, honey, you brought it all up here. It's a little crowded, but we can snuggle up to each other. Come over here, girls. Pass the green chile, please."

"You get them yourself. Today is Felipa's day off, and she's already left. If she leaves late, she gets upset. Are you going to drink milk or coffee?"

"This is great, woman, just great! Would you cover me up with that blanket your mom made? After breakfast, I'm ready for a little nap. Sit up, would you? I want to put my head on your lap. Now, rub my head."

"Now I've got to clean up this mess. I don't like to leave dishes all over the place."

"Darn it, I can't get anything from you. You're always finding some excuse. That's it, now you've got it. I love it when you rub my head."

"Shoot, the telephone. And the kids are playing outside. Let me up, I'll answer it. Or do you want to get it?"

"No way. I'm worn out."

"Hey, Chubby . . . it's your mother. She wants to speak to you."

"Tell her I'm fine. Invite them over for dinner."

"Chubby! There's no food in the house. Maybe there's some coffee," I tell him in a low voice.

"We can do whatever. Let's just buy something, or we can go out, or we can order Chinese food."

"You talk to her; it's *you* she wants to talk to."

"Damn it, I can never rest in this house. Don't you understand that I'm tired? Sure, sure, while you spend the week loafing around. Hurry up, you still have to rub my head. Tell her to come to dinner! And bring the tweezers. I want you to pull out some gray hairs."

"Hey, you're an old man: that's over forty gray hairs. I'm tired of doing this; besides, I don't want to watch soccer. I'm going to water the plants in the garden. I haven't had time for two days. Come on, help me with this stuff!"

"Are you crazy? I'm just fine right here. Okay, then, order take-out. My parents should be coming soon. Why don't you set the table out in the garden . . . and make a pitcher of lemonade."

"Hey, they said they don't deliver today. What now?"

"Here are your choices: open some cans of food or pick up a couple of roasted chickens."

"Did you enjoy the meal? It was great, wasn't it? Now we'll have some coffee. I love staying at home on Sundays. The restaurants are always full, and the service is lousy. Maybe you can come next Sunday, too. Tell my brothers to bring their kids, too. Wherever there's food for eight, there's enough for eighteen. We really enjoy spending time at home now. Yep, on Sundays we rest. Right, honey?"

Through a window I can see the mountains dotted with houses in the far-off distance. Yes, this is all very nice, to have all this beautiful scenery and this attractive fireplace, but once you're out here, there's no place to go. It's all houses and nothing else, not even a bakery, or anyone out walking. At night, not even a soul is out. What the hell are we doing here? How did I come to end up here? Just because this is the popular thing to do these days? I live miles and miles away from my sisters and my parents. The closest store is three miles away, and if the car breaks down, you're finished. Whenever the seamstress comes to the house and she runs out of thread, I have to take the car to a nearby town . . . which I love to do, especially on Sundays. There's always a Sunday market, lots of people, food stalls, and games. Then get back home and there're no cloves, so off I go again, another three miles there and five to get back. But I'm a quick learner: before I return, I remember to buy what we need to eat: tortillas, bread, milk, or whatever else I can find; and, of course, I come racing back to fix something to eat. Now we need a refrigerator; clearly, we'll have to learn to live more efficiently.

"Look, you live in the country now," says my mother. "Why did you choose to live at the end of the world? And such a big house! You'll spend your life cleaning it."

"Every woman who sees a psychoanalyst ends up getting a divorce," theorized Mari, when she heard that I've been going to therapy.

Ever since he's been criticizing me for playing cards, things have gotten worse between us.

"What classes are you talking about now?" grumbled Lalo.

So what the hell am I supposed to do at home if all the kids are at school? Sit around and imagine things? I should be using my imagination *for* something. And there's him, looking at himself all day long in the mirror, having just bought three new suits.

"Do I look good in these suits? Do you think anyone notices me?"

He and his friend Jacobo flirt a lot now, as if they were single. It's their age: they just turned forty.

How dare he ask me those things! I try to be happy, but my life is totally dependent on the way he feels at any given moment. Maybe this is normal among married people. I need to reread that poem by Borges that says, "I have committed the worst sin that a man can commit: I haven't been happy."

For him to say that at eighty years old is tragic; if my life doesn't change soon, I'll rewrite that poem at seventy and add a few stanzas. Borges and I will be co-authors of the same poem. What matters now, though, is that I'm alive, still young and attractive—well, maybe not that attractive, but I can compete.

How can I explain to you, Mom, that time destroys everything; it's in the air, like dust. It's illusive, it envelops us, it buries us.

In two years, I'll be forty. It's time now to be what I want to be, to become something. If not now, when? What I want more than anything in the world is to stop time; that's why I take pictures obsessively, in order to capture and preserve my kids' childhood.

That's why I asked her what she did yesterday.

"Nothing. Took a walk. Went to see a neighbor. We talked all afternoon. I killed some time that way," she explained.

While Lalo is asking me—that is, forcing me—to transform myself into his personal slave, I'm busting my brains thinking about what I can do to achieve that celebrated state of economic independence without destroying my life. My husband's frustration continues to grow; he attacks me instead of thinking of something that allows me to grow or do what I like. And I don't like to make love anymore; I'll use any excuse to say, "Not today."

"Are you still working on that book?"

"And what am I supposed to be doing? I'm not sleepy, and what's it to you anyway? Instead of tossing and turning, I'd rather take advantage of this time. There's no noise anywhere; the kids are in school. It gives me great joy to be able to read in the mornings. If I get up, I won't read, because then I'm trapped with so many things to do."

"What? Can't you do anything else? Don't you get bored? Why hasn't she brought my fruit to me?" he protests furiously while turning the TV on at full volume.

"I'll bring it myself," I say, struggling to put my robe on.

I come back furious, with the serving tray and the newspaper.

"I'm sick and tired of watching you read all the time."

"Reading and learning make me happy. Susan's mother said that if I want my children to be happy, the first thing is to be happy myself. Yes, Lalo, I want to learn to be happy, to discover what it is that gives me pleasure, satisfaction . . . you should as well. Go out and find your own happiness, look beyond just me."

"To be happy . . . what makes me happy is to make money for you and the kids. That señora is crazy; her daughter, too."

"I don't want to knit anymore. Do you remember how I used to knit so much?" I tell him, putting down the newspaper and covering myself from seeing the news on the TV.

"That wimp Ochoa is a jerk," he says.

"I've already said it, but I can't believe how they squeeze so much out of the news, and the people just fall for it."

I watch Lalo eat his fruit and drink his coffee ever so slowly, without taking his eyes off the television screen.

I hate television; I would like to destroy it, beat it to death. I hate it more than . . . I don't know.

Little Esther has piano lessons on Tuesdays, gymnastics and swimming on Mondays and Wednesdays. On Fridays, the older ones take sculpture classes. Fortunately, Dori's children do too, so we carpool. It's far away, but it's worth it: today they made little dogs and faces out of clay; sometimes they paint them too. The things they make just fascinate me. Then, after I drop them off, my littlest one and I go either to the park or to the movies.

"Doctor, I'm trapped. No, I just can't up and leave that man. He has told me over and over again that if we get divorced, I'll spend the rest of my life in misery. Just now, for him to give me enough money for the kids' classes at the beginning of every month, I have to see him almost spit in my face. Jessy is really advanced in her piano classes; she's been at it for four years, she's given several concerts, and this year I would like to send her to music camp."

"And what is going to happen to those kids if they don't take piano classes, swimming, gymnastics? Anything?" asks the doctor seriously.

" . . . it's true, nothing. Nothing will happen to them. One can live without those classes. When I was young, I did my homework in the afternoon, played outside, and watched TV. It's true . . . they'll survive without all those extra activities. I just want to give them everything: when Jessy turned two I started her on ballet lessons; when she could draw a circle and a straight line, I figured she was ready for art classes. I found a super teacher, and she was the only child among a group of adults. Everyone marveled at how well she could draw. And I was her mother. I'm so proud of my children, it's almost embarrassing to say it. I'll show you her drawings someday. I have them framed. It's been . . . let's see, yes, I've been doing this for fifteen years. This change is going to be difficult for them and for me. But if their father punishes me by taking away their classes . . . then he'll have to live without them."

My God, what a relief! I just alleviated the fear that they might not have any more classes.

I remember now, it's true, that I was prevented from moving on because I was worried about paying for camp, and I didn't want them to be stopped from going. Last month, it was having to buy books at the beginning of the school year, and now I'm held back because Felipa's salary has to be paid. From the looks of it, this has been like dieting: there's something every day that hinders me from doing what I want. There will always be expenses.

I'll never escape.

I'm glad I went to see *Waiting for Godot* at the theater. They had talked about this play at the Institute. I, too, am waiting for Godot in order to do what I want to do; it's just that life is going to pass me by while I'm waiting. Paralyzed by pretexts, lacking protection and security, says Samuel Beckett, I'll neither leave Lalo nor confront the unknown. I want Serafín to grow up a little more; I don't want to separate him from his father while he's so young. Jessy should finish out the year, and little Esther . . . on our way back from Acapulco will be better; to go on vacation without a husband won't work.

We're back, but how am I going to tell him now, Rosh Hashanah is coming up soon, and the whole family will know about it. Better afterwards. If I don't want to lose anything, I'm not going to gain anything either. I have to take my chances.

I'll get a divorce so that the unknown will become a part of my life, too. And this "something unknown," will it come if I continue waiting for Godot? And what if it comes when I'm old, and this freedom is of no use to me? My mother has said, "When you turn your face, you've gotten old." And here I am turning forty. It's better now than when I turn fifty.

This is the third time I've taken something I've written to the writing class. I wrote about a dinner at Sabbath.

"What does *atavanado* mean?" asks Elena.

"Something like 'upset, mad,'" I responded. "It's Ladino, the way my mother talks. It's strange that no one here understands it. That's why it came to me so naturally; I had no idea that they wouldn't understand those words. It's the old Spanish that the Jews spoke when they were expelled from Spain in 1492."

They thought those words sounded quaint. They seemed melodious, and interesting. Next time I'm going to write something using a lot of those words. They might find that amusing.

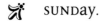 SUNDAY.

I brought home some delicious goodies for breakfast. Lalo didn't even hear me come in. He was on the telephone with his mommy, feeling sorry for himself. I sat down and listened.

"She doesn't listen to a thing I tell her; I eat alone, I watch TV alone. Who wouldn't be interested in watching Mannix, soccer, or like right now, a billiards competition? She doesn't like to be with her family; she just goes to her room. She's just like her brothers and sisters, they only care about themselves. She never does anything for me. But it's all going to end soon, because I'm going to give her hell. She goes to that Institute three mornings a week, and she still wants us to go out. She can go out if she wants. Two of her friends from the apartment complex are already divorced, and that's what she'll end up doing, too. Last Sunday she went with her cousin Alegre to a show at a club, because she got bored with my being tired all the time. 'All you'll find there are deadbeats, I'll show you,' I told her. This woman won't stop; she wants me to take her on trips, to the movies, and to the parks, because she likes to see the greenery. She won't let me live my life! Ah, yes, she wants me to have a hobby. Why? If she only knew how hard I work, she'd stop pestering me. I don't have any clothes anymore. The servants steal us blind. One of these days I'm going to send them packing; then let's see what happens. They serve Mexican food for breakfast, can you imagine? At that hour? I'd prefer to go to some restaurant; after all, I can pay for it now. She's losing me, and she's going to regret it. For some time now I haven't even been coming home to eat dinner, and it's been at least two months since I've had breakfast here. Who does she think she is? She's going to end up alone with her books. Why do I go on like this? I could be happy with another woman, who would treat me like a king. She's not even a real woman."

◇ ◇ ◇

I was surprised to get a call from Daisy Asher inviting me to participate in her photography class; Becky must have told her that I had taken a course at the community center. She doesn't live far from home, and it's twice a week. I really couldn't say no, so I went.

I arrived at 5:50 P.M. Her maid let me in. Becky's brother, Enrique, was already there with his two kids. I felt out of place, but I was ready to begin the class. Just about everyone knew each other, so I just walked around looking at the house. The chauffeur was taking Daisy's daughter, who's about four, and her two older children, to the club. As far as I can tell, she's divorced. Then I saw a bunch of posters, one of which said in English, "Long Live Sex!" Another one had pictures of a couple in all the positions. How embarrassing to look at them in front of Becky's children, even though they didn't seem to care in the least. My God, how can you hang posters like those with kids around? I guess they're used to it. On one table there was a collection of nice candles and a Turkish pipe that made me imagine nights of lust, smoke, music, and darkness. The ivy growing across the ceiling hypnotized me. Her house is certainly different from any other I've seen. Becky always talks about her friend Daisy, who had been a model. She must be beautiful, I thought as she came down the stairs, petite, wearing jeans, a tightly fitting T-shirt, small breasts, no bra, long black hair, brown eyes, and a cute smile. Everyone there seemed to be good friends of hers. After introducing her assistant, she explained what the course was all about; the last month will be dedicated to taking pictures of nudes, all models. If Lalo knew about Daisy, he'd kill me. I won't mention anything about the nudes.

Her first class went well: we learned how to use the camera, put in a roll of film, and choose the lenses. I grew to like her—

she's so sweet. But how can she walk around without a bra on, in front of her friends, and her assistant, and have books of nudes everywhere?

The next morning, the girls came into our bedroom. I was so tired that I couldn't get up. They tried to talk to me; they poked me.

"Maybe she's dead," said little Esther nonchalantly.

I woke up from fright.

I hardly ever see my cousin Lety anymore. She moved to Polanco, and since she's not allowed to use the car on the Sabbath, she can't eat at my grandparents' house. I told her to bring her child to little Esther's birthday, but she can't ever go anywhere on Saturdays because they've become completely orthodox. Well, that's religion for you! It pulls people together who are like themselves, but it separates them from those who aren't.

"You don't respect those who aren't as religious as you," I told her.

"But you don't either, Oshinica," said Lety. "Really, my husband and I enjoy Saturdays. They're different, they're special days for us. We take a break from things, they're our days to be together."

My friend Frida is a congresswoman representing Jalapa. She was just here for a few days and took me to see the Camus play *The*

Just Assassins. It takes place in Russia, but I'm not sure if it was before, during, or after the Revolution.

As I watched the play unfold, I began to feel a need to find new inner strength. The protagonists were ready not only to lose their car and home but also their lives in order to defend their ideals. I don't want to remain quiet in order to preserve *my* security.

I felt like my head was being pulled from my neck. Even thought I tried to look normal, my neck was beginning to look like a swan's. At the end of the play, two people were dead: they had chosen it over betrayal.

I don't know how long it had been, but I was sitting up so straight that it seemed like I had swallowed a stick.

"*You're* upset? How can you leave such a good husband? You've got a house, a car, two servants, a man, and everyone respects you. You live like a queen. Listen to me, you're not dumb, but get a hold of yourself, you're just going to create a lot of problems—money problems—for yourself. He'll just find a young girl and even give her a dowry. Somebody else is going to reap everything that he's built up with you, because when you married him, he wasn't rich. Wake up, Oshinica, where are you going to find a husband like him? No one wants to marry a divorced woman, and even less one that has children. The other women will attack you. Just look at the pretty things he brought you from Houston. And he's a good father. Do it for your kids. Many women would love to have a man like yours. That's the way it is. If you separate, all the women will treat you like dirt. For Heaven's sake, Oshinica, in the name of our great Father! Have you lost your head? What does your mother have to do to make you open your eyes? Dear Father, when is she going to smarten up?"

And she was crying the whole time.

As I walked down a path, I suddenly felt something moving beneath my skirt: it was the same little dog that I had petted here yesterday when I was wearing a jogging suit and tennis shoes. Today, it was a spring dress. How did he recognize me? He just kept following me, making sure he wouldn't lose sight of me. Saying goodbye was an ordeal. That's why I like the street dogs more; they're smarter. Pampering them just paralyzes them. It's the same with birds: if you let one go that's been caged up, it'll just die.

Whenever I'm likely to come here, I'll know I'll always find a friend. A dog's life is dominated by indifference, which must be boring. Even *they* like to receive a smile.

Daisy is teaching things about photography that we didn't learn before. There are only ten of us now. We've already learned to use photo lamps, and we've taken pictures with flickering candle light. The results are fantastic: they create so much mystery.

She gave us invitations to her nude exhibit, which is going to be held at the Alianza Francesa in Polanco. How exciting! And we're going to have a real model for our next class. She has asked us to treat her kindly and with respect. "Just remember, we have clothes on and she doesn't, so she's vulnerable. A big difference."

Our model was a fragile-looking girl. Even though we had placed a portable heater next to her, she had goose pimples all over her body when she took her robe off. It was a beautiful afternoon. I wouldn't mind being less timid with my own body, but I've always been that way; I never liked showering with the other students in high school. I was the shyest of them all.

Lalo and a friend opened an import-export store. They have to travel all the time, and I'll bet they flirt a lot. I know they do. Lalo goes with him to Liverpool to do business, and they probably get all the girls they want. Whenever he gets back from Houston, it's like a circus around here. He usually brings me formal, exotic-looking clothes.

"Guess what I've brought you this time?" he says, grinning with those sparkling green eyes.

I never could have guessed that he would bring me a Hasseblad, which came in its own case. It's the best camera in the world! The same one they took to the moon. I can't believe he bought one for me!

Daisy's exhibit opened last night. Unbelievable! What great pictures! Most of them were taken with special lenses that create a dreamlike effect. I just love them! Some of the pictures were of a model in bed: you could see a woman's body among the folds of the sheets. Or it was a man, or a long-stemmed rose. I'm proud I take classes with her. A lot of people went to the opening. She's so courageous. I would have been embarrassed for my parents to see all those nudes, but hers seemed quite happy. They're no different from us. How strange!

Nevertheless, some parents whose children attend the Alianza Francesa were indignant that their children had to see those nudes there. Lalo didn't see the article, but as soon as he left, I called her: "Hi. I just read the article. I'm so sorry," I told her, as if I were in mourning.

"On the contrary, I'm happy about it. It means more publicity. What dirty old men! Don't let it bother you. Come on over. We're here dying from laughter."

I'm speechless. Never in my life would I have thought of reacting like she did.

This Sunday, as always, we go out to eat. Lalo always takes us to an expensive place. Little Jacob is so funny: when the elegant waiter is ready to take our order, Jacob always asks the same thing, and he's serious about it, too.

"Do you have a skillet?"

"Why, of course, young man."

"Butter?"

"That too," he responds ceremoniously, notepad in hand.

"Put the skillet on the stove, add the butter, and crack an egg in it. I want a fried egg."

My choice is silence, and I've listened to you for years now, maybe centuries, not wanting to hear you, but even after all those miles of wasted words, I'm the one who has learned to go the furthest, seeing what I wanted to see, yet there you are. I see you, but I don't see you, I laugh at you without smiling, I just wait for you to wear down, and you'll get tired, you'll give up before I will ... you think you see that I'm here, but I'm not here, and now I can fool you into thinking that I'm condemned forever to listen to you, but you shall never possess me the way you want to, you'll just go crazy trying. And then I hear, "Don't do that, you're not going anywhere, no, we're not going, don't say any more, why do you think that way?" Then you break a chair, and the noise reminds me of your yelling, which never ends, nor will it stop until you don't live with me anymore, but even then you'll need me to listen to you, and when I leave the bedroom, I know you'll force me to return, you'll close the door so my body can't escape, and I return without resisting as you pull me down and I fall into bed, cover myself up, and try to leave again, but you continue making demands on me, your eternal complaining, your demands; but traveling through my memory, disappearing, I spy on you from the bed, watching you come and go, your broken voice, your ugly face, almost screaming, "You just laugh at me, you laugh at everything I say, you make fun of me." "No, I don't make fun of you," I respond, bored to death. "Yes, you laughed," he says, pulling back the covers. "I didn't realize it, I didn't know." So, I'm trapped, and my false smile and I go into hiding again; then I walk around the room, and from the expression in your eyes and pale face, I can tell that you're still talking and gesturing wildly, but slowly, I undress, turn on the faucet, and feel the water begin to cover my body, my face, I can hear it, I close my eyes ... but then you jerk the shower curtain back, I'm taken by surprise, nude, more than enough proof that I'm there, even though you make sure once again that I have no choice but to be there, where I see you but I don't see you, while you complain about my family and my friends, so now my bath will take longer, it starts to fill up, I add some bubble bath, I sink, but now you'll have to leave for work, you've only got ten minutes left, I love taking baths, and it's time for you to get dressed, I can hear you opening and slamming drawers, five must be pulled out by now, all with violence, there are three left, and I know that next you'll say, "Nothing's right in this dump, the servants and the lady of the house are bitches," so you must be about finished, and before hearing you slam the front door, which is your way of saying goodbye, I hear you repeat, "I don't have any money to give you, and don't use my car," as I cover myself with a towel, go to the record player, and choose a record that will fly me away from your world of complaining.

Then, that evening, you'll return to interrogate me, forcing me to explain how I used my time and repeating after each answer, "And what else? Then what? Who were you with? Who was there? Who called you? What else? Why didn't you call me instead? What do you mean I wasn't there? The normal thing to do was to ask me! Then what? What do you mean, 'nothing else'? You never tell me the truth. I'm tired. Get me something to eat. Why do you have to talk to the servants so much? They're playing Cupid, aren't they? I'm going to fire the whole lot. You know I'm capable of doing it. Ha, you don't care, you say? You'll be up the proverbial creek without them. Isn't there any Turkish coffee? Well, I'll be damned, you actually thought of me? These cookies are good. Where'd you get them? You didn't go out anywhere? Didn't you tell me you were there? That's a real coincidence! You always say the same thing. So why did you go by there if you were on your way to Colonia del Valle? To the dry cleaners? You're either dumb or trying to get away with something. Change the channel! The soccer match is coming on, and we don't even have cablevision. You do whatever you want all day long, and you don't even let me enjoy a little TV. Watch the game with me. You'll enjoy it. Quiet, everyone. See! She's already asleep. She only cares about herself. Why can't she knit, at least? Hey, don't go to sleep. So, what did you do today? Why did you do that? Who did you see? What do you mean, 'nobody'? You couldn't have just thought that up out of the blue! That's what I've been asking myself . . . who is she knitting that for? You mean you ran into her by coincidence? Of course I'm watching the game. Do you think I only worry about what you do all day long? That idiot doorman is a liar!"

That crazy Susan really likes this story:

> Once upon a time there was an ant and a grasshopper that lived in the North Pole. Winter was approaching. The industrious ant gathered wood for his home, knitted woolen clothing, and stored food. That way he wouldn't have to go outside when it was cold. While the ant went back and forth, sweating from carrying wood on his back, the grasshopper played music with his guitar in the streets. The ant, in turn, was eyeing the grasshopper as he was singing.
>
> "Look here, Mr. Grasshopper, you should be getting ready for winter, because when you need something to stay warm, I won't give it to you," she vociferated.
>
> But the grasshopper just kept on singing, and the ant kept on working. Upon returning from his last trip one afternoon, he saw that this time the grasshopper was singing with a friend. He smiled ironically and went inside his house. Even though he had enough provisions, he thought one more trip wouldn't hurt, so the next morning he went out for more wood and flowers. As he was returning, he noticed that the two grasshop-

pers, who were now three in number, were still singing. The ant closed the door, lit his chimney, put on some warm clothing, and turned on the radio. Just as he was about to drink some hot chocolate, he heard a knock on the door.

"Ah, ha, it must be the grasshopper."

And, in fact, it was.

"Okay, Mr. Grasshopper, if you're here to beg for something, the answer is No!"

"Oh, I only came here to tell you something."

"Well, if that's all it is, come in and sit down."

"I only wanted to tell you that the owner of a ship that cruises the Caribbean was here, and he hired us to work for him. So, I've come to say goodbye. Can you imagine it? Singing and dancing on the high seas every night? Then we'll go to the Mediterranean, and on to Greece, where we'll visit Athens."

"Athens, are you sure? Well, then, I'd like to ask a big favor. See if you can find someone by the name of Aesop, everyone there knows who he is. Once you find him, please tell him to go fuck himself."

Today, when I was at the photo shop where Amparito works, I made a confession to her.

"I want a divorce, but I don't know how to support myself. I only know how to raise children and take care of the house. I haven't earned a red cent in my life."

"Why don't you become a photographer and take pictures? You're already good at it."

I began thinking. That wouldn't be so bad. I could take pictures of my neighbors, my children, and my cousins.

When did Lalo begin yelling at me? And to be so demanding? It must have started when it occurred to that dreadful psychologist, who had been recommended by my husband's psychoanalyst, to tell me that I was too authoritative. I became so worried about it that I lapsed into submissiveness. So, when I began to remain silent, he'd yell at me even more. And since I was made to feel like I was to blame, I didn't answer back. I just thought that the sooner he'd get it out of his system, the sooner he would calm down. To the contrary, he just yelled and screamed even louder. I started wasting more and more time just taking care of the daily chores. Soon it seemed normal to me that husbands would simply yell at their wives all the time. I had learned that this is the way they treat their wives.

Not long after that I found myself repeating the same things that my grandmother used to say: "The Señor will be here any minute. The Señor has just arrived! Don't make any noise!" Or I might say, "Daddy is sleeping, he has a headache." Or I would convince myself that I shouldn't say anything to him, he's had a rough day.

And I had already warned my friends: "Don't call when Lalo's at home."

There are numerous empty lots in this neighborhood where the weeds grow all by themselves. In September, they fill up with bright wildflowers that are always facing the sun; they turn their heads, flirtingly, with no shame, to follow the sun crossing the sky. They're called sunflowers. They produce color everywhere.

They're so majestic that I'm always taking my children and their friends to see them and to take pictures. I use all the special filters that I can find. Why haven't I noticed this rebirth—these changes—before? Where could you find sunflowers growing in the city? That's why I like to look for empty spaces; I know I'll find places just covered with these flowers; one only has to stop and walk through them. The flowers are absolutely stunning. And our Saint Bernard loves to run through them too, and he tries to knock us down. Then I begin searching desperately to find new subjects that are in bloom; by November, they will have dried up, only to sprout again the following year.

"The Señora went to her photography class," Felipa tells Estela.

"You mean you have to take classes to be able to take pictures?"

No matter how much I insisted on taking advantage of the open fields, my neighbor wanted me to take still life pictures inside. So I fixed up the living room by putting up a rod to hang a black sheet for the backdrop, hiding the cycloramas behind the curtains, and putting some wood on the floor for the cycloramas to stand on. After I finish taking the pictures, I put the living room back the way it was.

When I found my notebooks, which were in total disarray, I discovered that some pages had been ripped out. Of course, Lalo had done it. The other day he saw me writing in them, so I quickly put them away.

"What are you writing about in that notebook? Give it to me! I have a right to know everything that goes on around here. Who says I don't? If not, then what kind of marriage is this?"

One day, the rabbi told a story.

The time had finally arrived when it was possible to give a man his only opportunity in life to go up in a rocket, but only for two hours. His family and friends encouraged him to take advantage of it, so that when he came back he could tell everyone what he had seen, what he had felt, and how much he had enjoyed it.

Once inside the rocket, he pressed a button and felt his seat move forward; then he pressed another button and it went backward. Hey, this was great! So he pressed another button, and a bell sounded; another, and some lights started flashing; another, and he went forward again, and then backward. He was having a ball!

But suddenly, they interrupted him: his two hours were over.

"What? We haven't even taken off yet! I still want to fly."

"No! Get out! Right now! You had your chance just like the others, but you wasted your time pressing buttons and pulling levers. By playing with all that glitters, you've prevented yourself from taking that desired and unrepeatable trip called life. There is no second chance. Your time is up."

I guess we fill our lives with distractions instead of taking advantage of our two hours of life. There are an infinite number of hours and days of distractions preventing us from making our dreams come true. For most, those many distractions only serve to fill a void; they stop us from thinking, from questioning the way we live, and from asking ourselves if we're actually living the way we want to live, or whether we should change directions in order to learn how to enjoy our solitude—that is, to hear the effusiveness emanating from that spring inside each one of us.

Life is too short. Heads up! I don't want to lose it. Today I'm saying it in the present tense, and if I'm not careful, one day I'll say "I lost it" in the past tense.

And today, like every day, I'm putting the sweet bread in the breadbasket and the ham and cheese on the serving tray. And, like every night, I'm asking Lalo what he would like to eat, and, like every night, after they finish their homework in front of the TV, the children go to bed. And, like almost every night, the maid and I take a bucket of hot water upstairs to my husband for his tired feet. And, like every night, I watch programs that I don't like. And today, one more time, I try to convince my husband that we should go out on the weekend, or take a class together, or whatever, but at least try something. And, like every night, I wait cautiously for a commercial in order to ask him, but they are so short that by the time I finally get ready to ask him, the program comes back on, and I don't dare disturb him. Soon he'll be asleep.

But tonight is different, because I'm finally asking myself if I really want to grow old with this man. Ten years from now, I don't want to be sitting in front of this TV, still watching the same programs and only talking when there's a commercial on . . . and without any kids around me. Donna and Levy, Levy and Donna.

I read somewhere that "we have been punished for not having learned how to be alone." We've been punished, and now we're living with someone whom we don't even love. And the reason why is because we haven't learned how to live alone.

NINE

I've been so involved in everything that I didn't even realize when or how my kids began forming an alliance with their father. All of a sudden, there were two groups in the house: them against me. Now they talk among themselves and leave me out of their conversations. I've been pushed away. They've taken up sides with him. I knew something was going on, but I couldn't put my finger on it. When little Jacob is with his father, he acts differently. And I wasn't aware that every time my husband criticizes me, he's undermining the admiration and love they have for me. I was also so sure that they'd never see anything bad in me, all of which seemed so unnecessary to defend.

Lalo and I are prisoners to each other; neither he nor I want to live the rest of our lives with each other. Why don't we just call it quits? If one of us could leave the other, we would probably end up applauding it, but neither of us has the guts to do it, or to carry the burden of guilt for having left.

I go to work now as if I were having to sneak out, as if there were something wrong with it. As a result, my children hate everything: my photography, my friends, my books, my parents, my sisters . . . anything involving me.

When I got married, there was only one path for me to follow. Larger than life itself, my mother had prevented me from choosing anything else. Even though the path that I was given wasn't very illuminating, everyone had declared that it was mine, nonetheless. And I was pushed along to take it. I didn't oppose it. I just moved forward, thinking I could start over anytime. Just to think that I could is what kept me going. Perhaps I had thought that there were too many options and that none of them was for me.

No matter what path it was, I began to walk alone, ever so slowly and carefully, with a watchful eye, measuring every step. I became accustomed to this new environment, this new direction I had taken. Without even realizing it, I began internalizing things more and more; I learned to travel with a different compass. I realized that many people were on the same path with me; sometimes we would laugh, and sometimes we were even happy.

On one particularly dark night, I dared to look back, for I wanted to see the tracks I had left behind in life: they had disappeared.

My house is spacious, and it's usually full of laughter and toys. The lights are on. The living room is the same way it was when I got married. I have a husband, children, a TV, and Odilón, our dog.

But then I look forward, and suddenly a wide, marvelous

horizon comes into view. Where am I headed? Who will I run into?

I had already started out, walking, and not knowing where I would end up or who was going along with me.

Walking . . .

Today, after reading one of my short texts in the writers' workshop, I happened to mention that my dad owned a store in Lagunilla Market, and how I was always embarrassed about having to barter to sell anything.

"Why don't you bring us something that describes how your father sells his goods," suggested Elena, "and then follow up on it. Be sure to bring something new each time. I sense that you're going to write a novel. We'll help you put it together."

Every time, she made correction after correction on what I had written.

"I don't know why you construct your sentences totally backwards," she said, returning my work full of little marks that I didn't understand.

The portraits I took of my cousins turned out so good that my sister-in-law is going to give her sister a darkroom.

"No way, it's all mine. Are you trying to say your parents gave me something? Nothing. . . . I'm like a dog . . . not even a house or a business. Did they think I was some jerk? Do you know I was offered my choice of the best girls in my mother's community . . . and businesses, houses, trips to Europe for the honeymoon? No, stupid me, I have to hook up with you. Every last thing in this house is mine: the children, the car, everything. I earned it with my own sweat. If you don't like it, pack your bags and get out. Leave us alone! I can raise them just fine. We don't need you. Or do you want them to decide which one of us they would like to live with?"

I said yes, feeling absolutely positive about what they would say.

"I'm going with my dad," said the oldest. The others followed suit, and even the youngest one repeated them.

"I'm going with my dad."

They didn't realize he was talking about something more important than simply going to the park.

I was paralyzed. My eyes popped out as I watched Lalo revel in the glory.

After becoming a married woman, with servants, maids, a gardener, and a seamstress at home, I went back to being the daughter of a family.

As soon as I left, Eduardo told the kids that I didn't love them anymore, that I never took care of them, that the only thing that mattered to me was studying, that he's going to hire a governess, that he's going to take them to Japan, and who knows what other fantasies. I refused to provide them with a litany of things about him, because I didn't want to confuse them any more than what they already were. They'll find out for themselves.

So, who'll take them to the club? The only classes they have are held there.

"He won't last, very soon he'll give them back to you," my father declared.

I hope I can endure the wait. In the meantime?

Like my grandfather, I had acquired many habits: saving money; going to the Farmer's Market for fresh vegetables, to the butcher shop for meat, and to the corner deli for fish; looking for wholesale prices if I was going to make a dress or curtains. Now it looks like everything I had saved was for him. What a fool I was!

The goal was to arrive home before evening and to be faithful to just one man. Now, I suddenly have neither home nor children. I don't know what to do with so much free time on my hands. Like a robot, I find myself going to the store right at six o'clock, and buying ham, cheese, and a large loaf of sweet bread. By the time I'm carrying everything out of the store, I remember: Why so much bread, ham, and cheese for just one person?

How can my mother live with such bare walls? And then she snaps back at me, saying that it must be impossible to live in a house full of junk. She likes her house to be "neat as a pin."

"I don't have a lot of things so I don't have to clean them, my dear."

I'm going to stop by my house to pick up a few pictures.

My siblings came with their children to see me. They're so cute and cuddly.

"Do you like your little sweater?"

Seeing them together really makes me sad. I called Susan and

Mari, whom I haven't seen in a long time. Ever since the two of them got divorces, Lalo prohibited me from seeing them. After spotting them at La Herradura one day, he went around mocking me: "Aren't you going to invite them out again? The little di-vor-cees?"

I'm going to find out what Frida's up to these days. I wonder if she's still living in Xalapa or if she moved to Mexico City? No, I'm not going to get sad. Despite her constant traveling, she's still close to her kids.

My parents and my brothers and sisters keep insisting that I should look for a steady job.

"A regular job, you know, one from ten to seven, a normal person's job, like everyone else."

My mother is already tired of seeing me with a camera all the time.

"Are you some kind of a tourist? Just treat it like a hobby. Don't take it so seriously."

No way, José. If I'm going to get a divorce, then I'm going to do what I want; if I don't, I'll just go back to married life. I don't want to drop out of my fiction writing class either. If I get a regular job, they're not going to let me off for the Thursday meetings. I want to make an attempt to do it my way. Photography isn't a great moneymaker, but I can set my own schedule.

Now that my brother Moshón has built a building on Amores Street that has space for two businesses, I told him that I would like to set up a photography studio there.

"My pictures will sell well, but let me have the first year's rent free."

He agreed. He's having the architect call me to see what I need to get started.

I remember the way Lalo would give me money at the end: "Is this enough for you?"

And he would put a large bill down on the table. Then he would put down another, and another, and look at me with hatred: "Not even with this?"

I would almost have a seizure just thinking about it. I never want to allow anyone to have that power over me again. Absolutely no one!

When I told everyone at the writing class about my situation, I broke out crying. They all gave me a hug.

"You'll make it," they said.

I was hired to take portraits of Alicia Trueba's nephews, and the others are going to tell their friends about my work.

Alicia's husband, Pancho, built a house, taking into consideration the fact that her classes were important to her. Our classroom, which is on the ground floor, is a large open space. It has some paintings on the walls, and it looks out onto a garden full of azaleas. Alicia is very pretty, and she's my mom's age. She never had children, and she's president of several different clubs.

I found a picture in our photo album of our proud and handsome grandfather. He was walking through the old Chapultepec Park at a time when there was one road going in and one going out. It was called the Promenade. His first grandchildren are well taken care of, and he loves us, too, because we have the names of his parents. My mother, my Aunt Chelita—who was still single at the time—and my grandmother are standing behind him. Next to the women is his only son, the one guarantee of the future of his surname. Both the women—and my grandfather, naturally—have always known that they must defer to the patriarch, whether they want to or not. My grandfather always used everything he could muster to quell his granddaughter's rebelliousness.

At the same time that Moshón began to demonstrate his manliness and I my womanhood, my grandfather's pride in his grandson began to grow. Moshón, also growing ever so proud of his new role, imitated his grandfather. Nowadays, they like to eat the same things, and they appreciate the same things.

They depreciate us.

One evening, I met Susan at Sanborn's at eight. I had also talked to Mari to see if we might meet in the afternoon, but she couldn't. Newly divorced, she has to work during the day; they only have the evenings off. I had some dessert and coffee. I got back home a little after ten.

"This isn't a good hour to be getting home," said my father, who had become enraged. "This is a decent house. There are rules to be followed. No one can come home later than ten o'clock! If you are willing to follow the rules, this is your house, too; if not, make your own arrangements."

My mother didn't say anything. Obviously, they were in agreement. Being back at home is worse than being with my husband; at least there I had my children, and I could seek refuge in their room. Besides, my mother has this obsession for wanting to talk all night long, and she makes me sit with her while she knits and watches TV. If I go to my room, she calls me out to watch some program or other. She can't understand why I want to be alone; she demands to know who I was talking to on the phone, what I've said to them, and to top it off, I have to consider her opinions and then comment whether I did right or wrong.

Live like they want me to? Without anything from before that filled up my life? Now I'm being forced to substitute for that something as uninteresting as TV. I have to go out and find some clients, take out an ad, look for a boarding house to live in. But how will a client let me know if they want some pictures taken? Maybe this will be more fun, I'll make new friends, and I could even meet someone there. I would like to fall in love, or have a lover. Balzac wrote about life in those places. It has to be interesting.

Susan is beautiful, really beautiful. As usual, she interrogated me; she must have been a detective in a previous life. I spent the whole time crying while she tried to give me some advice, that is, orders. She even got furious.

"Defend your rights!"

"I didn't come into this world to end up fighting. I'm going to die before I ever get anything out of my husband. He told me in no uncertain terms."

I miss my children. I want to see my baby . . . well, he's not a baby anymore, he's seven years old, but I like to say that he's my baby.

I met a woman who interrogated me about everything, from A to Z, from top to bottom, my mother used to say. She likes my work. There's just one other young woman, who works in a bank, living in this place.

"You can use the kitchen to make some coffee, but that's it."

My room is dark inside, and it only has one closet. Will my

camera be safe there? I had to give her my mother's phone number as a reference.

"Since this is a respectable house," the landlady added, "no visitors."

Darn it! Here I am fleeing from all this respectability and now it's coming out of the woodwork. How does it find me? It won't leave me alone. I'm going to have fun *here?* Never! Besides, with such a horrible closet, I won't even be able to smile in the mornings. Just thinking about living there makes me cry. I'd rather go back to La Herradura, even if I have to live with this demon that's inside me. At least there, I would have my garden, my hammock, and my Saint Bernard. And, of course, my children, even if they don't miss me, hmm . . . do they miss me?

I told my cousin Alegre about the boarding house.

"Come and stay at my house," she said. "I've taken in so many of my friends at one time or another, so why not you too?"

"It'll only be for a month," I assured her, with a voice that was about to crack, "just until I can find someplace else."

"What do you mean only a month? Stay as long as you want. Let's don't worry about it."

I don't like calling people to see if they want photographs taken. Once again, the embarrassment of being in need and then some of them feeling sorry for me. However, it's great when they show enthusiasm about hiring me, like that good friend who lives in La Florida and had called my house three times.

"The Señora does not live here anymore!" Lalo answered.

I hadn't even thought of calling her myself.

When I got to Camelia's street, I noticed that there was a swimming club in front of her house. I saw some mothers going in with their babies. A disaster ensued: I broke out crying, so I couldn't take any pictures.

My family thinks that if I don't have the resources to take care of the children, it's better to be without them.

"At least with him they'll have everything they need." To have, to have, nothing but *to have* wherever you turn. What's my problem with money, anyway? Why didn't I save any if I was so thrifty when it came to household expenses? How could I ever have thought that everything we had belonged equally to both of us? Every time I got my allowance or I saved it, he would just borrow it from me. And just try to get it back!

"It's ridiculous to try to save pennies; I earn a lot of money," he used to say.

Long before I turned fifteen, I had already thought about how I would treat my children. It was going to be different from the way my mother did it. Now they're confused.

"The truth will always win out," my father assured us.

"And you have to wait until you're sixty to find that out?" Susan responds in a high-pitched voice. "Don't be a jerk, Oshinica!"

It's horrible not being able to see them, hear them, or see other children and their mothers. Of course, my children hear the cutting comments that their father makes about me . . . those same comments he makes about anyone else he doesn't like.

But then I heard that the children have been repeating the same thing.

"That classical music is so boring . . . you and your books . . . Borges again? . . . your friends are crazy . . . daddy isn't giving you any more money because he doesn't have any, so don't ask . . . he's right . . . you're never at home."

My kids have rejected what I have to give them; none of that is important to them any more.

For so many years, my entire life had been surrounded by kids, classical music, and the Magnavox. Was I stupid or not? I spent all my time taking them to classes, and then more classes. Three years per child for swimming lessons. Three times four children equals twelve . . . twelve years of my life taking the older ones every afternoon and the youngest one two mornings a week.

It'll never, ever, be the same between us again. How stupid of me to have given more importance to them than to myself! How did I ever reach that state of placing myself last and believing that we were all the same? I didn't understand that they eventually become their own selves. They aren't me, I'm not them. How crazy to think that I was getting fulfillment through them! Instead of taking them to classes, why didn't I spend that time preparing myself for the future?

Adults aren't any more dangerous than children. I need to go into the adult world now, a place where I can use the same tactics and speak the same language, even yell if I want to, because they're just kids and I'm supposed to be the model for them. Educate, educate . . . take care of myself.

And now what? Let's see what I can come up with.

Meanwhile, I'm going to stay with my cousin.

My father caught me leaving my room with a suitcase and my paintings. He couldn't believe it; he looked at me almost with hatred, but he said nothing.

I thanked them and told them where I was going.

I arrived with all my belongings: the car, the camera, my clothes, and a little money in my purse. Alegre gave me the bedroom where her friend Patty was staying. Patty moved to Alegre's room. There's a wall-to-wall window and a record player next to my bed that I play all night long. The only bad part is that we're far out in the suburbs.

Now I can come and go pretty much as I please. When I'm there, we talk. Patty is an architect, and she gives photography classes. She recommended that I take a course on studio photography, like the one I'm taking now.

Two weeks ago, the space was divided into the reception area and the lab, which has windows to allow the smell of chemicals to escape. And there's a place for the rinsing bins, too. It's going well, but my family can mess things up anytime. I need to learn a lot more in order to become a true professional and make a decent living.

"What are you going to do now that your children are grown up?" she asked. "You should take control of your life and make your dreams come true."

Alegre looks a lot like me: straight hair, small mouth, square nose. I like her smile, but her voice is deeper than mine. One day, while I was at the club, someone came up from behind and covered my eyes.

"Guess who?"

I went down the list of friends, and when I finally managed to get loose and look, I still didn't know who it was. He thought I was my cousin. I'm a little fatter, but we look alike. She's been divorced longer than I have. She knows how to earn a living; she's a fighter, and I hope to learn from her how to shed all those prejudices that prevent me from enjoying life's pleasures, especially the ones belonging to my body.

"We all have to work," Alegre assured me. "And those who are forced to learn to put up with their masters, their husbands? Are they happy? Brush the cobwebs from your brain! Every one of us has the same needs: house, food, etc. So you work with pride to support yourself, and that's it. You have your dignity, dummy," she said, giving me a hug.

It was crazy to believe what my friends used to say, like "I don't have any necessities, I just live this way to keep from getting bored."

Her son and my Aunt Mati are still in Monterrey, but they'll always spend long periods of time with Alegre.

I signed up for the course on studio photography with Camilo and Tinajero. The teacher is good, but his poses are too stiff. His portraits look like the ones they take of presidents. I can't stand stiffness in my pictures. I hope my brother doesn't back out on giving me the studio. I already have a ton of customers on the weekends.

Living so far away can produce a lot of problems. I barely leave the house and I run into the first obstacle: traffic jams. The free time that I once had has gone up in smoke: there's no way to move forward. My God! Every morning I get the feeling that I'm trapped. I've decided not to return to the house until nighttime; if I go back in the afternoon, there's no way I'd go back into the city later. The best part is that the trunk of my Ford Galaxie can hold a bunch of stuff. It's my motor home. I change clothes wherever I can, and I take everything with me: makeup, sweat clothes, tennis shoes, and high heels.

I called Andrés. I wanted to know what it would be like to do more than just kiss him . . . to make love to him. Have I separated from my husband to find out? I've never forgotten his phone number. I've dialed his number many times just to hear his voice. Today, however, I didn't hang up.

"It's me, Oshinica, I want to see you. Lalo and I have separated."

"I don't live with my mother anymore," he said, "I just happened to be here when you called. Here's my number."

We agreed to see each other on Monday, and he'll call me to set the time. He must have noted my nervousness, because he calmed me down.

"Just pretend that time has stood still."

I felt better after he said that.

I didn't leave the house all day Monday. I nervously answered every phone call. The day went by and he didn't call, so I dialed his apartment. No one answered. Then, finally, he was at home.

"I was sad all day long because you didn't call," I murmured, trying to dominate my shyness.

"I was going to call you, today or tomorrow. You know, I have friends whom I call every six months, but that doesn't mean that I don't care about them. Why don't you come over? I'll tell you how to get here."

Excited, I got dressed up. I don't know why I asked Luisa to go with me; I guess it was because nothing seems to faze her.

I arrived at his house. I liked it. I could tell it was neatly kept. He's still tall and thin like a pole from his head to his toes. I saw a serene smile, a sweet look, but not the one I desired so much, not the one I thought was mine.

Luisa sat down by the telephone in the bedroom; Andrés asked if I wanted a drink. Wanting to appear relaxed, I kicked off my shoes, and I took my thesis down from the bookshelf.

"You still have it . . . and my graduation ring?" I asked with anticipation.

"No, not anymore."

What a letdown! That ring had meant so much to me. True, once I got married, I had distanced myself from him, but I had given it to him as an expression of my love for him.

He took out some photo albums, and I nervously flipped the pages hoping to see a picture of me, but the only thing I saw was the girl he's going to marry in two months. He showed me a picture of her in a bathing suit, which made me feel ridiculous . . . as if I could share his happiness.

I got up from the couch. I felt stupid and old, even though I'm a little younger than he is. I set my drink on the bookshelf, put on my shoes, and went into the bedroom to get Luisa. She was talking on the telephone.

"Let's go," I said.

Andrés looked disconcerted.

I opened the door and went out. My friend was right behind me.

"If the gate downstairs is locked, I'll come down and open it," was all that he managed to say.

It's been twenty days since I've seen my kids; every time I see a pregnant woman or something that has to do with raising kids, I get torn up inside. Without them, who am I? I wish I didn't have to see children anywhere.

My cousin has gone to Cuernavaca, so I put on some music, turn on the light next to my bed, and stretch out face up on the bed. I stare at the ceiling. Where did I go wrong? When did I do anything wrong? What did I really want to do before I got married? Study? Change the world? I remember going to the women's jail with Frida and to the insane asylum with Dori. I had barely discovered what poverty was. I had ideals, I wanted to help, I wanted to be a better person, I wanted to go to the university and to Israel . . . work the land . . . see the world . . . study, fly away, I wanted to be . . . what? And what did I do? I got married in order to be free. It never occurred to me that I was jumping out of the frying pan into the fire. I threw away my ideals. Where did I lose my way? I lost my way through my children. I was misled by their smiles, their faces, their seductive eyes, the sound of their voices, and the joy of seeing them learn to do something.

It was always quite an event when they learned new words and began to think for themselves. Then we could talk about things together, or go to the movies. We were always cheek-to-cheek, and I marveled at the color and shape of their eyes, their eyebrows, their noses, their mouths . . . what beautiful children! I was the vainest mother of all! They became a magnet to me. There was never enough time to be with them. One year went by, then two, five, and ten. I could have remained trapped by their seductive beauty.

I went everywhere with them. I avoided listening to my body. I just let it go. In order not to look at others, to be faithful, I took refuge in them.

Yesterday, I couldn't stand it any longer: I went to see little Jacob. When I saw that jerk's car pass by, I honked the horn.

"Hi, sweetie, it's your mom, get in."

"I can't, we're going home to watch *I Love Lucy* now," he yelled from the car window.

Feeling like crap, I drove back out to the house. I couldn't believe it. How can they not miss the world we built together?

All of a sudden, I felt like not loving them anymore. I had discovered that soon they would become unmerciful adults.

I was bedridden for days. When I finally got the energy to get up, I drove to their school to give them some candy that they always liked. Then I was off to see my new friends, the ones who had not given in to the system—that is, Cortázar's friends, the ones from his novel *Hopscotch*.

I prefer them. I don't want to live among people who judge everything.

"Oshinica, how are you?" asked Alicia Trueba. "You know that we're here for you. We *are* your friends."

"I'm so happy you came by! It was about time you remembered that your old neighbor had a baby and that it was time to visit me. Come in, let's have a cup of coffee. Just let me rinse out the baby's bottle; she's about to wake up, and if her bottle isn't ready, she gets furious."

Fortunately, I don't have any more babies. It's been eight years since I last performed those rituals: rinse bottles, eight nipples in all, put the milk away, then the dish soap and the nylon brush . . .

Chely gives her a multicolored rattle and makes her laugh; then she picks her up and lays her down in the little tub for a bath.

"Señora, the Señor is calling."

"Hand me the phone and get the diapers off the line, it might start to rain. Hi, honey! How're you? Really? That's great! Didn't I tell you? I said everything was going to turn out all right, right baby? Oshi, please hand me a diaper; they're in the bottom drawer, no, on the other side. Yes, yes, honey, I hear you; no, no, I'm not doing a thing. . . .

"Señora, it's the drugstore delivery. Should I sign for it?"

"Yes, but make sure they brought what we needed. I said yes, honey, Oshi is here, she says hi, of course we miss her. It's almost time for her to eat, but we're still sterilizing the bottles. Do you hear the others playing? They never stop fighting; I'm going to feed them dinner early so they won't make such a fuss later on. So, honey, what are you going to do while you wait for your meeting? Oh, sweetie, please bring some ham and cheese home with you; I wouldn't want our visitor to go hungry. He's something else; he watches everything I do. Nothing, I said, just fixing the baby's bottles, talking with Oshi, got something from the drugstore, watching the other kids. No, are you kidding? I'm not doing anything! And then at night he says, 'What? You're tired? So what did you do all day long, woman?'"

Graciela puts a clean diaper on her little daughter, then some pink pajamas, baby cream, and finally, into the crib with a blanket. She comforts her, winds up a music box next to the crib, places some toys around her so she won't get bored, and then says, "Wait a second, my dear, I'll be right back. I'm going to bring your bottle."

"Oshi, let's go to the kitchen just for a moment. Now I give her canned milk, because powdered milk always creates a mess. Would you like some yogurt?"

Then we finally sit down.

"What's she supposed to eat now? Peas, I guess," she says, looking at the doctor's prescription. "The best part is that I give her Gerber's and half of a fried egg yolk. Oops, it's already cold!"

She goes back to the stove, puts on a pot of water, and reheats the baby bottle. She grabs a small spoon, the mashed peas, and the bottle, and we go back upstairs.

"Martina, bring the fried egg!"

She puts a bib on her, and begins to feed her the mashed peas, which she devours instantly. Then she eats the rest.

"Tell me, Oshi, how have you been? Tell me everything . . ."

"Señora, it's the doctor. Should I bring the telephone to you?"

"I can finish feeding her while you talk," I offered.

"Okay, the call's important."

I get settled in a chair, put the baby on my lap, and feed her; meanwhile, she gives me a dirty look, squints her eyes so as not to look at me, and makes some nasty gestures. She refuses to eat and pushes the baby bottle away. No matter how much I smile, hug her, and give her love, she remains unconvinced. Finally, Chely comes back.

"Maybe she won't take the bottle because she needs to burp."

She takes her in her arms and rests her little head on her shoulder. Very soon a sound emerges from her stomach, followed by applause from my friend.

"Bravo! Now you'll see how fast she finishes her bottle; she's a perfect baby."

Sure enough, she polishes it off quickly. Chely gets her to burp again, and then places her in a little tub while she changes the sheet in the crib, puts a clean diaper on her, and lays her to sleep face down. She winds up the music box again, says good night to her, and turns out the light. As we're leaving the room we hear the melody of *Bailarina*, which the baby will store in her memory forever.

"Oshi, let me get that book I borrowed from you. I'll bet our coffee is already cold. I want to hear all about what you're doing these days."

◇ ◇ ◇

I ran into Susan's mother at the club. She ended up making me go with her to her house, which, basically, is a dress factory.

"The only thing I asked of my daughter was not to forget about herself. I'm suggesting you do the same. You *are* important, Oshinica, my darling, and I've always said it, even when we lived in the apartment building together."

I've found myself now. If I was reluctant to take charge of my life before, I have no alternative now.

First: "When are you getting married?"
Second: "When are you going to have a baby?"
Next: "When is the second one due?"
Then: "And the third one?"

I wasn't going to be happy until Lalo got a son. And now I'm getting a divorce, so I'm asking myself if I'm going to start over. Isn't that exactly what I'm trying to do right now? I had already answered myself. For many who ask themselves these questions, starting over means getting married again.

And here we are at my cousin's house: my camera, my Galaxie, and me. Those things are indispensable, for I depend on both of them. My Hasseblad maintains me, and my car is home to my camera and me. We sustain each other.

I really don't like my psychoanalyst, because he defends marriage at all costs, to the point that any day now I'm going to get the divorce over with. He wants us to get back together . . . for the kids' sake. He must be a model husband himself. All that matters in life are his wife and children. That's boring! I would change therapists, but that's who Dr. Toledo recommended. According to my husband, he's God on earth.

No matter how much I try not to think about my kids, I still break down and cry. The older kids call me on the phone, but not little Jacob.

This past Thursday, when I went outside after my writing class, my car was gone. Alicia insisted that I call Lalo.

"What do you mean they stole it? Damn it, you're so careless."

"Well, that proves it wasn't him," I assured her.

Everyone in the class was distressed over it. Alicia went with me to the police station.

Without my car, my camera and I were unable to get back to my cousin's house. The psychoanalyst recommended an antidepressant and told me to go back to my real home.

I went back to my kids, my bed, and my dog.

I had been defeated.

Oh, how sad! No sooner did I return but I went out into the garden, and instead of the colorful posts that supported the hammocks, I discovered some ugly holes, haphazardly filled with a mixture of dirt and cement. They're gone! I loved the idea so much that I spent my last allowance on putting them in. To see the posts yanked violently out of the ground pained my heart; I felt as if that's the way I had been thrown out of the house. I couldn't bear to go into the garden.

The children are loving to me, but they're sad to see how slow I am because of this medicine that's made me drowsy. They wouldn't allow me to drive. But I'm happy to be at home once again. Ah, and to think I can sleep with them!

That's all I want.

After two months of taking antidepressants and watching the grass grow over the spots in the garden that represented anger, resentment, and hatred—who knows what else—Lalo, who was feeling embarrassed, brought my Galaxie back, just like that. He had kept it somewhere all this time. If I hadn't become so weak, I would've hated him, but I have no desire to oppose him. He doesn't even remember that moment when I called him, when I was crying, to tell him about my car being stolen, and he just acted dumb.

But, now, finally, I can use it.

I went back to the studio. In the afternoons at the club cafeteria, I still run into a lot of mothers, who all take their kids to gymnastics or swimming. I enjoyed seeing everyone—Beatriz, Clarita, Annette, and my sister. They're all finishing high school, and no one can forget Gabriel Weiss's classes. One of them has two children, another has three, but they have the support of their husbands. It's no big deal if they take classes. I wouldn't be able to do that, because it would just trigger more fighting. Who wants that, now that it's relatively peaceful.

I thought it was funny how the waitress reacted to the way some friends from Turkey were talking; a woman and her adolescent son were speaking Ladino.

"They speak just like the Indians," she said.

And it's true, because that's the same Spanish the conquistadors taught them. The discovery of America and the expulsion of the Jews from Spain occurred the same year.

I had breakfast with Trueba the other day, and it was hilarious to invent some lines for the pictures in the album that she had made for Pancho for their twenty-fifth wedding anniversary. It was a picture story of their lives since they were born. Their stories became one the day their paths crossed. Next to the pictures, she added comments in little balloons like in the comics. It's obvious that they have a good marriage. How strange! And no children either! I wanted to see the whole album.

"Take it home with you. Look through it at your leisure," she offered happily.

I was amazed they would even think of lending it to me, but I gleefully decided to borrow it.

"How have you managed to make love the most lasting part of your marriage?" I asked, without even wondering what the answer might be.

"I'm not sure, but perhaps, contrary to what everyone believes—that is, that children bring marriages together—many times they actually destroy marriages. I just don't know. And who am I to say? Still, I love this man, because he gave me the freedom to become who I wanted to be. He has supported me all along the way. He does what he has to do, and he doesn't stop me from doing the same. Simply put, I love him."

As I drove up, I saw my husband's car. Damn! What am I going to do now? If he sees me with this camera, he'll blow his top. He doesn't want me taking photographs of people I don't know. The only thing I could think of was to leave my equipment at Chely's house, which is nearby. I went into the dining room all smiles and feeling guilty. His brother was there, so he had to control himself, but you could tell by his eyes that he was livid.

"Where have you been?"

"At my mom's house," I blurted out, frightened to death.

Facing a full-scale interrogation, all I could do was tell him a bunch of lies.

Alberto, who is my cousin Alegre's son, came to visit me.

"A friend of mine who is studying medicine wants to meet you. He loves photography, he's seen your work, and the other day he was going to do a portrait of a woman who at the last minute said she preferred to have you do it. So, he wants to know who is this person who is stealing his clients. Let's go to his house. He doesn't live far away."

We went to the place where he has his pictures developed, and I met the owner. We're going to do the work at my house, as if the studio could be just about anywhere. Victor showed me where to buy cheaper film. He has as many books about photography as he does about medicine. I had a good time with them.

"I took a course on studio photography," I told him, "and I have four photo lamps and two cycloramas. If you want, I can show you how to use them. You've got a lot of room here. Do you want to take some pictures?"

"Nude?" he asked mischievously.

"That's fine . . . if you have a model."

Victor is the only son of an older couple. My mother would say he's "an unexpected gift." He's thirty years old, enthusiastic, and blond; he uses an intellectual's glasses, and hence he looks like one. His studio occupies the entire top floor of his house.

It's been several times now that I've left the kids with the maid at the club while I go by Victor's studio. I'm learning a lot. Then I pick them up in the evening. My friends are studying so hard that they're always tired, and all they talk about are mathematics and biology. They'll graduate next year.

"You said you would do it with us. You're the one who got us into this," Beatriz reminds me. "Yes, yes, we've got to finish this preparatory work in order to get into the university."

"It's hard, with my husband and all; besides, I'm kind of out of it, you guys are closer to it than I am; plus I've always been bad in math, and I barely passed physics."

"Just come with us, it's the last month. You can refresh your memory a bit."

"If I were ever to leave the house at eight in the morning, my husband would slash his wrists."

"I'll bet if we ask the director to . . ."

"No. What I need to do is take pictures, tons of pictures. Even if I have to do it behind his back. I've got to generate some clients. Would you like some portraits of your kids?"

"Sure. And I told my sister-in-law about you, too," said Annette. "Do you have anything with you to show her?"

"You can take pictures of my kids this Sunday," added Beatriz.

And right there, on the table in the coffee shop, I pulled out some samples for everyone to see.

I suddenly remember that butterfly that was trapped in the spider web. It hurts to think that it can't fly anymore. I suffer because of its suffering; it was beautiful, watching the orange-colored pollen fall from its trembling wings.

We set up the equipment, and I made some portraits of one of our friends. But the lamps get so hot they burn out fast!

"Let's buy some better equipment together," suggests Victor.

"Why do that? It might take you away from your career goals."

"Frankly, I've got to make some money in order to buy my books."

There's always something we can do together. I look at his pictures, I take mine to show him, and we examine our errors. Or then Alberto comes along, and he brings some of his friends from the university. They're photographers too; others have made videos.

I could tell that my friends were really enthused that I had shown up by eight. Even though this place is for adult workers, they still treat the students like children; for instance, my sister, who is a mother of three, had to recite the same poem about spring as her son did, who was in first grade. They don't let them out until exactly one o'clock, not even when a teacher is absent. Who knows if I'll be able to put up with it? The place is freezing inside, but women are allowed to wear pants.

I was sitting down with my pencils, colors, compass, and drawing triangle on my lap, when the school principal rushed into the room. As if we were mentally retarded, we were supposed to stand up and say in unison, "Good morning, Mr. Principal." I tried to fake it as best I could without being disdainful, but all my school supplies fell on the floor. When I finally stood up, everyone else had already sat down. Either I'm dumb or life is just too complicated for me. I felt really stupid.

Jenny, the one we ran into on her honeymoon, is also studying here, but she too is having problems with her Lebanese husband.

"They're the worst. Poor thing, what can she do?" says Beatriz in Ladino. "Poor dear, may her husband be removed from her eyes!"

"I didn't marry a student."

"True, but when we got married you promised you wouldn't be against it."

Once again, we started arguing.

"Get out of this house."

"You get out."

"This is my house."

"Since when? You've never worked here."

This house.

Neither of us will ever leave it. Does the one who leaves the house also lose it? Lose it? Is there anything to be gained from it?

And what if I regret it? Should I regret not having gotten a divorce?

Are we going to live under the same roof until we kill each other?

I stopped going to school with the girls. I decided to do whatever he wants me to do: be a good wife, take the kids everywhere. He's really happy when I go to the club. And I haven't been taking any pictures either. Even though he gives me more money, my sadness grows daily.

The exquisite roses that my father brought over yesterday have totally withered. I felt like I was them. How can he say he loves me if he doesn't care if I'm withering?

"You don't love me. If you loved me, you wouldn't let me wither away like this," I told him.

He's still stubborn. He says that if I want a divorce, then we should get one.

And we've been living like this, day in and day out: screaming at each other and showing constant anger, to the point that one day a tripod slipped from my hand and I just about hit him in the head with it. When he realized that I had the other one ready and that my eyes were afire with hatred, he ran out of the room.

Part Two

TEN

"From now on, Faith, I'm the Señor and you're the Señora. I have to learn how to earn money, and I need someone to do what I used to do. Being the matronly mother for twenty years is enough."

The following Monday she didn't let her niece, María, come in, because María returned at midnight.

This is great having a wife! What a shame I didn't become aware of this while I was one; I would've felt more important. I hadn't realized that to take charge of those things that are only noticed when they're not done had allowed my husband to put all of his energy into his business. And now, since what we've saved came from what he earned, I'm learning at forty to create a budget, calculate costs, and sell my work at a loss.

I tell my daughters to learn to go to the stores by themselves. I don't want to be the one who always takes them every time they need a notebook for school.

"You can catch a bus at the corner, and come back on the same one. When I was your age, I used to take my dad's lunch to him in La Lagunilla all by myself."

"No mother makes her kids go on the bus," they snipe.

"We have to learn to help each other. Okay, let's do this: sit in the back of the bus so you can see me while I follow you in the car."

I managed to get them to do it once; I'd send signals to them from my car. The result? They hated me even more, and of course, they accused me of this and that. And, of course, they found support for it all. Being independent frightens them to death.

I took them to Victor's house, so they could see how we had made it into a photography studio. Before we went in, I asked them not to mention that their father had left home.

I just love it: since no one in the writing workshop knows my family, I can write whatever I want. Before, I had only Jewish friends, and if this group had been only Jewish, I would've followed my father's advice that silence is golden. Here, it doesn't matter. I spent the entire day at Angélica's house. I made her a leather photo album of pictures of her family doing things they do on a typical day.

All the women in this group are great! They are real characters! And what families! They give me confidence. I feel like I could give them everything I own. It's strange that I had only Jewish friends before. I wonder if I would get upset if one of my kids married outside the faith? I don't know, but . . . where did I ever get this idea that Jewish guys were the best husbands, and that they were the only ones who respected their women and the home? Or that the Gentiles were the only ones who had loose women? Frankly, these women's husbands seem like good people too. I feel like I've been misled. Trueba's husband, Pancho, is a real gentleman. When I was living in the apartment, I wasn't capable of making friends with Gentiles . . . well, it's true, because there were a lot of us.

"I've never made love to anyone but my husband," I told Angélica. "How could I dare do it with someone else?"

Maybe that's why she insisted on taking me. We agreed to meet in the plaza in Coyoacán, and then meet a friend who was a poet. I didn't even know how to get to that famous plaza, and I was born in Mexico City. What's more, I didn't even know it existed. I arrived an hour early, so I sat down to read on a bench in the plaza. It was a pleasure to escape from the humdrum of the big city, because Coyoacán seemed like a small town. Even though it's next to the large Insurgentes Avenue, life is different there. I had only known the areas around La Condesa and Satélite. I always thought I could never live anywhere else. In comparison, neither area has much charm; none of the modern neighborhoods could even come close to this one.

Bells are ringing in the cathedral. In the plaza, there are large old trees, dried branches scattered about on the grass, and a kiosk in the middle. The municipal buildings are on one side. People who are out walking around the plaza stop to sit on the benches for a moment and watch the people milling around, as if they were waiting for something to happen. An old, but not old-fashioned, man with a beard, who looks like a painter stares strangely at me; a plump, sweet mother tries to teach her baby to walk while he struggles to capture some pigeons; a little girl with pigtails was having fun throwing bread to the birds.

I see my friend parking her car. She looks pretty as she approaches, sashaying and smiling, her breasts bouncing up and down under her blouse that's held up by two thin strands. She's so sexy without a bra! Did her husband see her leave like that? Her children?

"Let's go in here and buy some wine and cheese to take," she says, pointing to a store. "What do you think about this brand? I sure hope it's good! It has to be: it's Chilean, and you know they have some of the best wines anywhere."

Although I hadn't ever tried any, I'll bet it's good, I thought to myself.

"We need to take something else to fix to eat. Let's see . . . sausage, parsley, cheese, eggs, olive oil. Let's get going; he must be desperate by now.

"Don't you think it might be better if you went without me?"

"Don't be silly, my dear, I want you to come too. I don't like to go alone. You're going to have fun. I want you meet different, interesting people. You'll see. I'm going to ask him to read some of his poetry."

Never in my life have I been a friend of a poet. I would like to talk to one, though, and learn about how he lives, what he talks about, etc.

This famous poet lives on one of those less fortunate streets in the area. There's a tobacco shop underneath his apartment, and that's where he's been waiting for us. He doesn't seem to be desperate or upset, like I thought he might when he realized that the person he had invited was coming with a guest. He's short, thin, wears glasses, and is almost bald. As we go in to buy ciga-rettes, she kisses him, and then gives him a sensual look. I blush. When I was single, I would barely dare to flirt, and if I did, I made sure no one was around. I thought it was shameful, as if those feelings weren't supposed to be desirable. After I got married, it never occurred to me to be anything but a decent, faithful—completely faithful—wife . . . to the point that I had forgotten what it was to flirt.

Now, after a few months without a husband, I was feeling lonely; even my body ached, but I still haven't dared to flirt, not even with a damn dog. It's been so long that I don't even know what to do. I really can't look a man in the face, and it's even harder if he's good looking. While they're paying, my friend keeps making sexual advances toward him.

"What, my love, you really thought we weren't coming? We're late because we stopped to pick up some food. And this is my friend. She loves literature."

Other families live in the same building, not just poets who wait for women to visit. On the stairs, we ran into his neighbors. Will they start gossiping?

He has a nice place: a round table in the dining room and two stuffed chairs facing a window. The sun coming through the window creates a cozy atmosphere.

"Mario, open a bottle of wine, and put the other in the fridge. And you, my dear, help me put some cheese on a plate."

"Damn, that's an attractive blouse you've got on; you look sexy."

"With these nasty little things underneath?"

"That blouse makes me want to see what's there."

"Really? Well, here, take a look."

She pulls up her blouse, and we see her "nasty little things."

"See, there's nothing underneath. Well, just about nothing. Here's to you, my dear Oshi: I hope this new life will bring you much happiness. So, you big macho, read something you've written. Oshi, pull out those books by Borges."

Mario goes to his room.

"See? He's really nice, and he was happy to see us. You'll like what he writes."

It's getting dark outside. All of a sudden, as if by magic, an illuminated, three-foot fish tank appears in the room. Everything inside is pure movement, a vibrating sensation. It's the most fascinating thing about his place. Then I notice a little school of fish inside. When I put my hands to the glass, they quickly dart away. They go back and forth, from left to right, I'm amazed at the power of my hands. I can't stop playing with them. Really, I'm bewitched, because when I simply move my fingers, they dart around, creating a kaleidoscope of colors. The way they make formations looks like something from an Escher drawing: they change into birds, fleeing to the sides like doves flying through the air. The mirror behind the tank duplicates everything moving inside. The insides of the tank become a lunar landscape with mountains, the coral becomes rocks in a river, the air bubbles that climb to the surface are clouds.

Mario puts on his record player. Wow! He's got fantastic speakers.

"Now you'll see how pretty this can be," he says, placing colored cellophane paper—green, blue, red—over the top of the tank. A yellow cloud floats along, and as it extends, it touches the other side and then changes color. And there's a large purple sponge with green branches inside, with blue and yellow birds, and some white and black tiger fish. And there's a blue one, too, with a white phosphorescent sheen to it that changes colors according to the changing sky above it. The fish seem to dance while they scurry about. When the dark blue fish swims under a blue sky, he becomes a deeper blue. I love the magic of the colors when the fish stops on top of the wine-colored sponge. The anemones are virtual flowers under water; another plant conforms in sleepy fashion to the anemone's lap, falling asleep in its cradle of multiple arms. Everything is transformed. The anemone's petals caress the blackbird fish. All the while, just imagine medieval chants as background music. The invertebrate anemones expand, shrink, change their shape. One of the anemones in its idyllic state flirts with a fish that hovers in wait, and a thousand fingers make love to it. The blue fish darts around among the roots of the reed mountain, the stalactites, a rock grotto, a coral tree that was once alive; and a bird-like fish with large white spots scurries past a black fish with a yellow mouth. It all looks like the work of a painter.

Even though I would love to sit there and peer into the fish tank for hours on end, I look away and see that my friend's eyes are hypnotized by the poet's eyes.

Any movement on the other side of the glass causes the butterfly fish to ripple its tail and fins.

I quickly come back to reality when I hear my friend's voice.

"Read us something," Angie says to her poet.

I feel like I'm in another world, one in which my friend is someone else, someone I don't even know. I adore her sense of confidence. And silly me, I didn't even dare stay at a party at school once, for fear someone would ask me to dance, or that no one might've asked me. I was dying to be unfaithful, but I didn't want to create any problems—but no matter, I had them anyway. What a waste! I just put up with it, and I continued to put up with it. What I began to discover was that with the passing of each day, I had to put up with more and more.

Angélica caresses my hair.

How in the hell did I come to believe that fidelity was for life? It's fine if it's for true love, but I possessed an overabundance of prudence—better yet, decency.

"Do you like the wine? Not bad, eh? I'll bet you don't know why it tastes better right now? It's because we're sipping it while we read poetry. Is everyone hungry? Would you like me to fix something now? Mario, you cut the parsley and tell me when the skillet's hot. And you, my dear, beat the eggs in that bowl, then look for a tablecloth and set the table."

As I set the table, light streams across it and reflects off the plates. The omelet she's making smells divine. It's going to be delicious. Either I'm just normally clumsy, or I'm that way when I'm around Angélica. I don't know how else to help, and I can't even set the table correctly.

We're barely finishing when Mario begins putting the dirty dishes in the sink.

"Don't bother with that, we'll do them together later."

Instead of leaving them, he rinses them. While he's in the kitchen, Angélica decides we should try to hide somewhere. This seems ridiculous to me, and I'm sure it is, but perhaps that's what these people do.

"C'mon."

"Where?"

"I don't know, under the table, anywhere," she says, already underneath. The tablecloth is covering her.

While I get under the table too, she holds back a big laugh. Mario is too busy finishing the dishes to hear us. What a tidy poet!

"Let's try somewhere else! I know, his bed," she commands.

And all of a sudden we're lying down face up in his bed with the blanket pulled over our heads. And then this guy doesn't even come. Are we going to just stay here? He takes a while, but he finally comes and lies down on top of us; we begin to laugh. I feel a body on top of me, and for the first time, it's the body of a man who isn't my husband. The more we push up, the more he pushes down. I like how it feels. We finally manage to pull the covers from our faces, get up laughing, and go over to see the show in the fish tank.

We put some throw pillows on the floor. Angélica explains to him that I've just separated from my husband.

"It's time to go. My husband will be back anytime now."

I make a move toward the door in order to give them room to say goodbye to each other, but she follows right behind me.

"I forgot my books!" I remember, going downstairs.

I rush back up to get them.

"Don't take them with you now; that way I'll have a pretext to see you again. Write your telephone number down in one of them."

I went dashing down the stairs, still feeling the impact of his lips on mine.

The telephone rings. It's the poet. Will I be able to drop by tomorrow? Well . . . of course!

"Look, Angie . . . do you remember that I left my books at the poet's house? He called . . . do you mind? . . . "

"Oh, my dear, I'm so happy for you. All I wanted was for you to meet him. Go to him. Enjoy."

I hung up and flew out the door. I hope I remember how to get there. Sure I do!

It's been one obstacle after another, but my interest is piqued; it's been too many years of suppressing my curiosity, not knowing whether all men make love the same way. And yes, it must be the same, but it's another body, another smell, another presence, another man. And not knowing where his hands or his kisses will take him.

This is the only picture I have of my parents with all their children. One day, the group just came together, and it's interesting that it happened like that and not another way. When our dad sat down for the picture, Clarita and I ran over and stood on either side of him. Then he put his arms around us. Next to Clarita was Rafael, smiling with his sparkling eyes. My mother stood directly behind us. Moshón, who had crossed his arms and whose eyes were bulging out, was next to her; just like any kid, he was biting his lower lip, looking impatient. In strategic fashion, he was as far away from Rafael as possible, because they weren't getting along then; but he was very close to Freddy, who was more sensible. And he was shorter than the others (despite all the vitamins our mother had made him take). And, finally, there was Zelda—she's so pretty—who stood next to them, but not all that close, really. I'm hugging my dad, who shows a great deal of love for his three daughters.

It's so beautiful to know that you love us! You've got such a nice smile and loving hugs. You *are* the center of the picture, the main trunk of the family tree.

Our parents have transmitted their values to us. I guess we could say that each one represents different sides. Everything seems to be a conflict based on money. While some people despise it, making things even more difficult, just about everyone gives it too much importance.

Little Jacob is totally absorbed by his father. I can hear Lalo speaking from inside him; in fact, I can still hear him speaking through all of my children. This is horrible! Will I ever be able to separate myself from him?

"There's not going to be any divorce," said my husband's psychoanalyst one day. "You can get a separation, but he's the father of your children, and he's going to be the grandfather of your children's children."

Becky's daughter, Lina, is getting married. Victor and I want to take the pictures, so to get her interested I asked her to do some modeling in our studio. The girl changed clothes a thousand times, and put on and took off what seemed like a million hats. We dimmed the light to create some special effects; then we used the black and white cycloramas, with moving subjects. We were fascinated by the possibilities.

We were eating breakfast the day I took the proofs over to Becky's house, and when I told her that Lalo had moved out, she gave me some suggestions on how to take care of myself. And now I'm not sure how it came out that I liked Victor. What seemed funny was that while he and I were showing her the proofs, she detected that he had been looking at *me* the whole time.

"You like him, don't you?"

"Now that's absurd! He's so much younger than me. The idea sounds ridiculous."

"Too bad. Because of your hang-ups you can't enjoy something that could very well be a beautiful experience. If I were you, I'd go for it. It's better to feel guilty for something you did than for what you didn't do."

Do I really like him? I've never thought of it that way. No, I don't think it'll work.

As soon as Lalo left the house, I got our carpenter to make me a desk. He brought it today. Never in my life have I had my own desk. Well, I had one when I worked in the lab, but that was when I was single. It's a dream come true! My own desk! And now I can write without worrying about someone reading it, which is why I had to have it made behind everyone's back. A desk!! I have the same feeling as the time when they brought the piano to our house. It changed everything. Does furniture have a soul? Now I feel important. This desk is mine and no one else's. It's big and majestic looking, with three drawers. I've already put a lamp on it, and paper clips and a stapler in the drawers. Now I have everything it takes to be a writer.

Makeup, rouge, eyeliner. My hands are trembling: the eyeliner on the left eye isn't the same as on the right. My daughter comes into the bathroom; I don't want her to see how nervous I am, nor do I want her to ask any questions. I'm not fast enough to invent a story. I can't wait to see him, and I hope he's alone. I grab my purse and the things I had promised him. As I ran down the stairs, I realized that this time there's no one to stop me.

"I'll be back soon. Bye."

My God, my heart is pounding. I get into the car, put it in reverse, and then take off. We don't live far from each other, but it seems to take forever to get there. The closer I get, the more nervous I get.

What is he going to say when I get there? What will I say to him? I guess I should arrive happy. But why? Talk about my work? No, I don't think that's the way to handle this. My skirt's pretty. These high heels make me look slimmer. I should buy some new clothes, something different, not those dresses that make me look like a wife, the ones Lalo chose for me. That's it: slim down . . . flirt more . . . dress sexier.

I got to Victor's house with the negatives. After driving like crazy in order to arrive on time, I found him still working away as if I weren't even there.

"Hey, why did I hurry so much to get here? You're ignoring me."

"You're in love with me, you know, and I'm in love with you," he blurted out.

I began to tremble. My hands were shaking. I couldn't control them. They weren't mine anymore. He saw what was happening.

"Why do you say that?" I asked, barely able to respond.

"It's the way you're looking at me."

"Oh, really," I said, suddenly embarrassed.

"Yes, really. You look at my mouth and then what's inside my pants," he said, looking at himself.

I couldn't believe it; I never thought it was possible that I would look at him like that. I wasn't even aware of it.

"Give me a kiss."

He kissed me on the lips for an eternity, or until my hands stopped trembling.

"I've always liked you. . . . I love you."

That was the end of the conversation.

About a year ago, when I first met him, I had been reading Cortázar's *Hopscotch*. My world revolved around La Maga . . . Oliveira . . . "Pola, a new love . . . a new sensualization." A new sensualization in my life! Marvelous!

Hopscotch is a novel made of gunpowder. It awakens the desire to break with the establishment: to destroy, to invent new schemata. A fragile book made of crystal? Not in the least. It's a book with the force of a sword, one that lacerates. It's a dangerous book; it demands change. It's a book of magic that ignites and explodes. It's like a jalapeño: it burns . . . it bites back.

All these years dreaming about a lover.

"And I'm it," he assures me.

"You called me three times yesterday. Was it about work?" I asked.

Only when he's kissing me will he confess that he wanted to see me, and that he got mad when I went out with friends the night before.

"I really like you a lot, Oshinica, but please don't fall in love with me."

A little later, he explains himself:

"I didn't fall for you because of your looks, but because you make me laugh, you're fun to be around. And besides, you don't even know how to make love. Since you were older and had been married all those years, I thought you could teach *me* something."

My eyes almost popped out.

"Even if you were ninety years old, I'd still be in love with you. I think I'm in love with you."

I wonder how long this will last?

"However long it takes," we say to each other.

I turned forty today. Victor gave me a little orange-colored stuffed baby chick, which made me feel like I was a little girl again.

He reads the novel about my childhood and adolescence with interest, but I don't think anyone else will be interested in it. He's going to New York to take a course on homeopathy for two months. I'll miss him, but I should just brace myself for it. And, to top it off, his family has some marriage prospects for him . . . they're all desperate: by now, he's supposed to be married and have children. They want to become grandparents.

But he wants to become a famous surgeon with an office full of patients and charge a lot of money. He wants to study overseas, but his parents don't want him to do it alone.

"What do you want me to do? You know, they don't just say 'May you become a bride' to women; they also say, 'May you become a groom.' We get pressured too, you know, and not only to get married, but also to earn a lot of money. Don't think you're the only victim in this game. They bought me a new car because they figured no girl would ever get into my old one. I need to specialize in the United States somewhere; if I don't, I'll be eaten alive here. I'm going out with this girl today."

"Don't worry about it," I said. "Our thing is *while it lasts*. We've already made that clear to each other."

Victor stopped by during breakfast to leave some flashbulbs and to check out my new desk.

"Aren't you going to invite me in?"

Just when I said, "Well, of course," I lost it. I was going back and forth from the kitchen, bringing him some ham and eggs with beans on the side and a little *trusht*. While he was eating, I jumped up to bring him something else: a sandwich, a slice of ham, sausage, and papaya and watermelon.

"Hey, you don't let me finish one thing and you bring something else."

I broke out crying.

"I'm nervous; it's just that I suddenly relived all those moments at breakfast time when there was no way I could please anyone. Look, I'd like to ask you a favor: please come to eat anytime—lunch, dinner, whatever—but not for breakfast. Reliving all that makes me want to get sick. I don't know how to calm down; I'm going to take a walk in the park. I'll see you later."

This path that I take over and over is totally different each time when I know I'm going to meet you. It's more beautiful, and I can see things more clearly. Everything seems to shiver out of excitement; it all seems eternal. How does this happen? I don't know, but maybe it's the anticipation, the idea of promise, a fluttering sensation inside, in your gut, but sooner or later, it comes to the surface, infiltrates your brain, crimson-colored. I just don't know.

I haven't even parked my car, but I know you're watching me from your studio window. I see that you're with a friend. I look away and you look away, indifferently; then you wave to me without turning around, as if I were just leaving, not arriving. I can smell your presence throughout the room. The phone rings, you sit down to answer it; meanwhile I walk back and forth, snooping around. I see things that are familiar to me, and others that aren't. Your friend is feeling uneasy. He says goodbye. I walk past where you're talking. You grab me, put your hand up my skirt, and all of sudden you're inside me. I'm immobilized, struck by lightening. While you utter monosyllables over the phone, you continue to penetrate me with your fingers. I'm paralyzed. You hang up and begin kissing me the way you know how. I'm a ripe fruit dripping nectar from between my legs; my mouth becomes soft, succulent mango. You pull me down onto the small throw rug you bought especially for making love. Leaving me poised to receive you, you lock the door and shut the blinds. You unzip your pants and enter me; I kiss you, salivating down to your toes and stopping to catch my breath at your belly button. You're the lover about whom I dreamed for so many years; I look at you and smile. I've waited a thousand and one nights for you, and now you're here next to me. My fantasies have been made real. I have you, we have each other. After hugging me tightly, you force me to turn over, and I feel the weight of your body on top of me; our eyes, now wide open, look at each other intensely; then we close them tightly. I cry, and the tears roll down my face. You smile, feeling them wet against your face. When I open my eyes again, I find you smiling at me tenderly. I want to keep watching you, so I can remember you like this always; my eyes dance happily, and you smile back at me. I say your name, I wake up repeating it, it becomes real, and now I have your name every time I wake up in the morning.

I'm looking at the strangest thing. I'm so happy that I didn't sleep with Jacob Zabludowsky or wake up with Mamoncito Ochoa. I'm so happy I'm not going out with them anymore!

Using the tips of my fingers, I glide my hands across every last part of your body. They begin with the nipples on your chest, move slowly downward toward your inner thighs, and then find surprises that make you tingle. It's hot outside. We stretch out on *our* rug, and the street lamp outside the window illuminates your body, creating new sensations. Your body, partly seen and partly unseen, moves me to tears. My fingers explore everywhere. While my eyes absorb your body and my tongue licks your succulent skin, you yield to my moves, waiting with closed eyes. With anticipation, your mouth avidly awaits mine; they touch, and I return again and again, tasting and nibbling, then following the curves of your lips with mine, pulling away.

I run my hands all over your body, up and down, always starting over. Electrified, the tips of my fingers pursue every last inch of your body. Before, they didn't know what to do, but now they've learned to respond to your heat, to the blood running through your veins in silence, listening to what we don't say, looking at your eyes, focused on your eyelashes. My lips travel your body freely; you quiver, and I reach ecstasy when you're on top of me, but I feel no weight. Nor do we think; we're fused into one being—I refuse to say anything, for the sound would destroy the magic of this moment.

I only hear us breathing in unison.

"Hey, don't be lazy, get going."

"But I'm worn out . . . okay, I'll just stick them in my coat pocket. After all, I live only a minute away."

Chely's chauffeur stays inside the car while I open the door to my house. There's my dog—happy and excited to see me. He jumps all over me and bites at my handbag. I struggle to remove my shawl, then my coat. My impotent smiles are no defense against him. The chauffeur wants to get out and help me.

"No, it's fine. He's like that every time I get home. He's very affectionate."

"I saw the dog pull something from your pocket."

"Yes, I think you're right," I said, sticking my hand inside and finding nothing.

After doing to me whatever he wanted, the damn dog decides to run away; no matter, I've left him out all night before. He doesn't go very far; besides, it's the only time he has any freedom. It's impossible during the day, because as soon as anyone sees him coming, they run inside, jump in their cars, or run for the closest bus.

Poor Odilón! He doesn't realize how big he is. He's always causing a ruckus, but I try not to let him attract too much attention. Why in the hell doesn't that guy get back in his car and leave me alone? I should have put them on at Victor's, but he told me to get moving.

"What a beautiful dog. What kind is he?"

"Saint Bernard," I respond dryly.

Now what should I do? Someone's going to find my new panties in the street in the morning. I don't care about them so much, but my daughter was with me when I bought them, and I don't want her to find them in the gutter when she goes out to wait for the bus.

"Odilón! Odilón. Give it to me. Come here, please."

"Allow me to help you, Señora," insists this jerk. "After all, I'm already here, and I have to wait for my boss anyway."

"No, thanks, I'm going inside to bed."

And what if my neighbor comes outside and sees the dog parading around with my underwear in his mouth? Just because I was too lazy to put them on! I'm almost falling asleep. It's past one o'clock in the morning, and here I am creating a scandal in front of my house.

"Odilón! Come here. C'mon you monster, here, try this. You'll love this meat."

Whenever I have to show the house, I get so upset. I can't even smile at the people who come by to see it. But Lalo keeps pressuring me, he needs his share, and I should get out anyway. He thinks it would sell faster if it were empty. He's threatening to cut me off if I don't do something fast.

He hasn't sent any alimony for six straight months. We barely had enough for gas, Felipa's salary, telephone, tortillas, eggs, bread, beans, rice, and meat for the dog. It's absurd to have a Saint Bernard . . . but then, what would the children say? We've learned how to get a lot accomplished during the light of day; it's free, so by nightfall they've done their homework and I've finished my work. I didn't realize that without electricity the water pump won't reach the cistern on top of the house. Felipa unclogs the bathroom drains, fixes the curtains, and irons. Somehow her energy is transmitted to us. That's the only way she knows how to live.

Last night, as I was walking down the hall with a lit candle, I came upon little Serafín with a flashlight getting his uniform ready for school the next day. I got a big knot in my stomach, but it went away as soon as I detected that he was pleased with the way it looked. It's not easy, but one can learn how to cope without the basic necessities.

I arrive at the studio, and Victor's touching up the picture of a young woman. I see that he's upset about something. He applies one color, then another. I see that he likes the person in the picture.

"Who is it?" I ask.

"I went out with her on Saturday and Sunday."

I notice how he's looking at her. I begin to understand.

"I don't want to lie to them. It's better to end it."

𝕏 THREE WEEKS LATER.

It's time for him to say goodbye. There are flowers, a bottle of good wine, two glasses, and a card: "Thanks for your love, your tenderness, and your friendship."

And I bring him something wonderful too: a tape of all my favorite music. Elena contacted Susana Alexander for me, and I asked her to sing some of the songs. Even before he started the ritual of what was going to be the end of our relationship, I was already working to stop myself from breaking down and sobbing.

There he was: Victor, the future doctor and youngest son of the family, now ready to begin his career. And me, a woman who's stubborn about defending herself, refusing to succumb, making a living doing what she wants to do. That's what my triumph here is all about.

Ever since the beginning, when we dared to admit our fears, we knew that this goodbye would also be a part of our story.

I made a list of all the thoughts I had underlined in my books by Octavio Paz, Pablo Neruda, and Julio Cortázar that expressed my fantasies about his love for me. The result was a collage. I transferred them to transparencies, and if it's true that I didn't write those poems, they became mine after I had met him.

We got out the projector, adjusted the sound, and he sat down beside me. Together, we could feel the emotion Susana had put into her readings.

Skyward, a bright heat, tarnished gold, greenish clouds turning yellow: the world begins to rouse. I get up feeling an enormous presence all about me, and I say: 'A toast to everything that flourishes and then falls to the ground! Here's to yesterday and tomorrow, to everything that changes, survives birth, grows, returns to the earth, and grows again! Here's to night and day, and the four seasons of the soul!

I look at the luminous blue morning that hangs over the plants, now diffused. A tree stands erect, the course of a river makes a curve, zigzags, circles around, but always returns home. I'm paralyzed by an immense sense of well-being! Ah, love . . . love . . . that is the word.

But what meaning hath these ardent desires? Why—in darkness—these feelings? What moves my spent body? Why must I press on? Why are there trees under whose shade I am unable to remain without being enveloped by vast, melodic thoughts? I sit down on the ground, look around, and see those trees whose beauty begs me to ask why is the splendor of their roots hidden from view? Patches of sky stream through the branches of the trees, the air tastes deliciously wonderful, and I run wildly through this October forest.

I never tire of looking at you. It's so strong, it's like the way moss covers a rock. The sun delights itself in announcing the dawn in your hair. Of all the things I have ever seen, I only desire to see you; of all the things I have ever touched, I only wish to touch your skin. Yet, my emotion grows even more, especially upon seeing such beautiful scenery: flowers, waterfalls, leaves, paths, couples. After a while I will go home, and enveloped by the vigor of my solitude I will draw your face, and recreate your smile. Do you know what? No one even suspects that I have it here inside me and that I remain awake reconstructing every moment I've spent with you.

Do you know what I did yesterday? I spent the entire day thinking about you. And that simple fact makes me happy. Without even realizing it, time goes by and your radiance grows in my memory. You are everywhere. Absolutely everywhere. Ever since I began to think, I only think about you. You penetrate the way I speak, the way I look at things, the way I kiss you; you have even penetrated my clothes, you have filled me with smiles.

I only want to talk about you. Everything reminds me of you. Sometimes, I think my words are only audible to you, and I hear you speaking amid the silence around me. I imagine that your words caress me, touch me, cover my face, come and go, and glide past me tenderly. I love to hear them, they stimulate me, they create me, I listen, they're mine, they're for me only, your voice touches me, gives form to my mouth, reaches my tongue, embraces me. . . . I love you. I love you so much.

I tell you these things, and even though it doesn't seem possible, I know that you hear me, see me, and spy on me with a certain indifference. I know your silence is filled with love. You look at me in that special way. I see strange worlds. I see your hands resting on your legs. Where is the little kid I used to see in you? Is he still there, or is he gone? I kneel by your side and put my arms around your legs and hands; I raise my face and see the eyes in the depths of which you live, the eyes that not even you know or understand.

I see myself rediscovering your body, inch by inch, which fills me with pleasure.

Behind your eyelids, I see some memories that have been forgotten. I never want to lose sight of you. I believe this is a game that I will eventually lose; nevertheless, the beauty of playing it remains. And, with sadness, I ask: what are your eyes seeing now?

I know that nothing lasts forever, not even the pain nor the happiness that you have given me, but I fear that I need you immensely.

You look my way and smile. It's your smile that I love so much. I would give anything for just that smile. I want to preserve that which I love, the smile that I'm sure you aren't aware of.

The story of my love is not the same as yours. You have given me love without even knowing it. It just is. I have invented you in order to continue living . . . and I've never been this happy.

I ended this homage to love with the "Ode to Joy" from Beethoven's Ninth Symphony, and a card in which I wrote: "Thank you."

I try to stitch together those precious moments when our bodies enveloped each other in love. I felt safe under your wing.

Today, here in Villa Alpina, swarms of birds cover the tops of the pine trees, perching on the most fragile parts of the branches. And me, a flower, a single flower, bowed by the weight of this beauty.

I toast my classmates in the writing workshop.

"Here's to the young people, the cowards, the slaves, the poets, your eyes, your kisses, your back, the tone of your voice, my trembling hands the first time you kissed me, the shape of your eyes, your beauty, my eyes that search you out, my defects that cause me to suffer, my insecurities . . . and to me, you, today, and my new, marvelous, and confused life."

❖ ❖ ❖

When we finally had to move away from La Herradura, I didn't want to say goodbye to the neighbors. I don't know how, but they knew everything. Did they spy on us? Did they notice that we were without lights for a week and that we ran garden hoses from the cistern down to the bathtubs? And they were nice enough not to ask us what was going on.

We drove out of the neighborhood behind the moving van that carried all of our possessions; oddly enough, after the movers had loaded the truck, one item had been left outside in the driveway, in full view: a portrait of our wedding. That seemed like a strange way to finish off twenty years of marriage, with nothing to show for it except four children.

Having to move to a new house is one of the worst things that can happen to anyone! How had I accumulated so much stuff? Maybe all I used to do was go shopping!

Felipa was already pregnant when we moved to an apartment on a busy street closer to the center of the city. We decided it would give us certain advantages: we'd have less work to do in an apartment; we don't need a gardener; and the kids are going to learn to use the bus.

"See the difference! If I hadn't been chauffeuring you around out there, you would've been trapped."

When Tacho was born, we put his crib right next to Serafin's bed. She puts him there during the day, because the maid's quarters are up on the terrace, and we're on the first floor. Felipa is very happy with her new son, and it seems like every five minutes she's calling me to come see how he's growing.

She never asks permission to visit her hometown or go out for one of her numerous "engagements," either in Chalma or

ROSA NISSÁN

Uruapan. She's a dancer; well, I like to kid her about it, for in reality she directs a group of folk dancers, and she's always busy organizing everything and making the outfits, the feathers, and the tambourines. Once they did a show in the Santuario de Los Remedios, and I went along. She looked like a peacock with all those ostrich feathers and the typical red Mexican dress covered with sequins. While the other dancers were getting ready, we sat on the stairs and ate some Mexican food that she had bought at the corner: barbecued meat, tortillas, guacamole, and hot sauce.

Whenever she gets ready to go away for a while, she'll fix food for five days and give us instructions on what to heat up on Monday, on Tuesday, etc., until she returns. She always comes back with baskets full of blue tortillas, mole, corn on the cob, avocados, and prickly pears.

My children are angry because they can't ride their motorbikes around the neighborhood like before. And Odilón isn't with us anymore; the owner of the apartment wouldn't allow it. If we open a window here in Culiacán, we can't hear the radio or ourselves talk, only large trucks and ambulances. Daniela is so upset that she won't even leave her room; she says we live in a fishbowl, because all we see are the Dolphin-brand trucks. I'm pretty sure the problem is that she's embarrassed at school to tell her friends where we're living. She'll get over it. It's not that I wasn't upset myself about having to leave, but there was no alternative. It's not worth wasting your life fighting over it. The worst part about it is the traffic, especially when I come down Jamaica Street. I can't stand not being able to find a place to park. At least the apartment is fairly spacious.

Yesterday was little Tacho's baptism. Rafael and I were the godparents. They told the priest that my brother was my husband, because, like anywhere else, you're not much if you don't have a husband. An unmarried woman is worth about half of what she would be if she were married.

I got worried when the priest said that if one day Felipa was unable to continue, that we'd be responsible to take care of Tacho and provide for his education. Felipa presented her cousin as Tacho's father. Even the father is fictitious, but when all is said and done, the baby's real.

The food Felipa prepared was fabulous. They borrowed a record player and rented a space, and everyone danced and toasted the new baby and the godparents.

Felipa seemed so different from when she's working for us in the apartment. Acting the queen, she gave orders accordingly. It occurred to me that it was an honor for me to have a woman like her help me become independent. I thanked God for having sent me an angel.

I just received my part of the sale of the house. As soon as I opened the envelope, I took it straight to Moshón. I'm afraid to keep it, because I've never seen so much money; I only had enough money to keep the house running. But I'm going to spend some of it now, before I feel guilty about it. I want to buy a tripod for my camera. Mr. Vera has a used one. I asked my mother to go with me to get it. I know I'll never regret it, because every time I'd take pictures of a large group, I always had to borrow Victor's.

I told Angie that my mom went with me.

"And why did you do that? Is she some expert on photography?"

Hoping to have a good time, I invited the kids to go to Mazatlán and La Paz, just like we used to do in the past. And we did have a good time. Jessy's boyfriend, who also came along, helped us a lot; now they want to get married. That really sent shivers down my back, because she just started at the university. Isn't that just the way life goes? I'm trying to get out of a marriage and she's trying to get into one. They've been friends ever since they were fifteen. I don't want her to stop studying. I want her to be older when she gets married. Just hold off, damn it! What's the hurry? And I've been so proud of the fact that I haven't pressured them at all to get married. On the other hand, it's also sad, because he's so nice. But I can't forget that I've lived my entire life wanting my children to be educated. Please wait, my child! You're driving me crazy!

Although it's been hard, I've decided to go to Italy with my friends from the writing workshop. They've got everything planned, and I don't know how to tell my mother. She's going to explode. Why didn't I learn the Commandments? How could I forget them? But if I obey her, I won't have any fun in life. Dear God, please help me disobey her, even at my age; please don't punish me for defying her. She's going to say that I just let money slip through my fingers, but I'm only spending some on this trip and the tripod.

Five women and two men: Carmen, Angélica, Meche, Magda, me, and the two teachers, Vicente and César. This is a different trip for me, because I'm free. I don't have to ask for money or permission from anyone. This group not only doesn't criticize me, they also like me. Just think: traveling around Italy! And on a train no less! And, what a surprise, the Italian guys like me. They're unbelievable! However, since we're going from place to place, there's no time to do much more than flirt and act naughty a bit. And who wants more than that?

I wouldn't recommend starting in Venice, because you won't see anything more spectacular after that. Built on fantasy, Venice is a city that wants to be real, a grandiose dream that materializes before your eyes. When I travel up and down the canals, I look avidly at all the palaces. I get the sensation that the whole place is made of cardboard that will disappear when we leave, but a closer look tells me that it's been around a while. Venice is the irrefutable proof of the eternal existence of magicians and incantations; it's a city of voices and bells that loom in the mist surrounding us. Everything there seems improbable. Its inhabitants foolishly insist that the city actually does exist; in the same vein, they argue that they aren't actors but citizens who live there. At times, everything is so real that I believe it, but after a few days there I begin to doubt again, saying this can't be true, it's only a spoof on reality.

This morning I get up really early with the idea that I'll surprise the Venetians before they actually begin play-acting; so I sit down on the steps of the canal near my hotel. A small motorboat draws near, stops in front of me; and the guy steering it has the audacity to tell me I'm blocking the gas pump. Surprise! I look around and spy a hose on the ground. I pull it toward him, he pretends he's filling the gas tank, and then he pulls away with the most serious look on his face . . . this is an illusion!

Without the right music to create a feeling of melodrama, another boat, looking like it's the local fire department, comes up the canal with bells ringing and screeching sirens. The firemen look so funny that I almost feel like applauding them, but they're taking the whole thing seriously.

The next day another boat—in reality, a floating garbage truck—comes up the canal. They say it comes by every day amid the yelling, laughter, and reprimands as the boat fills up with bags full of waste. Whenever I can, I get on a little steamer, which takes me around to see all the local spots of interest. Here, you can't go around with your head buried in the sand or be caught reading a book; frankly, it's too hard to sit down and read, and I can't even stand losing time by having to sleep. I want to spend the entire night in San Marcos Plaza, stay there forever, wake up during the night, turn around and look at everything that's going on around me, then watch the sunrise. I don't want to get tired just to have to rest later; I don't want to have to go to the bathroom just to have to take a bath. It's during those moments that the Venetians work behind the scenes, making plans to keep the big deception alive. They organize those who actually carry it out: presidents, policemen, even a boat with a crane for building a building. Their dress should be impeccable, for this is a society of actors from the outer limits, but they're also from here, too. They're people who seemingly believe in drama. This is the place to which everyone, from everywhere, gravitates; it's surrounded by the sky of eternal fantasy.

Here, you find daily drama that's totally alive. In essence, Venice is the harmonious result of a group of dreamers from many past generations; they have invented something that requires them to keep alive the most exquisite city ever created by mankind. And they play out the drama of this city that has no time or place. Shakespeare, Molière, and Pirandello, no doubt, are still here, somewhere . . . perhaps working as waiters or gondola drivers.

I get up early every morning; in fact, it's been earlier each day since we've been here. We only have six days in Venice, and it won't be enough. I open the window in my room, and I can barely make out strange shapes in the fog; everything's mysteriously hidden, but little by little I can perceive what's out there. I don't want to stay in the hotel room, so I begin walking along the narrow, winding streets near the hotel. I don't care about the stores, so I'm not interested in what they sell. This city has overwhelmed me. I return to my hotel, and I put on my best dress because I'm embarrassed by what I've been wearing; it just didn't match the elegance of the drama that takes place here every day.

I decide to take a ride in a gondola carpeted in black. I lean back in the seat and close my eyes. I can hear the oars knifing the water. The steamers don't travel along the narrower canals. Everywhere, the sounds of life invade me, they get inside my pores. Right now, just about every Venetian mother is probably washing the breakfast plates in the sink, all at the same time. I smile at my gondola driver, who's waving enthusiastically at a friend who's taking tourists somewhere. When I open my eyes and look up, I see all kinds of laundry proudly hanging from the windows: undershirts; pants; and red, yellow, and blue underwear. Diverse sounds—the oars slicing the water of the canal, and dishes being washed—collide simultaneously. And, of course, there's a myriad of voices, speaking not only Italy's national language, but also what's spoken in Venice. Everything drifts from the windows and floats down the canals, sticking to everything in sight, even the laundry and my ears that delight in hearing the everyday music of this vibrant city.

My boat ride, which has taken an hour, is over. Feeling elated, I remember that San Marcos Plaza is still there, at all hours of the day and night, every day, every month, every year, and every century . . . and it will continue that way forever. So I sit down at a table in a small café and wait to order something, even if it takes every last cent I have; no matter how expensive it may seem, it'll still be cheap. Before that, however, I'm going up into the Campanile. Ah, there's an elevator, and all of a sudden I'm overlooking the entire city of Venice. From here, the laundry hanging in the windows is below me, out of sight, hidden under the eaves. The lack of the magic created by such an effect from below is compensated by the view of the red-tiled rooftops that replace the commercial signs adorning the rooftops in other cities. Everywhere you see the slanted roofs that hide from view all the hanging underwear of the world, a world built on canals, gondolas, and gondola drivers, a city that's constantly floating, but now hidden from above.

My Venetian-style coffee has arrived. At this hour, I have the entire plaza to myself, and for as long as I want. Then some smooth-talking Italian guys who are real playboys show up and start staring at a group of tourists. It's easy to talk to anyone, and these Italians are really passionate.

If, after spending a few days here, you begin to believe everything you see, it's time to pack up and leave quickly; that is, if you don't want to go crazy, or assume some meaningless role, or even invent one, and then find yourself trapped, and finally, you find yourself dressed in a blue and white striped shirt like the ones the gondola drivers wear, singing as you row and watching out for your luxurious ship. And why not? They're showing wide-eyed tourists, like some American couple, who are film experts, let's say, the beauty of a city without automobiles or parking lots. Or those tourists who want ever so fervently to relive a love story like the ones that are filmed in Venice.

Here, the lighting engineers are incredible. They invent the nights and days at their will, angelically controlling the sun, the moon, and the stars. You don't really notice them, because their work is near perfect: the sunrises and sunsets are unlike anywhere else in the world. Whenever these guys get tired, they invent cloudy days and gray afternoons, like the ones when you can't take any pictures, for instance, returning on the little steamer after having spent the day on the beach of the Hotel Excelsior, reliving the film Visconti made.

On the other hand, plant life isn't all that great here. Venetians aren't experts on gardening, but the tourists don't seem to notice or even care; instead, they're mesmerized by the stories they hear, the narrow streets and canals, the laundry hung in the windows, this floating island. It's a world unto itself, a world inside another world, where artists—the ones who dream—must go when they die. It's a country where dreams come true.

It seems like that for centuries now, Magda has been talking about the importance of a couple's relationship. She's been hung up on this for a long time. I listen to her, but the last thing I want now is to get trapped in another relationship, to have to go everywhere with only him, or to have to include him in everything I do. No way! I don't want any of that; well, not for several more years. At one time I believed that my world was naturally determined by the man who would be at my side forever; now, however, I want to stand alone. I don't need to hide in his shadow; I need my own light. Given the education I received from my parents, I know that it's my duty to show my devotion to him; in fact, I did it automatically, not necessarily because he wished to impose himself on me, but because I've been taught to obey men. Just the force of their voices controls me. I'm tired of it.

I remember the day my sister-in-law died: I arrived at their house just as everyone was leaving for the cemetery. My brother, who neither said hello to me nor gave me a chance to give my other sister-in-law a hug, blurted out: "Get in the car!"

Naturally, that's what I did. When I discovered that I was among people I didn't even know, I said to myself, "What am I doing here, if all I wanted to do was give my sister-in-law a hug?" Is it my second nature to blindly obey men? Maybe that's why I'm not anxious to get married again. I know that I'll begin to get nervous if I sense that the man I'm with demands some coffee or if he didn't like the lemonade. I'll end up obeying his orders before I have a chance to think for myself. I'm used to him waking up and making all the decisions. Once again, I'm facing the danger of disappearing, just when I'm beginning to experience a resurrection.

So, when did I choke up? Why did I let myself shrink into a nobody? Why did I inundate myself with so many chores? I want to use what's left of my life to meet the rest of life head on; not like before, always standing to one side, half-hidden, half-lived, feeling sorry for myself, as if I hadn't been invited into this world that somehow was organized without me but was letting me fill a small void somewhere and paying me to exist. My life didn't seem important, and that's why I wasn't concerned about myself. It hurts to think that since childhood they've squelched my imagination, clipped my wings, and prevented me from building my own house of fantasies. I've always tried to make my house look exactly like my friends' houses. Why didn't I build my own house? I didn't even have anything to do with the one I presently live in.

I'm going to invent a new style of sweater: I'll start out with red yarn, change to blue whenever I want, alter the pattern, create new ones, all just for the pleasure of being the one making the changes. I want to create my own clothes, love affairs, food recipes, dance steps, ways of kissing, laughing, wearing makeup, singing, running like a crazy person, sitting down with my legs apart, having a birthday without a cake, writing a novel or a short story without a plan or a structure—that is, without any exposition, rising action, climax, or denouement.

Well, it was on one of those Italian mornings that I met Giorgio. We drank a glass of wine together at my hotel so that my friends could meet him. They approved. He's so handsome and friendly. Suddenly, he stopped in the middle of the story he was telling.

"I must go home. I forgot to feed my dog! Come with me! I don't live very far away. It's only five minutes from here."

My friends waved me on. As we were leaving the hotel, I stuck some sandals in my purse. I can't stand to walk very far in high heels, which is what I was wearing because I hadn't planned on leaving the hotel.

After driving a while, I realized that we were leaving the city.

"Just how far is your place? Isn't it nearby?"

"Just one more minute," he said stiffly.

But we just kept going and going. Florence was now a ways behind us. The lights of the city got smaller and smaller.

"I don't want to go to your house. Take me back to the hotel."

"*Aspeta!* We're like *vichinos.*"

By now, it was deserted outside.

"Either you take me back now, or I'm getting out," I said after a few minutes.

He stopped the car, and looking indignant, he grabbed me with both hands and yelled at me in Italian:

"*Aspeta!*"

Oh, oh, I thought, this is starting to look ugly. At that point, I realized that it was next to impossible to get out of the car. We kept driving. There were fewer and fewer houses, no other cars. He turned a corner, and we stopped at the only building on the block.

"Who do you live with?" I asked calmly.

"Who do you think I live with? I live alone! With my dog! That's why I had to come back. He hasn't eaten since this morning. We won't be long."

I followed him up the two flights of stairs, looking for ways to escape. When we went into his apartment, I saw piles of recently washed dishes on the dining room table. Didn't he say he lived alone? What if his friends come and they all rape me? Or what if he locks me inside the apartment and leaves? All those horror stories that Magda told us about terrorists and men with turbans who enslave women came to mind.

"I'd like a glass of water," I said, taking off my shoes to make him think that I was at ease there. Then, as soon as he went into the kitchen, I took off down the stairs, opened the gate below, and ran off into the surrounding darkness. Giorgio flew down the stairs and got into his car. He used the car lights to search almost everywhere for me, but then he left. I took out my sandals, put them on, and cautiously left my hiding place.

How was I to find the road back to Florence? Not knowing where to go, I started to cry. I spied some lights in the distance, which had to be Florence. After reaching a road, I heard a motor scooter coming . . . two young boys. If they had wanted to, they could've dragged me to the side of the road and done whatever they wanted to me. Now who's going to help me in this dark, deserted place?

They made some advances and joked to themselves. I started bawling, only able to respond with, *No parlo italiano.* I hoped they would feel sorry for me, so I begged them however I could to take me to the nearest bus stop. The youngest one offered to take me . . . well, in exchange for a kiss on the cheek. The kid in back got off the scooter, I got on, and I put my arms around the young boy who was driving; then he accelerated hard.

Not far away, there were signs of life—some houses and a bus stop. The sign said the last bus left at 11:15 P.M. What a relief! It was still only 10:30. I was lucky. It looked like I was going to make it back. So, out of gratitude, I gave him a kiss. He left with a smile on his face; after all, it was a good kiss. Then I hid among some bushes near some trees that created dark shadows.

They must have had second thoughts about letting their catch go. They came back. And there wasn't a soul around, but then someone opened the door of the house in front of the bus stop and came out. I asked him for his help, and he started laughing at me.

"They're just little kids," he said, indicating that it was ridiculous for me to be afraid of *them. Non paura,* he blurted out, but I grabbed him by the arm and made him walk with me to the bus stop. I was determined to make him wait with me until the bus came. And it wasn't long. I was relieved to see the word "Ferrovia." That bus went within a block of my hotel! I was so happy to get on and, finally, sit with the other passengers.

When I got off, I was worried that Giorgio would still be looking for me. Not wanting to look conspicuous, I tried to blend in with a family that was walking by. True to form, he was already there trying to spot me with his car lights. He'd swerve from one side to the other on the street, just like he did out where he lives. Within half a block of the hotel, the family turned up a side street. I started running.

Since it was late, the door to the hotel was locked. I panicked and started banging on the door. I knew that Giorgio had seen me. The door opened before he could stop his car and get out. He almost got me. I ran all the way to my room on the second floor, and I could still hear Giorgio banging on the main door downstairs. They wouldn't open it for him.

My friends hadn't returned yet. Trying to calm down, I took a hot bath. Meanwhile, Giorgio continued to bang on the door, screaming that I was crazy, because all he wanted to do was return my high heels that I had left in his apartment.

After that experience, I was a little wiser about things, but there are professional Don Juans roaming around everywhere. From then on, I didn't let my friends out of sight, except for my last day in Rome. I had wanted to get out and do something by myself, be outside, enjoy the sun, go to museums (all of which seemed like cemeteries to me). I wanted to invent everything: streets, plazas, and cafés. I wanted to live it all, so I went to see the sunset at Castelgandolfo, where I met a young student who gave me a rose. That gesture restored my confidence in men!

Well, I'm back in Mexico, and I've been hiding in a fetal position under the covers. I've become afraid of so many things; for instance, our fragility as human beings. Suddenly, the accumulation of emotional stability that I had stored up inside me came tumbling down like a house made out of playing cards. It fell on top of me: the psychoanalysis, self-injections of energy, the uncontrollable laughing, and the painful crying . . . everything that means life.

While we were on the plane on our way back from the trip, Magda continued telling her horror stories. Ever since she was a child, she told stories to her siblings and cousins before bedtime. While we were in Italy, I didn't know about her fondness for fear.

And what about this place? Was I really in danger? Or were my fears being driven by her stories?

The stone-faced owner of the building where we live informed me that he was raising the rent. Darn it, that triggered such a horrible feeling. I did everything I could not to let on, but my hands were trembling. It was difficult for me to say much as we walked to the door. I resolved I would do whatever I could to pay it. When Felipa saw him come in, she could tell something was fishy. That's why she gave him such a dirty look.

We moved to a smaller apartment in the Condesa neighborhood. I collected all the money I had, and along with some help from my parents and my siblings, I scraped together enough cash to buy it outright.

"Money just slips through her fingers," said my mother, referring to me. "If you give her a chance, she'll lose it all. She should just buy the apartment."

I wasn't thrilled about the place, but at least we'd have a permanent roof over our heads. It seemed like a toy house. There was a time when I couldn't have imagined that a family could live in such a small place, much less have running hot water, or an oven that actually works. But the neighbors seem happy: they sleep, cook, and bathe there in those apartments.

As long as I didn't have to turn in the key at the other place in Culiacán, I'd go there to take my baths; but it was bothersome having to go back and forth with shampoo and conditioner. My kids and Felipa started using the new apartment immediately, and Tacho had started to walk. Little by little, we decorated the apartment with what we had; nevertheless, it was difficult to make enough room for all of us, have my own little special area, and find the sunny spots. It wasn't long before we had some plants, which we hung from the ceiling, and bookshelves, paintings, and music.

Without Victor, I don't think I could have continued living in the other apartment. Our relationship ended with our first move. But I'm so happy to have had a lover, and I have to congratulate myself for not having let myself be dictated to by my hang-ups. And I'm not unhappy without him; in fact, we talk on the phone. He says he's pleased about the girl he's going to marry, and he asked me to take the wedding pictures.

"No problem," I told him. Yes, I know. . . . I'm not crazy, and I'm not a masochist.

Now, this is strange: one day Susan told me that my apartment was starting to look more and more like me, the way I dress, even the way I talk.

Tacho, who runs all over the place now, makes it impossible to find a moment's rest. At the other apartment, Felipa could take him upstairs to the maid's quarters at night, and we wouldn't hear anything. I'm starting to get nervous with him around all the time. There's no place to hide.

"Here's the problem, Señora," said Felipa. "My room is too cold for Tacho. And I really want him to be able to get out and run in the countryside. Besides, I was only going to stay until you got settled in this new place."

I felt ashamed, but obviously she had already decided to go home. She said she'd get a niece to take her place.

"Grandpa, how have you been?"

"I'm better," he responds, rubbing his stomach and gesturing on cue. "I'm better. I had an appointment with Ernesto yesterday. He switched my pills," he adds, taking them out of his pocket. "Listen, Shamuel, I want you to come over early in the morning and get the car out of the garage. It's bigger than I thought, and I can't get it out."

At the time, I didn't know why, but his right hand had begun to shake. Now I know that a proud man hides it right up until the time he dies. True to form, he opened the newspaper and began to read. The TV program that he had chosen for the moment was the one we watched until he decided to change channels.

Why am I still here? So, I say goodbye and take to the street, anywhere, Mexico Park. I need a place where I can talk freely.

Without Felipa's help, life is almost unbearable. As for the new maid, every time she goes home, we never know when she'll come back. That means that I have to do all the work around the house. I decided to warn my little cherubs: "You're not going to school unless you make your bed."

As it is, they can barely get ready on time.

"I'll-do-it-when-I-get-home," they yell in unison as they walk out the front door.

Since they don't get home until three o'clock, there's no way I'll leave the breakfast dishes in the sink until then. I gripe to myself while I'm straightening up the place. At times I think I've become their worst enemy. And they don't turn off the lights in their rooms, which I hate. And when I get home, they spend all their time on the telephone with their father, the one who dominates everything they do; and, of course, the person held in the lowest esteem in this movie is *me*.

🏃 ANOTHER SUNDAY.

As usual, my parents eat at my grandparents' house, but only after they've taken them to Chapultepec Park and to see houses, which is my grandfather's hobby.

I ring the doorbell. My dad comes from the back of the garage with some keys in his hand.

"I'm so happy you came," he says with a smile. "We just took your grandparents out for their ride."

I give him a hug, and arm in arm we walk back to the house. The fig tree is filled with fruit. I pull one from a branch. Then my father puts a few eucalyptus leaves in my hand.

"Smell them," he says, and I break them into little pieces to get their full aroma. As I inhale deeply, I suddenly feel surrounded by a forest that my father had managed to stuff into his pocket.

Back inside, everyone's already eating. I give my mother a kiss. Today, for a change, I'm feeling at peace with the world.

LIKE A MOTHER

"Grandfather, how did a piece of crystal get broken?"

"That crazy, son-of-a-gun painter did it, but we're having it replaced. He can go to hell."

After moving to this new neighborhood, I've been worried that my children might get depressed, because they don't have their motor scooters, their dog, or the quiet neighborhood from before. Nevertheless, I'm still happy that we made the move, because out in the suburbs, if the car ever broke down, that was it: you'd have to have it towed to a mechanic, take a taxi back to pick it up, or ask for a ride from a friend. Here in La Condesa, on the other hand, everything is a lot easier. Now, whenever I get a flat tire, I go to a place just around the corner; or, if they don't fix something right, I can go just down the street. And if there's nothing to eat? Or if I get bored late at night and want to go out? I simply go for a walk and find anything I want to eat: quesadillas, hamburgers, you name it. The burgers they make at the corner are really juicy. Or I can go to the movies. I've gotten to know the local locksmith, plumber, and electrician; and they know just about anyone else I might need to fix something. I always see the glass shop owner arrive in the morning and open his store. He parks his car, and then he blesses his children. They leave for school but return to work with him in the afternoons. I'm going out to buy the newspaper from Pifas. And I take a picture of the shoeshine guy sitting next to all his equipment. He has a funny sign: "I'm not here. I'm out to shine at the billiard table."

" . . . mind if I take a look at the newspapers?"

"Say, do you know so-and-so? He's a photographer like you. Look! Here he comes now. I'll introduce you to him."

Pifas has introduced me to several people in the neighborhood.

Whenever I don't have time to take a walk in the morning, I'll go in the evening. Mexico Park is well lit. I don't really like those gated communities with only houses inside. Sometimes I'll take walks through them, but it'll be five months, or longer, before I do it again. They're too monotonous.

Back then, I had a single plant in a flowerpot; since it was mine, I only watered that one plant, nothing else. The rest of the garden dried up and died.

Recently, I ran across a poem by the Venezuelan poet Andrés Eloy Blanco. I wrote down parts of it.

When you have a child

You have not only your own, but everyone else's too:

The one strapped to the beggar's back;

The one pushed along in a stroller by an English governess;

The white one cradled by the dark-skinned woman;

The fair-skinned child carried by the black maid;

The Indian child carried by his Indian mother;

The black child carried by the earth.

When you have a child

You have so many children that your house fills up.

And when you have two children

You have all the children in the world;

You have one child, or two, or a thousand

Or just one, and you say, "my child," or "my children."

Suddenly, I felt so egotistical for wanting to see the perfections in only my children, for wanting to love only them.

We're redecorating the living room with new drapes and new furniture. We still have a Persian rug, but it's a different color. The largest object in the room is the record player. When we didn't have one before, I always wanted to listen to one. And we never got to listen to my grandfather's, because he was the only one allowed to turn it on. We were always on the verge of asking him to play it. The same knickknacks are above the chimney; only the TV remote is different. We have the same pictures, but we added one more: Golda Meir. Who knows where it was taken! But the picture of all of us together is priceless. When it was taken, I thought we looked ridiculous: my grandparents sat in the middle—the patriarch and the matriarch; my Aunt Chela, who was pregnant, stood behind a stuffed chair; and on either side, my mom and dad. All the grandchildren stood wherever they could find a spot. My! How we've changed! There's Moshón, but he's handsome now. Clarita's mouth is hanging open. Freddy is as thin as a rail. Rafael, who is fair-skinned, always looked mad. And Zelda, with that ugly straight hair, and I mean really straight. Poor thing! We'll never forgive dad for that one. And we're all wearing those green Scotch-plaid velvet dresses that we wore at my aunt's wedding. The table in front of my grandparents is piled with newspapers; even today, he stills buys the *Excelsior* and *Novedades.*

Someone started singing on TV: "My love, oh, my love/you're so mean to me/who would have ever thought/that a lie would find its way/into a song." Ah, we're going to watch a great movie. It's just starting, and we don't want to miss anything. We like the movie star, Emilio Tuero. No one dozed off, not even Moshón, who is such a sleepyhead.

" . . . who would have ever thought/that a lie," he sings with that familiar voice, "would find its way/into a song."

"Man," comments my dad while we're watching, "is the king of his house. Eve was made from Adam's rib and given to man as his companion."

"See what these women can do to us," adds my grandfather. "It's better without them," he continues. "You have to be careful not to give neither the good ones nor the bad ones everything you have. They'll take over, and then they clean you out. Even if they're beautiful, and only God knows how much I adored the woman who gave birth to me—my mother—you have to be careful; they'll deceive you every time."

"Knowing me pains you . . ."

"They'll drag you down, just like what happened to that unlucky Carlos Durán. He wasn't a bad person; he was duped. She sidetracked him: he fell in love. That vile woman led him astray, and look what happened to him: she destroyed him. Did you see that diamond necklace he gave her? All those jewels, furs, petticoats? He ended up in jail. What he wouldn't have done for her! Ruined because of a woman!"

" . . . for so much love/in my moments of desperation/the voice of my heart will vex my conscience."

"And when he got out of jail, he ran into *that woman,* who was with someone else. A jealous man is capable of doing just about anything. So, when you think you're falling in love," he told his grandson, "be careful. Remember: don't give up all your love nor all your money."

" . . . now all I am to you is a vagabond/wandering aimlessly like a criminal."

"And after all that, she becomes the wicked one. He goes back to the cabaret to look for her, because he can't forget her. Did you hear what the pianist said he should do? He felt sorry for him. He said, 'Let her go, you've already lost her once, just forget her.' The love for a woman can turn us into the scourge of the earth."

This isn't the first time we've seen that movie. I listen to my grandfather, and I realize he hasn't changed his opinions since we were little kids. He's never questioned his values to see if they're still valid; if, at one point in his life, they seemed reasonable, then he'll continue thinking that way until he dies.

Moshón and I look at each other; he knows that I get furious when I hear that kind of talk, which is all the time. Of course my son just laughs, because everything we hear favors the males in the world. He likes that. But what he doesn't realize is that men also have their defects; for instance, the one who thinks he needs to become rich.

At this point, I'm about to blow up. I turn to my dad, but he's afraid, along with my grandmother, of my grandfather. He tries to stop me, or at least soften my interminable disgust.

"Grandfather, why do you say that women are bad?"

"What do you mean? Bad? Why, they're the most beautiful creatures in the world; they're cherished everywhere. I just love my daughter Chelita, and Lety and all my granddaughters too. Our religion requires that we respect our women. They're the ones who educate our sons. They're very important."

"They tell us that we're important, but I don't feel it."

My grandfather gets up from his chair and sticks his hands in his pockets.

"Samuel, come here. I want you to help me open the door to my bathroom. It gets stuck with the humidity, and I want to be able to take my bath in the morning."

Obediently, my father goes up to my grandfather's spacious bedroom.

So, we destroy men. We trap them in our claws. We betray them. We're the seductive, perverse hunters. We squeeze them for all we can get. We seduce them and take everything. I, for one, have spent my life trying to show that it isn't just because we're women that we're also dependent; otherwise, I wouldn't have married a poor guy (fortunately, he became rich). Perhaps we seek security in a man because we are taught to be dependent upon men. But there are men who are just as dependent as we are.

" . . . I will continue waiting for your love/even though I'll suffer forever."

My dad comes back downstairs. He's laughing at my grandfather's antics; he's in awe at how creative his father can be in finding so many ways to torture them.

The movie makes us emotional.

"What a life those women lead who get up at noon every day. They live by night and end up with whomever they run into," adds my mother, feeling repulsed.

"Mother," says my dad, "I'll call the carpenter tomorrow to fix the door. I opened it for him, but it's going to be difficult for him to close it." Then he joins in the conversation.

"Work is what we're supposed to do during the day, and I've always believed that the early bird gets the worm."

"And those women: what kind of love will they have if their lovers are from anywhere? They'll never see them again," adds my grandmother slowly.

"Behind all that beauty there's a sinister soul," concludes my Uncle Isaac.

"They cry, they pretend they're weak, and then they trap us."

My Aunt Chelita doesn't say a word; she just smiles.

"Every pretty woman is a potential saboteur . . ."

Just as the news is starting, Uba brings in the tray with the Turkish coffee. Teresita, who wears thick glasses, is sitting on a small chair with her eyes glued to the TV. She's here, but she's not here; she's a part of the family, but she isn't a part of the family. Her wicker chair is always waiting for her; fortunately, it hasn't fallen apart yet.

On TV, they're talking about how women were able to vote in Mexico after 1952.

"That's ridiculous. The whole thing is crazy. Why would they want to vote? In Mexico, that law is worthless. Now you tell me, just what good has it done? Chelita or your mother is going to vote? It's just one more thing that hasn't done any good for women."

I'm still without a maid; in the meantime, though, I've got a plan: since every one of my kids is going to school now, taking classes, going out with their friends, or whatever, and since today is my writing class, I'm going to get ready before they do. The one who is going out is *me*. Let's see how they manage on their own now! The girls are getting older, and little Jacob is going to be ten soon. Even he should be putting his own dishes away, but he won't; he won't even turn the light off in his bedroom at night.

When they saw me running out the door, all dressed up and clutching my manuscript, they were stunned. In rapid fire, I said to them what they always say to me: I'll-do-my-bed-as-soon-as-I-get-home. And then I was gone.

I returned home to make my bed long after they had made theirs and left that morning. But they had already talked at length with their father, who of course told them repeatedly that I'm just that way, that's why he left me, that I was completely irresponsible ... and all the other things that husbands say about their ex-wives. Now they hate me even more, but I refuse to be their slave.

"I propose that we divide up the work around here; besides, I still have my photography work."

They agreed to make their beds.

I don't know how this is going to end. Right now, though, they feel for me what I feel for them: hatred.

Part Three

ELEVEN

A loud explosion wakes us up. I open my eyes and remember that I'm at Gloria's house in Acapulco; she's the Cuban woman in our writing class who lives up on a mountaintop above Las Américas Hotel. Then another loud noise. Nothing moves; the roof hasn't fallen in. Then another one.

"Hey," yells Angélica, "let's find out what's going on. We can't just stay here in bed."

Once we leave the room, we can see the bay down below. I get down close to the ground in order to make my way to the edge of the balcony. I pull myself along with my hands, skirting the swimming pool.

"Angélica, get down on the ground, you're too visible."

Her standing up like that in her nightgown makes me nervous. I claw the ground to get closer.

"Get down, please! We're being invaded."

"But we're not at war. It must be the San Andreas fault."

More explosions. The rumbling off in the distance continues.

From my vantage point, I can see the entire bay. I don't see any war ships.

"Angélica, please, get down; it must be a surprise attack."

"But we don't even have any enemies."

More artillery fire, and we freeze. The noise stops. Total silence. I still don't dare to stand up; meanwhile, all the others are still in their rooms.

"Okay, get up, honey. It must have been an explosion of some kind. We'll find out later. Let's go back to our room."

"What's this about the San Andreas fault?"

Once we get back into our beds, my heart stops pounding, and she explains to me that Acapulco is situated along a fault line and that's what it's called. I try to go to sleep, concerned that I don't know more about this phenomenon. At breakfast, Elenita comes in with the newspaper, smiling.

"Did you hear the cannon shots? It was the beginning of the Cinco de Mayo celebration, and they let loose with a bunch of rockets at daybreak."

Angélica and I just look at each other.

"Now isn't that something, dear? And here you were flat on the ground."

"I don't know why I reacted that way."

"It's because you're Jewish. The Jews always think someone is going to attack them."

"But I've never been in a war."

"True, but you'll never get rid of your paranoia either. Let's go to town to buy some food. Do you know how to drive a stick shift? I don't."

As we were leaving the supermarket, I just about ran into someone. I didn't even see them. I hit the brakes and almost fainted. I think my teeth were chattering out of fear.

"Did you see how that person cut me off? Did you see?" I yelled at Angie.

"Yes, honey, but it wasn't because you're Jewish. That happens all the time."

When a new friend of mine, René, heard where I wanted to go, he tried to talk me out of it, but I wouldn't listen to him.

"To the King Kong."

Near the Teatro Blanquita, an enormous rubber chimp with his hands outstretched toward the front door greets us. We park the car, and the guys in the parking lot stare at me. I take off my jacket and straighten the neckline of my yellow dress while we walk. We buy two tickets, and they give us a couple of flyers at the door: one has the prices of the drinks they serve; the other is a list of the types of bottled liquors they sell.

We go into the main ballroom. The orchestra is on a landing above it. Everywhere women walk around in long, low-slung black dresses, selling tokens for requesting songs. There are young women, working women, and secretaries. Since we're sitting near the coatroom, I can see the girls who are still arriving. They bring their evening clothes in a small bag, change in the bathroom, and leave the bag with the attendant. Two of them, who aren't very pretty, are sitting near us, each at her own little table. They're comparing themselves to the others who've arrived. They're not only ready to dance, but they want to be paid for it. They're brave souls. When I was single, I was deathly afraid that no one would ask me to dance and that I would remain there, sitting alone. One of the happy things about marriage is that I didn't have to put up with that any longer. This orchestra plays the best dance music of all time; no wonder just about everyone comes here at one time or another. We danced to *Nereidas,* the *Cumbia Macondo,* which I love, and the songs by Bigote. René gets up, excuses himself, and goes to the bathroom.

And what if he leaves me here alone? If this one guy, a good friend of Freddy's, had up and left a girl whom we all know at one in the morning, why couldn't René do it to me now? Time stands still. I'll bet he's left, and here I am without my coat in this dive where they pay women to dance. I have no car, this place is on the outskirts of the city, and I'm wearing this low-cut yellow dress. If I stay, though, for sure someone will ask me to dance. And if I leave by myself, for sure those guys in the parking lot will see me. Will I be able to get a taxi at this hour? I turn to see if he's coming out of the men's bathroom. No sign of him. What am I going to do now? This is what I get for going out with someone about whom I know absolutely nothing. I shouldn't have done this.

Feeling desperate, I start looking around everywhere, but then I try to hide myself between my crossed arms on the table. Then someone grabs my hair. He's probably got money in his hand. Frightened to death, I turn around. It's René. I get up, hug him, and start crying. My mascara must have been running down my cheeks.

Dori called last night; she said she wanted to see me. How about tomorrow?

"Tomorrow is Saturday. I'll have to wait and see what Rafa is doing; if he goes out, I can have breakfast with you."

Does she have to wait to see what her husband is going to do before she can do something herself?

I called Luisa and Regina; since they've been divorced for some time now, they can decide what they want to do with their own lives. Luisa's funny; she doesn't read books or ever get sick. She's a little spaced out.

We met at the bar in the President Hotel, on Juarez Avenue. To them, this is having fun.

"Okay . . . I'll learn how to do it too," I told them.

We crossed the ballroom, followed by a lot of staring, as if we were in a fashion show or a beauty contest. I made a beeline to one corner and didn't dare look around; I just kept my eyes on the show, trying to hide my nervousness. Damn! They're really turning it on, and Luisa is even fatter than I am. In a flirting manner, she grins from ear to ear and says "Cheers" to God knows who.

The Chicontepec Trio comes out to play popular music with a harp, which is fascinating. While they're setting up, I quickly look around. I'm enjoying the feeling of silk stockings. Between numbers—El Querreque and La Bruja—three guys come over to us; we make room for them at our table, and they pull over some chairs.

"I'm Luisa, she's Regina, and that's Oshi."

"They want to buy us a drink. What do you say, girls?" asks Luisa.

In a matter of minutes, they had taken over our table. I guess who was going to dance with whom had already been decided. I get the one who's left over. He doesn't say anything to me, and I'm really not interested in talking to him either. He only made some comment about race horses. I hate gamblers.

Then, all of a sudden, I find out that we're going somewhere else to dance. Forget that! Luisa suggests that we all go in one car, and pulling me aside, she says, "C'mon, dummy, we'll be safer in our own." Even though my Galaxie is the biggest, the other two couples are jammed into the back seat; in fact, they're on top of each other. I hate turning around to look at them. I just didn't imagine they were like this, especially Regina, who was such a saint when she was married and never felt like doing anything.

"Let's go to Satélite, that's where Los Yorsys are playing," orders Luisa.

This is horrible. I don't even know how to dance; I've never danced with anyone but my husband, not even with my brothers or my dad. Fortunately, I was saved from the ordeal by watching the others. Who would ever want to return to this way of life?

It's already one in the morning, and by the looks of my friends, they've just started. Through my rearview mirror, I see that the Saint is really getting it on with the guy she's paired up with. It's amazing! And this guy who is in front with me is glued to the door; frankly, I'm glad, because if it occurs to him to get any closer, I'll find a way to dump him and go home.

Spotting some neon lights, we finally arrive at this well-known dive. I can't imagine the type of music. My God, if that's what I'm hearing from here, I'll die. What am I going to do with this guy?

"Luisa, my dear, listen, please, I want to go home. This guy only talks about betting and cars. Let's get your car, and you can stay here as long as you want. You're not going to enjoy my company."

"But, Eugenia, geez, I never thought you were like this. C'mon, with a little music and a drink, you'll loosen up. If you like my guy better, you can have him; I don't think your guy is so bad. You're not sure now; you seemed apprehensive earlier this evening."

It's three o'clock in the morning. When will this torture end?

◇ ◇ ◇

I continue writing what Elena believes is going to be my novel. I have no idea how this material will ever take shape.

Every Saturday, our grandparents invite us to lunch at their house. This time I went up to my grandfather's bedroom. And what a room! I would like to inherit everything in it, but I could never propose that to him, or could I?

"Grandpa, please leave me at least the chest of drawers in your will."

That's going to be the title of the novel.

I talked with my sister-in-law for a while; I like her a lot, and I've already pardoned her—thanks to my psychoanalyst, a feminist, whom I chose, by the way—for the fact that Moshón loves her. The truth is that I never wanted to put in my diary that I was jealous that my brother . . . no, not yet, I still can't write it. The good part is that I'm being forced to let go of my possessiveness. I like her, and she likes me. I'm happy that my brother has brought her into our family; otherwise, I might not ever have met her.

I got a laugh out of Angélica, who drew up a list of things required to start a voluntary separation, with an eye to bringing about a divorce. This is the minimum you should expect from a husband from whom one might separate one day, even though, frankly, it's horrible to think that they would still love each other. The idea is that if he doesn't accept all of it, there's no way you could grant a divorce.

1. Begin with the idea that he's completely despicable.
2. If he's at all sensitive, the least he can do is speak well of you.
3. Make sure he's always the guilty one.
4. He must act like a gentleman.
5. Whenever I go out, he'll help the children with their homework.
6. He should lead an austere life so as not to waste our savings.
7. He should never forget to tell me every time he sees me that he regrets his errors and that I'm prettier than ever.
8. If I get depressed or have problems, he has to be ready to help. He must say, "I am here to help you."
9. I can have a boyfriend. He can't have a girlfriend.
10. All the women have to be attracted to him, but he'll be eternally in love with only me; in fact, if it ever happened, he would die with my name on his lips.
11. He will dedicate himself to his work in order not to feel lonely.
12. There has to be a picture of me in his living room.
13. Every time we see each other, he must repeat with a sigh, "You were absolutely right."
14. My friends and my courses are sacred. We already know what his sisters and mother are. He should be aware of the class of animals that his sisters are. He will always keep in the back of his mind that he was just a poor guy who was born in a snake pit.
15. He should make comparisons to my family so that he'll see reality and become aware of the fact that mine is marvelous.
16. During my honeymoons, he'll be in charge of our children with the loving heart of a good father.
End.

"Señorita, is the lawyer in?"

"No, Señora, he'll be here soon."

"That's strange. He said he'd be here. I'll wait a little longer."

"He had to attend a commencement."

"That would be great to attend a commencement," I add, to make small talk. "They say it's an incredible experience."

" . . . Señora, just what kind of commencement do you think he went to?"

"Why, to a school commencement . . ."

"I'm afraid not, Señora. He had to attend the commencement of removing squatters from some land."

"Oh, my dear, how sad! What kind of world am I living in, anyway? You know what?" I add, after an embarrassing silence. "The lawyer told me that in order to process my divorce I had to bring the marriage certificate and my children's birth certificates. May I leave them with you?"

And I fled the building. I feel so stupid.

I wonder why people become so paranoid about divorce? Several times I've had to tell myself not to be afraid. Several times I've had to state that I no longer have a husband, and everyone reacts as if they've touched the most vulnerable part of my being. They apologize, change the topic, get nervous, spill their coffee, squish their pastry, and drop their underwear.

Last night I went to a nightclub with Susan, and a young guy asked me to dance. He was handsome and looked at me a certain way . . . to the point that I hoped to see him again or go to some party with him. His friend came over to us while we danced and said something to him.

"I'm going."

"You're leaving?" I said, already back at my table, showing indifference.

"Do you want me to stay?" he asked. I smiled, which was an invitation to stay. "If you invite me to stay, I'll stay," he added cynically.

I didn't want to ask him to stay, but I invited him again with my look. There was a brief silence.

"Leave!" my mouth said.

"Really?" he answered, unable to believe what he heard.

"Yes, leave!" I repeated, convinced that he wouldn't leave.

I stopped smiling when I saw him leave. Then I thought that he'd be back in a few minutes. I felt abandoned, as if I had been offered an apple, allowed to smell it, and when I was about to take a bite, it was jerked away from me, mockingly. I tried to act like I didn't care, but my self-esteem went out the window.

"What were you expecting from that little snot?" criticized Susan. "You think he's going to fall in love with you for the rest of his life? Don't be so conceited, Oshinica; he wanted you to beg him to stay. They live out these situations every day of their lives; they have other options. And you arrive for the first time; well, at this place your purity isn't worth a red cent."

I turned to see if anyone had been looking at us.

"Dance?" the guy at the next table asked me.

I looked at him; he was older. He looked very serious.

"Don't let something like that happen again," I told myself, getting up from the table.

"Do you enjoy dancing with me?" he asked after a few numbers.

He dances well. I let myself get closer to him. I feel better; I'm almost happy again. He holds me a little tighter, then a little more, and the lights go down.

"You're very pretty. And you're so sweet. Why don't you answer me?" he murmurs while we dance.

I answer negatively with my head. "I don't want to hear any more lies," I repeat to myself.

"Eugenia, I like you very much. Do you believe me?"

"The one who just left said the same thing," I answer back faintly.

"It's been a long time since I've met someone as pretty as you."

A glassy sheen came over my eyes.

"He's just a young kid, a dumb kid. I know him, he always tries the same stunt; I was watching how long it would take before he left. Please, he's not worth crying over. Would you like to do something together tomorrow? Let's dance a little more. You are very sensual; it really doesn't matter if you've been married, had children," he said, as if he were acting altruistically. He was probably married too, but in his case, that doesn't matter, does it?

"Let's sit down with your friend. Let me kiss your hands; it's been a long time since I've kissed a woman's hands. I feel like I can give you a great deal of love. I want you to be mine and no one else's. But what kind of a world have you been living in, Eugenia? I get upset seeing you like that because of some young kid you've just met. If he were still here, I'd slug him. I'm an older man, I'm responsible, and I'd never treat you like that. That's what happens when you deal with kids who are only out for fun."

The lights above the dance floor start to hurt my eyes. I feel like I'm being watched, but I rest my head on his shoulder anyway.

I've spotted his shirt with tears.

"Do you have a car? Let me drive you home."

We park the car.

"If you want, I'll wait for you here, and when you can leave, I'll be waiting for you. Don't be afraid with me, I want to protect you. Are you able to travel? We can go overseas."

"Call me tomorrow at five, like you said. We can see each other then," I said.

I went to the department store to buy some sexy underwear. At four in the afternoon, I sat down next to the telephone.

It was six o'clock. I had already given up hope at 5:20. And I was ready: makeup, perfume, and a dress. All the while, I was repeating what he had said to me. I wouldn't let anyone get on the phone, and I answered all the phone calls quickly and desperately.

There's no way you could fix dinner for the women in my writing workshop without appetizers, wine, and other alcoholic drinks. That wasn't ever done in my family or with our friends after our marriage. I remember when Lalo drank at two or three weddings, and I gave him hell for it—it was so disgusting.

"There are no drunks in our family," my parents used to say with assurance.

But now I would like to drink some alcohol and feel what it's like to get drunk. I tell Angélica what better place than Trueba's house in Cuernavaca at New Year's. If I'm going to get sick, better with them than anyone else. They can just haul me to my room. And if I don't do it then, when? I mixed all the drinks together I could, and I gulped them down as fast as I could.

"What an animal!" screamed Olga. "Oshinica's gone crazy."

Surrounded, I felt happy and safe. I didn't get angry, I didn't vomit, and I didn't make a fool of myself. Now it was time to stop seeing life as a source of trauma, to stop being a hypocrite . . . and a prude.

Fifteen of us stayed over to sleep. After midnight, they put on some Arab music. We got up to dance, and feelings of limitless sensuality flowed from my body, emotions that I had never allowed myself to express. I closed my eyes; I slowed the rhythm of my body, moving more slowly each time, turning, letting my hips take over. Those horrendous hang-ups had kept those oriental melodies out of my heart; so many years of getting mad at my grandfather and my husband because this is all they played, and now it emanates from me as if I had danced it all my life. I've always detested this music, but now I realize it's inside me. Magda not only plays flamenco on the guitar, but she sings as well.

"Look at Oshinica dance!" yells Elena, laughing enthusiastically.

"It's in her blood," says Alicia.

"How do you do it?" asks Angie, trying to imitate me.

I continue to move rhythmically, turning myself around, tossing my handkerchief, and letting my hands fly. My hips, shoulders, and hands move in unison. My wrists and fingers are agile doves. The tide comes in and goes out. The negative comments about Arabs became a wall which Arabic music and language could not penetrate—not even their food, which is what my husband ate as a child and what I never learned to prepare, could penetrate. I became drunk with the music; I plopped down exhausted. I dreamed of colored veils and gold and silver thread that fluttered like butterflies.

◈ ◈ ◈

I had gone to Angélica's house in Tepoztlán. When she returned from the market, she arranged the green vegetables in a large wooden bowl and placed it on the kitchen table. It was beautifully done. I was horrified to think how I usually store vegetables at my house. I had never learned to appreciate the beauty in vegetables, or in things like *chile poblano,* radishes, watermelon, or pineapple. To me, a head of lettuce wasn't ugly or pretty, it was just a vegetable for making a salad . . . and it wasn't fattening. The tomatoes should be firm, and that's why they cost more. String beans have to snap when you break them. Everything had to be done as quickly as possible, no lingering, because otherwise there would be no time to fix dinner and have everything put away before the TV programs came on. On Mondays, which were market days, I would always smother beautiful heads of lettuce in a plastic bag in the bottom drawer of the refrigerator. I would do the same with peas, piling them up in one place so they wouldn't take up a lot of room, and the same with the squash, the green beans, and everything else. I'd never take the time to arrange the fruit in a basket; I'd just pile it all up in the refrigerator. What's the difference between that and stuffing a bouquet of flowers in there? What terrible things I did with such beauty!

And how is it possible that I never got to know this other world beyond the capital of Mexico? I'm the same as a foreigner in my country. I was always looking at a single tree and missing the forest. Was I really living my life through a magnifying glass? Is that why I didn't see the rest of the world? It's so beautiful to look up and see the horizon in the distance, to see Tepozteco surrounding us. This land, this country, is much bigger than the place where—with my head buried in the sand—I had focused my life. The creative writing class opened a door for me that has led to another, larger door, and beyond that to another, and

another, each time opening up new worlds more vast than the last
one.

I haven't taken anything to the writing workshop recently; everything I write seems boring. Who could possibly be interested? I
read to my dad the passage about how he sells his wares in La
Lagunilla, including how he barters. While the participants in the
writing class laughed out loud, he got furious.

"You made me look like a swindler. Look here, I'm just trying
to make a living. Am I the only one?"

"Señorita, I have an appointment with Dr. Castelazo."

"Your name?"

What should I use? Mataraso or Matalón.

" . . . Señora Mataraso."

"Is this your first visit?"

"He's been my gynecologist for eighteen years. I would like to
update my file. Eugenia Mataraso. That's all."

The secretary gives me a cold look. While I'm waiting, I'll
make a few phone calls, one to find out if my camera's fixed.

"Is Señor Vera in? This is Señora Mataraso. . . . Señor Vera? How
are you? I'm Eugenia Mataraso."

"Who?"

"This is Señora Matalón, but from now on I'm using my
maiden name."

"Why, kid? What happened?"

"Nothing, but in order to get a job I think I should use my
maiden name."

"Don't make me laugh. I think something else is going on here. . . . Don't jump the gun, little girl. I'm here to help you. Let me make an annotation in my book the way you want your name."

Little by little, people will get used to it; so will I. They're going to be surprised at the lab; after working with them for two years, I change my name. Well, that's life. I get mad when they keep using that other last name; I've always had my own, the one with which I was born and with which I'll die. I'm already tired of having to explain my new marital status. I've got to make new calling cards; and if I ever get married again, I'll make sure never to hide behind some other name, despite how much I might love the man. No woman belongs to anyone. Why do we have to accept that new surname? Many people who are close to my ex-husband won't even realize that he's not married anymore. He made a million cards that say, "Señor Eduardo Matalón and Señora." When he gets married again, they'll still be valid.

🏃 august.

Elena was invited to go to the fiestas in Huamantla, Tlaxcala, and she invited me to go with her. They sent a van with a driver to pick us up; every time he braked, we went flying forward, but we decided to have fun instead of gripe about it. As we drove through Puebla, my head started to hurt, so the driver offered to stop at a drugstore in Apizcaco to buy some aspirin. I took some right then and there.

At the cash register, there was an advertisement for carrot cream. Since Elena has always had a weak spot for creams, especially the natural ones, she bought a jar and immediately started to put it all over herself. She was quite a sight, with those pigtails and all. She had found the time to prepare an article for . . . and another for the presentation of . . . and so it worked out well that they picked us up a little late.

We went into the main church in Apizcaco and left before it got dark outside. Back inside the van, we were thrown from one side to the other.

It was night when we arrived. As we opened the door to the van, we saw that a large group of "important" people from Huamantla was waiting for us. In a most ceremonious way, the chronicler of the town helped us get out. The Director of the Cultural Institute of Tlaxcala and someone else also welcomed us.

"This is Oshinica Mataraso, photographer and writer," said Elenita.

The welcoming committee showed us around the Cultural Institute, the archives, and the paintings. I could see the honorable chronicler giving explanations to my friend Elena. After walking in and out of several rooms, I ran into Elena's thickly creamed face. The orange color made her look funny. I looked at the group accompanying us; they were all acting very ceremoniously. I almost broke out laughing. I almost lost it. How was I going to tell Elena that her face still had a thick coat of carrot cream all over it? The chronicler continued narrating the history of the area, and Elena, who was acting with all seriousness, just nodded. I couldn't stand it anymore, I had to tell her.

"Elena," I interrupted out loud, "wipe your face, it's covered with cream."

She broke out laughing, and so did I—I couldn't wait any longer. While I laughed, she wiped her face with Kleenex. We had never laughed so hard.

I really like her; she's so funny.

◇ ◇ ◇

My life and my kids' lives have changed drastically: there's no set time when we eat or when we come home. They talk to me or call me anytime they want; there's no one around to get mad or make them stay at home. The TV isn't a part of my life anymore; I'll let someone else watch gangster and police movies.

Little by little, this same disorder and chaos have also been taking over the bathrooms, the living room, and the dining room. There's no husband around to scold them. I love it!

One of the participants in the writing class wrote a story about an Indian who goes to work in the capital. I don't know if Elena doesn't like our classmate, but she tore into her after she finished reading her story. She said it sounded false.

"When would you ever know what it's like to feel what one of them feels? Have you ever made love with a bricklayer? A plumber? You've never ventured beyond your neighborhood or your own family."

You could tell by the expression in her face that she was angry.

"None of you people has to work; you don't live real lives, you only fake it! I don't see any of you finishing your novels either. So far, only Silvia Molina has published hers. Alicia Trueba's novel sits in a drawer, Oshinica has stopped writing, neither of you is doing anything with what you've written. As for the rest of you, it's the same old thing. If you don't write, there's no use in coming anymore."

She frightened us, so we asked for a second chance. We'll finish our novels, who knows when, but at least for the next class, come rain or come shine, I'll bring something to read to the class. Alicia ran to her desk where her novel was gathering dust. Was it true, like some of them believe, that we only came to socialize?

Daniela turned twelve today. I rented a place for a party that had the latest games and a portable swimming pool. After having read *Hopscotch,* I want to do everything backwards, or just the opposite of the way it's supposed to be, even if I do just a little bit. At five, I called everyone inside to cut the cake, but I quickly realized that several children had already left and others were about to leave. Alarmed, I got on the microphone: "Please, don't leave yet. We're going to have some refreshments."

But no one heard me, they were already leaving. They've been programmed to go home as soon as the cake has been cut. I screwed up, they left, and all the food was uneaten. No doubt they're going to say that all I served was a piece of lousy cake.

I went to La Lagunilla today. Goyita has gained weight and she's gray-haired; in fact, everything around there looked older. My grandfather's store doesn't shine with the elegance that it once had. A sign made of a fine linen fabric that had his name stitched into it has disappeared. Now it's just an ordinary sign. The fancy wood and glass door separating the front of the store from his office is gone. It was so beautiful! The beveled glass was so elegant. All of that is gone now, in the name of spaciousness, simplicity, and practicality.

The only part that remains intact is the mannequins; they seem to have drunk from the same fountain of youth as my grandfather.

Like princesses waiting for the arrival of their princes, they are still as beautiful as ever. They were always dressed with fur coats and nightgowns; their age hasn't been a pretext to let themselves go; their physical permanence permits them to continue to act like exemplary ladies of high society.

At home, it's the same old story.

"Haven't you thought about changing your life? Once the children get married, they're going to leave you. Loneliness sucks."

TWELVE

Clarita, Beatriz, and Annette are already enrolled in the National University. They've been together all their lives. That's really neat—I'm so envious. My parents aren't upset with Clarita, who studies like crazy, because her husband is proud of the fact that she will be a psychologist soon.

"She's serious about her studies, but you just go to waste your time. Nothing you do is normal. She's going to be a doctor," says my dad, who is extremely proud.

My brother-in-law is a super guy: he says that he has to help his wife become all that she can become. I'm so jealous.

When I got home, my children's friends were looking at the photo albums for each child that I have spent so much time on over the years and given so much love to. When those got filled up, I had larger ones made out of leather with gold lettering. Those albums have been one of my proudest achievements, but ever since the children have chosen to be with their father, I haven't been able to add any new pictures, poems, or commentaries. That's the way they've come to an end, or will end up . . . I guess.

I don't spend time on those things anymore. I can't deny that I was really hurt over it.

It was my turn to read at the writing workshop today. I read for an entire hour. Since there are several of us working together, I won't have to read again for another month. It's hard to correct a novel this way; who is going to remember what we read the last time?

I finally understood why I construct my sentences backwards. Do you say "construct my sentences backwards," or "construct backwards my sentences"? It's hard for me. Somewhere I wrote what my mother had said once:"Being smart, will you get it?" Elena corrects me by turning it around. I defend myself when it absolutely has to be said a certain way. As we go over other sentences, I realize that I write this way because that's the way I heard it said at home. That's the way Ladino is. When I ask a question, for instance, I'm always saying something like, "You are upset?" or "You are a tourist?" Or like my mother, when she says, "That way, it has to be." That's why I write that way; it's a mess, hard to change. So, my mother would probably say, "You write backwards everything, everything upside down."

Now Agustín Monsreal is going to conduct a novel writing class.

I invited everyone from the writing class to have dinner at my apartment. I really wanted to show everyone the tape about love that I had made for Victor. Along with Elena came two veteran teachers, Gonzalo Celorio and Magda, who are also avid fans of *Hopscotch* and who had transmitted their enthusiasm about the book to us. During coffee, Trueba proposed that each one of us say something very special to someone else.

When Gonzalo got up, he began praising my tape.

"It seems incredible to me, having just heard your tape, which demonstrates so much sensitivity, that you have such a plain house. How can you surround yourself with such bad taste?"

While he was making that statement, he was surveying with great incredulity the walls of my apartment. I was sitting on the floor, leaning against the chair on which Angie was sitting. She gripped my shoulders tightly before responding to Gonzalo.

"She's making a lot of changes in her life. Soon she'll make changes in her house, too. Leave her alone!"

My eyes filled with tears. Never had I thought that someone would see my house like that. Gonzalo would stop to gaze at certain objects, and then he would continue his tirade, each time with stronger words about the same thing.

Days later I sat down in my living room to observe everything around me. I had figured it out. It's full of things from my previous lives, bits and pieces from eons ago, like a trio of porcelain angels playing heavenly harps and zithers. At one time I had liked them very much. Since Mari had bought some, so did I. And there were little dolls, lying on their sides with their heads propped up, three little babies with diapers, and some bronze tables with marble eating utensils. I've always loved all kinds of little tables; frankly, I had bought a lot of things over the years. There were wedding gifts and other things marking our tenth wedding anniversary, like painted plates with Louis IV figures hanging on the walls, and a lot of cut glass, which for the intellectuals represented crystallized money. My house was no different from my friends' with whom I had played when I was young. Why is it that a rich person's house signifies bad taste?

It's true that when we moved to La Condesa, there were some things that weren't attractive to me anymore. But I didn't completely get rid of everything. I kept some things, because I wanted to make the place pretty like it was before, and also to reduce the blow of not having a garden, a tree, or a hammock. But it's true, the porcelain figurines, the plates on the walls, and the dolls were pretty ugly.

My world revolved around the same habits as everyone else's, the same way of decorating our houses, the same way of living, the same way of getting married, the same way of having fun. We trained our maids to be exactly the same, we went to the same pediatrician, and we went to the same gynecologists.

Now I'd rather experience the effects of change on our lives, like in Cortázar's novel. Why stick to the same sea all your life? The same beach? The same soup? Why?

I wrapped up some of the decorations in newspaper and put them in a basket.

"Here, take them," I said to my mother. "They're not a part of me anymore, and you've always liked them."

Why have I always gravitated toward doing the same thing as everyone else? Every restaurant has its clientele. I'm happy that at least I'm the only Jewish person in the writing class; the way I see and hear things around me is distinct from everyone else. Yesterday, when I was arriving at the club, I suddenly saw everything differently, even though it was all the same: The club members were exactly the same people as always. It's wonderful to belong to a club, but I don't want it to be the only thing in my world. The real world is much bigger. I'm from a family that, as soon as it crossed the ocean and settled down, there was no way to change them. They're sedentary . . . I mean really sedentary.

Dori wants us to go to Acapulco for the weekend, but I have hardly any money, especially after buying the condominium. I'll go on one condition: if they want to stay at a more expensive hotel, that's fine, but I'll go to one that I can afford.

My daughters and little Jacob were excited about going. We stopped to look at several hotels, but they refused to get out of the car. They kicked and screamed. In the end, we stayed in the Marriott. They refused to make meals in the room, so instead of staying the entire weekend, we went back home the next day.

No matter what goes wrong, they blame me when they call their father. Why would they do that? To feel closer together? He doesn't live with us, but he still controls everything. They even ask him if they can go out. This is crazy! And since I refuse to get involved in a fight with him, I keep my mouth shut. He keeps threatening to take the kids with him. Okay, then, I wish he'd take them and leave me alone!

"You're going to be sad," little Jacob warns me, "but I don't want you to take our pet to school for me."

Why that little! . . . I actually had to laugh at the fact that he said something as painful as that with such pertness.

"What are you doing?" said my mother, who had just called.

"I'm working," I answered.

She seemed bewildered.

"What do you mean, working? Doing what? You mean work work?" she said sarcastically.

Sometimes she can be so obnoxious!

Five of us joined Agustín Monsreal's writing class. One guy is really arrogant, but he's got a good novel. The scenes are really intense, well constructed. I was frightened to death when it came to be my turn. You're supposed to read about half an hour. I was afraid to look up at them, so I just stared at my text while I was reading. Time seemed eternal. The first thing I saw when I looked up was Javier González Rubio's face. He was visibly affected by my reading. I'll never forget that moment in particular, or his face. When I got home that night, I was feeling more than happy. They wanted me to read another segment for the next class.

Every time I sneeze, I get worried. The other day, when I was at the University Plaza, I coughed and left a puddle at my feet. My mother is going to ask a neighbor who is a doctor at the State hospital to recommend a good doctor for me.

It's difficult to write in such a cramped space; there's an adolescent in every room playing loud music.

"Why don't you use my apartment on Hera Street," offered Alicia Trueba. "It's just a block away from the Insurgentes Theater. My niece won't be back for three months. Here, take the keys. I'll make sure someone cleans it for you."

Before taking my walk through the park, I packed up my novel and went to inspect the apartment. It's small and pretty—a lover's hideaway. If Victor were here, it would've been perfect for us. It has a bedroom, a tiny kitchen, and a living room. But the best part is the terrace—it's as big as my living room, and it has a table with an umbrella. I sat down and got comfortable. I worked for two hours. The only problem is that directly in front is a building under construction, and by the looks of it, they've just begun. They've got several more floors to go. I write. When I look up, I see the vines growing everywhere on the terrace. The noise from the construction site distracts me. Too bad, really! I thought I was escaping from a lot of construction work in La Herradura, which is a new neighborhood, and now this! The good part, though, and even in La Condesa, is that there are no more lots left to build on. I'll come back on Friday.

I've got to get more done before they operate on me.

It's true, this apartment reminds me of Victor. Now I remember the only time we went to a hotel, and I became frightened because, after two hours, I saw that there were mirrors on the ceiling. I scrambled to get under the sheets, and I didn't dare move after that.

Today I woke up with his name on my lips and I felt happy.

Three pens: red, blue, and black. I just love new pens! What else? Ah, yes: *El apando, El agua y los sueños,* the Sunday supplement, a few issues of *Material de la lectura,* two short stories that need revising, two nightshirts, a robe, slippers, stockings, a notebook, and some beauty cream.

I don't want to wear this nice slip, but it's getting late; there's no use in changing now. Clarita is going with me. I didn't say anything to my children, because they're worried about me being operated on in the State hospital. Their fears would be enough to drain me of what strength I have left. Besides, I don't have a choice. They say it's a good hospital. I can't afford a private hospital anyway, so I'm not going to make a big deal out of it. They operate on millions of people here. Why not me, too? And I've got some contacts here.

We go to the admissions office on the gynecology floor. Everyone just stares at us. I just smile back; perhaps I get carried away. Clarita is the strongest one in the family. She was also hospitalized in a place like this.

We walk up to the reception desk. We laugh. I'm carrying my small bag. They stop my sister, who laughs nervously when she sees that I'm frightened. We give each other a kiss.

"Señora, remove your watch, and you can't take that bag with you either. You'll get it back in the morning."

"And my books? What am I going to do in the meantime? They don't operate on me until tomorrow morning."

"Don't worry. You're going to be quite busy. There'll be no time to get bored."

"At least my stockings, I get cold easily."

"No, honey, it's warm inside."

"Let's go, Señora, hurry up! You're the last one," says a nurse from inside.

"If that's the case, I'm going to leave my things in the car."

We ran to the car and ran back again. My slip was flying everywhere.

"Eugenia, take something with you. Don't be so obedient."

I grab my notebook, the literary supplement, two books, and some money that my father gave me, and I stick it in my purse. If they steal it, tough luck.

"Sir, will you let my sister stay here for a little while?"

We peek inside. The waiting room. We see some women wrapped in tight-fitting green wrinkled gowns. I try to act natural. I go in, look at them, and stop laughing. I remembered my visits to the insane asylum and the nurses who were wearing those oversized uniforms.

"Quickly now, honey, take off your clothes. Here, put this gown on."

Clarita laughs. She's amazed to see me obey orders. They give me a green plastic bag.

"Don't leave," they say to my sister, "you'll take her clothes with you."

I go into a small dressing room.

"And, honey, be sure to put your underwear in the bag too."

Once I put the gown on, I feel humbled and humiliated. The effect is mysterious: I feel like they've exchanged my skin for that of a wrinkled old woman. So many changes! From young to old, from rich to poor. To enter one world, you have to leave the old one behind. Here, I'm just a body, nothing more. And my soul? What if something happens to me? Where will it go? Do they realize that we're more than this material body? How horrible! I've been stripped of everything. They're only getting a body . . . my body.

"Honey, come and sit over here with the other sick ladies. Soon I'm going to take everyone upstairs."

There are three rows of chairs, squarely arranged in front of a desk, just like in kindergarten. A woman welcomes us and talks about family planning. In addition to operating on my gall bladder, they're going to tie off my fallopian tubes. I keep thinking about being naked. If my children were to see me now, they probably wouldn't recognize me. From this point on, I don't have anyone else but these people who are here beside me.

"And you, Señora, why are they operating on you?" I asked the lady next to me.

The social worker says that two people have to donate blood for me. One of the women who looked like me has olive skin, but she is much younger than me.

"If you don't have anyone to donate blood for you, ask my husband. He has lots of blood, and he'd love to donate some more. His name is Germán."

She gives me his telephone number, and I write it on my hand.

"Honey, please hurry up, we're waiting for you. Why are you taking so long?"

Trying to hold my gown in back so as not to expose my butt to everyone, I run to get in line behind the others. We get into the same elevator, both men and women, that everyone in the hospital uses, and I worry that I might run into someone who recognizes me in the middle of this sea of green.

We get out on the seventh floor. I've been assigned bed no. 8 in the second wing. With my bag hanging from my shoulder, I say hello. Feeling mentally and physically well, as the sun turns Mexico City into glittering gold, I get into bed, straighten my pillow, and cover myself up.

There's another woman in the bed next to mine. That's a relief! I feel like trying to get out of here, but I can't, because I don't have any underwear or money. I wonder what time it is? I get panicky. I think about when they took all of my possessions, everything; instead of a watch, now I'm wearing an adhesive strip with my name in green letters.

I check out the other beds in the room. Three more women are across from me. The woman next to the window smiles at me; her permanent has fallen down around her brown skin. The other two must be in pain: they hardly move. I turn and look to my left: a thin woman is sleeping. And next to me is Conchis. There are curtains between the beds for privacy.

Oh, my God! Once again I'm thinking I've gotten into something without considering the consequences. I remember the time when my three daughters and I got on a bus going to Cozumel, and I had no idea that in order to get there, you had to cross the Gulf of Mexico!

There's a light above my bed. I don't have much that I can call mine, but everything here is important to me: a light, a small chest of drawers, this robe, and the few things they wouldn't allow me to bring that are in my purse. I can read and write. Right now, I feel pretty good. Come tomorrow, though, I'm going to be like my neighbor: I'll have an IV stuck in my arm and no desire to smile.

A nurse shows up pushing something that looks like a dessert cart. I hear my name on the PA system. Disconcerted, I look around, but I don't see anything.

"They're calling you," says the woman with the permanent. "Go down to the nurse's station. Talk to them!"

"Who?" I ask.

On the wall above my head, I spot a microphone, so I say to the wall, "I'm coming."

Then they call Conchis. We get up in a hurry. The others who came in together are all standing together. I'm glad to see them again.

"Come this way, girls, we're going to take some blood."

"Oh, no, please, they already did that yesterday."

Submissively, all my new friends roll up their sleeves.

"I want you to understand something: when I found out I was going into the hospital today, my doctor sent me to the laboratory, and they took some blood. No, I'm not going to do it again."

"What are you not going to do again?" asked the nurse, astonished.

"Not this again. Look at my wristband. Who do I have to speak to?"

"The doctor's over there; his office is in front of the cribs."

"Damn it, he's not there. Is he going to come back?"

"Look here, Señora, if he doesn't, they won't operate on you."

"Do them first. I want to be the last one."

"Honey, please don't let the tube slip out; I'll help you stick it back."

We're all laughing together; we've become instant friends.

"Don't leave us, girls, they're going to prep you now."

What! Again? I haven't been to a beauty shop in a long time; I wonder how long I'll stay shaved like this. This is the pits. Damn it!

It's starting to get dark outside. You can finally see the city lights. Shadows overtake the French Cemetery. My neighbor, who was asleep when I arrived in the afternoon, gets up. She says that in a nearby park her old friends from where she grew up are gathering to play something or other. We go over to the window, but we can't see anything.

Smiling like the others, another nurse comes by pushing another cart. It's strange that everyone here is always smiling.

"Okay, honey, it's enema time."

"I can't do it. This, too?"

Conchis steps to one side.

"Try to wait as long as you can stand it, and then go to the bathroom. It's just down the hall."

I don't have any choice. And what if I don't make it to the bathroom?

"Tell me again, sir, is the bathroom far away?"

I'm so afraid to move that I can't even get out of bed. I wait as long as I can, but then comes the urgent need to go. Rolling to my feet, I start down the mile-long hallway toward the bathroom.

I have to stop half way. At this point, I'm not sure what's going to happen, so I start running. My fate has been sealed.

When I'm in Acapulco, I always request a room with a view of the ocean; in these hospitals, you have to request a room next to the bathroom. I close the door. I've been sweating. I can hear the rest of them coming toward the bathroom. Some are screaming out of desperation.

"Is there anyone out there who doesn't have a toilet?" I manage to ask in a low voice.

"It's me, Pati," responds a raspy voice.

"I'm coming out right now. I guess I wasn't in that much of a hurry."

We all look at each other again. What faces! We start to look worse and worse. I wonder what we'll be like in the morning. I wonder what the concentration camps were like.

Since she arrived, Pati has grown more pale and frightened.

"What else are they going to do to us?"

"Oh, I don't know," she answers, looking even worse as she comes out of the bathroom.

I'm exhausted.

"Excuse me, I'm going back inside one more time."

When I come out, I lie down face up on a bench.

"Anita," said Pati, "is getting some sun."

We're wrinkled and green, like green frogs.

"Hey, girls, is everyone okay? Time for bed. They're bringing your food to you. Tomorrow you'll have a bath at five in the morning."

Since I have no idea what the future holds for me, I write the following:

It's ten o'clock. We're being held hostage. Ever since we checked into this hospital this afternoon, we've been subjected to all kinds of assaults: first, we were stripped of our clothing and then given these green hospital gowns that magically turned us into submissive robots. Next, they poked us intravenously. Then they sent us to the barbershop. Not stopping there, they subjected us to a massive defilement, claiming hygienic reasons. Finally, the pay phones are on another floor, which means contact with the outside has been cut off completely.

"For those being operated on, it's bath time! We'll be by for you shortly!"

They give us soap and clean, wrinkled hospital gowns.

"Girls, there aren't any towels, so use your sheets to dry off."

Once again, we're huddled together in the bathroom.

"See you after the operation."

My attendant rolls me into an elevator. I try to figure out where he's taking me. We enter a labyrinth, going down hallways and finally arriving at the operating area and the world of masked doctors. We stop in the recovery room. Many other women are there. They're going to park me somewhere, but it seems like there's no space left. A little to the left, then to right, and he backs me into a small corner . . . obviously, he's had practice at this. I turn over and see Conchita. She looks terrified. More beds coming and going. If this keeps up, we'll have a traffic jam on our hands. One of them coming back in raises her head. Her eyes are wide open.

"Hello."

It's Pati.

This is a waiting and recovery room all rolled into one. Some of the women have IVs. A nurse is checking on another woman who just had a cesarean birth. She's in pain.

I just remembered my teeth. Now I really begin to worry; other times when I've been in the hospital, I've left them with my mother.

"Okay, girls, did everyone leave their false teeth at home?"

I almost fall out of my bed.

"Sir, I didn't leave them anywhere, I have mine right here. How could I leave them at home? And go around without them?"

"You should've left them somewhere else, sweetie. But you can leave them here. Is there anyone here who will keep them for her?"

I start crying.

"Sir, how can I do that? There's no guarantee I'll get them back after my operation. Stop the operation." I sit up in the bed, crying even more. Several nurses come over to me, offering every type of assurance. Gently, the head nurse takes them from me and puts an operating mask over my mouth.

"Now you can talk without feeling embarrassed; I will keep them safely for you. I'll be here when you get back."

"Listen up, girls," says a nurse pushing a cart full of medicines. "I'm your horoscope, and I'm predicting that today is your lucky day; everything's going to turn out fine, but you've got to cooperate with me: I'm going to give you a shot in your rear end and put an IV in your arm."

They take me out of the waiting/recovery room and push me toward the operating room. I see my doctor.

"There's my patient," he says.

This is a world of green and white mummies. They begin by covering me with a green cloth. I look straight up at the ceiling. I can see my reflection in a light fixture. Two women wrap my legs and my head. I'll bet I look like a crumpled birthday present. Someone opens the door.

"Doctor, this gal is in her second phase, she's going in right now."

Then all I hear is a voice describing what's going to happen. Two hands hold my face.

"I'm your anesthesiologist," he says with a big smile. "Tell me, Eugenia, why are you so chubby?"

I guess they've finished operating on me. I can see the lady who kept my false teeth for me. Will I be able to talk? And if I say something, will anybody be able to hear me?

"Miss, can you give me . . . ?"

She smiles and returns with a small package.

"Oh, thank you, thank you," I say, clutching her hand.

As they were getting me ready to leave, I saw Conchis; she looked like she was in pain. Then I heard someone say they were taking me up to the eighth floor.

"But my room's on the seventh."

"Yes, yes, honey, take it easy. We're taking you to your bed. Here's a gift for you."

It's a bag with my toiletries. Once again, they roll me out, and along with an IV and a catheter, they put me on a stretcher. I look around me: a sea of green lumps. They're newly arrived. They smile. I can barely react.

Why have they changed floors on me? I wonder how Conchis is doing? She probably thinks I've died, because I didn't even go back for my bag. There's a similar light on this floor; it's the same view, only a bed less because we have a bathroom this time.

I begin to meet some of the women on this floor, and I recognize others. The one to my left moaned all night; she hasn't given birth yet. They just brought in the one to my right. The one in front of me has a lace robe. Why is she smiling so much? She seems happy. There's a pretty flower arrangement next to her bed. I'm too tired to talk to her. The others have become my friends.

"Hey, can't you take me down to the floor where I was before? I have some friends down there."

"No can do, honey."

The woman in front of me gets up out of bed and goes over to the window.

"I think my husband's here. I can see his car. Visiting hours are from four to six."

She's young and pretty.

"They didn't operate on me today. I was on the operating table when they realized that my sugar level had gone up. Off the scales! They had already done the prep work; the skin on my stomach hurts where they shaved me, but I was ready to be slit open. I'm having a hysterectomy. I've bled a lot. I can't go home now, and my husband doesn't even know they didn't operate on me; he won't be bringing any clothes, so I'll have to stay here until tomorrow."

My eyes pop open.

"And why didn't you call him?"

"There aren't any phones on this floor, and they wouldn't let me go down to five."

Her poor husband. He's going to be so surprised to see her just like he left her. He'll be coming in any moment now. That's what I thought, anyway. He tiptoed in gingerly, fearful. He brought a bag with shampoo and creams.

"How are you doing?"

They murmured to each other, as if they were in a movie theater. They were trying not to bother anyone around them. While she was explaining what happened, he repeatedly kissed her arm.

"Pardon me," he said as he pulled the folding curtain between our beds.

I've also received some visitors. Terrified, my daughters come in one by one, because they allow only one visitor at a time. Having been educated with liberal ideas and in another economic class, they found it difficult to adhere to the rules. They're furious that I had to come to be operated on in this hospital instead of the British hospital, where I could've had a telephone, flowers, unlimited visitors, and a TV. I didn't want to get mad or play the victim, although I very easily could have done so.

After visiting hours are over, María Félix, my new neighbor, asks to me to draw back the curtain because her husband has already left.

"A question for you," she says. "How did you manage to keep your bag and some books?"

"I'm not sure. No one said anything to me," I said, knowing that I was lying to her. "Perhaps they weren't paying attention, and since I didn't know either, I just brought them in with me. I guess I was lucky, eh? Say, had you known that you had a high blood sugar level?"

"Not a clue. I have no idea why it went up on me. Maybe it's because of what happened on Sunday when we were at La Marquesa: the old man who had taken my son on a horseback ride didn't come back on time, and I thought that maybe he had been kidnapped. So many things crossed my mind that day! My husband and my daughter went out looking for them, but they didn't find anyone."

"Honey," says a nurse, "we've got orders to put you in a private room."

Now I'm in a real hospital; there's no difference between this and the English hospital. It embarrasses me to receive special treatment, because I was determined to go through with this just like anyone else. Now I must seem different to them. They're probably asking right now, "Who is she? Why have they given her a private room?" I can read more in here, but then, I was able to read in the other room, plus I could talk to the others.

I'm making an effort to be friendlier with the nurses, but it tires me out. I'm even mad at myself. It's like deciding to marry someone with leftist ideas, understand his position, be proud of him—and then when we return from the honeymoon, someone offers him a job at the National Bank of Mexico and he accepts. In here, I have no one to talk to, no one to tell me stories, and there aren't even any decorations on the walls.

"Crying again, honey?"

Some of my friends from the time when I was still married came to see me; they had attended the Sephardic school with me. My children had never met them. They were all happy to see each other. I opened up a package of cheese soufflé that Hanna brought me. It was delicious, and we even licked our fingers.

"Our gin rummy group just celebrated its eighteenth year together," said Dori.

"We haven't changed a bit," said another.

"It's been over thirteen years since you stopped playing with us, right? Just remember, we didn't chase you away; why don't you come around some afternoon? We never bet a lot of money, of course."

"Would you be interested in joining our group again?" asked Hanna.

"Sure. After all, what one learns well, she never forgets. Do you remember when Daniela gave us such a scare? If you hadn't been there, I would've died. How's Miriam? And her kids? I've never seen her again."

"She's fine: pretty as ever, always on the go, doesn't have time to play with us, but we'll see how long she lasts. For her, everything's either this way or that way. There's no confusion."

"Really? What I liked best were all the possibilities. How does it go?" I asked, making a cross with three horizontal and three vertical cards. "Is this the way you do it? I can't remember anymore."

"Right. Just pull out the one in the middle. Who's next? I'll pass. Don't ever think that nothing changes here," says Lucilla, as she quickly deals the cards with not only dexterity but also her usual enthusiasm. "And three really nice ladies joined the group; I'm sure you must know them: Leonor's sister-in-law and someone who says she knows you. She belongs to the Ashkenazi community. Did you know that my daughters are married now? I'm a grandmother already. And the best part of it all? Why, my granddaughter. Look at this picture! Here she's six months old, here she's a year, and in this one, she's two. I'm such a lucky grandmother! We're all crazy about her."

"Now most of us play bridge, and we go to tournaments. For that, you really need to know what you're doing," interrupts Mari.

"And what about you, Oshinica, are you thinking about making some changes in your life?" asks Lucilla.

"I'm already in the process. That's precisely why I got a divorce."

"No, I'm referring to remarrying," she says impatiently.

"I don't know if I'll ever find a man who'll leave the doors and the windows open for me to get out if I'm ever suffocating from the relationship. Frankly, so far no one has asked me, and I'm not really dying to get married anyway."

"The sooner the better, I think. It'll be harder when you're older . . . especially after forty-five. Being alone when you're older is no fun."

Ah, we'll see, I say to myself. I've got a ways to go before I get old. What should I do? Will it cost me or not? I wonder, reluctant to step into the unknown.

"Go ahead, take a chance. Do whatever you want. You still know the game."

"Very good," adds Hanna, "now show your card. Of course, you pay. You're in bad shape, but at least you're not losing your capital."

"Exactly! See, I still know how to play. I like to play, but I won't let myself get trapped. Or who knows? . . . it's fun, nevertheless. I shouldn't play, though; the temptation is too great. And what about this: does everyone still believe that if you don't play cards you won't have any friends? After repeating it so many times, you actually begin to believe it. Well, it's true that at one time I believed it too; but years ago I got rid of my green tablecloth, plastic chips, and dozens of decks of playing cards. And now I have *more* friends than before. Listen to me: stop thinking like that. I have a deck of cards here, true, because my neighbor in the next bed was going to have her baby."

While we visited together, I got all the latest gossip: who got married, who got divorced, and—may God bless them—who's died. They told me about the latest dress styles and their trips abroad, and they gave me some upscale cooking recipes. Everything seemed great; I even believed it.

"Oops, it's seven-thirty already. My husband gets upset if I get home late."

I ask myself: What's the rush? Of course, I had forgotten that it's the hour that good wives are supposed to be at home. Their husbands don't like being alone; besides, what if they would want to eat then, or even go out somewhere? Yeah, what if!

They picked up their purses and flew out of the room, giving me pecks on the cheek. They came like a flock of geese and they left like a flock of geese.

THIRTEEN

Even though I could barely drive a car after the operation, I went to Hera's little apartment to work on the novel. I couldn't even remember where I had left off. I began reading it from the beginning, revising the chronology as I went. Then I realized that a character that began as Dori ended up with some other name. The bricklayers across the way continue their work: the building has taken shape.

Yesterday, I dropped off some photographs to a client who lives on the corner of Mexicali and Cholula, just around the corner from where we lived before the earthquake in '57. Our building, from which we were allowed to retrieve only our furniture, was on this very spot. I went up to the sixth floor, and as I looked out from a balcony, I saw that the street below was lined with jacaranda trees full of purple flowers. I guess they existed when we lived here. It's strange to think that, having had a balcony that stretched the full length of our apartment, I never paid much attention to those blooming trees, which should have reminded us of springtime. I'm sure I was always doing things to show my mom that I was busy; as a result, I never saw anything around me. At my house, tranquillity and idleness were shunned. Even today it's hard for me to sit down and read during the day. We were always in a hurry. From the moment we got up, we ran from one thing to another. Well . . . enough of not seeing anything. Enough of always being on the run!

The kids are excited that their father has purchased an apartment. I didn't think he would ever do it. He must be happy now that he doesn't have to pay any alimony. And this is what they call justice! My foot! After all these years of marriage, everything belongs to him. They're going to decorate it together, from top to bottom. It'll be ready in two months.

"The elevator isn't working yet, so we're not leaving all at once," said the little monsters.

Once again, I'll have to adapt to a new way of life, just like when Lalo left me. I guess we'll all adapt somehow. Who knows, maybe they'll learn to appreciate me more.

"I'm scared to death," I told my psychotherapist.

"You have two options: sink or swim. It's your choice. You have lots of friends. If you're feeling lonely, call them up."

I'm afraid that my relationship with the children has taken a turn for the worse: they feel so protected by their father that they don't even obey me anymore. He rules them by remote control. He'll call them at ten or eleven at night, just to see if they're at home yet. I'm not going to police them. I want them to be happy and to have fun; discipline only goes so far, but when they let their father govern them, it makes them feel like he cares more about them than I do. And there's no way of getting that idea out of their heads. If they want that kind of control, fine, they can go and live with him. I'm against having to brake at every turn, because when you really have to sometime, it can cause a wreck. Instead of going to a mechanic to have the brakes fixed, it would be better to go somewhere and do just the opposite. It's turning out to be harder to free myself of all this than the work it cost my parents to strangle our freedom when we left them. If they leave me now, I'll be happy taking them out on Sundays, like he does with them now; then they'll learn to love me again. But maybe . . . just maybe something else is in store for me.

When I walk into his store, my dad has his lunch spread out on top of a sewing machine. He's examining what his wife has sent him, and if he doesn't like it, he gets upset with her. His assistant, Enriqueta, is showing a coat to a client. We smile at each other, because I find it amusing when she mimics the same persuasive techniques that my father uses.

"Oshi, honey, sit down here beside me; your mother sent me too much food today."

"No, Señora, it's not imitation, it's real wool. Señor Samuel! Do you have a match on you?" asks Enriqueta.

"Why, of course. Look, Oshi, here's that plantain-and-meat dish. I've already tried it. Your mom sent some yesterday."

Enriqueta finds a place in the lining between the stitches, pulls out a thread, and lights it.

"There you are, Señora," she says, as if it were the first time.

Now it smells like burnt sheep everywhere.

"Here, serve yourself some on this plate. And take some of this eggplant and cheese; it's really tasty. Why haven't you called to go for a walk? If you could only see the tree nurseries; they're like forests now. We've gone there on the weekends because they're closer, but with all the damn cars these days, I couldn't get back to the shop before eleven. And there are always two or three customers waiting for me, and fortunately, they wait. They know me now. I'm so glad your grandfather just left. I was starving to death."

The employee wraps up the coat.

"Señor Samuel, she's ready to pay now."

"Since he didn't sell one coat this morning, he left here fit to be tied," continues my father. "No matter how much Enriqueta waited outside to snag someone while she swept the sidewalk, no one came along. And he can't understand why, as he says, 'even though I have the best merchandise in La Lagunilla, I still can't make a sale.'"

"Oh, Dad, how can he honestly believe that? Everything he has is from the Stone Age."

"But we have to sell something today, make at least that first important sale, if anything. I told him to take a few days off and go to Acapulco. He could stay at the Sultana or any other hotel. Nope. He doesn't like that idea; he prefers Agua Hedionda in Caútla. And he's so nervous and fidgety; I can't even get any rest. Ever since he bought the Volvo, things are even worse. Did you see it? It's not very big, but he's afraid to put it in the garage, so now he calls me every day to go over and get it out or put it back in. Did you like the eggplant? Finish your plate. It makes you healthy. You look worried. Is something wrong?"

"Shoot, Dad, when are you going to stop being the obedient

son? It's too much, and then you make yourself believe that you're happy doing it."

Well, I guess that's the way you are, Dad.

Let me explain it to you: Lalo bought a condo in Polanco; they're all going to live there with him. The older girls, who are still in Israel, don't know it yet, but he's already written to them, explaining that each one of them has her own room waiting for her. Daniela and little Jacob are delighted.

"Child, why do you want to create so many problems? I don't understand why you got a divorce. Your husband isn't such a bad person; you're crazy to get rid of him. Who wants a woman who goes to school, anyway? If my wife had come up with these stupidities, I would have sent her packing. Did you like the eggplant? Your mother still sends me good food. And are you sad?"

"Not much. It's just that they don't treat me very well. The only important person for them is their father. They can go with him. If you could see how happy they are, coming and going as they load up the car with their stuff; then, they give me a kiss, saying they're going to invite me over to eat with them tomorrow and that their house is the prettiest ever. Everything is new: the living room, the dining room . . ."

"Let them be! They don't know what they're doing; they're confused, they'll come back to you. Would you like a little more, or should I put it away? I need to return some heavy overcoats that I received today. With this heat wave, I'll never sell one of them. I'm sure there was no one to take them off their hands. Come with me. We won't be long. Fortunately, my help has already had her lunch. Enriqueta, I'll be right back. Don't let any customers get away. Please, come in, Señora, it costs nothing to look . . ."

And he pulls in some customers off the street as we're leaving. All smiles, he pulls out an overcoat and helps a lady put it on, adjusting the shoulders.

"Picture perfect! Tailor-made! Couldn't fit any better than that."

A beggar shows up at the door, so my father waves to him and signals Enriqueta to get some money out of the till. Standing outside, the old man gestures with gratitude and continues on his way. Meanwhile, I stroll around the store and can't help but notice that the coats are out of style. Ever since they removed the street vendors, it's been strange without their stalls nearby. Goyita, for example, is gone, but Chucho, who sells flowers, is still around; we saw him near the public urinals in the Market.

I walk over to my grandfather's store. His assistant, Rosa, is bored: she hasn't sold a thing, and as she waits to snare a customer, she's been sweeping out in front all morning long. I see the same mannequins with stiff wigs and false eyelashes. How is my grandfather going to sell those fur coats if every year it gets hotter and hotter in Mexico? Who's going to buy those old styles, the ones with collars made of silver fox fur? I can't believe it! His store is completely out of step with the times. I feel sorry for my father.

It's frightening to think about trying to make it on my own without the alimony. How am I going to pay the monthly bills? My family insists that I look for a real job. They're worried, but to have to take on a business venture will kill me; I'll feel like I've lost the battle. I have to keep fighting to do what makes me happy. I'm going to put an ad in the sports section of the newspaper, or wherever. And I still have a few clients who like my work. This month I'll make do however I can; next month, as my dad says, God will be generous. I'm lucky that I own the condo. As for the rest, I'll find a way. I know all too well that one can survive on rice and beans.

Agustín says that my novel is overpopulated with characters. He thinks I should reduce the number of Oshi's friends from five to three. Whatever I like about what they say in the novel, let the remaining ones say it.

The bricklayers keep going higher and higher; they arrive every single day to continue their work. Now they're at the eighth floor. After taking a while to sit down, I finally observe that the plants on the terrace are in bad shape, so I try to spruce them up a bit by pruning them. The little clusters of white flowers with yellow pistils have dried out, and their petals droop down next to the healthy ones. As soon as I remove the dry ones, the others come to life in their entire splendor. The dead parts had overshadowed them. Using my alphabet-camera—that is, my pen—I write a picture of them. Using my other camera as well, I can produce a graphic-poetic feature article.

If I read my novel from beginning to end and remove the dry parts, it will begin to radiate like this garden.

We barely had five sessions with Agustín when he suddenly suspended classes until further notice. And I was so excited about adding what everyone was suggesting to me and getting ready to read my new material. What a shame!

I haven't gotten in touch with my married girlfriends, not even Beatriz. I get the impression that their husbands don't like their wives hanging out with divorced women. I guess we're a danger to them, and maybe they're right. Then, what a surprise! Beatriz called to complain about how I had abandoned her. I had talked to her just last week, but I talked to her anyway.

"It's just that I don't want them to think that I'm brainwashing you, that I upset things," I said apologetically. "Lalo, you say . . . well, why go over the past, my family, too . . ."

"I'm sad," she responded. "I've been separated for two months, and it wasn't because of anything you said or did. I want to see you. We've always been friends; we've changed together, and you were the one who encouraged us to continue our studies."

"I'm also happy to have you as a close friend. I'm going to Acapulco with Meche and her children next week; she's a friend from our writing classes. We're not going to spend a lot of money. Do you want to come along?"

"Are your children going with you?"

"They live with their father now! But I did invite them, although they're not going to like the idea of doing it on the cheap. They can't understand that when they go with me, there's no staying at the Hilton; and since their father promises them the world, they turn up their noses at me. I wonder if that famous trip he's taking them on to Japan will ever happen; in the meantime, they won't be going anywhere with me. That's their problem. At first I thought I shouldn't go alone, but I decided that if I didn't go, I'd be frustrated, bored, and resentful."

"My kids would love to go," said Beatriz, feeling reassured, "especially the youngest. When are you going?"

With our tickets in hand, we went to Sanborn's on Aguascalientes Street. It's the closest one to both of us.

"Tell me, Oshinica, do you feel sorry you got a divorce?"

"It's not that I'm perfectly happy, but I didn't have any other option: I was dying on the vine. If he had been more flexible, I would have stayed married. Do you know about Annette's husband? While it's been hard for him to accept the fact that his wife is more than someone who just raises his children, he's been more intelligent about it; as a result, they're still together. Their family isn't broken up like ours."

Spending the same vacation in Acapulco year after year, in the same hotel, at the same beach, with the same view, is like making love the same way every time—at the same hour, in the same bed, with the same man.

Acapulco needs to be turned upside down. We need to change our schedules, go at different times of the year, walk it, sweat it out, go up, go down, swim it, grab it, kick it, smell it, contaminate it.

This time, obviously, I couldn't stay at the Acapulco Hilton, much less think about ordering room service on the balcony of the room that looks out over the ocean; instead, we stayed at

Hipólito Fajardo's boarding house that's on Pie de la Cuesta. Since we had references, he rented us one of the three rooms that look out onto a parking lot. The most luxurious part of the room was the oval iron grating over the windows. Luxurious, because when the sun filters through them, changing designs are projected onto the walls of the room. That's the main decoration during the day. The designs reminded me of the mosaics we used to make with our compasses in geometry class. Circles, especially the ones that touched each other or overlapped, or were placed inside one another, always fascinated me. I loved to color them, using different colors, like a dark blue next to a bright orange. The houses along Pie de la Cuesta Street look upward toward the sky, toward the ocean, toward the waves. Reflected in the windows, they became poetry.

My room has walls of two different colors, a dark blue one and a lighter bluish-green one. Along with the two double beds, they gave us an extra mattress to throw on the floor; since there are seven of us, we'll take turns using it. This seems to be the best arrangement, because I also want a light above my bed. A corner of the square-shaped room was divided off with a low wall that formed the bathroom. A plastic sheet hanging from a rod served as the door, and the bothersome part of it was that every time someone would go into the bathroom—which was about three hundred times a day—the rod would fall down, but we'd just put it back and do our thing.

"Don't go out alone after dark," says Marita, who is serving us some soup, shrimp cocktails, and snacks. "Do you want to bathe outside tonight? There is a lagoon just across the highway."

The little kids prefer to be sprayed with the hose. I wish my kids were here now. How we spoiled them!

There's a full moon, and all the stars are visible. We're wearing our bathing suits. We have shampoo, conditioner, and soap in a little bag. We dance, sing, and jump around in the water. The bubbles from the shampoo and soap on our bodies shine in the dark. I imagine myself as one of Gauguin's women, who combs her hair at the edge of a river. Beatriz takes off her bathing suit and goes to the edge of the water to rinse off her body. Then Meche does the same. And I, never having been able to overcome my shyness, simply deny myself the pleasure of feeling the water all over my body. We linger longer than normal, because the water doesn't turn cold like at home.

"I bathe down here every night with my husband," says Marita, "and then we jump into bed and snuggle up to each other. Our children have already moved out."

We were still in the water when large drops of rain started to fall.

"What rotten luck!" says Marita. "Poor Bertha, and to think she spent so much on Paulita's party! I hope it stops raining soon; they've been getting ready for this for weeks. And all that food and drink! Let's get going!"

We wrapped ourselves in our towels, crossed the highway, and went to our rooms.

Amid thunder, lightening, and total darkness, I go out to look for the famous Hipólito for a candle. He gets up lazily and then wanders aimlessly around the room before heading for the kitchen. As if he were being goaded, he returns with the same impetus, carrying a little plastic cup with some sand and a small candle inside. He lights it. I thank him and begin to leave.

"I would like to use the bathroom without anybody seeing me," I say, "but there's no way they'll wait outside in this storm."

"And being that shy, you still wanted to go out for a sail on the *Acalli*? All it has for a bathroom is a hole looking straight into the sea."

I resign myself to reading by the light of this candle. Bachelard says it's very romantic. I look inside the little cup, trying to find the wick; there's about half an inch of wax left. I search frantically for my book; I don't want to lose any time. I stretch out next to the little flame, and read as fast as I can. After a matter of seconds, darkness overtakes everything . . . but we can still hear the rain.

"Be sure and lock the door!" shouts Hipólito. The lights had come back on at two o'clock in the morning; Paulita's party had been postponed until noon today.

"Could you please take pictures?" they ask.

"Hurry up!" says Marita. "I have a table reserved for us. And make sure you dress up."

The orchestra and all its equipment are right in the middle of everything. The speakers are turned up full blast: tropical music by Rigo Tovar. Some partygoers came on their bicycles. A little girl is selling bags of popcorn that she carries in a basket. The Italian Ice man is right outside the door. Dogs come and go at will. I see Paulita throwing up behind some decorated palm trees. Señora Bertha brings us some folding Coca-Cola chairs, and after sitting there a while, my chair breaks and I crash to the ground. And, of course, it didn't matter if I had broken my back, but my precious camera, never. Those folding chairs cause more problems! If those jerks in the orchestra would've had the decency to keep playing instead of stopping the music and laughing at me, no one would've noticed.

Ocean and sky are the two basic party colors, and multicolored ribbons crisscross the patio. Just about everything else is blue: the cake, Paulita's dress and hat, the employee's uniforms, the doors to the hotel rooms, the palm trees. The seven-story cake is next to a sink, where Bertha washes her feet and puts on her high heels. I take a picture of her with her children. As soon as she hears the click of the camera, she puts her sandals back on, reaches for some keys in her apron pocket, and opens the refrigerator with "Coke" inscribed on the side. Many guests have been lined up with their money out, and we thought that drinks were going to be free! It looks like the cake is about it. I go outside to get an Italian Ice with anise. Meche orders a rum mixture.

The master of ceremonies, who is from the school nearby, announces that the girl celebrating her coming out party—that is, her fifteenth birthday—will first sing a waltz and then a contemporary song. The musician playing the saxophone suffers the same fate I did with his chair, only he goes down with his instrument and everything. The schoolteacher continues his speech by congratulating Paulita's brother, who "choreographed" the party. Humbled by the applause, the twenty-year-old kid, who is wearing a Batman T-shirt, takes a step forward.

"And now, it is an honor for me," says the teacher with a firm voice, "to say a few words to our honored lass: July, month of renewal, the month of green and exuberant trees whose shade protects the coastal lass from the hot sun. The lagoon, with its peaceful movement and that soft, almost monotonous, melancholic sound, gently massages her bare feet, while her fragile figure emulates the litheness of the palm tree and her gait communicates the music of love.

"Young people, your presence at this party gives it the right atmosphere. Señores and señoras! On behalf of the Alarcón Cruz family, please accept this most hearty welcome. [Applause]

"Fifteen years ago, this charming little girl barely made gurgling sounds, but with the passage of time, she has been transformed into a beautiful señorita. Now she is the pride and joy of her parents and the admiration of her young friends!

"Paulita! Be careful of the road paved with roses. Don't be fooled by the tinsel, because temptation can pull you toward the abyss, toward damnation. Your loved ones have worked hard to give you this party, mainly your mother, who with a smile on her lips has cried joyfully in silence. For her and for your brother, who is a new teacher, show them that you can meet the challenges that lie before you.

"Paulita, those visible tears that dampen the faces of the ones who love you must be dried with the white handkerchief of your purity."

Hugo Fajardo Santiago

I gave in to the whims of my friends and to the temptation of mystery: we left this paradise and struck out for Acapulco's underworld of quaint hangouts for eccentric bohemians.

First, we went to a restaurant with noisy ceiling fans, loud music, and harried waiters running from one table to another as they held their trays up high. They insist that you order right then and there, that you eat with the same speed, and then leave as fast as possible. There were families all around us: children, grandparents, maids, and strollers. We tried to prolong our presence in those idyllic surroundings, but it was impossible. Outside, on Pie de la Cuesta Street, you could hear the silence; beyond the party and the ocean waves, there was nothing. Besides going to the lagoon, there's not much else to do at night but sleep and read; in fact, I've never read so much.

Out on the street, though, we've been assailed by crying babies.

We gobbled down some tacos, and after talking for a while, we decided to go somewhere else.

Everything that moves in the streets has musical rhythm; every car brings its own version of noise and chaos, and it's almost better to go back to the excessive silence of Pie de la Cuesta and its lack of alternatives, where Paulita's party was the event of the month. Then we ran into one of Meche's friends.

"What's up with you guys? Things are jumping at the discos. That's where it's happening."

Those places fill me with terror. I'm not even dressed for it: my hair needs fixing, I lost my sandals at the beach, and the ones I'm wearing are so loose that they keep falling off my feet. I became distressed, because I remembered that Pie de la Cuesta was now far away.

It wasn't long before we entered a large tube in the shape of a seashell that was decorated with flashing lights. But the place looked rather exciting. At Armando's Le Club, things were starting to come unglued.

We were in a world of magic, another galaxy, with extraterrestrial beings dressed for some other world that you'd never see on Pie de la Cuesta. I don't know which way to turn or look: sideways, upwards, at the floor, at the tables, at the people who are dancing, jumping, running in and out, hands in the air, back and forth. When do they change direction? At one moment, everyone seems happy; at another, disenchanted. Oh, God, I've been transported to another world: four flashing green lights are rotating around and around, everyone on the dance floor is inflamed; then red lights go on, the green ones go out, and four other colored lights start flashing. Dazed by it all, I hear a bullhorn hooting, something like the Cry of Dolores, but in English. Everyone responds in unison. I guess they're all together. That's good. The whooping stops, but the music rages on; then a voice begins again, everyone is frenzied, and a call to arms sounds again. Since I don't understand what they're saying, maybe there's something else to it. The intensity of the music continues to grow. It's contagious—bodies go crazy, delirious; there's screaming, then howling. The place is about to explode.

I can't take my eyes off of a woman who is dressed like a little girl, her fuchsia dress barely covering her lace panties, her toothpick legs moving stupidly to the expressions in her face. My friends decided to dance. From across the way, a young guy in a black shirt communicates via some secret code with his fingers that he wants to dance with me. He comes over to me. I don't know how I'm going to dance with these sandals on. I pull him out to the center of the dance floor so that no one will notice that I don't know how to dance. I try those steps that Leon Escobar, the gymnast, taught me, but there isn't enough space, and I can't really do them right. This is horrible! I can't get the rhythm. I can't move like everyone else. After all these years of married life, I only danced occasionally at weddings and, if I ever went, at a New Year's party. I feel stupid. I want to get out of here, but I'm afraid that my friends will think I'm boring. I search for my partner's eyes . . . I try to smile; after all we *are* dancing together. After three numbers, I still can't see his eyes. The lights go down, he holds me tight around the waist, finally a slow piece. Without looking at me, and after a long silence, the guy squeezes me even tighter.

"Which hotel are you in?"

"Pie de la Cuesta."

"What do you say we go there and talk a while?"

Oh, *Dios mío,* what a smoothie!

I go back to our table, and even though I don't smoke, I light a cigarette, then another. The movement of the lights hypnotizes me as if I were looking at a trapeze artist doing flips in the air. I must really look stupid.

Meche went to the car with her lover over two hours ago; we'll have to wait for her to come back. Meanwhile, I'm nailed to my chair. It must be getting late, the place is clearing out a bit. Speaking English, another guy wearing overalls comes over and invites me to dance. I say "no spik inglish." Then he introduces me to a friend from New York who asks me in her native tongue if I'm an American. I tell her I'm Mexican.

"Then why don't you speak Spanish to me?"

I wake up. I'm the first one. Without making a noise, I head for the beach; I prefer to continue dreaming in a hammock with the sound of the waves beating close by. I put my shawl around myself and close my eyes. Some birds are singing nearby. The endless string of food vendors starts coming my way. Wow! The bread this kid sells is delicious!

"And your friends?" he asks. "I didn't see you yesterday, so I thought you had probably left. Do you want the same as yesterday? Don't forget that on Sundays Bertha sells food at the lagoon."

I'm going back to see if they're awake yet. Beatriz meets me with a broom in her hand.

"Sweep up in here! The room is dirty; we can't live like this. We've already made the beds. Hey, kids, don't track sand in here. Can't you see our friend here is sweeping the floor? Go outside and brush the sand off your shoes."

Señora Bertha, Paulita, and two little girls are at the edge of the lagoon serving food. They've all become little girls, or that's the way they looked at the party, wearing their dainty little lace dresses. They looked pretty then, but now even more so with their regular clothes on. They serve fried fish, meat, and shrimp soup. Paulita gives me a copy of the teacher's speech, reminds me to send her the pictures I took, and says they're going to cut the cake at five. We don't even believe them anymore, because all they say is that they're going to cut it later. It must be as hard as a rock by now. I've never felt such a craving to try some cake; I'll bet we leave here without getting to try any. We're going home today.

With no children at home, I'm afraid to go back.

I tell Angie that living alone is difficult, mainly because there's no one at home to call and say where I am.

"Don't worry, honey, your problem is that you're accustomed to telling somebody. Listen, call me whenever you want to . . . every day, if it makes you feel better."

"But I can't do that."

"If you're going to feel better that you've told someone where you are, I don't mind you calling me at all."

"But you understand, don't you, Angie, that ever since I was born, my mother always knew where I was; then my husband. And now . . . well, it doesn't seem possible that no one knows where I am."

"For that reason, be sure to call me at least twice a day; if you don't, I'll start worrying about you."

Like the game of Snakes and Ladders, in which you can suddenly have to retrace your steps, I've had a good run of luck and I've met Elena and Alicia, both of whom have been important to me. If I hadn't opened up my own world, I wouldn't have met them, and I'd be just that much more the worse off, not to mention that I probably wouldn't have pursued my writing either. There's no doubt about it: I've had great mentors, from Elena in her garden in Cerrada de Pedregal to Alicia in Chimalistac, in whose garden I also learned about the beauty of plants that lived freely. I'm learning to live without so many necessities, without having to scurry around to make a living, which has been important to me. I still like what I'm doing . . . well . . . this week I took pictures of a Melamine vase, and last week it was an advertisement for learning foreign languages. It took me hours. . . . I began with natural light, but then I decided artificial light would be better. The object shines in this light, but no, it's better the other way. I detest having to photograph objects that will become a part of a process to promote consumerism. No, I neither like this type of work nor do I want to waste my time doing it.

To think: sink or swim. Better to swim, for I've got a lot of people supporting me. All I have to do is pick up the telephone.

I love sitting in the sun at the club for hours on end, just like my dad likes. There, I can usually read the entire Sunday paper. Surprise! Wrestling matches are going to take place right across from the club at the bullfighting ring, El Toreo de Cuatro Caminos. I'd love to go, but I've never tried. And to think I was an expert at applying wrestling holds when I was young! I used to be able to put a hold on my opponent and keep her pinned down until the referee clapped his hands three times. I was one of the best, and my brother Moshón always had me to defend him.

Then I see Beatriz walk toward me in her bathing suit. She's carrying her kickboard and fins in a bag.

"Do you want to watch the wrestling matches?" I asked.

"Ugh!" she says, putting on her bathing cap and goggles before she jumps into the water.

After we eat lunch together, I walk across the road to the arena. Just inside the entrance, there are people selling masks of the wrestlers. I'm tempted to buy one of The Saint, but really, why would I want one? I couldn't decide where to sit, close to everyone or far away. No one even looks at me; they're too busy rooting. And they're very passionate about it. There are lots of women, children, and old people in the crowd. Strangely enough, they're the ones who scream and yell the loudest. It's so funny to see a little old lady screaming at the top of her lungs, "Hit 'em! Poke his eyes out! Kill 'em! Harder!"

It's fascinating to watch them root for their favorite wrestler. I can't resist buying a white mask with red holes and putting it on. I laugh at myself, but not even with a mask on will I start cheering. It feels good to act a little crazy and not wait another ten years or all my life to do this. Even today, I still remember what it was like to wrestle, and how strong it made me as a young girl. It's true, I wanted to be a wrestler, but in those days women didn't have that opportunity. Fortunately, things are a little different today. In my family, the men still continue to be the ones who protect, decide, and judge everything and everyone; in effect, they have the last word.

This year Clarita, Beatriz, and Annette will finish their studies in psychology. They're really excited, and so am I. Within a couple of months, they'll be doctors.

I landed some work taking pictures of the ballet festival at my girls' school. I had to hire an assistant because there were too many girls to photograph; nevertheless, I still made good money.

The table I'm sitting at looks out onto the pool at the club. While I wait for Susan, I read *The Sunday Journal*. Then I see Andrés. It's been four years since we've talked to each other. He has some gray hair now, but he's still handsome. He seems like he's looking for someone; then he smiles at me as he surveys the tables to the back.

"Your everlasting friends are over there," I say to him when his eyes fix on mine.

"Yes, but Isidoro is with them; I'll eat breakfast with you."

"I'm waiting for a friend, but pull up a chair."

"Lupita, bring me some fried eggs and a glass of papaya juice," he says to the waitress while he continues to look around. "Do you know who's playing in the Super Bowl today?"

"Me? No."

"Everyone knows. More than seven hundred and fifty million people—Japan, Norway, and Canada—are anxiously watching. Incredible!"

"Why is it so incredible? Twenty million cows eat grass, but that's no reason why I should too."

"Well, this is what I like to talk about," he responds.

"Then I'm not the best company for you."

"No, you're not," he says ironically.

And you aren't for me either, I thought. The waitress brings him his breakfast.

"Let me see your newspaper," he says, taking it from me. "This rag never has anything important," he adds after thumbing through it quickly.

"See what I mean? Not everybody is holding their breath."

"Several countries have sent their own satellites to watch the game in the United States. I'm going to finish eating with my friends. See you later."

He picked up his plate of eggs and went to the other table. When Susan finally came, I asked her if she knew anything about the Super Bowl.

"Me? No."

Andrés goes to the cash register to pay. When he returns to his table to leave a tip, he walks by and smiles.

"Susan, I'd like you to meet Andrés. I was in love with him fifteen years ago."

"Yes, really in love, but they married her off to someone else."

"They arranged your marriage?" asks my friend as her eyes pop out.

"No . . . they didn't force me, but if I hadn't married Lalo, I would've had to marry some other guy. Enough! Is that how you see it, Andrés? You think they coerced me?"

Andrés becomes visibly tense, says goodbye, and leaves the restaurant with that strange gait of his.

"You can't imagine how much I loved him," I tell Susan. I remember how nervous we'd get when we'd meet each other. I was always with my children. I would be speechless, and our eyes would be glued to each other. It was his passive look that I fell in love with. Someone asked me why didn't I marry him? So many times since then, I've wanted to stop him and say, "I've never forgotten you."

But I never dared. I would have felt guilty for betraying my husband. But the first thing I did when I got the separation was to call him.

How could I have ever thought that he would continue waiting for me and that all those years really amounted to nothing? He probably had the chance to meet lots of women, when in reality he was my only love. That nostalgia allowed me to face so many problems and the routine of marriage. Whenever Lalo refused to go to the country, I always remembered that Andrés wanted us to live on a kibbutz. After our nocturnal walks along the streets in the neighborhood came to end, our lofty discussions about the stupidity of making too much money came to an end too.

"What would it take for you to feel like a millionaire?" I used to ask him.

During all those years, I had this image of Andrés waiting to give me his love. What an illusion!

Someone told me that men and women sat together at the Bet-El Synagogue, so for the next Sabbath I went with Susan and Enrique, her boyfriend. I liked their singing, but not as much as at my synagogue on Monterrey Street. At the last *Kipur,* their singing that afternoon almost made me cry, and even more when the entire congregation sang. What feelings of emotion! Here, on the other hand, things are pretty conservative. At the end of the prayers, everyone has some coffee and sponge cake (that the Ashkenazi simply call "Spanish bread") in the hall to one side of the synagogue. It was a splendid layout, and we all sat on chairs.

"Susan's already told me," said Enrique, "that you feel trapped and about your conflicts of identity. Please don't worry about it, you're not the only one. Don't be harsh on yourself; there are many ways to be Jewish, and you can do it however you want. I don't agree with the Orthodox sect, for instance, so you have to differentiate between what is the religion and who are the religious people. I'm Jewish because I love the history of these people. Judaism isn't just a religion; there are other aspects: its history, its music, its philosophy, and its art, which is a part of its culture and very rich in its own right. Oshinica, you might not be recognizing it, because if you did you wouldn't say it's a hassle to be Jewish. I think you are confusing its religion, which you may find superficial and based on mandatory formulas, with what it means to be Jewish; you need to discover its true essence."

"That's just . . ."

"No, my friend, you just don't understand what religion is—you've gone astray. To be Jewish is something much more profound; if you would only live it and study it more, you'd feel proud, like me. But that doesn't mean I don't have a profound love for Mexico too. One's religion doesn't have anything to do with one's loyalty to his country. Enjoy it; don't anguish over being a Jewish Mexican, or a Mexican Jew. No matter what, you're enriched by this relationship."

Susan makes fun of me for struggling with this double identity. She's less concerned about it than I am. She lets other people deal with it.

"You've created a lot of turmoil for yourself," she says.

"When our parents came to Mexico," continues Enrique, gathering a second wind, "the Jewish community was pluralist. By that I mean that different ideologies—Socialists, Bundists, Zionists, and others—coexisted. Our generation has tended to homogenize things too much, even though we continue to be divided in other ways by our communities. We have lost that enriching aspect of diversity. Why don't you check out the group that calls itself the Jewish Humanists? They don't distinguish between the sexes, they oppose repressive organizations, and they support the idea of pluralism. They don't see it as a threat but rather as a guarantee for our survival."

"I've never met one of these people, and I've always been an integral part of the Jewish community. In my circle of friends, we're all the same; I'm not like a mushroom that suddenly appeared out of nowhere."

"Let me see if my friend Bill is around somewhere," he says, getting up from his chair.

"It's fascinating to talk about these things. Where did you meet this guy? Does he have a brother?"

"I've known him forever," responds Susan, smiling. "We studied together in our community school. How was I to know you were interested in other ideas? As for me, it's in one ear and out the other."

Enrique comes back with his arm around a short, gray-haired man, who smiles at me when we're introduced.

"And it just so happens," Enrique continues, "that I've interviewed one of the founders of the movement. The Humanists defend, above anything else, human rights; for them, Judaism isn't just what the rabbis have to say. The Humanists want to be free thinkers, remain open, and respect the fact that there are many ways to be Jewish."

"What a relief! Because in my family, on my father's side, there are many very religious Jews who, I think, are basically fundamentalists. As a woman, it's no fun to be sent upstairs in the synagogue; to me, that's discrimination, and I resent it. I feel inferior."

"They have their own way of thinking," Bill adds, "and they have a right to; remember, you can't become intolerant. Judaism has always permitted freedom of thought, and that's why it's still strong today; it's never stood still."

"Well, that's not true, because what I'm asked to do is what they've been doing since the time of Moses."

"If you study the history a little more, you'll see. It's not my fault that you haven't taken the time to study your roots."

"Everyone says that I should study history and philosophy. Why? Will I ever learn to embrace the insults inflicted against women?"

"There are far more differing positions than the one held by the fundamentalists. They alone aren't going to define what it is to be Jewish; nor will they have the right to make you feel like you have to obey the letter of the law. Besides, every religion has its fundamentalists; we're no different."

"Good! What you're saying helps me reconcile my position with Judaism, because I want to belong to a group that defends the dignity of men and women."

"Judaism is relevant to our times as well; the values and principles that came into being thousands of years ago are still valid today, and the important part is the essence of it all, the significance of each thing, each celebration, not just the habit itself."

"Wait," jumps in Enrique excitedly, "listen to what I have to say! Why do they have to tell you what's right and what's wrong? We're all old enough to make our own decisions. That's okay for those who need a father. To follow another path is more difficult."

"You should understand," adds Bill, "that we come in all stripes and colors, tutti frutti. Those of us who want to decide what is good and what is bad have no option but to try to understand why things are the way they are."

"The fundamentalists really bother me—shoot, we have the right to be different from them; I bought into their idea that if I'm not a traditionalist, then I'm not Jewish."

Children, young people, parents, and grandparents are dancing the hora, accompanied by the accordion.

I'm so happy to meet Jewish people who think like I do, who are like the type of Jew that I want to be. I still insist that it isn't easy being Jewish, especially if one belongs to a minority.

Fortunately, we stopped talking for a while and admired the dancing, the words to the songs, and the sometimes slow dance steps.

"Nevertheless," says Bill with an illuminated face, "I find my Jewish roots in this music, in the food. You can't tell me it's not a beautiful way to find one's identity. Perhaps we should dance."

"This Humanist group has a cohesive way of thinking: they respect the social customs, but they really understand what those social customs are and what they mean; perhaps you were brought up in an environment in which you were taught only to respect those customs. Perhaps you didn't learn what their purpose is. For example, next week is Sukkoth. The origin of this agricultural celebration is the harvest. I asked my children today what they had harvested this year, and my youngest one said he had germinated some alfalfa. But everyone always harvests something in his or her life. Did you know that one of the most important aspects of this celebration is being hospitable? You are supposed to invite some-one to eat with you and your family, both rich and poor friends, in the traditional hut, Sukkah."

"No, I didn't know that, but I'm interested in getting to know this group you're talking about."

"They meet every two weeks; in fact, next Wednesday. They're going to discuss the different types of Judaism that exist in the world. You'll see a lot of young people there; you'll receive a lot of support from everyone. We can go together. Where do you live? We'll work that out later. Let's dance now. You too, Enrique."

"Susan, give me your hand!"

"I'm trying, I'm trying. Hey, take it easy, you're going to jerk my arm off."

I left very happy. So, Judaism isn't just my family's authoritarianism. Where have I been? I'm fascinated with the way my perspective on the world is expanding.

On a sad note, I informed Trueba that Agustín Monsreal had stopped his classes.

"So, why don't we ask Agustín Ramos? We could meet once a week and finish our novels. I'll talk to him."

"That's fantastic! I love the idea."

Half asleep, I began thinking. I could hear my father saying, "The early bird . . ." I'm not going to get up; if I were to obey him, when would I start to think for myself? Once you're in the middle of things, stuck in traffic, the day goes by and there's never time to reflect on things. I can hear the rain falling. Why is it that even now, without my children at home, I don't have enough time to read? My friends do it before they get up, and they're always ready to go. I began to enjoy reading on my own when I was in high school, but they always nagged me to finish those endless chores. To read was to immobilize your body, to take your soul and your fantasy on a walk. We never see the internal revolutions that can take place. I squeeze my eyes shut, I don't want to get up, and the words and the light disappear. I don't want to know anything, not even what time it is. It's morning, I don't have any early appointments; the daylight erases my ideas like the moment when a roll of film is exposed to the light and the images disappear. My legs ache. I make an attempt to look at myself, letting my thoughts flow through my veins to the farthest reaches of my body. See less, but soak up more. Recover the image, and listen to the bells ringing, the drums beating.

I have an appointment with the dentist. I have the worst teeth of anyone. I'm glad my children didn't inherit them from me. I showed the dentist my portfolio of accomplishments. Photography is my principal source of work.

"Don't you think I'm too good for this camera? Do you remember the first time you saw me with it you said, 'Señora, don't you think this camera is too much camera for you?'"

It seems like ever since I became a photographer, I do things more slowly, and I've learned to be patient. It's true, I like to move slower, and I don't like to be in a hurry. I drive my mother crazy when we go to the market together. The guys who used to carry our groceries and call out to me by my name don't even come around to help out; they all say I'm too slow.

At the fruit and vegetable market where I used to have my orders filled, many of the vendors who know me are accustomed to having me around, watching me carefully choose my avocados with my Konica hanging from my shoulder, ready to take pictures of the piles of recently washed jicama fruit, papayas from Hawaii, and banana leaves. At first I was embarrassed to get my camera out, but it was a seductive process.

"What! You didn't bring it with you?" they say when they don't see the camera on me.

When I talk to them, I look at their faces, their eyes, their hair, and their bodies. The vendors arrange their produce in an aesthetic way; it's something that comes naturally to them. I like the roundness of the sliced pineapples. To come upon four neatly wrapped apples, three cucumbers, and a bag of beans at the supermarket just isn't the same. I've spent the majority of my time trying to convince those who look at my pictures that paradise is here and now.

I look at the sweet bread that's been decorated with roses and green leaves. I watch how a vendor carves open a mango, turning it into a flower, a flower that tastes like a mango. I watch the cotton candy maker spin his magic on a stick, creating small, different-colored clouds that instantly dissolve in your mouth. I watch how the crates of milk sway back and forth on the delivery trucks. I'm participating for the first time in the Day of the Dead. I'm moved by the way the living arrange flowers on the tombstones of those who have departed.

And I'm beginning to transform my house. And my face, my hair, the way I walk, my smile. I've expanded my limits. I've changed the way I dress: dark blue miniskirt, and purple, yellow, or green scarves.

Agustín Ramos got excited about our novels. Only Trueba and I were able to keep going.

How stupid! In chapter four I said that television had made it to Mexico, and eighty pages later I wrote that only radio was available. If I hadn't been able to finish this uninterrupted, unswerving single reading, in which I paid attention to every detail and concern of our workshop leaders, I wouldn't have caught the error. My God, I'm so careless!

The text has to have movement, action, and sound. One must be able to hear the bricklayers yelling from the top floor. "Look out below, you jerks!" Then a loud thud! People were running around everywhere. Cement covered everything. The bricklayers work, eat, go up, go down, and balance themselves on the reinforcement rods they just installed. The frame is already up.

I'm constructing my own work, watching it take form, one day at a time, the way I want, and the way only I can do it. I believe some people are going to feel comfortable in my building.

✡ General mayhem.

We were in the Sephardic school auditorium to see a Turkish group sing in Ladino. Everyone was there: those who came on the ships from Europe and those of us who belong to the first generation, born in different neighborhoods such as Condesa, Roma, and Polanco, who studied Spanish grammar and Mexican history. We got our start in this country, and we fell in love with its people. We were the ones who would go rowing in Chapultepec Park. And the third generation, our children, have cars, go to discos, and aren't presented with "good boys" for marriage because they meet each other at dances at the club, at the university, or at the Jewish youth organizations.

The words of some old songs contain references to the customs of our parents who came from the Old World. Here, in Mexico, they raised us, found us those "good boys," and married us to them.

They had an old saying:

"This one smells bad, and that one doesn't suit you. Guess what, my daughter? I'm going to introduce you to a tall groom."

"But the tall one is out of my reach."

"Well, then, my daughter, I will introduce you to one who is shorter."

"But the short one is way too short."

"Ah, then he'll be very handsome."

"But the handsome one will never belong to me, and with the jealous one, I'll never be free."

Why am I crying?

I love the Ladino dialect because of my mother, not because of my father; my grandmother on his side spoke Farsi, and if he spoke any Ladino at all, it was because he learned it from my mother and her community of friends, and because it sounds like the way honey tastes sweet. Whenever I hear someone speaking it, I feel like they're a part of my family, that I can trust them, that they understand the way I live, that they were educated the same way I was educated, and that in their homes I would find special dishes made with cabbage and spinach.

Some of my friends who are in the writing workshop have parents who were in the Mexican Revolution. Alicia Trueba's uncle was the director of the military academy, and when he marched down Madero Avenue mounted on his graceful steed, he would wave to her.

"The one on the white horse, see him waving at me? He's my uncle," she said proudly.

Angie, the one who went to school at Sacred Heart, had a grandfather who fought with Pancho Villa or Carranza. While girls like her were used to living on large estates in the country (or they would go to their country houses on the weekends, where they'd prepare chiles in a special nut and spice sauce that I just tried for the first time in my life recently,) I was learning to embroider using patterns from Istanbul, to dance the hora instead of the mambo, to make cheese and eggplant turnovers. Whenever they talk about those times, I can't really participate.

But on this beautiful night, I'm able to appreciate their singing in the old Ladino Spanish from my mother's side. I give her a hug and a kiss, and I feel happy, because her friends surround me: Rashelica la Puntuda, who is sobbing, and Mrs. Bulizú, who plays in her bridge group. I can see the nostalgia in their faces. Their tears make me sad. Where were their thoughts when they were listening to that music? I imagined so many things as I looked into their watery eyes. Then they sang together: "Dark eyes are what I want/I would die for them/but when I see those green eyes/I can find no solace."

How heartbreaking those scenes of goodbye in Istanbul must have been! I hear everything like sharp jabs, and my eyes go from the singer to the ladies in front of me, to those next to me, to my Aunt Mati, who said nostalgically, "Nowhere in the world, my dear, would you find better singers. Nowhere . . ."

"I've got a silly daughter," they sang, "who has to be watched/ for when she's out on the street/she wiggles her you-know-what, her you-know-what, her yooooooou-knooooow-whaaaaat!"

"Is it true that the Turkish girls would go out wiggling their you-know-what? You never told me that," I said to my mother, who was weeping.

As the beautiful evening was drawing to a close, the singer spoke to the audience.

"Even in exile, the Sephardics wanted to continue to belong to their adoptive mother. The umbilical cord that connects them to Spain has not been severed."

Sefarad! Which means "Spain" in Hebrew.

Last night I had a dream that my book had been published. A bunch of copies were on top of my desk. The telephone was ringing off the wall, people wanted to interview me . . . the club, the Jewish community. I began to tremble. Fortunately, I woke up.

Fear shot through me: I ran to my desk to make sure the draft with the corrections was still there. I relaxed. It hadn't been published yet. What a relief!

"Ele, I had a horrible dream. I'll never be able to turn this manuscript over to a publisher. I kept imagining it, so I couldn't sleep after that."

"Don't worry. If you don't want to, you don't have to. But make sure you finish it. Don't stop now. You'll publish it when it's ready. And if not, you won't."

The divorce was the only thing that I really did without any help. After the chaos, the hurricane, the tidal wave, the earthquake, the soul searching, the personal crisis, I went from being an orchid to a wildflower.

Disaster. Pain. The children.

I struck out on my own, without orders from anyone. But how was I not going to follow orders, when at seventeen I found myself in a situation about which I knew absolutely nothing? I had wanted to work with my hands on a kibbutz, to be a part of the drive for equality among all human beings, to learn about the rest of the world and its inhabitants.

"You went wild," said my daughter Daniela.

I became like strawberries, or sunflowers. No longer was I like a rose, an orchid, or a greenhouse flower. I had acquired an aura of freedom, which compelled me to find myself and to seek happiness in providing for myself.

My God! What a monumental task!

We're working exceedingly well with Agustín. Elena is pleased that we're moving speedily toward the end. She has already told an editor that soon she'll be giving them our final drafts.

"So, hurry up. I'm going away for two months; when I get back, let's give them to the publisher."

I had been trying to come up with a title in Ladino, something referring to a daughter and who she is.

I wake up, but I stay in bed, vigilant. I write down what comes to me. Where is it coming from? I don't know. Nevertheless, I listen: if there isn't silence, there's no way to hear.

Silence is the principal ingredient for writing; it's like the flour for making good bread. How much you have to knead it depends on the consistency of the dough. I wake up with what I want to say in my head, and I add new passages here and there to the text. My building is also taking shape. First, the framework, then the structure, and then the siding. If I work on my novel every day, I'll eventually get it done. Floor by floor, chapter by chapter.

The apartment is cleaned every day. If I leave dirty dishes, the cleaning lady does them, too. I should keep coming out onto this deck, but now that my children are gone and there isn't any noise at my place, I'm too lazy to come over here; still, it's here where I get the most done, because no one calls me here, and I get inspired watching the building across the street steadily going up, now blocking the horizon and changing the view. The bricklayers work with me, day after day, so I don't feel alone, although I'm always facing the temptation to have a man over. But they didn't loan me the apartment for that; it's to finish the construction of my building.

While revising, I become aware of so many errors. When I got bored with it, problems arose: desire fed on fantasy; I imagined myself with a lover. I've never been adulterous. What a pity! No one has ever believed me. Simply wanting to have one was never a problem, but if I had ever dared to . . . my life depended upon my husband's moods.

I must finish by September. The framework is done. I'll paint it with vivid colors, hang curtains, put down throw rugs, buy some plants, use fine wood paneling. The bricklayers, who build places in which to live, are like writers: they build worlds out of nothing. We need comfortable places to live. Alicia's novel is going to be called "Original Colors."

When I went to Cuernavaca for three days, I took the novel with me. I couldn't leave it behind. It would get cold. I get anxiety attacks when I'm walking down the street, and all of a sudden, ideas come spilling out, as if from a cornucopia: the bananas won't fit, the apples fall out. So I go back home and weave the pieces into the text, where it's appropriate. This process frustrates my friends who are with me. They must think I'm crazy, because I always have to go back home.

Poor Daniela has assumed the role of maid at her father's, mainly because her sisters haven't come back. From the beginning, they weren't entirely convinced about going to live with their father. They knew they would have to take charge of the house, so they decided to stay longer in the kibbutz. They didn't completely rebel against him; they're not stupid. Now they're almost finished with getting settled in their new place. Their father gives them orders, and between his work and putting on airs, he keeps them entertained.

I went by to see them, and I could tell that Daniela was very proud of her choices of the dining room set and the refrigerator that made ice cubes. Now the one who's poor is me. It doesn't matter; I feel more at ease being with them for a while, although I don't know quite what to think about their independence.

Of course, I feel rotten to see them getting along so well without me. It's hard not having them with me while they're growing up. It's been like fast-forwarding parts of their lives. Nevertheless, it's best for me to accept it and understand that I'm not their owner.

Damn it, what a rotten feeling!

Today, finally, I was able to buy a skirt that will go with the black and yellow shawl that I bought in Florence. It's a strident canary yellow color. I decided to show it off, so I took a walk and went by some bricklayers who were tossing coins on the sidewalk. One short little guy saw me coming.

"Hey, you're like a . . . flower." I would've smiled at him, but my better judgment took over, so I just kept walking, trying to look dignified and serious. But then he followed me.

"A sunflower!" he blurted out, feeling happy that he was able to remember.

His poem left me smiling as I continued to walk home. I felt as if I had been blessed with sunlight. I was a sunflower.

Yes, a sunflower, a sunflower. Of course! A sunflower!

I had a dream that I was a trapped butterfly. It was hardly daybreak when I called my sister, because my dad picks her up early to go to the Bosque del Pedregal Park even before the sun rises. The climb has always been hard for me, so they have to go slower. My dad likes to hear his echo in the mountain darkness.

"Goooooooood morniiiiiiing!" he yells.

A few seconds later, we hear his voice over and over again.

"Goooooooood morniiiiiiing!"

Then it's our turn.

"We're heeeeeeeeeeeeere!"

Then some dogs come running out of nearby houses in the gorge. Once on top, we can view the sunrise and then follow some uncharted trails that my dad and his buddies have created on previous outings.

The imaginary butterfly of my dreams is pursuing me. I have to find it. I know that there will be many of them, and during the rainy season the dew covers their wings, illuminating them in the early morning haze and making them easier to see. I step among the muddy rocks while my dad collects prickly pears. He forgot his knife again, so I don't know how he keeps from getting needles stuck in his fingers. A luminous light from the sky peeks through the trees of the forest. Precisely at that moment, I spot a beautiful two-foot-wide spider web, also illuminated by the dew. A Monarch butterfly is perched on the edge of the web. A distracted butterfly will have an unfortunate fate. I get closer to the jailer. Should I kill it? What if it stings me? I can't go without helping the butterfly. And what if I rescue it and it gets trapped somewhere else? I guess that's what it desires.

"Dad! Do you think if I try to save the butterfly, the spider will sting me? How do I do it?"

With his customary agility, my dad makes his way over the rocks to where I am. In desperation, the butterfly flaps its wings.

"Yes, you can save it. If it were farther toward the center of the web, it would be more difficult. Fortunately, it's on the edge. Let's see what kind of spider it is, because if it's a black spider with an orange marking on its belly, it can sting."

"Dad, don't get too close, it might jump on you."

"No, I don't believe it's one of those kind. It'll probably just scurry away, because it doesn't jump. It hangs from the thread it spins and will try to escape. They use the web to trap their prey, which they'll eat at some point. Wait, I'll look for a long stick. Do you see the design on its wings that splits into two parts? Just lightly grab it by its wings."

"I'm scared."

"Silly. Give me the stick to stop the spider while you nab the butterfly. If you're afraid, leave it alone. There's no reason to create problems. Just grab it by its wings. Go on, Oshinica, or we'll end up spending the whole morning here. The forest is full of trapped butterflies. Thousands of them!"

"Dad, I can't leave it like this. Not this one . . . it called out to me. This butterfly doesn't have the strength to get loose. Good! I got it!"

"Okay, let go! It's fine now. Time for us to go. It's getting late."

"Clarita! Look, it's free. See? It's flying away. It's free! Freeeeeee! I just hope it knows where it's going."

At one point, I didn't like being a woman. I had figured out that I could never go anywhere alone, never be director of a large company, never make a lot of money, never learn how to invest money, never learn how to buy a house, and never learn how to travel alone. I heard a woman say once that without men, women are worthless. My God, that's atrocious. But that's history: three months ago, I went to Acapulco, walked around by myself and went to bars with the others.

Even though I'm a woman, what is there I can't do?

That despicable psychiatrist who had said I was too authoritarian really seemed to enjoy herself when she talked about penis envy. That idea seems stupid to me. Penis envy? Who in the hell wouldn't be envious of all those privileges? It was terrible to feel the disdain of men, their disgust in women. Is it disgust because of our periods? We're dirty? Why are we dirty? Feeling repugnant, I couldn't possibly respect myself, or other women. And they were my daughters, sisters, sisters-in-law, my mother, Eva, serpents (female), snakes, the evil one, the rejected . . . the impure. Who would ever want to be a woman?

"Thank you, God, for not having made me a woman," states the Book of Prayers at the synagogue. And every time I reread that phrase, what can I say to God? A simple Thank You? Yes, thanks! But it can be beautiful being a woman if you don't close all the doors to yourself like those who went before us. I can do anything if I have access to the same education as men. That's it: to be content with oneself. My brothers were forced to become professionals so they could carve out a future for themselves. And I thank all those women who have fought to free us from this oppression, and I'm thankful for having lived in the era of contraceptives, because it has given us the opportunity to know other men without exposing ourselves to danger, and to enjoy our bodies without the fear of getting pregnant. Now we're not as burdened with so many children. Now even husbands have to ask us to have their children, because if we don't want to, we don't have to.

Something else that the women in the writing class have helped me with is to reconcile myself with women in general. They have been a driving force for me. Elena has stimulated me, given me direction. Do you think any man has done that for me? Thank you, God, for allowing me to start anew. If my children hadn't left me, I would have been forever trapped in my love and devotion for only them. Even though the wound caused by their departure will never heal, they saved me . . . despite myself.

I'm going to make a family collage. I'll divide it into two parts: on the left I'll put pictures of all the women in our family—the old, the young, and the babies, but only the females; and on the right, the men, beginning with my grandfather, his relatives, my brothers, cousins, husband, and son. I'll divide the two groups by drawing a wall of plants like the ones they use in orthodox weddings. I will put a title on the collage: "The Pure and the Impure."

I won't put a picture of my father. I wouldn't want him to be a part of them.

While I was picking out the pictures and arranging them on a large piece of cardboard, my brother Rafael—my grandfather's legitimate grandson—came by. He misses Israel, but as soon as he's there, he misses Mexico. Obviously, he's got an identity problem. He never did want to be just another merchant, but he did nothing to change his destiny either.

"Hey, go figure! You've got to understand that you don't have to choose between your Jewishness and being a Mexican. It's just fine to love both. By the way, I'm really mad at you. Your girlfriend just called me and told me you've been acting like a jerk with her. You're just a typical macho. So, leave me alone; I've got other things on my mind right now. Elena is leaving in two weeks, and she wants me to finish my novel."

"Listen, sis, no one's going to want to read a lot of gossip. Don't wash our dirty underwear in public. You're going to make all of us look stupid, and besides, you don't understand anything that I've told you about living on a kibbutz. It's wonderful. You don't use money; I didn't see any for weeks on end. And I see how you suffer with all your bills. If you'll leave within three weeks, no, a month, I'll pay for you to go to Israel. I'll bring you the money tomorrow, but it's not for buying a better car or whatever."

"Right now, precisely at this moment, I was writing about machismo and how men discriminate against women. And you're the direct descendent from my grandfather."

"Of course I'm a macho. And you women *are* impure, right? Ha, ha! Anyway, I'll be by tomorrow. Remember, if you don't go within a month, you have to give the money back."

I've just finished reading Yourcenar's *Opus Nigrum*. Zenón is dead. Silence. Jesus Christ has just died, at least the Jesus as I understand him, who was like Zenón, or like that Oshinica that I used to be when I got married. I cry, because he couldn't live with himself. He couldn't live with his free will that he should have known how to exploit. He killed himself in order not to be assassinated by the so-called justice of the masses that believes what others say is always the truth, the masses who don't think for themselves or even ask questions. They believe that truth is the will of the majority.

Oshinica got married at seventeen. What could she have done with no experience? Forever "like a bride." How could she oppose putting on a wedding dress even though she wanted something else? Like a bride. Like a bride . . . like a bride. I can visualize her, crucified . . . with a wedding dress on.

But she didn't die on the cross. The cross sustained her while she worked to grow up. She was resuscitated. Afterward, a vine started to grow all over her, and she turned beautiful. Then she continued down the path she had visualized for herself.

Is it any different to sacrifice young women in the sacred lake? What about "Like a Bride" for the title of my novel? Even though it's painful, it's exact. Elena isn't going to like it as much as the other title. But I see now that it can't be any other way. This novel already had its title; it just had to be discovered. And it should end with the words "Like a mother."

I'm finding it painful to get inside my novel; that is, to relive and rediscover the pain and jealousies that seemingly had been forgotten—that is, to write it down with the commitment to tell the truth like the person who stimulated me to write in the first place. It's damn hard. It hurts.

Poor Moshón. I must admit that I feel for him, because he was the one who was chosen among us to become the knight in shining armor, the one to go out and conquer the world and return to distribute the booty among all of us. And he *did* conquer that world, but I'm not sure he's willing to share it with those who outfitted him to become that knight. Precisely because he didn't come to my aid, I've had to find my own way. I've done that now, and I don't need him anymore. I'll never need him again. I have removed the obstacles that were in my way, the ones that prevented me from seeing farther down the road. Now, the fruits of my labors are sweet. He's not to blame, but sometimes he makes me mad, and I get furious. I hope God will remove this abscess soon. I need to get well. Now!

"Divide your novel into two parts," advised Elena, "before Oshinica gets married and after. If not, you'll never finish it. See how the first part flies. Leave this part for a second novel. I'm sure you'll finish it someday."

"I want some water. I'm going to the kitchen."

Uba and her daughter are heating up some tortillas. They smell delicious!

"Would you like to eat something, honey? We have everything."

I remember how my grandmother and my dad, while they were standing in front of the stove waiting for the coffee to heat up, would share secrets with each other and make all kinds of plans. My father would tell her about my grandfather's antics at work that day.

"Just put up with it, son, what else can you do? That's the way he is, very strong-willed, so don't answer back; if you do, I'm the one who pays for it. You get to go home to your wife and kids; he takes it out on me. Just ask Uba how he makes me cry."

"Child, you're not listening to me. I asked you if you wanted something to eat. You're not paying attention today," interrupts Uba. "At least take your plate to the dining room, because your grandfather gets upset if you don't."

"No, thanks, Ubita, I've already eaten."

I return to the dining room. The sun coming through the window makes it warm in the room, and my dad begins to doze. My aunt, who seems to be shriveling up, sits in front of the TV. I sit down to enjoy another late afternoon. I observe each and every thing around me and think about all the years that porcelain rooster has been pulling on the little girl's dress. In a few minutes, shadows will begin to take over the room. I want to take advantage of the sunset to see how everything changes, to watch how everything—each little figurine—begins little by little to disappear around me.

Even though many years have passed, this same scene, despite the warmth, has been frozen in time. The only changes I can see now are my aunt's hairstyle and my father's gray hair. My grandfather's stuffed chair is empty; he still hasn't come downstairs. He always takes a long time to get ready and put his cologne on. Outside, the world is spinning out of control; in here, absolutely nothing is happening. Day after day, it's always the same. I also learned to depend on my habits, just like my grandfather, but I've acquired some new ones that will allow me to experience new things. I remembered something I had read by Pico della Mirandola that I put in my diary. "Little by little, in the same way that day after day a person consumes a certain type of food, he ends up altering his composition and form; that is, he either loses weight or gains it, but he also receives from that same food his strength or some bad effects that he didn't know about, proving that there are invisible changes going on in his body that are the result of acquiring new habits."

When I started to attend the writing classes, I began taking in nutrients heretofore unknown to me. God has sent me Elena, a tiny woman with an easy, deep, different laugh, who has a profound look about her. One weekend she invited me to Huamantla to write about the fair going on there, and we went to Tequisquiapan, where her "mommy" lived. Seeing the way she treated others, I admired her generosity, her purity. To be an idealist at fifty is admirable; at twenty, anyone can do it. As I watched her conduct our classes and live life to the fullest, I knew my life had gone awry with all those diapers, all that love for my children, so much fear, so many chores, all those cookies and frying up food, all those closets to clean. Despite those banalities, they are what life is all about; little by little, I'm practicing forgiveness for their having abandoned me, even though I've never been the same since then.

Or perhaps it had to happen so I could find myself. I'm following my own instincts now, the same ones that back when I was single had passed before my eyes. When my children are grown, I want them to know that, apart from being proud of them, their mother had her own life to live.

Now that I'm about to finish, I can't even go outside. I went to the movies and it was extremely difficult to tell everyone that I didn't want to eat dinner afterward. My novel awaits me at home, and I leave home with the same fear that a mother feels when she leaves her child at home. A little time goes by and I have to return home. On the other hand, I'm so happy. From the beginning, I had no idea what it was like to write a novel; it's been such a long and arduous road that, having known this before, I might not have tried it at all. And now, I have no choice but to finish it. I've spent the entire day sitting at the typewriter.

The family patriarch is beaming with pride, because his triumphant grandson Moshón has exceeded all expectations. It fascinates him to have his successor stop by to see him. Nothing else matters. Now a well-dressed, flourishing architect who is in the know, my brother stops by to see him. They eat their favorite fruit together: watermelon, which is followed by a steaming cup of Turkish coffee and a conversation based on questions about the profession and how others are doing. That way, they avoid having to say how each one of them is doing. They're deathly afraid of personal questions. Conflict and torment aren't even tolerated in the movies they watch. They like to talk by themselves; I mean to say, without women around, even though I've always felt that there's been a place for me whenever my dad's around.

Conclusion: if my dad isn't around, I leave them alone, despite the fact that, since I was the first granddaughter, my grandfather has always had a soft spot for me.

This grandfather of mine has always lived in the same house, with the same servants. At nine o'clock in the morning every day, he eats the same thing: cornflakes and milk. He takes the same route to get to work, and the car radio is always on XEW. He parks in the same place, and when the newspaper boy brings him the newspaper, he sits down at his desk to look through it until a customer comes in. He always takes the first customer in order to show his assistant that he continues to be a better salesman than she is. At precisely two o'clock in the afternoon, when he's gotten fidgety from working all morning, he crosses the street to begin his return home.

Since my grandfather was late in coming downstairs today, Moshón and I both ran to sit down in his rocking chair; well, we didn't exactly run like two little kids to get into it, because we're adults now. To run would've been ridiculous.

"Were you going to sit there?"

"No, go ahead."

"It's okay, I'll sit over here."

"Don't play games," said my father. "You both want to sit there, don't you?"

Then we both dived at the chair.

"I got here first."

"No, I did."

"We both did, but now the two of us don't fit," I said.

"Auntie, I saw my dad get there first," said his daughter.

"No," said Daniela, "my mother was first. It's true, grandpa."

The rocking chair.

We've always fought for that chair, the one that belongs to the one who controls every member of this family. All of a sudden, as if Moshón and I were receiving orders, we jump up from the chair as our grandfather makes his grand entrance: tall and erect, with the customary hand in his pocket. Then he ascertains what we're watching on TV. It won't be long before he changes the channel.

"Grandad," Moshón and I say in unison, "sit down in your chair."

León Felipe, you are no longer with us, but I had the good fortune to meet you once. I, too, have learned that history repeats itself: it's always the same, no matter where you are. However, here in Mexico there's a house where time has stood still, and although there's nothing glorious or noble about it, my grandfather lives there and is always sitting in the same green leather chair. Without leaving the room, he fights off long hours of idleness by watching, but not seeing, silently, little women scurry around doing their chores.

He's my grandfather. While he's very handsome and gallant, he lacks a sword, as well as a genteel or dignified home. It hurts me deep down inside to see him like that, so proud, as solid as a mountain, with his hands in his pockets but unable to look you in the face.

It pains me to harbor that image of him, so distant, lying on top of his wood-carved bed, in that spacious and bright bedroom, the largest one in the house. I'll always have that image of the large windows, with the clear, harsh light streaming through, making one appreciate in great detail the embroidered comforter on his large bed.

What a shame, León Felipe, that you can't achieve heroic feats, have a green leather chair, or a wood-carved bed. Being a woman, I'm a pariah, and I don't deserve that he should even have to look at me in the face.

It's impossible for you to understand that, even though I have no sword, nor the strength to brandish it, for some time now I've been in the midst of a battle. Yes . . . what a shame, León Felipe, that having what I have, I'm still unable to sing of great deeds. As a woman, I'm an outcast, and I'm forced to recite things of little importance.

Beatriz, who is without her children, wants to go to Oaxaca.

"I'll go in two weeks," I tell her. "By then I'll be done with my novel. The timing's perfect."

After I had been working two solid days, Susan came by to see me.

"You look like you're lost," she comments.

"I'm pushing myself to finish. Right now, I'm typing up the final draft so I can give it to the publisher. Agustín says it needs more editing, that it's not ready. He even called Elena about it."

"Don't worry, Agustín," she tells him in her adorable, high-pitched voice, "just have her send it in. That's the way she writes. There's nothing we can do about it. It's her first novel. She'll write others. The important thing now is to get her book published."

I left the manuscript at the corner to have a copy made. Since it's late, they'll give it back to me in the morning. Without "Like a Bride" sitting on my desk, I feel disoriented. This is horrible! I can't bear to separate myself from my baby. And now what am I going to do with my life?

I wake up early, but the copy shop doesn't open until ten. I wait at the door. I can see it on the counter. What a great feeling of security to hold it in my arms again! Bound with a black cover, I'm ready to write the dedication. It's so pretty this way, nice and neat. I stroke it with love, and then again. And what will it be like when it's finally published?

Full of illusions, I dig out the box of yarn that I've been secretly hiding. While knitting my last sweater, I had started to use imported yarns of different colors. After gathering up everything and sticking it into a paper bag, I grab some wood and lighter fluid and head for the patio outside. The fire quickly consumes it all.

I never want to knit or embroider again. During my entire life,

I have staved off my anxieties and desires by weaving like a mad woman. I won't try to fool my body's needs again. No more sedatives! The knitting needles had been like aspirins. My body hurts from hunger, my heart yearns for a touch, and it aches for having virgin skin and a chaste body. Never again will I suffocate my desires. I never want to extinguish my passion with flimsy excuses. I've knitted an indeterminable number of bedspreads, jackets, skirts, dresses, sweaters, and blouses. I've embroidered tablecloths and doilies. Ah, yes, I've forgotten to throw all the knitting needles into the bonfire. And all those knitting brochures, too. And *Family Magazine.*

I only want to do what my desires tell me to do.

I go back down to my apartment, gather up the rest of it, and throw it on the fire. As I watch the flames jump around, I feel like the healing process is already underway. Hypnotized, I watch the smoke drift up into the sky. Never again do I want to see a flower embroidered from so much pain and so much desire. The television set! I want to burn it too, forget about Zabludowksy and Memito Ochoa, five hours a day watching that garbage. During that time, I could have become a doctor several times over, obtained numerous masters and doctoral degrees. My God, what a waste! In order to become the old lady that I want to become, I'll never let myself get sidetracked again.

The skeins of yarn have made a great fire. Yes, they were made of wool, just like the overcoats in La Lagunilla.

Everything smells like sheep.

In my own timid way, I'm becoming a writer.

Now I'm wondering what the Jewish community will think of my novel? And everyone else in the world?

I'm really frightened. I leave you now; it's time to say goodbye. And, as my mother always used to say, "may your road be paved with gold."

The End